CROSSING THE LINE

By the Author

The Stick McLaughlin Novels

Stick McLaughlin: The Prohibition Years

Crossing the Line

Exchange

Night Voice

Nantucket Rose

CROSSING THE LINE

by

CF Frizzell

2018

ISBN 13: 978-1-63555-161-7

This Trade Paperback Original Is Published By
Bold Strokes Books, Inc.
P.O. Box 249
Valley Falls, NY 12185

First Edition: August 2018

CREDITS
Editor: Cindy Cresap
Production Design: Susan Ramundo
Cover Design By Sheri (hindsightgraphics@gmail.com)
Cover Concept: Deb B.

Acknowledgments

For those of us who *have* to write, I think we all experience the nagging storyline or character that won't go away, and we wrestle with the wisdom of lending it too much attention. But authors occasionally create realities that refuse to be put to rest. There once was such a young woman who refused to settle, back in 1920s Boston, and she turned the tables on those who'd taken from her. The wily well-intentioned characters Stick "Mac" McLaughlin wove into a family have been nagging to have more of their story told for several years now. *Crossing the Line* acknowledges their perseverance, their guts, and their love for each other.

But behind the scenes, recognizing their story, constructing it, and spelling it out for readers wouldn't have happened without support from this author's "family." I owe such gratitude to talented Bold Strokes Books authors Kris Bryant, Sophia Kell Hagen, Fiona Riley, Holly Stratimore, and Jean Copeland, among others, who stood by *Stick McLaughlin: The Prohibition Years* from the beginning and rooted for more.

Encouragement from *Stick* fans, my family, best bud Bill, and most of all, my wife, Kathy, meant the world as I pushed through this during the holidays—and the life-changing addition of puppy Chessa to our household. Deep appreciation also goes out to BSB publisher, Radclyffe, for taking a chance on this story, and to my editor, Cindy Cresap, for smiling on the relationships, the action, and even the villains.

From conception to completion, there's a lot of "crossing the line" in this story, and I trust that everyone who's played a role will approve of each one.

Dedication

To Kathy, who gives so much to so many.
Thank you for giving the world to me.

CHAPTER ONE

Gentlemen!" Out of patience and out of time, Mac yanked her fedora into a steep angle over her forehead and stalked out of the woods. "Enough stalling," she groused, raising the collar of her topcoat. Delays weren't acceptable. She stopped in front of the old truck, awash in its yellowed headlamp light, and focused her ire on the men in the cab she really couldn't see.

"Ridiculously outnumbered and *still* you refuse to get out?" She grabbed an associate's Thompson submachine gun, racked the bolt back into firing mode, and leveled it at the windshield. "Want an invitation?"

She squeezed off three rounds and glass exploded into the cab. Just for good measure, she sprayed bullets from one headlamp to the other, puncturing the radiator between them in a burst of collateral damage. Now she could easily see that both truckers were in custody.

The driver cursed her and an associate kicked him to the ground. As Mac approached, he spit toward her shoes, and she scuffed the wet patch of gravel back into his face.

"Don't press your luck." She signaled her associates to begin transferring his truckload of whiskey into their vehicle.

The driver swiped at the dirt on his graying stubble. "You son of a bitch. You'll be sorry you picked *this* load."

"I appreciate the tip." She ordered his hands tied to the back of his belt just as a shotgun blast from the rear of the truck startled everyone.

Evidently, the bootleggers had packed an escort with this load, and she fumed at having been outsmarted. Several pistol shots rang out, then another blast.

"Stand him up," she said. "Hurry." She spun the driver around, gripped his belt, and rushed him forward with the tip of the Thompson. "You'll stop this right now."

Suddenly, a pistol barrel pressed between her shoulders and brought her up short. A man barked in her ear, his breath short and heavy.

"You're done! And we're done getting the short end of the deal. You got that?"

Mac whirled on him, Thompson high in both hands, and smashed the gunstock against his head. He crumbled at her feet with a whimper.

Another whimper followed, then a soft whine, and she thought she heard her name in a meek, high-pitched plea. Then came several soft pats to her cheeks.

Mac blinked repeatedly and shifted against an odd pressure on her torso.

Reality materialized slowly in the refined sitting room of her hotel suite, complete with one impish toddler on her lap. Curious azure eyes peered at her from behind disarrayed blond curls, and the little girl brightened, her turned-up nose crinkled with excitement when their eyes met.

"Mackie seep."

Mac forced herself to wake up. She counted her blessings that *this* was her life now, that her past sat where it belonged, and such vivid dreams rarely recurred. Today, this little girl and her mother mattered above all else, a family that was meant to be. Forever.

"Yes, my Katie Rose," Mac said and wrapped her in a bear hug. "We took a nap, didn't we?"

Katie nodded with enthusiastic pride. "Katie seep." And she patted Mac's chest. "Mackie bed." She slid off her lap and waddled purposefully toward the doll on the settee. "Baby seep, Mackie."

"Well." Ellie leaned against the doorframe, her grin and sparkling eyes the mirror image of her daughter's. "It's about time you two woke up. We're meeting everyone for dinner within the hour."

Wearing a simple cotton sundress of cobalt blue, her hair styled up into the latest fashion by the hotel salon, Ellie radiated a contentment Mac could feel in her own heart. That's just how it was when two hearts blended as one. They'd been lovers since their teens, and despite leading separate lives for a time, they'd migrated back to each other as if by fate. Mac took full advantage of this moment to appreciate every inch of her and the life they'd built. *You and Katie will always have everything I can give.*

"God, you're so special."

"You're not awake yet, *Stick* McLaughlin."

"Am so." Mac smiled at the old nickname. She looked down at herself, slumped in the leather armchair, her tailored dress shirt and trousers now wrinkled. "Not skinny old Stick anymore, honey."

"Oh, you were my Stick when you were just a bag-of-bones hobo," Ellie said, crossing the room to her in a graceful, leggy stride, "and you're my Stick today, all dashing and wiry muscle." She leaned on the arms of the chair and lowered her head. Mac melted into her slow, luxurious kiss until Ellie inched back and spoke against her lips. "I don't care if the world knows you as Mac or even Elizabeth. You'll always be the Stick I fell in love with years ago and that's never going to change."

Katie thrust her doll between them, face down on Mac's chest. She carefully positioned Mac's arms around it, then stepped back to assess her work.

"Mackie go seep."

Ellie crouched beside her. "Sweetie, it's almost suppertime."

Katie promptly placed a tiny finger on her mother's lips. "Mama, ssh. Mackie go seep."

Heavy and lazy, rich with lake sweat even at this midnight hour, the humid air suspended Mac's cigarette smoke like a flimsy barrier just beyond the brim of her Panama hat. Unusually warm for early

September in the Adirondacks, she thought, a bonus for their much-anticipated retreat on Lake George. Her little family's fifty-three acres were only a few hours away, but this escape to the grand resort hotels of "Millionaires' Row" felt like a fairy tale. Having spent the past two years adapting to anonymity and rural seclusion, they deserved a vacation. Ellie deserved a "honeymoon." Mac was thrilled to arrange this prolonged stay at the glamorous Sagamore Hotel.

She walked silently on the banking's soft grass, an eye on the gently undulating water. Such a serene way to unwind after that fabulous dinner and wild poker session with old friends. Smiling at the prospect of returning to the hotel and giving her significant winnings to Ellie, Mac relaxed in the quiet companionship of her best friend, Jersey, at her side.

Jersey ran Mac's old operation now, more in alcohol distribution than hijacking, and Mac liked knowing that her old second-in-command kept the money flowing for that loyal bunch. She hardly saw her old gang anymore, so having several favorite cohorts up from Massachusetts made this getaway all the more precious.

"All right, already. Out with it." Jersey's short blond hair wafted across her forehead as she grinned up at Mac. "You've been thinking too hard by yourself."

Mac tossed a hand toward the dark lake and the glittering Sagamore ahead, lit so brightly white against the night sky. "Look at us, at all this. Who would have thought?"

Jersey chortled. "I remember when you said that about our Victorian in Dorchester."

"And this is a far cry from that." At times, she missed their closely-knit household, the responsibilities, and the daily tasks, but not the lethal dangers. When Ellie reentered her life, and Mac stepped away from hijacking Boston's ethnic mobs, she brought wealth and a full heart to the family of her dreams.

Jersey lit a Chesterfield and her blue eyes flashed at Mac over the flame. Mac could feel her reading her mind, just like the old days. "Ellie doesn't want you concerning yourself with *the business*."

"She'd prefer we left it behind us, and I can't blame her, but it still comes to mind every now and then."

Her family had been a long time coming, and required Mac to keep Ellie and Katie free of the worry that the Feds or the Mob would someday corral her, the elusive "Hijack Mack." Not long ago, her phantom-like operation enjoyed legendary status, and the Feds still held outstanding warrants on the "man" they couldn't find. For damages and lost revenue—and blatant disrespect—the Mob still sought revenge. And always would.

But Mac's due diligence wasn't limited to herself. Ellie also sat high on the Mob's "most wanted list," for testimony that put many thugs and their political connections behind bars. Mob outfits as far away as New York City suffered massive financial and organizational losses, and, as with "Hijack Mack," the name Eleanor Harrison acquired permanent "enemy" status.

"Sh." Mac turned abruptly. "Did you hear that?"

Jersey pulled the cigarette from between her lips and stood motionless, listening. Severe coughing and a low-pitched groan broke the silence, followed by cursing, thrashing, and muffled grunts. She pointed to the boathouse. "Serious disagreement."

"A woman's voice."

They bolted toward the small barn extended over shallow water.

Jersey pressed against Mac's side. "Boss, you're still carrying, I hope."

"Just the little .25mm on my ankle. You?"

Jersey tapped her jacket near her left shoulder. "Always."

They stopped before the doorway to listen.

"I don't answer to you!" The peculiar, gravelly voice sounded near panic.

"Shut the hell up," a man said. "We just took you for a little swim, Rey. Mama Bear needs a little practice holdin' her breath, doesn't she?" He and another man laughed at his words, while the gender reference confirmed Mac's suspicions. "Next time you pull something stupid, you might not—"

"God dammit!" Rey said, her scratchy voice roaring. "No more 'next time'! I don't do business with your kind."

"You just keep running product down the lake."

The second man snickered. "Yeah, we'll be seeing you."

Mac stared at Jersey as they listened, the familiar topic clearly striking both of them.

"Oh no," Rey countered. "I defend my loads on this lake and I'll defend 'em on roads through the woods, if I have to." She coughed deeply. "I'm not afraid of you clowns."

"Even for a bruiser of a woman like you, Rey, that's a ballsy claim."

Mac and Jersey peeked around the corner in time to see the large figure raise a hand and yell. Broad shouldered in soggy shirt and pants, Rey rushed the smaller man, her size advantage obvious even in the poor light. Mac gripped Jersey's arm and stopped her from reaching for her gun. She estimated that Rey topped her own five foot ten by several inches, carried far more than two hundred pounds, and was quick for a woman her size. Rey grabbed the man's shirtfront and hauled him off his feet like a rag doll.

From one of the boats, his partner pumped a shell into a shotgun. "Hands off him, y'dumb bitch!" He directed Rey away with the gun. "Move!"

Rey straight-armed the man backward off the pier and down onto his partner. The pair landed in a pile on the boat deck, but had guns pointed at her before they even found their feet. Now, Jersey had her chromed .45mm poised at the edge of the doorway.

The man pushed his partner to the controls. "Get us the fuck outa here." He shook his head at Rey. "You do as you're told, and don't be stupid again. Think of the consequences, Rey. Broads don't win this game."

"I promise you, your time will come," Rey snarled as the boat motored out. "And I don't play games, you son of a bitch."

The men puttered away from the boathouse before accelerating toward the village at the southern tip of the lake. Rey stood in place, watching until she couldn't, then dropped to her knees, head in both hands.

Mac's blood pulsed like it hadn't in years. Such action was in her past for good reason. She'd promised Ellie "no more bad guy stuff" when she left her operation, and the idyllic life she now cherished meant far too much to risk coming close to this kind of heat.

She edged them away from the doorway and waved off Jersey's gun. "Enough. Should have minded our own business."

The idea of returning to her hotel rose inviting and warm with each step along the lakefront path. Ellie and Katie slept, safe and sound in luxurious comfort, and now Mac couldn't wait to join them.

"Jesus," Jersey said on a breath as she matched Mac's longer stride. "Figures, we'd come upon something like that."

"Looks like she's in a really bad spot."

"Yeah, that's serious heat on her. You can smell that type a mile away."

Mac resigned the boathouse incident to something she should not have seen and could do nothing about, and looked ahead, relishing the sanctuary of the majestic Sagamore. So regal in its posture overlooking Lake George, the hotel reached out from a central columned structure with two-story wings of suites and acres of manicured lawn that sprawled down to the private dock. For a moment, she lost herself in its grandeur and thought it suited a king, and that the lake's namesake would have approved.

But footsteps in the gravel behind her caught her attention, and she kicked herself for not noticing sooner. *Shit, when did I get so soft?* The crunching stopped, and as she turned, she heard Jersey do the same.

Her shoulders sagging, Rey stood outside the boathouse studying their departure. She watched with eyes Mac could only feel, her bulk an imposing shadow, her intention impossible to read. Beyond the immediate curiosity of spotting them, a volatile mix of defeat, sadness, and rage had to be boiling inside her. Mac's personal experience told her so and explained why Rey's looming presence didn't intimidate her now. Mac had a healthy respect for volatility— in herself and others—and saw far more in Rey's bearing than Rey could ever imagine.

Mac looked beyond the threat to the commonality Rey didn't know they shared, and acknowledged her with a nod. *I get it.*

CHAPTER TWO

Hoping she wouldn't regret this decision, Mac returned to her old friends at the table.

Jersey eyed her curiously. "I'm shocked you let her cut in."

Mac hadn't wanted to, but she hadn't wanted to frighten Ellie or make a scene, either. She forced herself to sit and, for the third time, looked back at the dance floor where that boathouse woman, Rey, now danced with the love of her life. Mac glared at the large physique, unable to tell if Rey cut in to check out the person she'd seen the other night, or if she honestly couldn't resist touching a beautiful woman.

Mac locked onto Ellie's eyes from afar, ready to rescue her in an instant, no matter what, but Ellie seemed to be faring well. The others at the table watched just as keenly.

"They sure grow their women big up here, boss," Millie said with a smirk. "She's bigger than you described."

Jackson mumbled pointedly before taking a swig of beer. "She's fishing for information. Couldn't be more obvious."

"I think I agree. We worry her," Mac said, eyes glued to the dance floor.

Millie set a cigarette into her ivory holder and leaned toward Jackson for a light. "Ellie can handle her." She took a drag and sipped her drink. "See? El's smiling at her. Whatever they're talking about must be okay."

Mac just wanted the song to end and Ellie to return. She never liked that "cutting in" part of dancing, anyway, and *really* didn't like it now. Unlike Millie and Jackson, who were two of the boldest people on the planet, Ellie had reacted with worry and disappointment when Mac recounted the boathouse incident of two nights ago. Surprisingly, Ellie didn't appear worried or disappointed at the moment, but Mac nevertheless lived to spare her those emotions.

"I think she looks like a pirate," Millie said with an amused smile, "that salt-and-pepper hair tied back between her shoulders. All she needs is a sword on her hip."

"You've seen too many movies," Jackson quipped.

Millie gave him a playful shove. "Wonder how old she is?"

The six-piece band from Schenectady segued into another song, and Rey swayed Ellie to the new beat. Mac downed the rest of her drink. "If she gets too friendly—"

"She wouldn't dare," Jersey said.

Jackson gestured with his beer bottle. "Go cut back in."

Millie sighed, put her cigarette in the ashtray, and adjusted her silk scarf to the side of her throat, exposing a sensational amount of cleavage for her petite frame. "Leave this to me." She stood and smoothed her palms down her hips, her purple sheath detailing every voluptuous curve. "I'm too curious now to sit and stare." She primped her tight golden curls before sashaying onto the dance floor.

Jersey flashed Jackson a grin. "This ought to be good."

Millie strode up to Ellie, tapped her shoulder, and said a few words. Then she looked up at Rey, arched an eyebrow suggestively, and smiled. Mac could only shake her head when Ellie stepped away and left Rey gawking down at her new dance partner.

Mac drew out Ellie's chair and clutched her hand to her thigh. "I'm glad you're back."

Ellie dabbed perspiration from her forehead with a handkerchief. "What a dancer. She's very nice, Mac."

"Uh-huh."

Ellie sipped her cocktail. "And said she thought my *husband* and I made a lovely couple."

Jersey snorted.

Mac looked out to the dance floor again. "Did she, now?"

Jackson nodded at Jersey. "Told you. Definitely fishing."

"Oh, without a doubt," Ellie said. "I was shamefully obtuse about that issue. Two can play that game."

Mac set a light kiss on her temple. "I'm not keen on playing *any* games with her, honey."

Ellie stroked Mac's cheek. "I know, baby, but I couldn't help feeling sorry for her, after what you said she's up against. She's hiding some serious pain, too. My guess would be her ribs, and her right hand is swollen and discolored."

"She dances all right," Jersey observed.

"She's that desperate to figure us out," Jackson said.

"Well," Ellie said, "I was surprised she admitted running a shipping business, 'commodities,' as she called it, here on Lake George. She seemed proud of it, in fact. Of course, I didn't let on that I knew what that meant. I just told her we have a farm near the Vermont border and are vacationing with friends at the Sagamore for a while."

Mac toyed with her empty glass and waved to the waiter for another round. "She ask about us? What we do for work?"

"No, but I caught her looking this way a few times." Ellie tickled a finger between the buttons of Mac's vest. "She's impressed by your suit, thought we were up from New York City."

Jackson thumped his empty bottle on the table. "I rest my case."

Jersey nodded. "Manhattan's probably where her worries are coming from."

"If she thinks she's going to make you forget what you saw the other night," Jackson added, "she got another thing coming." His dark eyes flashed with promise. "We'll give her more than Manhattan to worry about real quick."

Mac noted the hint of disapproval on Ellie's face. "Thanks, Jacks, but there's no need for any of that."

"You only have to say the word."

Mac knew without asking that they'd brought more than luggage in Jersey's new Studebaker; just like she knew Jackson's trigger-happy spirit would never change. But the last thing she wanted was trouble. Plus, she could feel Ellie's anxiety mounting with such conversation.

They all looked to the dance floor again to check on Millie.

❖

"Well, hello up there. Thanks for letting me cut in." Millie set a hand on Rey's hip and let Rey take her other hand in her big, bruised paw. She quickly realized that dancing with someone this brawny and a foot taller required tricky, measured steps, and she appreciated the waltz pace. And she was pleased to unsettle Rey with the view straight down the front of her dress. "So, I couldn't help but notice you're a terrific dancer."

Rey took an extra beat to respond. She lowered her head to avoid shouting over the music, and Millie purposefully straightened and raised her ample bosom closer to Rey's face.

"Ah… Well, s-so are you," Rey managed. "A great dancer."

"This band is as good as any I've heard in Boston."

"You're from Boston? Look, I, uh, I don't mean to embarrass you or anything, but…well, you sure are one pretty lady. What brings a showstopper like you to Lake George?"

"Why, thanks." Millie feigned a slight fluster. "Just a little vacation with old friends. My name's Millie Anderson. What's yours?"

"Rey."

"Rey what?"

"Eh…actually, it's Camille Reynaud, but I go by Rey."

Millie scrunched her nose. "Camille doesn't suit you."

"My friends call me Rey."

"And we're barely friends."

"You're the rebellious type, aren't you?"

Millie shrugged. "I say what I think and I back it up. Folks can take it or leave it."

"I don't know you at all," Rey said, chuckling, "but I believe you."

To Millie's surprise, Rey's hazel eyes lightened, and the edginess of her wide, weathered face softened. Her full-bodied sound, drawn from deep in that barrel chest, rumbled like faint thunder. Millie couldn't recall ever meeting such a female countenance in her years circulating through city clubs and speakeasies.

And Millie could count on only one hand the times she'd been "believed." Once, during her struggle toward womanhood, when her schoolteacher agreed Millie *hadn't* thrown the first punch. And a second time, when a certain handsome, soft-spoken dyke welcomed Millie to a family of hijackers.

"Well, *I* believe," she countered, "that beneath this tough mountain exterior of yours lies a softy, a sucker for a sultry clarinet. I'll bet you're an independent soul, a hard-ass by necessity." She cocked her head and grinned. "Tell me I'm wrong."

The song ended and Rey rolled her eyes. "Saved. Any more dancing, and you'll be telling me my shoe size." Millie giggled as Rey escorted her back to the table and was pleasantly surprised when Rey pulled the chair out for her. "Maybe I'll steal another dance later, Millie?"

"You can try."

"Rey?" Ellie beckoned her around the table with a wave. "I'd like you to meet someone." She clutched Mac's hand on the tabletop and beamed.

"Oh, of course. Your husb—"

"My Elizabeth."

Rey's face went blank. "Nice to meet you, Elizabeth."

Mac simply acknowledged the greeting with a word. "Rey."

The waiter suddenly interrupted with drinks. "Would you like your CC over here, Rey?"

"Sure she does," Jackson answered for her. As Jersey spaced her chair to make room, he swiped a chair from a neighboring table. "She'll have a seat right here."

"Oh, I couldn't." Rey's eyes flickered around the table. "I mean, thanks, but I-I don't want to intrude."

Jersey stood and offered the chair. "But we insist."

"Get your mighty self over here," Millie said and poked Jackson's shoulder. "Move over one, Jacks. Rey's sitting next to me." She picked up her abandoned cigarette and turned back to Rey. "Now, come on over here and sit. My neck's starting to hurt, looking so damn far up. Got a light, or do you just want to watch me wave this thing around?"

Rey obeyed. She lit Millie's cigarette and reached for her own Canadian Club as soon as the waiter set it down.

"Thanks, Michael."

"They know you here, Rey," Ellie observed.

Mac drew a pack of Lucky Strikes from her suit jacket and kept a studious eye on Rey as she lit up. Rey was an intriguing contradiction, so ferocious and gruff yet remarkably conciliatory here in her pressed shirt and slacks. She had to be tough, a survivor, Mac thought. This line of work hardened you. *The thugs called her Mama Bear for a reason.* Credit to her, though, especially if she's being pressured by heavy hitters. And there was no question that those guys were connected.

"Most every place around the lake does," Rey answered. "It comes with the job."

Millie leaned closer and lowered her voice. "Ellie says you're in *commodities*? That's exciting stuff." Mac fought to remain straight-faced as Millie pressed her innocent act. "You have a boat, I assume, and lots of sailors? How long have you been at it?"

Rey had everyone's attention as, again, she glanced around. "We're small but efficient, and it's been ten years now."

From the onset of Prohibition, Mac calculated. Considering the wealth in the area, she conceded that she'd defend this goldmine, too.

Mac drew the ashtray closer. "These places must have huge needs," she said with a casual air, and intentionally looked down as she flicked her ash. "I'm sure you do well." Ellie squeezed her thigh, and Mac was tempted to change the subject.

Rey turned her glass thoughtfully and seemed to search for the right words. Mac wondered if she'd reference the boathouse incident. Finally, Rey looked directly at her through an exhale of smoke. "I'm lucky to have the best action south of the border. Sometimes we're a bit hard-pressed to keep up."

"It's all in who you know, I suppose." Mac held Ray's gaze. The weariness was evident.

Rey broke their connection and lifted her whiskey. "I'll drink to that."

"So will we," Jersey said, and everyone drank.

"So." Rey cleared her throat before continuing. "What about you, Elizabeth? You have a farm?" Mac noted the eagerness to redirect the conversation. "Because, I have to say, I've never seen farmers dressed so fine." She grinned at each of them. "Y'sure you're not straight off Madison Avenue? I mean, damn. I'd need a whole factory to get me a suit that looked that good."

Mac hated games like this and usually walked away from them, but Rey's obvious attempt to glean information via polite, social chatter intrigued her. She doubted Rey had much experience plying details, and knew their own outdistanced Rey's by a mile. A twinge of sympathy for Rey's predicament threatened her concentration, so she chose her words carefully. "Actually, we're not really New Yorkers, but we did leave the city for a quiet, healthy place to build our life, to raise our little girl."

Rey's eyebrows went up. "You don't say?"

"A long story," Ellie said, "but the greatest moments of my life," she flashed Mac an adoring smile, "having Katie and then reconnecting with my long-lost love."

Rey sat back hard. "Wow." She downed the rest of her CC and waved to the waiter for another round. "Well, I... Hell. That's just really swell, the two of you raising a little one."

"We're still learning farm life, but it's exciting," Ellie said, "and Katie is just thriving." She checked her watch and patted Mac's arm. "And we'll need to leave soon. The Sagamore nursery closes at eleven."

Rey looked a bit awestruck. "Does my heart good, a family of women living the good life. Just amazing. And changing from a city lifestyle couldn't have been easy. What kind of business did you have?"

Mac cocked an eyebrow at the loaded question and raised her glass. "Commodities."

CHAPTER THREE

Awake since dawn, Rey had her forty-two-foot *Jean Luc II* spotless for a joyride around the lake with her new friends. The opportunity to relax with like-minded folks was just as invigorating—and rare—as this spell of balmy weather, and she was glad she'd extended the invitation. The group fascinated her, and she attributed the attraction, *or maybe it was hope,* to what she had in common with Elizabeth. She'd spent the past two days thinking about their evening at the Lake Harvest Grill. Couldn't stop thinking about it, in fact, and worked up so much excitement about today, that she found herself moored at the Sagamore's private dock with plenty of time to spare.

She settled into a deck chair and waved to passersby out for their morning strolls, guests enjoying the picturesque hotel in ways far beyond her means. Elizabeth had the means, however, obviously had fared exceptionally well in the "commodities" trade, judging by the look of her, the talk of farm and family, and the very fact that they were vacationing *here* at the Sagamore. Knowing a woman triumphed in this male-oriented business lent Rey a spiritual boost. And, as if fate hadn't smiled on Elizabeth enough, she had a sweet, beautiful lover—and a daughter.

The others seemed to hang on her every word, too, and she pictured them working for her, following orders. Their pointed questions and subtle glances the other night had been intimidating, and there had been moments as she sat among them, that she'd felt snared by some spider's web. Oddly, though, the experience didn't carry the same anxiety she suffered around the mobsters who threatened her business.

No, this group felt more like a family, a generous bunch, and easy talkers. Somehow, they managed to get more out of her than she'd intended, while revealing little of themselves. She'd seriously tried to learn their reaction to the boathouse incident, and if they'd use that information against her, but they'd stayed tight-lipped about it and kept conversation direct, polite, and often funny.

Millie's brash personality certainly stood out among them, along with her quick wit and the most breathtaking pair of female assets Rey had ever seen. She wondered how many suitors Millie had back in Boston, and pictured a line of fashionable men and women at glitzy clubs waiting their turn. Rey took a bit of satisfaction in being a "terrific dancer" in Millie's eyes.

Two elderly men in suits and bowlers strolled along the dock, eyeing her *Jean Luc II* with unabashed interest.

"Mornin', gents." She tipped her cap. "Fine day, isn't it?"

"That it is," said one with a remarkable handlebar moustache. "Going out, I presume?"

"Can't wait," Rey answered as the other man ogled her boat.

"Bet your name is Rey," he said, and she straightened in her seat.

"Do I know you, sir?"

"No, but we've heard of the *Jean Luc II*." He turned to his friend. "Haven't we, Mr. Merriweather?" He looked back at the boat. "You must be glad to have this leisure time."

Rey squinted against the morning sun, not particularly comfortable with his implication. They simply could be businessmen interested in shipping, or maybe just nosy tycoons. Or Feds. Or worse, they could be snooping for the Mob. She made a point to look and sound at ease.

"How could you *not* enjoy a day like today?"

Merriweather injected, "Exactly. Not a breeze about and the water's smooth as silk. Have a fine day. Nice meeting you, Rey."

"You gents have a fine one, too." She tipped her cap again, her gut unsettled as they wandered across the lawn. All the locals knew her *Jean Luc II*, and kept its business to themselves, but these men weren't locals and she wasn't thrilled that they knew anything about her or the boat. Exactly *how* they came about that knowledge gave her pause.

However, seeing a familiar group approach, Rey stashed that concern away for a later time. Elizabeth, Ellie, and an adorable toddler led the others toward the dock, and the little family brought a smile to Rey's face, along with an unexpected pang of longing.

In a sundress of pink ruffles, the little girl chattered away as Ellie and Elizabeth each held a hand. They looked every bit the perfect parents, a perfect family. With a parasol on her shoulder, Ellie was radiant in a pale yellow dress that fluttered just below her knees, and Elizabeth practically glistened in a white linen suit, complete with that Panama hat.

Rey couldn't help but notice the love between the three of them, and the joviality among the trio of friends that followed. Teetering across the grass in not-so-short pumps, Millie glowed in her scarlet knee-length skirt and revealing scoop-neck blouse, and teased with a matching sheer wrap around her shoulders. Watching her laugh brightly at something Jackson said, Rey wondered if there was something special between them. But then Jersey took Millie's hand and guided her onto the dock, and Rey abandoned the thought as a futile waste of time.

She welcomed them aboard the *Jean Luc II* and smiled at the toddler in Mac's arms.

"Hello there. Are you Miss Katie Rose? You're a pretty little one, you are."

"Katie," Ellie said with a hand on Rey's shoulder. "This is Rey, our new friend. Can you say hello?"

Wide-eyed and obviously a bit overwhelmed by Rey's size, Katie opened her mouth but then cowered against Mac's shoulder.

Mac gave her a squeeze. "It's okay, Katie. Say 'Hi, Rey.'"

Katie waved timidly. "Hi, Wey."

Rey tipped her cap. "Pleased to meet you, miss." She swung a long arm toward the lake. "Want to go for a ride out there on my boat?" At Katie's smile, Rey grinned and clapped her hands. "Okay!

Let's go!" She offered them seats, and quickly shoved off from the dock.

In short order, Rey had them entranced, often laughing as they cruised among the many little islands and she told tales of the lake and her life on it. She motored north at first, turning around at her modest cabin in the cove at Gull Bay. She presumed Elizabeth calculated the duration of deliveries from this far north, and stood a little straighter at the wheel.

For their leisurely ride south, Rey brought out beer, lemonade, and cookies; boasted about having made the latter two herself; and warmed at seeing Katie enjoy them. At one point, Katie wobbled across the deck to her, cookie in each hand.

"Wey, cookie."

Rey cut the engine and went to one knee to accept her offer. "Thank you, Miss Katie." She took a bite and rubbed her stomach. "Mmmm." Katie mimicked her, ran back to Ellie, and mimicked Rey again.

"I think you've won her over," Elizabeth said, joining her at the helm. "You've got the touch with the ladies."

Rey chuckled as she put the *Jean Luc II* back on course. "If only cookies were all it took."

That deepened the grin on Elizabeth's sharp features, and Rey relaxed a bit more. There was a steadiness about her that Rey admired, a cool reservation that said she ran on an even keel, practiced in the art of control. Sensing a strong intuitive force, a craftiness about her, Rey understood how associates would grow steadfast and devoted. *Shrewd, savvy, and smart. I should be half that accomplished after a decade on the job.* The irony of meeting someone—a woman, thank God—who shared her experience didn't escape her, and Rey admitted she was grateful. Lately, with Mob pressure getting physical, she'd begun to fear her own isolation.

Hat in hand, Elizabeth just stared ahead, her dark eyes narrowed against the oncoming breeze, crisply cut auburn hair slicked back, severe jawline set and unmoving. Rather dashing in that suit, Rey thought, tall and with an athletic build, she probably attracted plenty of ladies. Whatever Elizabeth had been through, running "commodities" in Boston no doubt surpassed Rey's adventures on the lake. Rey found herself eager to hear her story, eager for a compatriot, and even though she knew little at the moment, she couldn't help feeling a bit envious, a bit in awe.

Elizabeth dashed away and scooped Katie into her arms before she toppled to the deck. "Gotcha!" The wind threatened the bonnet on Katie's curls and Elizabeth tested the tie beneath her chin. Katie countered by grabbing the Panama with both hands.

"Whoa!" Elizabeth laughed and snatched it before it blew overboard.

Katie giggled and twisted to study Rey's cap.

"Oh, no!" Rey said, eyes wide. "You want mine next?"

"Wey, hat!"

"Let Rey drive," Millie said, her steadying hand on Rey's back. The surprising touch sent a surge of warmth down Rey's spine. "You come to Auntie Millie, you little rascal." Millie slid Katie out of Elizabeth's arms and draped her wrap over Katie's head. "Where'd you go?"

Rey watched them retreat to the stern, where Jersey stole the wrap and wound it around her own head. Katie scrambled onto her lap.

"A good group you've got there," Rey said.

"The very best," Elizabeth said, "and thank you for treating all of us today. You know, it's so beautiful up here, Rey. You're all by yourself? Come on, now. There must be someone special."

"Aw, no. Not for a while now." Rey didn't care to think about the past four solitary years, especially when the odds of finding a female soul mate here in the wilderness were stacked against her. As much as she knew her present situation was her own doing, the prospect still hurt—when she let it. And that was rare, because she couldn't allow heartache to consume her, and there was no way to get it off her chest, no one who would understand. Until now. "I paid the price for doing what I do," she said. "I should've listened, seen the signs, but...this work, it takes a lot. Well, I-I suppose you know what I mean."

"I do."

"I was born up here, so the lake keeps me company. It's a part of me, and I guess that can be hard to understand and accept. I try not to let daydreams, wishful thinking, steal my focus. It's a decent life and things have been okay, I suppose."

"Really." Elizabeth turned to her. "Have they?"

Broaching the subject had been inevitable. The question was blunt, but the gentle delivery drew Rey's full attention. Elizabeth's direct gaze, commanding yet sincere, revealed an intensity Rey believed ran deep. She lost all reservations about leveling with her.

"They have until recently. My operation has become a target for hijackers," she glanced back, "and not local ones."

"New York City?"

Rey nodded. "And then some, as if it could get worse."

"Do you know who, exactly?"

"Yeah, pretty sure. They fear a guy named Charlie like he's God. Now, I may live here in the sticks, Elizabeth, but I read newspapers and I got a radio, and I know the name Charlie 'Lucky' Luciano well enough to be scared."

"Jesus."

"Yeah, you can say that again. And you ever heard of Jack Moran? They call him Legs Diamond."

"I have. He's that Luciano renegade, doing his own thing, never what he's told."

"Yup. The papers say Luciano's tried to knock him off a few times, he's such a pain in their ass."

"Shit. So, you're saying Diamond is up here, too?"

"Yeah. He's building his own empire, thumbing his nose at Luciano and his Manhattan boys. Obviously, they'd prefer he lay low, but he's taking over everything local." Rey removed her cap, scratched her head, and wiggled the cap back on. "Guess I'm easy pickings."

"All of a sudden?"

"Well, I think Diamond sniffed out the hotel-casino project, Dazzle, that's underway now in Lake Luzerne, not far from here. Everyone knows Manhattan's behind that because they already come up to Saratoga for gambling and the track. I guess they decided to build farther up this way, go after the big-money crowd that vacations in places like the Sagamore. Um... No offense."

Elizabeth looked across the water as she spoke. "You're saying *both* Manhattan and Legs are tapping your loads."

Rey snorted and glanced over her shoulder again. The others were waving and yelling to swimmers off a nearby island and weren't listening.

"The other night at the boathouse... God, that was awful, the worst they've been so far," Rey said quietly. "They were Diamond's men, and they made it pretty clear they'll take my stuff whenever they want. Between him and Luciano, I get hit on a pretty regular basis now. I've had to put some of my biggest hotels on hold too often, and the other joints along my route cry loud when I can't deliver on schedule. Then they all start demanding discounts." She shook her head. "So bad for business. And resupplying is costing me a God damn fortune."

"This casino, Dazzle, is it up and running?"

"By next June, they say. But Luciano and his pal...Lansky, Meyer Lansky, they're testing the waters in advance, making sure mine is an operation they can build around, dependable, and with lots of quality product. They came at me a few weeks back, demanding a load or they'd mess me up—or sink my boat. One of my crew learned the hard way that we don't have much choice. He ended up with a broken leg. And they offered me pennies, thirty percent. You believe that? What can I do with thirty percent?"

"I don't know this area or your connections, Rey, but I'd guess not much. Frankly, I'm surprised they offered you anything."

"I suppose, but thirty is basically nothing. When Legs interferes and swipes my load, Luciano's men get resentful, like it's *their* stock getting lifted. Hell, it's near to impossible now to even sneak my own loads through to my customers." She sighed hard. "My product is just too damn popular. Those guys all know about each other, and it sure would be good if they killed each other off, but I can only dream."

"God. I'm sorry to hear this, Rey."

"Hey, *I'm* sorry I got all carried away. It's my headache, Elizabeth. Today's supposed to be fun."

"It's all right. I asked. I'm familiar with the names and the tactics. And please, call me Mac. Y'know, as in McLaughlin. So…" Mac shook her head. "Jesus. With all this heat, how the hell are you managing?"

"Ah, dammed if I know. Won't be able to handle it much longer. That I *do* know. And the frustration, the anger keeps me up nights. I've worked damn hard all these years and just want a simple life, but I'm not blind. The writing's on the wall, Mac. If you've ever dealt with that kind, you know my operation's days are numbered."

CHAPTER FOUR

The late-afternoon steamer chugged its way from the Village at Lake George, rousing Katie from her nap in Ellie's lap. She quickly fell back to sleep, though, worn out by Rey's morning cruise and an afternoon of sightseeing, eating, and shopping on their own. This return leg of their excursion had all of them excited, because they'd missed taking in the magnificent daylight approach to the Sagamore when they arrived.

Leaning against the rail, Mac tugged the brim of her hat down more firmly against the breeze. She slipped both hands into her pockets and crossed her ankles nonchalantly, moved by the simple image of mother and child lounging before her. She scanned the busy deck and the dozens of preoccupied couples and families enjoying the scenery and abruptly ducked forward beneath Ellie's parasol. She lifted Ellie's chin with the back of a finger. "I love you."

Ellie pulled her closer by her jacket lapel and teased her lips across Mac's. "You're my everything." Mac claimed her mouth with a kiss that evoked a yearning moan.

"Ahem. Beg pardon." A young waiter stood nearby, awkwardly studying his shoes, his dark skin brilliant against his white uniform. "May I offer the gentleman and his lady a lemonade, iced tea, Coca-Cola, coff—" Making eye contact with Mac as she straightened to her full height, he faltered. "Oh, I-I mean—"

"Lemonade sounds lovely," Ellie said gently. She selected a glass from his tray. "This is wonderful. What is your name, please?"

"Edwin, ma'am."

"Thank you, Edwin."

Flashing a smile, he nodded and turned to Mac, his expression once again formal. "We also have a large selection of soda pop, Saratoga's mineral water, and...if you'd prefer something a bit stronger..."

Mac's blood heated. Remarkable. Even here, among tourists in the middle of the biggest damn lake she'd ever seen, alcohol still turned its nose up at the stupid Eighteenth Amendment.

"There's a saloon on the lower deck...m-ma'am. Cigars 'n all."

"Jameson, please."

Edwin snapped to attention with his new mission. "Yes, ma'am. Be right back."

Mac watched him disappear to a lower deck and she cast her eyes to the northern horizon, where the lake curled into the mountains. She envisioned Canadian Club whiskey traveling down this waterway on the *Jean Luc II*. With all these posh hotels, mansions, and Saratoga's thoroughbreds, there was, unquestionably, a serious demand for it and serious money on the barrelhead.

"Elizabeth McLaughlin. That young man didn't know what to make of you."

Drawn from her musing, Mac chuckled. "He won't be so presumptuous next time, will he, Miss Eleanor Marie Weston Harrison?" She winked at Jersey's smirk as she sat beside Ellie and removed her hat.

Ellie leaned against her shoulder. "Jackson and Millie already went below to find the bar."

"Speaking of whiskey..."

Ellie sipped her lemonade and shifted her gaze to the "Millionaires' Row" shoreline of mansions and hotels. "Sometimes I think I can read your mind."

Mac's mouth curled upward. "Money by the barrelful, Ellie." Jersey grunted in agreement.

Ellie nodded but wouldn't look her way. It wasn't a frequently discussed topic any more, but Mac took comfort in the fact that they would always share their thoughts.

"Money by the barrelful, true," Ellie said, "and no doubt people are already making it." She set her glass aside, wrapped her fingers around Mac's hand, and sought her eyes. "We have far more than we need, baby. Far more than anyone knows. After all that you—that *we* have been through...I know *you* know better."

Mac could only nod because, without a doubt, Ellie was right. Life hadn't been easy and they'd been lucky. They'd survived, and unlike millions of Americans these days, they had plenty of money to live comfortably. Home now couldn't be any safer.

Nevertheless, she was intrigued by the challenge she knew she could—but wouldn't—meet. A ripple of shame passed through her. She would never endanger, never risk losing the ultimate treasures she'd longed so hard to hold.

Edwin reappeared. "Your Jameson, ma'am. Anything else I can get for you?"

Mac withdrew a five-dollar bill from her billfold, deftly folded it with two fingers, and tapped it down into his breast pocket. Edwin went wide-eyed and shook his head.

"You work hard," Mac insisted. "You're good at your job and it's appreciated."

"I-I thank you very much, ma'am."

Mac set a hand on his thin shoulder. "You're welcome. Thank *you.*"

As Edwin hurried off, Ellie hugged Mac's arm. "I'm so proud you're mine. That meant the world to him."

"I've been where he is, remember. We lose respect for one another and the world will go to hell."

Announcements sounded from the loudspeaker, reporting they'd soon be approaching Green Island and the Sagamore's private dock. Ellie gathered a groggy Katie, and Mac slipped an arm around her as they stepped to the rail.

"And how proud am *I*," she said, "with two beautiful ladies in my life?"

"Just two?" Millie said from behind her. She waved an open palm down the front of her blouse and skirt. "This ain't just chopped liver, sweetheart." She hip-bumped Jersey aside and wriggled up to the railing. "Let the lady through here. I want to see, too, you know." She sipped her cocktail and ran a finger around Jersey's ear. "Absolutely *delicious* female creature downstairs," she said. "Go check her out before we dock."

From Jersey's far side, Jackson leaned his forearms on the railing, his drink dangling over the side, and shook his head. "Don't bother, Jers. That doll had men all over her."

Jersey sent Ellie a resigned look.

"Next time," Ellie said.

The ship's horn proclaimed its arrival and now all passengers crowded the rail. Katie squirmed and pointed in Ellie's arms. "It's hard to imagine we're staying here."

Rounding the southern tip of the island, the steamship took aim at the customized concrete docks that sat ready to receive, and onlookers took a collective breath. Acres of sprawling green velvet and flower-lined footpaths drew all eyes to the property. Scattered stands of mature pine and birch, clusters of brightly colored plantings, and appropriately located benches and wicker chairs decorated the grounds.

"Oh, Mac. It's spectacular," Ellie said as passengers bustled around them, eager to debark.

"The brochures don't do it justice." Mac downed the rest of her drink in a hurry.

"And seeing it this way," Ellie said, "I'm even more amazed that so many can afford it these days."

Mac kissed her cheek and hugged her and Katie together. "We can, my love. This and so much more." She took Katie into her arms. "Let's go."

The ten-minute process of leaving the ship took twice as long, once Katie decided to bid farewell to everyone—including the captain. A burly, heavily bearded fellow who looked better suited for the helm of an oceangoing freighter, he happily held Katie in his arm and they acknowledged every debarking passenger. Ellie and Mac stood close by, preening proudly.

Two elderly men teased the captain about Katie as they passed, and one wearing a white bowler clapped Mac soundly on the shoulder.

"Well done, young man," he barked on an exhale of cigar smoke. "Got yourself a pretty little pair right there."

Mac glanced at him through the smoke, coughed lightly, and decided to keep the peace. "Ah... They are lovely, yes. I am proud and grateful they'll have me. Thank you, sir."

The man puffed his cigar vigorously and stared just as hard. His friend's handlebar moustache twitched when he smiled, watching Katie toy with the captain's beard. The cigar smoker, meanwhile, maintained a keen, rude stare into Mac's face.

"First time vacationing here at the Sagamore?"

Matching his height, Mac faced him squarely. "Our first time, yes. And you?"

He held up three fingers, preferring to suck the cigar before speaking. His friend filled the awkward silence.

"Here on business," he stated, offering a handshake. "Name's Merriweather. My associate, Roberts. We can't get enough of these libations on the water. But so far this week, I'm afraid, we've thrown away too much money at the casinos."

Mac gripped the weak hand, careful not to hurt the man. Thin and graying, Merriweather at least was pleasant, polite, which seemed more than his friend could claim.

"McLaughlin," she responded in kind and stepped slightly aside. "And the lovely ladies are Ellie and Katie." Roberts's eyes narrowed and he appeared ready to speak, but Mac continued. "I've heard the Canfield is beautiful."

"Most definitely a sight to see," Merriweather said. "We've just hit a streak of bad luck at the tables, but I can suggest some places you might have success."

"Well, then. We'll make sure to connect with you." She tipped her head toward Katie. "Tell me, sirs, do you think we've lost little Katie forever to the ferocious bearded pirate captain?"

Merriweather laughed as he nodded. "Listen, McLaughlin. Serious poker in the saloon here later tonight. Uh...that is..." his voice dropped, "if the missus will turn you loose. You're welcome to sit in. Plenty of fine *refreshment* available, as well."

"What's your line of work, McLaughlin?" Roberts asked.

Mac grinned as her guard rose. "Your table stakes are that high you think I won't cover?"

"Oh, not at all!" Merriweather said.

Roberts scanned Mac's suit as he rolled his cigar between his fingers. "I'd say you do all right."

"Join us, won't you?" Merriweather seemed almost desperate. "There are six tables so far."

"Where are you from?" Roberts persisted. "And what did you say you do?" He exhaled into Mac's face, and this time, Mac blatantly waved the smoke away.

"Excuse me. I'd appreciate it if you'd send that elsewhere." Eyes watering, she coughed deeply as a familiar palm patted her back. The motion of Ellie's hand became a brief but affectionate rub.

"Okay. That's it!" Roberts stated with more volume than necessary. He pointed the cigar toward Mac's chest. "You're a woman."

Merriweather straightened and his eyebrows rose. Several passersby stared and muttered to each other.

Mac chortled as she wiped her stinging eyes with her handkerchief. "Jesus, Roberts. Of course I am. Took you long enough." She retrieved Katie from the captain and settled her into the carriage, then winked at Merriweather. Before Roberts could comment further, Mac staggered him with a jovial slap to his upper arm. "And here I'd thought an associate of Merriweather's to be more astute!"

Ellie started them toward the walkway. "Good afternoon, gentlemen," she said through a forced a smile.

Mac glanced back and offered a casual salute with a finger to the brim of her hat. "Thanks for the poker invite, gents."

Rey wrestled with the business numbers in her head, but they just wouldn't add up. *Booze has never been so popular, but between Legs and the Mob, there's no way I can keep either of them happy.*

She practiced her explanation out loud, over the growl of her boat engine. Damn shame, such a pretty twilight cruise had to be wasted on this meeting with scum. For a moment, she imagined an entirely different mood, and that Mac and the group were still with her—and someone with whom to commiserate. Because, truth be told, *this* run to Diamond Point was no joyride. Rey bent behind the windscreen and lit a cigarette.

The "businessmen" awaiting her in the hamlet weren't going to be happy about coming up empty-handed the other night. And they'd expect her to make good, instead of going after Legs, who hijacked that load in the first place. Just picturing those thugs, smarmy and cocky, flaunting guns like their dicks, turned her stomach.

She had confidence in the spiel she'd prepared, that it would fire them up to put another big hurt on Legs, but they wouldn't give two hoots that she'd been left too broke to resupply. Her problems weren't their problems.

"If I don't have it, I can't get it!" she shouted into the wind and sucked smoke from her Camel with a vengeance. "Sons of bitches."

Once again, she'd see no return, no working capital from the lost load, a shipment that had practically drained her finances to acquire. And her Canadian source wasn't about to lower his already rock-bottom price out of sympathy. She'd feared this nightmare would come true, after these New York heavies cornered her a while back. Rey yelled at the dimming sky, cursed the "agreement" she'd been forced to make. She knew full well that the Mob's minimal thirty-percent allowance would send her finances crashing. She'd salvaged her operation, albeit barely, but *had* to keep running shipments. Or else.

It spelled bad tidings all around, especially for the livelihood she'd work so long and hard to build—not to mention her health.

Rey exhaled in frustration, smoke blowing back into her eyes and making her squint. Ahead, village lights twinkled as night descended, deceiving in their tranquility. She pulled her loaded .38 from a nearby drawer, absorbed its heft and authority for a long minute, and then grudgingly put it away, never feeling more alone. She'd have to take whatever they dished out. She inhaled long and hard through her nose, stiffened her back, and knew she had no choice. She dragged heavily off her cigarette and flicked it overboard.

She docked at Diamond Point, then ambled toward the designated café and took a deep breath for composure.

Nearly all the cozy tables were empty at this hour. By the door, one hulking man sat with coffee and pie, while at a table against the far wall, three men in suits looked up at her approach.

"Rey. Have a seat." Dark and broad chested, Frank Bocci flashed a set of teeth whiter than his shirt and looked quite authoritative despite his loud green sport jacket. He summoned a thin, middle-age waitress, and she stood by as he spoke to Rey. "We already ate, so you hungry?" He chuckled when Rey shook her head. "Eh, figured not. We'll do a few rounds, won't we?" He patted the red checkered tablecloth and addressed the waitress without looking up. "Bring us a bottle of something decent. You gotta have at least one hidden somewhere."

Rey watched her hurry away, hoping she wouldn't gossip about this gathering. Rey liked being a friend to many here, enjoyed alliances earned through her integrity and generosity, but the locals would look at her sideways, maybe not return the helping hand when needed, if they thought she was in cahoots with this lot. Christ, she thought, these guys make this sweet little place feel sleazy.

She rested her forearms on the table, folded her fingers, and shrugged at Bocci. He hadn't taken his eyes off her and she wanted to kick him under the table and stuff her boot into his crotch just to erase the smirk from his face.

"You know my situation, Frank. There's only so much I can do." She paused to let the waitress put glasses and whiskey on the table. "You're a smooth businessman, a practical kind of guy. You can see it was true, what I said about trouble up here."

Bocci nodded at the skinny guy seated to his right, and the man poured for him and Rey.

"Have a drink," Bocci said, pushing a glass toward her. "Relax. We're here to chat about our little arrangement, not this other stuff. We're looking into that." He gulped the whiskey and set the glass in front of the skinny guy for more. Rey prayed they'd catch up with Legs and retrieve some of that product, relieve the pressure on her.

"Meanwhile," she said, "I'm supposed to hold up my end of the deal with what?" She tossed a hand at herself. "These good looks?" Bocci and the skinny guy chuckled. Even the guy with the crooked nose at Bocci's left snorted. Rey wanted to flip the table over on all of them. "This…this stranglehold of yours… Our *arrangement* has cut me to the quick, Frank, just like I told you it would." She set her full glass aside. "I can't go shopping with empty pockets. I know you get that."

"Now, Rey. You didn't get this far without your wits. You'll figure it out." He toasted her with his second drink. "Our little working relationship needs to establish reliability. Quality and quantity we can count on is the name of the game. I hope your promise is still good."

"My wits. What'll they buy me?" Struggling against her rising temper, Rey downed her whiskey. "The stinking thirty percent you forced on me won't cover another load."

Bocci selected a cigarette from his gold case and sent her a puzzled look. "Not sure what you're saying, exactly. You breaking our agreement?" He zeroed in on her over the flame of his lighter. "You going back on your word? Or have you blown the money and now you're begging for more?"

"Used every available cent on that last load, is what I'm saying, so it's not me who deserves this heat. We all know who took it, and if you want more from my end, you're going to have to up the ante."

Bocci looked to his left and right, met each man's steady eyes, and then pointed at Rey's glass. "Fill her up again." He leaned forward. "Listen, Rey. You have to be more resourceful. Look around, see what's worth cashing in to hold up your end. You got a car, right? That ought to be worth something, get you back on track."

Rey shook her head. "I can't be without a car." She picked up her refill and straightened. "Sounds to me like *you're* going to reneg on *your* end of the deal leaving me high and dry." She chugged down the drink. "Is that how you do business? Sneak out the back door?"

And she knew it was, just like she knew she was pushing Bocci's patience along with her luck.

"Guess I gotta spell it out for you," Bocci said on a sigh. He flicked ashes to the floor and leveled his eyes at her. "There'll be no more money. You make it work. We'll go after that load we wanted, but you come through by Saturday. You got a week, hear me? You don't produce," he hiked a shoulder, "we won't be meeting like this."

"A week?" Rey flashed a look to the henchmen at either end of the table, and forced down the knot in her throat. "That's just stup— er, well… You're being unrealistic, Frank, and that makes for lousy business, especially when you hide behind goons to get your way." *Be tough. They respect toughness.* "I don't scare easy. Go after Legs, scare *him*. Maybe *this time* you won't fuck it up and you'll stop him once and for all." She stood so quickly, the henchmen jumped up, too. "I'll hold up my end just as soon as I can, and maybe that'll happen by Saturday or maybe not. Either way, you'll just have to live with it."

She walked out holding her breath, past the now empty table at the door, and concentrated on where the thug had gone, not whether a gun was aimed at her back.

On the dock, her nerves in shambles, she stooped to free the bowline and jerked hard when a gun barrel stung her spine. Afraid to move, she awaited a command.

"Don't turn around. Leave it tied and get on the boat." Rey caught a glimpse of the large man who'd been seated by the café door. If she spun around and shoved, he'd be in the water. "Move!" he snapped.

When he shifted the pistol to jab her again, Rey spun and knocked his gun aside. But his punch felt like a brick to the face, and she fell back, tumbling over the boat rail and landing on the deck. He jumped down at her and Rey slung a nearby coil of rope into his midsection. She locked onto the gun with both hands, until he bashed her in the eye, and when he landed a punch to her mouth, she dropped flat.

"Just…delivering…a…message," he said, breathing hard between kicks to her head and stomach. "You…better…get…it."

Squeezing her ribs against the pain, Rey gagged on a mouthful of blood but refused to vomit. She drew up a knee, turned slightly away, and unwittingly offered her backside.

A savage blow to the back of her head sent her reeling, and the world went dark.

Several hours later, covered in evening dew, Rey worked herself into an upright position, and every bone in her body screamed for relief. One eye opened reluctantly, and the other simply refused. Gingerly, she assessed the goose egg above her collar, and the damp, matted hair she knew had to be bloody. A small dark pool had formed on the deck where she'd lain, and she spat out the foul taste in her mouth.

"Jesus Christ." With a hand on the dashboard, she slumped onto the wheel. Nauseating pain surged from deep inside, and she wrapped her free arm around her aching ribs. She avoided inhaling a lungful of air, afraid of the excruciating pain.

The blurry vision in her good eye gradually cleared, and she gave thanks that only empty boats had witnessed her exchange with the Mob. But she had to sit, lend her faculties a few extra minutes of recovery, and her battered brain time to reflect.

Still afraid to straighten, Rey found a clean cloth, wet it from a water jug, and carefully tended to the blood on her mouth, nose, beneath her closed eye, and down the back of her neck. The idea that her crew could be victimized next rumbled through her and began to shake her resolve. "Big, tough woman doesn't scare easily." She snickered at herself. "Fool. Tough talk doesn't faze them one bit."

Someone like Legs gave them fits, however, and she took a measure of satisfaction in that. All because he knew the game. He was sharp enough, had their kind of "wits." Was she desperate enough to ask *him* for help? She couldn't imagine having a sit-down with Legs. *Hell, I'd rather shoot that bastard.* She shook her head at that idea, but as she winced at the pain, she remembered someone else who was familiar with the underworld game.

It surely looked—and felt—like the time had come to learn from someone who'd played and won. Someone who'd have the right kind of advice.

CHAPTER FIVE

Upstart architect Reginald Lowry strolled into the elegant Adelphi Hotel in downtown Saratoga Springs feeling entitled and gloriously vindicated. The lavish Victorian décor reminded him of all he'd lost several years ago when Olivia Waters divorced him, and it felt good to be back in his proper element. If only that bitch, that perverted maid Elizabeth McLaughlin, hadn't turned his wife against him… He'd never forget her and what she cost him. He failed to send her back to prison, lost rights to Olivia's wealth, but somehow survived and worked his way back to this.

Confident and cocky, he was North Woods Consortium's "chosen one" now, designer of the flashy casino/hotel complex, Dazzle, and his future as the company's key man looked secure. Preliminary dealings had been with Manhattan-based lawyers, so this face-to-face with North Woods owners and investors had him eager to learn more, prove himself worthy of a permanent inside seat. He clucked with satisfaction as he was escorted into the ornate sitting room.

A man Lowry guessed to be in his late twenties, not quite his own age, stood like a statue in suit and tie by the velvet drapes, pretending not to watch his every move. A busboy arrived with a cart of champagne and flutes, and a man outside the door took the cart from him and pushed it into the room. Lowry appreciated all this propriety. It suited him, after all.

But when the door opened again and six men entered, his optimism promptly exited. There was no mistaking one face in particular, and Lowry struggled *not* to stare at the mobster kingpin America knew from newsreels and newspapers. Charles "Lucky" Luciano, complete with cagey smile and wavy black hair, all slick and shiny with tonic, settled into an upholstered chair, and Lowry might have relaxed right along with him, if those deep-set eyes weren't prowling the room. The piercing look wafted over him like an icy breath, knocked the knees out of his self-confidence, and rendered him motionless. Never having felt so naked, so vulnerable, he second-guessed the designs and calculations in the briefcase by his feet. He worked for *this* man now? When one of the henchmen handed out flutes of champagne, Lowry wanted to take two. *Is my hand shaking?*

"So you're our architect."

Lowry's mouthful of champagne stopped halfway down his throat. He swallowed hard as he jumped to his feet and extended his hand. Luciano simply watched from his throne.

"I am. Yes, sir." He decided against the handshake. "Reginald J. Lowry III."

Luciano grinned. "The third." Lowry almost shivered when Luciano scanned his body, the visual assessment creeping down his suit to his polished wingtips. "Sit down." Luciano jutted his chin toward Lowry's chair. "You do good work. I like what I've seen."

"Ah… Well, thank you. Sir."

No one spoke until Luciano selected a cigar from the humidor. "We'll get to details later," he said, puffing smoke toward Lowry's briefcase. "Right now," he turned his penetrating gaze on the older fellows seated directly opposite him, "these two gentlemen are the men of the hour. Merriweather and Roberts?"

Lowry felt the air return to his lungs when attention went to the silver-haired pair at the coffee table. Also dressed in fine suits, with hats on their laps, they sat completely still, side-by-side in brocade chairs, and appeared stricken by Luciano's presence. The bubbles in their untouched champagne were the only things that moved. Lowry figured these two were the investors he'd heard would be part of this meeting, although this hardly felt like any business meeting he'd ever attended. More like an audience with God.

"We appreciate this opportunity, Mr. Luciano," the one named Merriweather said, and his handlebar mustache vibrated.

Luciano nodded. "This economic depression the country's in makes for difficult times, gentlemen. So many of the high-and-mighty are falling by the wayside, shamefully overextended, but those of us with foresight? We continue to thrive."

The words barely registered. Lowry observed with growing fascination as Luciano held the pair frozen in their seats. He imagined that, like his, their earlier excitement had been stunted by the discovery of the notorious Mob boss at the reins of this enterprise. Whoever had persuaded these two staid men to part with their money must have made a terrific sales pitch, and Lowry wondered if it had been his own contact, the pushy, imposing entrepreneur Frank Bocci. That man had a "convincing" way about him. *How I rushed to sign that contract.*

Luciano addressed Merriweather and Roberts like the potential business associates they were, but Lowry thought they looked cornered, desperate to retreat.

"I vacation here now and then," Luciano said, and his foxy expression hardened when Bocci entered the room and interrupted. "You're late."

"Yeah, sorry, boss." Bocci adjusted his garish plaid blazer. "Just a little…ah, *Legs* trouble up there again, but we're on it."

The small man sitting beside Luciano leaned forward. "Frank—"

"Yeah," Bocci continued, "y'see, Jack *used* to have this snitch in the barbershop near his farm." He straightened proudly. "Oh, and we took care of that delivery problem, too."

The little man next to Luciano tried again. "Frank. Not right now. Let's—"

"But, y'know, there's this big moose of a broad who runs the shipping up there. We bounced her around pretty good. Didn't touch the boat, not this time, but she still got—"

"Bocci!" The small man stood as he yelled, and everyone except Luciano jumped. "Shut the hell up." He softened his voice. "These are our *investors*, Frank." He gestured grandly toward Merriweather and Roberts. "We'll straighten out the delivery situation *after* our meeting."

Bocci nodded and leaned against the rear wall.

Whoever this little man was, Lowry liked him. He had serious clout, considering Bocci was a scary combination of crude and mean. *"Used to have a snitch"? Beat up a woman?* Lowry made a mental note never to test Bocci's temper.

"Now, where was I?" Luciano shook his head. "Oh yeah, vacationing here." He rolled the tip of his cigar in the ashtray and began a stroll around the room. "I've been a little under the weather lately, so of course I chose Saratoga to recuperate. The horses are good to me here. So are the casinos." Everyone except Roberts and Merriweather chortled. Lowry didn't get the joke either. "The games were good to you gents today, I hear, and, if I'm not mistaken, Mr. Bocci's advice put a tidy sum in your wallets."

Merriweather cleared his throat as Roberts nodded vigorously.

"Ah...yes. Yes, sir. We're quite grateful for the wagering advice. It seems he's our lucky charm. Who gets 'fourteen red' to come up four straight times? And then the cards fell our way for two solid hours. Who would've guessed?"

Luciano studied him briefly and glanced at the untouched champagne. "Yes," he finally said and stopped at the fireplace to relight his cigar. "Who would have guessed."

Roberts looked up tentatively. "We're very appreciative."

"Oh, I'm sure you are," Luciano said without turning around. "Mr. Bocci has just the right instincts when it comes to picking winners." Apparently deep in thought, he nodded toward the tall arched windows, open to the warm, early evening air. The intense quiet in the room made Lowry itch. Even the sounds of Saturday revelers and traffic down on Broadway seemed to have fallen silent. "And he invited you gents here on another display of instinct," Luciano continued, returning to the coffee table. "Getting in on this project is a very wise move on your part."

Roberts inched forward in his seat. "When we first met Frank some time ago, we were struck by his gaming knowledge, but his insight about this project is what sold us, Mr. Luciano. We cleared fifty thousand this afternoon, and he indicated it would go a long way toward getting Dazzle construction moving, a real shot in the arm." Merriweather sent him a quick frown, and Lowry almost grinned at the choice of words.

"Yeah, that's right." Bocci stepped forward again. "See, I got this knack for picking good ones. Back in August, I just took one look at these good ol' boys and I—" Luciano's glare cut him off. "Uh, oh. Sorry, Charlie."

Luciano offered Roberts a winning smile. "Yes, Mr. Roberts, you're correct. Your investment will be put to good use immediately. Dazzle has terrific potential. My accountant here, Mr. Lansky"—the small fellow with clout bobbed his head—"he is extremely confident about Dazzle's potential, even though it will be seasonal for now. There's good money to be made—just in alcohol alone, not to mention gaming."

Roberts finally sipped his champagne, and Merriweather's mustache stopped twitching. Both men's breathless posture appeared to soften. *Regardless of the force behind it, they know the project reeks of profit.*

"Taking the old Drysdale Grove, that picnic area and dance pavilion, for a first-class casino and hotel is a brilliant plan," Merriweather continued, "and a nightclub in the hotel? It's perfect for Lake Luzerne. No doubt, it will require considerable effort, but the finest materials and amenities will make it a hot spot in no time. A big moneymaker."

Lansky pulled the magnum of champagne from the ice bucket and filled a glass for Luciano, then one for himself. He certainly *seemed* like an accountant, rather demure and mild-mannered, but to be the "numbers man" for Lucky Luciano meant there was a lot more to him, and all kinds of clout. *Newspapers have made him almost as famous.*

Lansky stuffed a hand into his pocket and focused on Merriweather. "What's your opinion of opening in time for the next racing season?"

Lowry's temptation to impress with his expertise flared and he almost interjected. But Lansky flashed him a look as if he knew, and

Lowry sipped his champagne instead and thought better of speaking out of turn.

"Well, it won't be easy," Merriweather answered.

Understatement of the year.

"But doable, I'd say," Roberts added quickly.

"I see." Lansky adjusted his tie as he sat. "And what does our architect say?"

Straightening in his seat, Lowry avoided Luciano's stare and looked from Lansky to the questioning faces of Merriweather and Roberts.

"I say correct on both counts, difficult but nothing we can't handle."

"You're ambitious, Lowry, just like our contacts reported," Lansky said. "You've done some great work in Boston and we liked your initial drawings. Put them right into play, as a matter of fact, but Dazzle is the biggest project you've ever had. If you think it might be too much, we need to hear it."

"Not at all. I've never been more excited, more eager to tackle a job. Of course there'll be challenges, there are in any project, but I go at them head-on and win. You can take that as a guarantee."

"Your guarantee is on paper," Lanksy said. "We've got it already."

"You have no choice but to win," Luciano muttered into his glass.

Lansky gestured with his champagne. "We heard you expect rough going this winter. It starts damn early, you know. The snow's fucking miserable up here. We've hit a few snags on the site already, so we're eager to catch up and get ahead of schedule before the white stuff starts."

"I'll look into those snags," Lowry said. "I'm sure they're nothing we can't resolve."

"You do that." Luciano pointed at him. "I don't want to hear about them anymore."

Lansky added, "Racing season will come fast, so make the most of the time you've got, cause if we're backed into a corner on this, you're gone like *that.*" He snapped his fingers.

"Oh, I-I understand." Lowry felt his scalp grow damp and cold. "Trust me. I'll get things on the fast track in no time." He held up his briefcase. "I tightened the construction timetable to make sure of it."

Luciano went to the window and Lowry risked a long look at the preoccupied stare. He couldn't imagine what went through the mind of a notorious murderer, especially this one. The world had to be black and white for him, his way or no way.

As the most dreaded element of New York's crime families, Luciano had the world by the throat, and the stock market's crash hadn't lessened his grip. He cruised along unfazed, it seemed, just like the diners, movie patrons, and well-heeled tourists who were spending money right now on the street below. And neither had the allure of Saratoga Springs been dampened by all the bank failures of late, and Luciano knew it. Lowry marveled at how Luciano always reached for more, how he created his own opportunities for sizeable financial gain. Dazzle was just the latest opportunity, and despite the force behind it, the project had everything going for it.

"Lowry," Luciano said into the breeze, "I want you on that site. Mr. Bocci will make arrangements." He turned, frowned at his cigar, and locked eyes with Lowry. "Get up there and ride this thing hard." He bent to the ashtray but looked up beneath thick, hooded brows. "There'll be no fucking setbacks."

Lowry managed to ignore his racing heart and nodded. "I'll be there tomorrow."

Bocci's voice rumbled from the back of the room. "Lowry, let's you and me grab a drink downstairs. We'll talk." Lowry twisted in his chair to catch the big man's eye and mouthed an "okay." *I'll need a couple.*

Lansky set paperwork and pen on the coffee table for Merri-weather and Roberts. "Your investment today will be well placed. Dazzle is just the beginning for North Woods Consortium."

Lowry released an inner sigh as the men scribbled their names and handed Lansky thick envelopes of cash.

Luciano's broad smile said he approved, but the glance he sent Lowry sliced down his spine. "All right, boys," he said, "let's make some serious money." He offered a handshake. "Welcome to North Woods Consortium."

Lowry stood with Merriweather and Roberts and they shook hands with the New York Mob.

CHAPTER SIX

Katie bounced her little stuffed horse across the linen tablecloth, up Rey's arm and down, and back to where Ellie waited with another spoonful of ice cream. "Let's not get any more on Bing, honey. Horses don't eat ice cream."

Rey couldn't think of a finer way to end their fun day in Saratoga than a treat at the famous Adelphi Hotel, right on Broadway. All the walking and playing with Katie had been tough on Rey's bruises. Relaxing here definitely helped, although she'd been struggling since morning to find time for more than just snippets of serious talk. She hadn't been able to say much so far and couldn't contain her nagging worry any longer.

"I hate to go back to my touchy subject," she said and toyed with the ashtray on their table, "but what would you do in my position?"

Mac swirled the ice cubes in her glass and downed the remnants of her sidecar. "Damn, you're in a tough position, Rey. For now, I guess I'd scrape up the cash to keep them happy, to have some product for them by Saturday, but beyond that..." It wasn't the magic solution Rey wanted, but she remained hopeful because Mac looked to be in deep thought as she leaned back in her seat.

Ellie wiped Katie's mouth with a napkin and frowned at Rey. "Friends and neighbors won't stand up for you?"

Rey lit a cigarette and studied the slowly healing cuts on her knuckles. She knew her black eye, scabbed lip, and hunched, tenuous posture screamed of defeat, and figured it seemed obvious that she was on the losing end of a one-woman war. She wished she could muster an army to retaliate, to at least stand in her defense. Mac shook her head, and Rey knew she understood.

"Even if she could beef up her crew with locals," Mac softly told Ellie, "they'd be in over their heads." She patted Bing in Katie's arms. "*Two* sets of gangsters, El."

Rey watched their interaction, saw calculated recognition appear in Ellie's eyes, and realized Ellie was no stranger to this stuff. They were quite a pair.

"Well, if one set is distracted enough," Ellie wondered aloud, and looked from Mac to Rey, "could you manage against the other?"

"Distracted?" Rey repeated on a burst of smoke. "Those guys?"

"You know, there *is* a possibility," Mac said, and a puzzling smile appeared on her lips as she gave Ellie's shoulders a quick squeeze. "If, say, trouble at that hotel construction site sent those guys sniffing in a different direction, some of the pressure for your product might lift."

Rey weighed the notion as she tapped her cigarette on the ashtray. The idea of sabotaging Dazzle sent a nervous ripple down her back. It *would* be easy, though. Even though many locals looked forward to Dazzle's success and the jobs it would provide, she still had a few allies who might help slow the project down. And it might lend her some breathing room, some time to recoup funds and resume a semblance of her delivery schedule. But realistically, unless they plagued the project for months *without getting caught*, the Mob's distraction would only be temporary.

"I suppose something's better than nothing."

Katie squealed when Mac snatched Bing away and began dancing it across her legs. "Meanwhile," Mac said to Rey, "I'd keep running your route, somehow. Put what you can out there. Think of it as bait."

"Bait?" The concept took Rey back.

"Let Legs and Manhattan fight each other for it," Mac explained. "War between them is already brewing. It's public knowledge that the big boys can't put a lid on Legs, can't hit a moving target even though they keep trying, and Luciano has to be boiling. And it wouldn't surprise anyone if Legs sabotaged their precious project, right?"

"If *Legs* did it?"

"Well, it could look that way. Dazzle's the reason Manhattan wants your alcohol, so it makes sense that Legs would hit it. Then, the big boys would throw everything at him."

Rey suddenly felt unusually dense. "So the damage looks like Legs's doing."

"Exactly. Combine sabotage with a product supply that keeps disappearing, and Dazzle will start costing Luciano a fortune. Chances are, he'll dump the whole project. Look at it from his perspective. It's way up here in the middle of the damn wilderness, for God's sake, a far cry from his Waldorf Astoria in the big city. There's nothing smooth and easy about it, which goes against his style, and he's too smart to keep pouring money into the woods." Mac downed the rest of her drink. "He's all about money, Rey. If he's forced to pull the plug on Dazzle, like any good businessman would, he'll take serious aim at Diamond to recoup his losses. They *all* might end up out of the picture, not giving a damn about you anymore. You're just small potatoes."

Ellie nodded. "It makes sense. So typical in that world, it's disgusting."

Rey crushed out her cigarette as Mac's reasoning settled in her head. *Bait.* She did have some savings, so she *could* scrape a few loads together. And it wouldn't take much to implicate Legs for any sabotage. A few well-placed comments among workmen in local watering holes, and rumors would travel fast. She sat back, staring at her empty glass.

"It's a lot to think about, Mac. So risky. They're a scary bunch. But...ah hell. I don't see any alternative." She stood, careful not to aggravate her aching ribs. "I'll order us fresh drinks at the bar. We need 'em."

Ellie watched her go. "I feel so bad for her." As Mac retied the red ribbon around Bing's neck and Katie excitedly looked on, Ellie saw contentment in her daughter, the joy they'd attained as a family after their own difficult times. She knew too well what

Mob association meant. "She's in over her head, Mac. Look what they've already done. You can see it when she walks across the room. What'll they do next?"

"Dare I say this, El? We have the resources to help her."

The thought had crossed Ellie's mind, too, although the implications weren't welcome. "Honey."

"I know. I know." Mac took Ellie's hand and entwined their fingers. "Not that we'd get *involved*, mind you. There's no way. But we could lend support."

Ellie held Mac's poignant stare as Katie climbed back onto her lap. The honesty and devotion in Mac's gaze didn't waiver and probably never would. Ellie trusted them implicitly, and knew that beyond Mac's physical attributes, her strength lay in her character. Ellie waited patiently for the words she sensed would come.

Mac stroked her thumb across her hand and spoke softly. "We have the money and access to plenty of experienced manpower. She needs it, El, and where else could she possibly get that?"

Ellie smoothed Katie's wild curls back into place as the grip of familiar, long-shed anxiety took hold. She'd felt it tightening when Mac posited that hypothetical scheme for Rey. Old habits died hard, but Mac's passion for their family underscored everything she did.

Ellie let Katie toy with her pearl necklace and kissed her sweet-smelling forehead. "I just can't believe we're even considering this."

"We are, aren't we?"

She knew Mac asked that of both of them because the answer didn't come easily.

"It's as if fate dropped us into this, Mac. Don't you think? Of all people to come into our life, why Rey? Is this a test of some kind?"

"I was thinking the same thing. Why us? It's not like a lifelong friend or a relative is crying at our door, I know. We aren't compelled to help her at all."

"We've only just met her, really," Ellie observed. "There'd be a lot at stake."

"True on both counts."

"You want to do this, I can tell." She stroked Mac's hair away from her forehead. "Despite all my perfectly logical reservations, something's pushing me to help her, too. It scares me, Mac, not knowing why."

"I think it's because she's like us, and I don't just mean because she's a lesbian. She's standing on her own two feet, living a life she wants, and someone's trying to take it from her. We've been there. And we wouldn't be where we are today without the support of 'family' who gave a damn. Am I being too idealistic, too corny, thinking this way?"

Mac turned in her chair to face her directly and offered the heartfelt smile that always reminded Ellie of their teenage innocence. So ruggedly handsome today, Mac stole her heart with that look every time.

"No, honey." Ellie rested her hand on Mac's arm. "You may have just answered my question."

"It's just that, a woman alone, up against it like Rey is... No one deserves to be used, woman or man, for that matter, and I can't stand to see someone beaten down. I know we have to be smart here, but it's damn hard to say no to this, El." Her palm warm on Ellie's knee beneath the table, Mac added, "Please remember: You and Katie will always come first, sweetheart. I love you. Never doubt that I'd give my life to keep you both safe and happy."

Ellie cupped Mac's cheek. The sentiment always made her breath catch because Mac meant it literally. Undying devotion, a love for the storybooks, Ellie mused, and mine is just as strong, as fierce as yours.

"Your safety and happiness mean everything to me, too," she answered. "Loving you completes me. Together we can do anything."

Mac set a light kiss into the palm on her cheek. "So we should do this? For Rey?"

Without question, Rey urgently needed a solution to her dilemma, could be killed without one. And in Mac's proposal, Rey would find none better. That was a fact. Ellie believed in Mac's innate sense of justice, her strength of command, just as surely as her promise.

"As long as the three of us stay removed from it all."

"I swear." Mac squeezed her knee to reassure her once more. "Then we'll talk details with her on our way back to the Sagamore and offer what we can. It's rightfully her choice to make. If she takes us up on it, I'll discuss it with Jersey and the others."

❖

"We're going to clean up the Catskills, all the small-time brewers Legs already has and the ones he hopes to get. Gonna show him who's boss," Bocci boasted, "but this supply we found on Lake George is perfect for Dazzle, once we nail it down."

Standing beside him at the bar, downstairs at the Adelphi, Lowry fought the crowd of patrons to catch Bocci's every hushed, guttural word. Lowry preferred a quieter place for talk like this, and thought Bocci should as well, but wasn't about to tell him what to do. After that unnerving meeting upstairs, he desperately wanted to relax in the Adelphi's decadent environs, collect himself, but knew better than to appear distracted. Bocci had steered him here with a leaden arm across his shoulders and a promise to provide "some necessary background" for the project. Lowry definitely needed details, so he played the subservient role to the hilt, and now sipped the whiskey Bocci ordered and absorbed this inside information with a dutiful air.

"So you're getting the Lake George supply under control?"

Bocci waved a hand dismissively. "Not a problem. We're dealing with a broad, remember? We reminded her that she's getting a fair deal." He ogled a redheaded waitress as she zigzagged through the crowd, her tray held high. "We convinced her pretty good, too. She won't forget that little conversation any time soon." His narrow eyes followed the waitress all the way to the dining room.

Lowry remembered the "bounced her around" comment Bocci had made to Luciano and wondered just how rough the interaction had been. The woman should have known better. "Guess she underestimated who she was dealing with."

"Got that right. We already got trouble at the job site. Guys are bitching for less work, more pay, and slacking off. One crew won't dynamite through the rock cause of neighbors. Shit, there ain't neighbors for a mile." He shook his head and drank. "And some supply deliveries have come up short lately." He glanced back to the dining room. "That waitress is some looker. You catch the redhead?"

Lowry gave the crowd a cursory scan and quickly turned back to him. "Not really."

"Eh, too bad. Anyway, like I was saying, they've slowed the project down. My gut tells me they're all in it together, so I'm looking into it. The last thing we need is a dumb broad giving us grief, too."

"You'll get to the bottom of it all in no time, I'm sure. And you'll have that alcohol flowing smoothly long before opening day. It'll work out perfectly."

"Atta boy, Lowry." Bocci clapped him on the back. "You get the picture. That's the attitude we need."

Lowry almost choked from the impact. "Well, I've built a couple contingency gaps into my timetable to give us catch-up time if necessary, but we can't have the little people slowing us down."

Now Bocci beamed. "For a young guy, you're all right." He raised his glass to him. "You'll work out just fine."

Lowry lifted his glass as well, more than pleased with himself. *I'm in this for me, you goon, and I'll do whatever it takes.* "If I have questions, if issues come up, I'm coming directly to you for help."

Bocci gulped his drink. "You bet." He thumbed his chest proudly. "I'm your guy."

Lowry extended his hand and fought back a wince when Bocci shook it. "I figured you for the man who gets things done. Pleasure to be working with you."

Bocci soaked up the praise, smiling when he poked Lowry's chest. "Get out a pen and I'll give you some names of guys to see on-site. We put up a small work shack you can use, got a table, some chairs, even a bunk and a little stove, in case they're needed. We got your blueprints hanging on—"

Lowry looked up at the interruption and found Bocci again staring into the dining room. Resigned to see the redhead, Lowry turned, leaned around bar patrons, and finally spotted her talking to a beefy customer at a table. "She is pretty."

Bocci squinted through the crowd. "No. That's the one. That's her."

"Who?" Lowry looked again. "Oh, the one the redhead's talking to? At that table with the kid? That's a *her*?"

"The broad from Lake George. Check out the way she's a little tilted in the chair. She's still hurting. Good."

Lowry studied the large woman and agreed she seemed quite uncomfortable. She might even have a black eye, he couldn't quite tell. "That's the rumrunner you bounced around?"

"The same." Bocci watched her over the rim of his glass. "Looks like she's got some well-to-do friends. Wonder if their money's behind her operation."

Lowry joined Bocci in surveilling the group from afar.

"Interesting thought."

"No kidding. That bitch, they call her Rey, she whined about not having the cash to hold up her end of our deal."

Lowry watched Rey wince as she retrieved her wallet and paid the waitress. Meanwhile, a striking blonde at the table spoke around a child bouncing in her lap to a man seated close by. He appeared to be the refined type, fancy white linen suit, dark hair slicked back. A Panama hat sat in the empty chair to his right.

"They have a little girl."

"The blonde is some doll, huh? See the pearls? The rack on her? Jesus, lucky guy."

"Too bad he isn't facing this way. You think you might know him or them?"

"Not yet, I don't." Bocci growled as he upended the rest of his drink. "Can't tell me that bitch has money problems. When you got friends like those, you're on Easy Street."

Lowry glanced back. The toddler stood on the blonde's lap, flung her toy at Rey, and shouted with delight, "Wey love Bing!" Then she spun and reached for the man in the suit. "Mackie!" She toppled into his arms.

Bocci probably was right. *Money begets money.* The rumrunner, Rey, picked up those bruises by crying poor-mouth to the Mob. Maybe she'd been trying to keep these wealthy backers out of the fray, keep such an ace tucked up her sleeve.

"The guy's apparently not the child's father. She called him Mack, not Daddy."

Bocci snorted. "Shit. That damn homo's probably the father."

Lowry offered a laugh, but the concept left him chilled. "You think she's one of *those*?"

"Fuck, you're kidding me, right?" Bocci rolled his eyes. "Look at her. What do *you* think?"

Lowry knew what he was seeing. He'd been scarred by a homo pervert before. He knew those twisted minds corrupted the innocent, contaminated life around them, and contributed nothing but trouble to the world. And he didn't appreciate that kind sharing the air he breathed. God dammit. He didn't appreciate that kind *breathing period.* Fortune and high living had been his once, and if not for the likes of *one of them*, he'd still be married to the Waters's estate, would never have had to make this climb to the upper crust.

He took a long look over his shoulder at Rey's hardened face. *A normal feminine beauty you're not, that's for sure. You're going down, you know, and your rich pal Mack won't stand a chance of helping you.*

CHAPTER SEVEN

Naked, Rey toweled herself dry as she trudged up the banking to her cabin in the woods, miles up the eastern shore of Lake George. She relished this freedom, a benefit of four years of living single. She'd never had to give a thought to propriety or neighbors in this remote piece of Heaven until today.

Mac's "associates" were due within the hour, and scaring them off with her hulking nakedness wouldn't do. She'd already spent the day cleaning the cabin's three rooms, the loft that spanned the second floor, and the outhouse, and had kept her anxiety at bay by working up a damn good sweat. She couldn't remember the last time she'd done such a thorough job, maybe the spring cleaning back in April, so she deserved that refreshing dip in the lake. She just wished it had soothed her nerves about what lay ahead.

She put on pants and a shirt from the haphazard stack of clothes she'd laundered in the village yesterday and stepped out of the bedroom to survey her home for readiness. It probably wasn't what these city folks were accustomed to, but Mac had said not to worry, so she hadn't. There was plenty of clutter to prove that, but at least everything was clean, and she figured even someone like cosmopolitan Millie might find the rustic confines "cozy." *God knows, I have more important things to worry about.*

With her aging sofa and two upholstered chairs by the fireplace, she could accommodate at least three overnight guests reasonably on the main floor. Upstairs, now that all the storage had been shoved aside, as many as a dozen could spread out blankets. Far from ideal, she knew, but Mac had assured her that her gang could handle the inconvenience, even if a few weeks were required. Anyone unhappy with the "community" arrangement could drive several miles back down the shore and stay in her storehouse.

What really mattered, though, was that Mac had offered hope, bolstered her confidence with "the plan." Rey had gone to bed nursing a headache after listening—and accepting—what she'd heard. Learning about the hijacking expertise Mac's gang had developed over the past years, the methods, weapons, associates, *and enemies*, left vivid, indelible impressions. But now her curiosity about them battled the jitters that came with bringing them into her life.

She'd just set out loaves of bread and a ham from the icebox when she heard the distant engine. Reality began to sink in. Jersey, Millie, and Jackson would execute the plan from her cabin, while Mac and family remained at the Sagamore, away from the action. At least Mac was in her territory to set things in motion.

Rey stepped onto the porch in time to see Jersey's Studebaker pull up in a cloud of dust. All four car doors opened and Mac waved from the passenger seat, but it was Millie who caught Rey's eye.

Sleek, bare calves swung into view, and shiny ankle-strap pumps settled into the gravel with a determined twist. Her bronze satin sheath, complete with fringe dangling below her knees, shimmered in the afternoon sun and accented curves Rey couldn't help but appreciate. The dress's meager spaghetti straps deserved credit for restraining an assertive, half-exposed bosom that beckoned to escape.

Chewing gum with authority, Millie primped her curls and planted both hands on her hips. "Some hideout you got here, Rey."

Rey found it impossible not to stare. The view from her porch had never looked this good. Millie was a humdinger, all right. And she was *here* in the front yard, in the Adirondack wilderness, as stark as a whistle in church. Rey simply didn't have words.

"Hey," Mac said and grinned knowingly as she strolled up the porch steps. Decked out in a tailored baby blue suit and vest, she radiated a nonchalant calm that Rey sorely needed at the moment. "You'll get used to Millie," Mac said under her breath. "Stun is what she does and who she is. Bless her."

Before Rey could respond, a large canvas-covered truck rumbled into view, and Jackson waved it into position. He tossed his suit jacket into the car and straightened his fedora before turning to Rey. "Afternoon." He obviously thought nothing of exposing his shoulder holster. He wore it like a fashion accessory, the tanned cowhide standing out against his sinister all-black look. "The second truck's due around suppertime, and the third, well after dark."

"*Three* trucks?"

The truck's rear canvas flipped aside and six gruff-looking characters jumped out, three women and three men of assorted sizes and ages. Another woman and man joined them from the cab, all grumbling about the long, uncomfortable ride.

"Yeah," Jackson said, hustling up the steps. "You ready? We borrowed them from our Boston outfit, and they overnighted in Albany. We staggered them for this last leg." He slapped her on the shoulder. "Didn't want a parade up here, did you?" He had such an unsettling smile, the white slash framed by black mustache and pointed goatee. And today his ominous dark eyes seemed to glow. Rey sensed he reveled in this adventure and enjoyed sending mixed messages.

She held open the door and let Mac lead the way. "Welcome," she said. "It's not much, but it's home, and you're welcome to it. I can't thank you enough for what you're doing."

Millie gave her shirtfront a tug as she passed. "Don't be fooled, honey." She winked up at Rey. "We're looking forward to this work. Like old times." Taken by the sway of Millie's hips as she walked in, Rey couldn't imagine what those "old times" had been like.

"We're glad to help," said Jersey, the last to enter. She stopped and tipped her fedora back when she looked up. With sleeves rolled to the elbows and suspenders supporting gray workpants, she was the grit to Mac's polish, and Rey saw a kindred spirit in her that she hadn't noticed before. Jersey tipped a thumb toward the cabin. "Shacking up here, we'll be in your way for a while, but it'll all be worth it."

Rey sighed. "You know, somehow, I don't doubt you."

Jersey leaned closer. "Listen, Mac's aces, and we're damn good at this."

"Well, I'm grateful. I'm sure none of you wanted to end your vacation with this."

"I heard that," Mac said. "Don't worry about it."

"Yeah," Millie added, turning in place as she checked out the cabin. "Seems like it was meant to be, us being up here at the right time, and all."

"You guys sure know how to make an entrance. I'll give you that," Rey said. "So how many all together?"

"Eighteen," Jackson said.

"Eighteen! Holy smokes." Rey ran a hand back through her hair. "It'll be cramped—"

"We'll survive just fine," Jersey said as the others filed in. "We're bringing plenty of provisions, too. This crowd could eat you out of house and home."

"Okay, everybody," Mac announced. "This is Rey. You all take a break, go stretch your legs, check out the lake down there while we get organized in here."

Rey explained what she had for sleeping quarters and grinned when Jersey deftly scaled the loft ladder, looked around, and came down.

"Well, the Sagamore it isn't, but we'll manage." She chucked Mac in the arm. "Although Millie might swim back down to the hotel."

"One hell of a long swim. She'll adjust."

Rey began to worry that Millie would object to the lack of luxury. The other women hadn't seemed fazed by it, but they weren't Millie.

"I hope you'll be comfortable here," she said. "I know it's nothing like the swinging scene you're used to, but it's quiet, relaxing." She dug Camels from her pants pocket and offered one to Millie.

"Don't mind if I do." Millie drew out a cigarette with practiced precision, her fingers delicate and peach-colored. "Thanks." Rey concentrated on steadying her lighter, on ignoring the sweeping cleavage that beckoned just below Millie's cigarette. She lit one for herself, hoping to soften her nerves. *Remember why everyone's here.*

"Mac, I don't know where to begin, thanking you. Everyone looks ready for action, men *and* women. I'm…well, I'm kinda dumbstruck by it all."

Mac set a hand on her shoulder. "A lot of the associates you'll meet joined after my time, but the outfit's drive and loyalty haven't changed. The business still runs the way it always did, thanks to Jersey. They're good people."

"Good people who've been through the wringer," Jersey finished. "When you've been used or beaten up or you've done time just so fat cats can get ahead, you end up with an ax to grind. That's what brought us together in the beginning, and what keeps us tight today." She winked at Mac. "We're a weird mix, but we're family."

Millie took in her surroundings with a bit of trepidation. This wilderness living was a far cry from her world of crystal martini glasses and brocade furniture. The Sagamore might as well be in Detroit, for all she'd see of it now. But their plan came first, and it was noble, typical of Mac. She grinned at memories of their many successes.

But it wasn't easy to wax nostalgic about the hefty icebox in the corner, the hand pump at the sink, or the stout pot-bellied stove with the battered pots hanging around it. The faded pattern on the furniture was nearly indistinguishable, and the plank walls offered stuffed animal heads, a rack of fishing poles, and charcoal sketches of everything from trucks to skunks. She eyed the clutter of newspapers and magazines on the coffee table, wondering how old they were and if she'd find anything worth occupying her time. Under the pile of boating gear in the corner sat several whiskey crates she hoped contained something useful. The battery-powered radio by the window was some consolation, but then there was the ladder to the loft.

"Well," she began, careful not to sound as apprehensive as she felt, "it's…quaint. It has that lived-in look. Is there more of it?"

"Sure. Over here." Rey went to the side doorways. "Odds and ends go in here, and this is the bedroom."

Millie peeked in as Rey hovered. The double bed looked neat, but that was all the room had going for it.

"Please don't mind all the clothes. I just did laundry the other day. And I've been meaning to replace that torn window shade but keep forgetting when I'm in the village."

Millie thought she'd prepared herself to "live without" for a while, but the cabin's clutter and disorganization distressed her even more than the crude accommodations. She prided herself on always being put together, always on the ball, and if she was anything, she was efficient, so *this* didn't bode well. Beyond herself, however, their large crew needed to function efficiently here, which meant some things had to change.

"Oh," Rey added, "and there's the loft, too."

"I see that," she said, looking up. "It's pretty high. Never wanted a staircase, I take it?"

"Hogs too much room. The ladder's easy enough. You'll see."

"Uh-huh."

"Oh, hey. I forgot I'd started making lunch." Rey went to the kitchen area and began slicing slabs of meat on the old wooden tabletop. "This ham's fresh out of the smokehouse in the village."

Millie glanced around for a cutting board or platter of any kind and riffled through Rey's cupboards until she found a plate. "It's nice of you to think of lunch for everyone." She had to admit, Rey was doing everything within her means to show appreciation and make them feel at home, even if "home" did feel like civilization's last gasp. After opening a few drawers, Millie located a decent knife and started slicing bread.

"Hell, Millie. This is the least I—oh, you don't need to help. You guys aren't here to do this. Go relax."

"No. I've had a week's worth of relaxation already, and I need to be busy." She slathered mustard onto each slice and passed it to Rey.

"Well, don't get anything on that dress. It's—" Rey cut herself short, and Millie bit back a grin, wondering what word she would use. "It's very becoming."

Rey didn't look up from her work, but Millie could see the blush on her cheek.

"Well, thanks, hon. I might change in a while. My bag's in the pile by the door." Rey looked out to the assortment of belongings, and Millie knew Rey could figure out which one was hers. A lone suitcase stood among the satchels and carryalls, just as what it contained would stand out in this wilderness. "A lady has necessities," she added before Rey could comment. "So, now," she held out a backlog of slices, "less talk and more work."

Millie didn't do this domestic thing often, and had painful memories of it as a child, but she did remember warm, aromatic kitchens shared with roommates, and then associates in their Victorian. But recollections made her restless, uneasy, and she was glad to focus on a task. She'd never been one to sit for long anyway, and had little use for those who did.

"Franny," she called out. "Make sure the eggs we brought go in the icebox over here." Franny stopped ogling the shotgun hanging above the fireplace and gave her a nod. "And, Sid? Please empty that basin and fill it so everyone can wash up. Outside." Sid slapped his cap over wooly blond hair and began removing miscellaneous hand tools from the little tub. "We might be a collection of toughies, but we're not savages."

She glanced up at Rey's rumbling chuckle. "So, you *do* have a water closet, don't you?"

"I do. It's around the back, just a short walk out."

"Outhouse," Millie said as her spirit took another hit. "Of course."

"It's clean and smells pretty good." Rey stacked two more sandwiches on the growing pile. "Well, I mean, good *considering*. It's lined with mothballs."

"The outhouse smells like mothballs?"

"Yup. And no critters ever come knocking."

"Oh." Millie lathered another piece of bread. "Well…that's important."

"Yes, ma'am. It is." Rey set down her knife and began stowing away the food. "We're done. These'll hold us over till supper tonight."

"And what's for supper?" Jackson appeared between them and stole a sandwich off the heaping plate.

Millie slapped his hand. "Pig."

"Hey, you three," Mac called from the sofa. "Over here."

Millie led them to where Mac sat in hushed conversation with Jersey, and nearly panicked when she sat—plunged—into the battle-worn chair. Jackson settled on the arm, while Rey took the other seat.

Mac lit a Lucky and eyed Rey through the smoke. "You're set to make delivery tomorrow night?"

"I am."

"Pretty much a given that the big boys—not Legs—will descend on your load, since they missed out on the last one. All that your truckers need to know is not to be heroes, that you're concerned they stay safe. We just want the normal pushback, remember. Nothing more. You're just doing what you've been told, holding up your end of the deal with Manhattan because you're scared of them. You, we"—she gestured to the others—"we *want* that load to get lifted so those big boys believe they've got you."

"Yeah," Millie said. "Manhattan expects you to be a good girl and kiss their ass."

"And the next night," Jackson added, "we take a few hammers and show Manhattan just how bullshit Legs is to have missed out, how he gets even."

"I'll draw you a map to Dazzle," Rey told them. "No one guards the place at night, so you won't have company."

"Good," Mac said. "The plan is to set that construction back weeks."

Millie grinned at Rey. "Guaranteed, they'll believe Legs made a statement."

"You'll probably get a demand from him for another load within a day or so," Jersey said, "and we have the green to make that happen. But the load won't get far, trust me."

In a tentative voice, Rey completed the thought. "Because after he lifts it, you're jacking it from him yourselves and bringing it back."

Millie patted Rey's shoulder. The concept appeared to rattle her, and Millie could sympathize. Talk about turning your whole world upside down. Rey's tanned face had gone rather pale.

Jackson loosened his tie. "Promise you, Legs will lift it right away—"

"Yup, and we'll take it right back," Jersey said. "We're the third party no one knows about, remember. So, those clowns will jump to blame each other and the war between them will ramp up another notch. Then, you'll get another order and can use the same product."

"When they keep coming away empty-handed," Jackson said, "and Dazzle's become a construction nightmare, things'll really heat up between them."

"Oh, I hear you." Rey shook her head. "But it's so... If I was at war with a neighbor, that'd be different. But these guys are a little more than that. The plan sure is clever, though. I'll grant you that."

"It's what we do best," Millie said with a smirk. "Well, *one* of them, anyway." She rummaged through her tiny clutch until she found her cigarettes and lit one off the lighter Jackson offered. "So, listen, Rey." She sat back and extended her legs, crossing them at the ankles. "What *I* wanna know is, who's the rat? You're going through booze up here like a sailor in the desert, so somebody in your distribution chain has a real big mouth."

"That's a sure bet, and I don't know who it is. Somebody's leaking details about my shipments, no doubt part of a sweet deal on the sly, but snooping around for the guy who's selling to either Legs *or* the New York Mob is tricky. Damn, it's fucking crazy. They both can make you disappear real quick, and up here, nobody'd find you. Nobody. Ever."

"Well, it's obvious," Jersey said, "that whenever you need a delivery and arrange a truck run, a source feeds one of those outfits."

"Practically every time now, yeah."

"Today, anybody would jump to make side money," Mac said. She looked to Millie. "Let's take our shot and hope we get lucky.

Whoever's getting paid off isn't smart. Chances are, not smart enough to hide it, either. In these tough times, money stands out."

Millie caught Mac's observation as the go-ahead for what they affectionately called "ratting." She knew the drill. She'd long since earned the others' respect for her talent and courage, and her success. This role challenged her in ways separate from everyone else, required more shrewd wit and "feminine wiles" than firepower and brute muscle, and she relished being responsible for a key to their plan. She tapped her cigarette on the ashtray, feeling all eyes watching, and sat back with a nod.

"Yup," Jackson said, standing and stretching. "Time to play with a snitch."

Mac stood. "I'll leave you all to it, then. Jersey's running me back to the Sagamore. We're up here for two more weeks, so be in touch."

Rey walked her and Jersey as far as the door, and Millie hustled out after them and stopped Mac at the car. "Hey, boss." The look on Mac's face said she was deep in thought, probably hoping she'd covered all the necessary details. "Ellie's seriously okay with this?"

"I'm not directly involved, Mil, so we're good. We agreed to help Rey this way. Besides, I'd never let this business get close to her or Katie. You know that, and so does she."

"Good to hear. We'll be sure to keep the wolves away." She patted Mac's chest. "I have to admit, though, I kinda miss our old days."

"I'm glad to have the good memories but relieved the bad ones are gone. It's nice to be excited about the future, seeing Katie grow up, knowing she and Ellie are happy and safe. You guys are carrying on so well, but don't be a stranger to the farm. We miss you."

Millie leaned up and kissed her cheek. "Miss you, too, handsome."

"Promise me you'll be careful, prowling the local haunts."

"Promise. Nothing I haven't done before, remember. I'm not worried."

"I know, which is why I am."

Millie snickered as she patted her thigh. "I still carry my own little secret weapon." She sidled closer. "And, honey, you *know* I have more than one. They make me irresistible."

"That you are," Mac said with a laugh. "Just try not to shock Rey. Please?"

"A little tease now and then—"

"Millie."

"Oh, all right. You did let her know things could get rough."

"I did. Whatever she doesn't know by now, I'm sure you guys can teach her."

"I wonder if she's not...you know, buffaloed by all this, *way* out of her element. I mean, she's one tough woman, but you know how rough it can get, and we can't go soft because of her."

Mac glanced back at Rey in the doorway. "She can handle herself. I just hope she can handle you."

CHAPTER EIGHT

At nearly nine o'clock, Rey dragged one of her chairs aside and sat, thinking it wise to just stay out of the way. The last two trucks had arrived, along with ten more associates and supplies for an army, and Rey's world now hummed with synchronized motion. Apparently, her cabin had to be transformed into "camp" before anyone called it a night.

Two young women moved the coffee table aside, and Jersey orchestrated a procession from the three trucks backed up to the front porch. Rey watched her parlor rug disappear beneath an accumulation of long, narrow wooden boxes, and it didn't take a genius to guess the contents.

She could see part of Jackson in the loft, stooped beneath the low ceiling, busy coordinating sleeping arrangements. Twice he settled disagreements without ever raising his voice. That associates accepted his direction without question came as no surprise. His reputation served him well.

However, in the little kitchen, Millie struggled for decorum. A man cooking some concoction for everyone's supper labored over Rey's finicky wood stove while a young woman maneuvered around him, stacking firewood, and two other associates created a mess unpacking provisions. Food covered every surface, boxes made walking nearly impossible, and Rey figured that the added unfamiliarity with the layout would probably push Millie over the top. She didn't dare offer to help.

"That's it!" Millie yelled, and slammed her hands to the only space on the table. "What happened to the system we had?" She didn't wait for an answer. Instead, she ordered all cabinets emptied and reorganized, their provisions added to Rey's usual stores and cooking wares. Rey sighed, knowing it would take days to find her way again in her own kitchen.

She returned her attention to the parlor and found the scene sobering. Associates sorted through an armory of rifles, shotguns, and handguns, breaking them down and cleaning them.

Jersey beckoned for Rey to join her behind the sofa. She squatted and opened two more crates for Rey's perusal.

"Shit." Instinctively, Rey took a step back. The first case housed a pair of four-foot-long Browning automatics; the second, four Thompson submachine guns. Shells, clips, boxes, and drums of bullets filled every remaining space. "Think I could use a good stiff drink about now."

"This is genuine heavy hardware," Jersey said from her crouch. "Trust me. When persuasion counts, you want a Tommy or a B.A.R., a Browning Automatic Rifle." She flexed her fingers around the Browning's wide wooden forearm and stood with it. One-handed, she gave the fierce weapon an ardent shake and Rey marveled at her strength. "This is a B.A.R.," Jersey said, as if introducing a friend, and handed it to Rey.

"Jesus Christ, Jersey." Thankful she'd accepted it with both hands, Rey ran her eyes the full length of the gun. "This would…"

"It would and it does. More like a machine gun, really. It doesn't take down a target. It erases it." She pointed to Rey's shotgun above the fireplace. "Your double-barrel .30-06 up there?" When Rey nodded, Jersey shook her head. "Imagine if it was a machine gun. The B.A.R's as fucking mean as it is big. Military only, so they're hard to come by. Don't ask how we got them."

"I won't." Rey handed it back gingerly.

Jersey put it away and picked up a Tommy gun. "Ever seen one of these?"

"The Thompson." Rey gripped it with two hands as if to fire. "Only in the news."

"We have a few drums for each of them. A hundred rounds each. You run them on semi-automatic, otherwise the drum empties in a snap. The B.A.R. magazine unloads pretty quickly, too, so fast your mind will blur, but the recoil's a little different." She grinned at that. "You can write your name with a Thompson, but you can blow up a truck with a B.A.R. I recommend you start taking one or the other on your boat whenever you go out. For anything."

Rey placed the Tommy back into the box. "It really has become a war."

Jersey dug a pack of Chesterfields from her pants pocket and shook out one for Rey. "Looks like you could use a smoke."

Rey accepted silently, thankful when Jersey lit it for her. She didn't think she could keep her hand steady enough. The impact of what would happen over the next week or so—of what *could* happen if things went wrong—struck her hard, and she wondered if she should be risking so much. Maybe she really didn't have to go through with it. Cripes. Who knew sticking up for yourself, asking a friend for help, could amount to this? *These people in my home could die because of me.*

She blew a stream of smoke toward the ceiling. The alternative, however, loomed just as unpleasant, because if she didn't keep the Mob happy…if Legs grew itchy and impatient… *Either way, it's just a matter of time before one of them puts his own guy in my place and I'll be…* She took another drag.

Jersey frowned. "Hey, you okay up there? I didn't mean to throw you with all this artillery. I just wanted you to see what you have going for you."

"It's all pretty amazing. I've seen a lot of blood and guts in my day, you know? I'm no babe in the woods, but this… Guess it's what's needed now."

Jersey tugged her toward a crate by the door and flipped open the lid. "It might ease your mind to know that these are our weapons of choice." She picked a police-issue nightstick from the pile and rapped it against her palm. "It's what we go to first. Nobody wants blood on their hands."

Rey selected one for herself and was surprised by the weight. Maybe knocks on the head *would* suffice, but something told her otherwise. "Who are we kidding here, Jersey?"

Jersey urged her outside and into a rocking chair on the porch.

"Not kidding a soul," she said. "Just so you know, we won't load those guns until we head out for Dazzle, even though we probably won't need them to put a beating on a construction site. But when we hijack your replacement load, we'll surely need them. This is big-time stuff, Rey. You're in deep, and the Mob, Legs, those guys only do business one way."

"All the guns just make it so... It's like a bad dream, when what you've seen in the papers, on the newsreels, comes into your home. When I think of what could happen..."

"Not 'could,' Rey. It already is. Mac said a couple of your people have been beaten to a pulp already, and you got the shit kicked out of you, so what do you think they'll pull next?"

Rey frowned as frustration and worry fed her rising anger. "I hate that my crew, their families, are scared. Shit, everybody knows that once the Underworld comes knocking, you're done."

"Usually, yeah. Because those goons don't ease up. And you won't be able to keep them off your back, not when your loads get stolen and there's no money to buy more. Do you have a gold mine hidden under these floorboards? You gonna call the cops?"

Rey exhaled heavily as she went to the railing and looked out, past the trucks to the woods and the lake beyond, and imagined losing everything. "What if it was just a matter of time, anyway?" She turned and leaned back, resigned to absorb some of the fiery confidence Jersey was trying to convey. "I know I'm lucky to have you all on my side. I doubt anyone in my position has ever had this kind of help."

Jersey leaned forward on her knees. "I know Mac told you what to expect, that when you saw it laid out in your house, it would scare the piss out of you, and now you see she was right. For someone who's never faced this, of course it's scary, but they're playing you, Rey, and you know what happens when they get tired of playing." She moved to the railing and set her hand on Rey's shoulder. "Look, you made a gutsy decision, asking Mac for help. You've got the guts to see this through."

Rey figured Jersey didn't need a response to that. Seemed a bit too late to back out now, anyway. But giving in to Mob games posed no future whatsoever, so yes, she'd find the guts to see this through.

"Thank you," she said and hoped Jersey hadn't detected the quake in her voice. "I can see why you're Mac's number one choice."

Jersey shrugged. "We go back, Mac 'n me. We learned a lot the hard way."

Jackson spoke through the screen door. "There's some supper left, if you two are interested. Millie made me leave you some."

Two plates covered with pot lids were the only items on the table when Rey and Jersey sat down. Two men stood at the sink, washing and drying, while another stacked dishes into a cupboard Rey seldom used. She took a longer look around and found her parlor rearranged as well, the coffee table in front of the sofa, and whiskey crates around her stuffed chairs. Seating for almost a dozen. Crates of guns now lined the wall, and her displaced boating gear sat piled in a different corner. She'd have some serious reorganization to do when this group left.

"Time for this little girl to get her beauty sleep," Millie proclaimed.

Jersey hurried to the parlor with her plate. "I'm claiming this," she said, planting herself on the sofa.

"Hey!"

"Closest to the door."

"Well, I'm heading up," Jackson said. He turned to Millie and pointed at the ladder. "Ladies first."

"You're a dog." Millie shoved his shoulder. "You just want a look at the goods. Uh-uh. I'll…" She scanned the room. "*I'll* take the sofa."

"I called it," Jersey said, stretching out, her plate on her stomach.

Rey looked on, amused but nagged by propriety. "Um…Millie, if…if you'd like, you can have the bedroom. I-I don't mind." She saw Millie's shadowed eyes widen. "I'm used to the big chair. It's okay."

"What a hostess. Thanks, hon, but—"

"No, it's really okay. I changed the sheets this morning and everything."

"You're serious? And I'm not putting you out?"

"No, you're not. We all need a good night's sleep."

"Got that right," Jersey said from beneath a blanket on the sofa.

"So true," Jackson grumbled from the loft. "Now everyone shut the hell up."

"Rey, this is awfully generous of you," Millie said and tugged on her shirt.

Rey bent to her, expecting a whisper, and Millie kissed her cheek. Rey felt heat rush to her face, and her leg and then her stomach muscles twitched. Not from a hard day's work. This was a physical reaction beyond her control, from some source inside that knew something she didn't.

"Hope you sleep well," she managed and stuffed her hands into her pockets. Her palms had begun to sweat. How dare mystery and random bodily functions interfere when there was such serious, dangerous work ahead? She tried downplaying the mystery of it all because Millie was just one of many here on business.

"Honestly, Rey. Thank you." Millie rose on her toes. "Good night, sweetie." She spun on a heel and left a hint of French perfume lingering at the door.

Rey wandered to the parlor and slumped into the overstuffed chair across from the sofa. She urgently needed to square away all the sights, sounds, and feelings of this day. She wasn't a particularly organized woman, but her head demanded some semblance of order for all this, especially when she had to focus on tomorrow night's delivery. She pulled off her shoes, and thumped her stockinged feet onto a whiskey crate—not the coffee table anymore. Damn if that woman didn't just take over everything. One minute she was giving orders, the next she was sweet, even suggestive. Hard to know which was the real Millie. Maybe both.

Rey shook a blanket out over herself and closed her eyes. Her mind raced from face to face, from guns to mobsters to seductive lipstick. Bustling organized chaos overtook rustic serenity, and bright, appreciative eyes upended solitary routine.

"She's a whirlwind, isn't she," Jersey murmured.

"And then some."

❖

"The truck boss said they'd already been hit and were on their way back empty when Diamond's men showed up," Rey reported the next evening. "When they saw that the city goons had beaten them to my load, they let the truckers go but said they'll be dead if there isn't another run in a hurry."

"So you've arranged for that within a few nights?" Jersey asked.

Rey nodded. "Done. The way things have been going lately, I'm sure they've heard about it already." She sighed and sat back. "My supplier wasn't thrilled about the extra work, but I told him I had double his problems. Hell, just a couple hours ago, one of Diamond's thugs stopped me in the village, walked right out of the tourist crowd, and bumped into me, hard. All he said was 'See you *real* soon, Rey,' and disappeared." She shook her head. "Damn tough to get product to *my* customers when those bastards take turns picking it off."

"Do New York and Diamond use the same spots, Rey?" Millie set her glass in front of Jackson and went back to filing her nails while he poured her more whiskey. Thinking Millie should be more attentive, Rey was surprised she even cared where the truckers were hijacked.

"They each have favorite spots along the route."

"You figure Legs will choose someplace different this time?"

"Can't tell."

Millie nodded as she sipped and flashed a look at Jersey. "We need to know."

"There's a lot we need to know," Jersey said and tapped the table in front of Millie. "Go with Al. There's bound to be talk, and the right stuff needs to be overheard."

Rey shifted uneasily in her seat. Apparently, Millie was going snooping. In Rey's opinion, their associate, Al, didn't seem big or tough enough to be her escort, not for the rough crowd that filled the area's hangouts. But then again, he was a bulky, gruff longshoreman by trade, so maybe he was more than just a quiet, background guy.

"Well, there'll be even more talk after tonight," Millie added, "so all the more reason for a few visits." She finished her drink and stood, then smoothed nonexistent wrinkles from her skirt. "I'll change and we'll head out. Rey, come up with a couple joints to check out, would you? And we'll take our shot while these guys play a tune on that construction site." She whirled away to the bedroom.

Jersey and Jackson rose from the table and Rey looked up at them. "In the meantime, I what? Just keep the damn home fires burning? There has to be something I—"

Jersey leaned down to her. "Easy, Rey. For now, please just sit tight. We went and got a good look at Dazzle today, watched what they were doing so we know what to go after. We won't be long."

"You sure I shouldn't go, too? I mean, I know—"

"No. We're not risking that. Don't forget: This is Legs being furious at New York, hitting them where it hurts."

Rey just nodded. "I heard folks talking today about the progress, that the third story is done and roofing is underway." Jersey just smiled and Rey's throat tightened. She seemed so sure of herself and her crew, and so sure of Millie and her mission. *Would Mac be as confident?* "And Millie's going to hit the bars? With only Al?"

"They're not new at this."

Rey followed her to the parlor, watched her strap on a shoulder holster and check to make sure that cannon of a Colt she carried was loaded. Jersey buckled a small pistol to her ankle and Rey recalled learning that Mac wore the same thing, regularly. Someone said Millie had a tiny one on her thigh, too. *So routine.*

Associates crowded into one truck, and Rey could see that the walls were lined with sledgehammers, axes, crowbars, and other assorted tools. Jersey arrived at her side.

"A few hours, that's all it should take us," she said, so matter-of-fact.

"Jesus. New York will lose its mind."

"Exactly, and go after Legs. And when Legs jacks your next load, which he will, we'll grab it back and make it look like New York did it. Then Legs *really will* try to hurt them. With Manhattan already bearing down on him, they'll collide like freight trains. Should be fun."

"I don't want any innocents getting hurt."

"Nope. That's just for the goons."

Rey turned at the soft grip on her arm. Millie beamed up at her, smiling lips a deep red, her cheeks highlighted with rouge, and those eyes masterfully outlined and shadowed for the kill. *Absolutely stunning, just like she's supposed to be.* Tight pin curls peaked out from beneath a cloche hat that sat jauntily askew and matched the slinky low-cut dress. Rey took a breath and forgot to move until Jersey sent her a playful nudge. Rey forced her eyes up as moisture beaded on the back of her neck.

Millie winked. "We've got a map," she said, waving it, and Rey finally noticed Al standing at her shoulder. "So come back in. I need you to jot down the names of some popular joints." Al held the door as she waltzed inside, and Jersey handed him the Studebaker keys.

Still trying to grasp the image of Millie at work, Rey met his eyes but hardly saw him. He tilted his head toward the door. "We're hitting the road, soon as you finish."

"Oh. Yeah. Okay."

CHAPTER NINE

Lowry wheeled his beefy Cadillac out of the Dazzle construction site and its evergreen environs, and headed north. To anywhere. The leather on the steering wheel creaked beneath his white-knuckled grip, even though he hadn't the wherewithal to speed. He checked his rearview mirror repeatedly. Frank Bocci roaring in his apartment this morning created a daytime nightmare that refused to relent.

And now Lowry had seen the sabotage for himself. He had no idea how to overcome such a setback and still meet his deadline, and he had reason to be afraid. *They call it "deadline" for a reason.*

He'd just spent several hours walking through the destruction with a foreman. Around them, workers cleared debris and salvaged what they could. He picked his way over splintered timbers, cracked cement, scattered bricks, and broken pipes. He stood in the same place he'd stood yesterday, when he gazed with wonder and pride at his masterpiece, and no longer saw the three stories of wood and brick beaming in the dappled sunlight. Gone were the broad oak double doors within the deep, covered veranda that he'd envisioned filled with satisfied, celebratory patrons. *How they'll meander in and out of the opulent foyer, linger in the magnificent dining and entertainment salons, repeatedly return for gaming and lodging...*

The pounding on his door that jolted him from a sound sleep had changed everything. On top of such traumatic personal loss, Lowry now faced a *real* bottom line that made him physically ill.

Bocci's breakfast message had been clear. *No matter what it takes, we open on time. You better make it happen.* Lowry cringed as he drove and wiped perspiration off his brow with a handkerchief. He'd always remember that meeting at the Adelphi, the way Luciano's threatening stare clawed into his stomach. *"No fucking setbacks."* A merciless board of directors hung over his head.

God help whoever did this. God help me.

Lowry checked his watch, surprised he'd been driving mindlessly for some time. Every damn minute of every waking hour was precious now, but right now, midday was late enough for the drink he needed to gather himself. On impulse, he curled the Cadillac onto the grounds of the Sagamore Hotel.

He chose a table in the sunny, glass-walled dining room and absently ordered food with his drink. He certainly had no appetite, but needed something to ease normalcy back into his body. There was so much work to do, this would probably be his last moment of calm for months, so he alternated between marveling at the bucolic view of the grounds and lake and looking at the newspaper he'd grabbed in the lobby.

Around him, couples and families occupied nearly every table, chatting and laughing about plans for the day, sights and activities they'd enjoyed, but he tuned them out and thought he really should start jotting work details.

From several tables away, however, a little girl's happy squeal distracted him and he scanned the room curiously. *I'll be dammed. It's them again, that rumrunner Rey's wealthy friends.* Once again, he found the blonde to be a vision in rose silk, the child bright-eyed and playful. And wearing a tan suit, with that Panama hat nearby, the man sat in profile, his jawline smooth and angular, his auburn hair slicked back and long enough to brush his collar. *Think it's the same guy. Mack was his name.*

Lowry peered over the top of his newspaper and wondered if the guy bankrolled Rey's business, where his money came from. He looked quite well off, so maybe he inherited his money or owned horses. However he came about his funds, he seemed none the worse for wear. *Liquor's the business to be in these days, but don't expect that big woman to make you money on this lake. That homo's product is already spoken for.*

But as Lowry continued to spy, the man, Mack, rose from the table, hoisted the child in one arm, and turned and offered the other to the pretty blonde. Lowry saw his face then, and sat transfixed as familiarity flickered through his mind.

My God. Is it possible we've met?

He watched as the trio left the room, his mind searching madly.

A waiter delivered his luncheon of broiled cod, and Lowry stared at it as if he'd forgotten he ordered.

"Your cod, sir."

"Oh, yes. Yes, thank you." Lowry held up a finger. "Before you go… That couple who just left with the adorable child, are they famous? Would you know who they are?"

"Famous? As in the moving pictures?" The waiter looked back briefly at the vacated table. "Well, I don't think so. They've been guests here for a while and I never saw anyone ask for an autograph or anything. I think the McLaughlins are just regular people, sir." He leaned closer. "But they're *very* good tippers."

Lowry sat back, eyes now past the waiter to the table in question. *"That* comes as no surprise. Thank you."

Lowry poked at his lunch for a minute, but then set down his fork and frowned toward the outdoors. "McLaughlin. Of all names." He'd only ever met one person by that name and that memory didn't sit well. "'Mack' McLaughlin," he sputtered under his breath. *Just my tattered emotions playing tricks.*

He drank more of his Chardonnay and wished he'd ordered a gin and tonic like he'd originally planned. It was just preposterous, the idea of his old nemesis here among big spenders in the Adirondacks. Besides, even if that lunatic Elizabeth McLaughlin finally went over the edge and decided to play a man's game, how would she ever end up with so much money? It was a far cry from being a pathetic domestic to living the high life here at the Sagamore.

Unless you know someone.

Lowry straightened in his chair. Elizabeth certainly knew his ex-wife, and Olivia obviously had thought enough of her to heed the garbage the pervert spewed at her. The divorce proved that. *And Olivia's father made his fortune bootlegging.*

Lowry left money on the table and headed back to his apartment in Saratoga, his head swirling with sketchy presumptions and desperate questions.

"It's all just too far-fetched, crazy, having *her* even remotely involved with my business." He pounded the steering wheel. "Dammit! I've got enough to worry about, trying to do the impossible—and for a bunch of killers, for God's sake."

How dare those bastards play with me like this? And now, what if... Well, if it ever turned out to be that conniving homo, I suppose I'd have a chance to make her disappear once and for all. Too bad Bocci isn't about to do me any favors.

"But of course it's not her."

Lowry thought back to when Olivia had nearly been shot during the police takedown of Boston mobsters. Not too long ago, and she and Elizabeth probably were still close friends at the time. Olivia had been among many federal witnesses, and he remembered being disappointed to see her face, the Waters name in newspapers, associated with that ilk in any way. If Olivia had her old man's bootlegging contacts, that damn pervert could've finagled from her all the details necessary to start her own operation. *Connecting with that rumrunner would make sense, two homos together.*

He suspected he was overthinking this whole "McLaughlin thing." Job stress surely had overloaded his capacity for rationalization and left him with only rampaging emotions, but his pounding brain wouldn't set it aside. After today, he'd be up to his neck in Dazzle work, his back to the wall, frantic that every calculation he made, every purchase, every directive led to swift project recovery—if the project could be salvaged at all. So he gave himself the rest of the day to exorcise his personal demon, to prove himself wrong, and drove to the Saratoga library with purpose.

By the time the librarian tapped her watch at his reading table, he had stacks of newspaper back issues everywhere. The yellowed copies of the *Boston Post* returned him to times when folks couldn't get enough of the mob trials, and he plowed hungrily through articles about the investigation, the massive shoot-out, and the arrests of gangsters and their political and law enforcement cronies. Key names rang bells he heard during his life at the Waters estate. There was Minsk, Weston, Flaherty, Harrison, Ambrosino, and even that Hijack Mack phantom who'd never been caught.

His heart banged against his ribs. *Can't be.* Despite his frantic research, only a few news articles about Hijack Mack surfaced— and only fueled his frustration. No wonder the guy had never been caught; every supposed witness had seen something different. Apparently, the guy towered over people, yet hardly stood five feet tall. Always in fedora and long topcoat, he somehow looked straight off the East Boston docks, in suspenders and flannel shirt. Reports claimed he spoke in a high-pitched crackle, as much the husky Irishman as the wispy German.

Disgusted, Lowry tossed the paper onto the pile he'd created, and a photograph of his glamorous ex-wife drew him back to a pre-viously rejected front page. Surrounded by reporters and photog-raphers, Olivia led a stream of witnesses exiting the courthouse, and clutched the arm of an attractive blonde as they descended the granite steps.

The caption identified the woman as friend Eleanor Weston Harrison, who later testified about crooked deals made by both her husband and father. Both men had been gunned down right before her eyes, and she'd bravely named names, then disappeared from the news. *And she'd been pregnant at the time.* Despite the grainy image, the pretty blonde looked *very* familiar.

❖

Mac slid her palms around Ellie's naked torso, flexed her fingers into the firm satiny buttocks, and drew their hips together. With an exquisite dinner now behind them and Katie nearly asleep in the next room, an evening on the dance floor awaited, but Mac couldn't have cared less about leaving their suite, not with Ellie standing before her like this.

"We don't have to go downstairs, you know," she murmured, lost in the luxury of Ellie's throat. "We could do our own dancing right here, once Katie nods off."

Ellie brushed her bare breasts against Mac's suit jacket, and linked her arms around her neck. "We've been looking forward to this orchestra, so let's at least go for an hour or so." She kissed Mac's ear. "Then we'll finish up here."

"As much as I want to show you off in that new dress, I want you naked like this."

Ellie laughed lightly and leaned back in her arms. "You haven't even seen me in it yet."

Mac cupped a breast and squeezed. "I'm partial to this outfit."

"Rascal." She brought her lips to Mac's. "You need to get out of here so I can get dressed." Mac grumbled and kissed her. Ellie's eyes were slow to open. "You *definitely* need to go. Now." She inched back and grazed splayed palms across Mac's chest. "Why don't you take Katie down to the nursery? I'll meet you at the bar in a little bit."

Urging her back, Mac ran her hands up Ellie's sides, forced her arms over her head, and held them to the bedroom door with one hand. "Dance with me now," she said and slipped her other hand between Ellie's legs.

Ellie gasped when Mac's fingers found her. "God, I love your touch." She hooked a leg around Mac's thigh. "I *so* wish you were nak—"

"Too late." Mac kissed her hungrily and reached deeper. She lived for this, thrilling them as one, sharing in this pleasure. Ellie trembled and the door rattled at her back.

"Oh, Mac. We'll wake Ka—Oh, please don't stop."

Mac released Ellie's hands to lock an arm around her waist. She reveled in Ellie's sex, so moist and hot, and slipped in and out so easily, just as she knew she would, just as she recognized her own rising desire. With her fingers hugged by Ellie's silky passage, she knew she'd soon have to devour the tender flesh with her mouth. Ellie clung to her neck, her hips eagerly meeting each stroke of Mac's hand. She twitched each time Mac withdrew, teased her, and Mac smiled against her lips.

"You get wetter every time I do that."

Ellie pulled Mac's mouth against hers. The bedroom door rattled beneath their weight.

"Mama."

The tiny query from the next room stopped them in mid-motion. Ellie breathed into Mac's mouth. "I'm so close."

Mac pressed a hard fingertip to her clit. "Come to me now." She wiggled her finger and Ellie surged against her with a long groan. "Yes, El, just like that." Mac pinched at her clit, tightened her arm around Ellie's waist, and drove two fingers inside. Ellie buried her face into the crook of Mac's neck and trembled as Mac pumped into her against the door.

"Mama?"

The hint of anxiety in Katie's voice nearly forced Mac to stop. She knew Ellie detected it as well. But then the leg hooked around her thigh shook and stiffened, and Mac plunged deeper as Ellie vibrated. She clutched Ellie to her, fingers perfectly positioned inside, and watched the orgasm shimmer through the love of her life.

Ellie's head fell back against the door with a thud and Mac kissed her way up from shoulder to neck to lips.

"I love you, Eleanor Harrison."

Ellie ran a limp hand through Mac's hair. "You, my sweet love, are so dangerous." She tugged her close for another kiss. "I might collapse if you let go, but we…"

Mac gently withdrew her fingers and traced a wet circle around Ellie's nipple. "I know. Before she gets worried." She edged away. "I'll take her to the nursery now and leave you to—"

Ellie ran a fingertip across Mac's lips. "Just wait till we get back here. You're in so much trouble."

Mac kissed her finger and opened the bedroom door. Katie's eyes widened joyfully and she reached up with both arms.

"Mackie, up." She rubbed her eyes with her fists as Mac hoisted her from the crib.

"You didn't fall asleep?"

Ellie snickered. "She will with some peace and quiet."

Katie grabbed Bing in a hug as Mac wrapped them in Katie's favorite blanket. "Time for some sleep, Miss Katie Rose."

Ellie kissed her cheek and smoothed back her curls. "Time for Miss Katie Rose to say good night."

"Ni-night, Mama." Katie rested her head on Mac's shoulder.

"Good night, my beautiful Katie Rose."

"Gonna grab my hat and I'll see you downstairs," Mac whispered before kissing Ellie. "Soon?"

"Soon." Ellie followed them to the door and plunked Mac's fedora onto her head.

Mac and Katie rode the elevator down one floor to the nursery, a trip far too short for the detailed saga Katie was conveying in her semi-sleep. All Mac could decipher was a memorable adventure with bunnies, cups, and, apparently, a lawn of "geen gas." Mac murmured appreciative responses and smiled at passing hotel guests along the way, until she entered the nursery and winked hello to the nurse on duty.

She lowered Katie into one of a dozen cribs in the warm, softly lit room. Katie squeezed Bing tightly as she looked up at Mac, blinking against sleep. Mac leaned over her, seeing in her expression a love and contentment identical to her mother's. *Peace, trust, and such a delicate innocence.*

"The sandman is coming, my Katie," Mac said, and lightly cupped Katie's cheek. "What does the sandman bring us?"

"Sandman seep."

Mac nodded. "We close our eyes to wait for the sandman."

Katie released Bing and stretched her arms to Mac. "Mackie, kiss."

Mac leaned all the way down to share a hug and kiss.

"Night, night, my Katie." She kissed the tip of her nose. "I love you."

Katie's eyes drifted closed as Mac tucked the blanket around her and Bing.

"Off to cut a rug tonight, Miss McLaughlin?"

She hadn't noticed the nurse behind her and didn't much care for being surprised in such a way.

"We are. We've been looking forward to the Timulty Orchestra since we saw the advertisement last week. Won't be too long of a night, though." She glanced back at the dozing Katie before stepping away. "Thank you for looking after her."

"Oh, heavens. She's never a trouble." The nurse gestured toward three other cribs with sleeping children. "And, y'know, I couldn't ask for a better job."

Mac crossed the ornate lobby and slowed as she entered the grand ballroom. The room was decked out for the occasion and sparkled from crystal chandeliers to the crystal goblets. Well-dressed patrons milled about, some already seated at the linen-covered tables that formed a horseshoe around the dance floor. Across the far end of the room, elaborately draped music stands lined a step-stage, and workers rushed to arrange seats and a singer's microphone.

Mac couldn't get enough of the massive mahogany bar, an intricately carved masterpiece that commanded one entire side of the room. Its backdrop of mirrored glass and impressive display of bottles expanded the room's dazzling effect, and she bit back a grin at the plentiful supply of alcohol. *Thanks to you, Rey.*

She adjusted her hat and gave herself the once-over, glad she'd worn this forest green three-piece suit. It made her look taller, and if she had to stare down some rude snob, she'd rather do it with a height advantage. But as she headed for a space along the bar, she conceded that during their prolonged stay here, no one had taken issue with her, her personal style, or their unconventional family.

She ordered a sidecar and settled into a swivel chair to wait for Ellie.

"Could use a loud and lively distraction tonight. Think this is the place."

The scratchy elderly voice caught her ear, and she turned to the tired but easy eyes of Gordon Merriweather.

She smiled as he took the adjacent seat. "Mr. Merriweather. Good to see you, sir. Back again, or would you, like me, rather never leave?"

The wispy ends of his moustache rose in an appreciative smile as he studied Mac's suit, and she detected a twinkle in his eyes.

"Back again, indeed. Thank you, young woman. Your name's…ah… Don't tell me." He paused, then snapped his fingers. "McLaughlin, am I right?" Mac grinned. "And I seem to recall a very lovely lady and cherub of a child at your side when we met some days ago. How are they?"

"We're all well, thank you for asking. We're enjoying the vacation of a lifetime. Hell, I think we're taking root here." His chuckle pleased her. "Confidentially, though, we'll probably never splurge like this again, but, hey, you only live once, you know."

Merriweather nodded vehemently. "I agree and I confess to envying your leisure. Business brings me here, but lately, it's become quite burdensome."

"Sorry to hear that, when the Sagamore offers so much luxury and relaxation."

He shrugged and drank a bit of whiskey, then stared into the reflection of the busy room behind them. Mac didn't want to press and looked back to the doorway for Ellie's arrival.

"My consortium has run into a serious roadblock," Merriweather mumbled. "One has to look out for one's investment, of course, and ours has been dealt a dreadful blow."

"Hope you haven't lost money."

"Terrible, terrible vandalism." Merriweather shook his head at his own reflection. "It's a grand project, you see. Dazzle's to be a most lavish hotel with casino and nightclub in Luzerne. But I'm afraid that difficulties are eating up what's left of this old man's faith." Mac's nerves crackled to attention. She sipped her drink and sent him a concerned look. "Yes, it's quite the undertaking," he rambled on, pride showing through his distress. "We've got a great young architect who'll get things back on track, I hope. At least that's what I've been assured by North Woods Consortium. They're, well, they're not easily discouraged."

Mac scrambled for words.

"I'm sorry to hear about the vandalism." Merriweather nodded glumly. "Well… You *do* sound as if you have faith in your company, so I'm sure it's solid. North Woods Consortium? They'll fix things, won't they?"

"Fix things?" Merriweather chortled and waved for another round of drinks. "We're lucky we don't have to start from scratch. Lost roofing, some walls, that gorgeous piazza. It's awful."

I'm sure it is.

She patted his shoulder. "Chin up, now. I have to say, the idea of operating a club in the woods sounds awfully hard—and *building* one sounds almost impossible—but your group must know what it's doing."

"We're confident that Dazzle will draw well, particularly if it gets a good foothold on the season." He snickered into his new drink. "We thought we had problems keeping it supplied...up to snuff, if you catch my drift. Ha. Supplying alcohol is the least of our worries now."

Mac leaned a little closer. "Surely, those resources are good around here." She gestured to the well-stocked bar.

"My associates are an impatient lot."

"Well, it's a bold and brave undertaking. When do you hope to open? Should I include Dazzle in my vacation plans for next summer?"

"June," he answered, "if our architect comes through."

"Will he have to redesign the whole thing?"

"My associates want the original design, come hell or high water but, personally? He only has ten months. It'll take his finest effort to redo everything by the deadline."

"Hm." Mac didn't doubt that Jersey and the crew had done a masterfully destructive job. "But your architect's good? He's a sharp guy?"

"Oh, sure, smart and ambitious, but he's young and never tackled something this big—or dealt with associates like ours." Merriweather downed most of his whiskey and swayed against Mac's shoulder. "If he knows what's good for him, he'll pull off a miracle." He held up his glass. "So, I'm crossing my fingers."

Mac clinked her glass to his. "I'll cross mine, too."

CHAPTER TEN

"This is number five on Rey's list?" Al let the Studebaker roll to a stop between a pair of dusty Model A's. He set the parking brake and they scanned the building's dreary cinder block walls in the headlamp light. "This one doesn't look like much, either."

Such a different world up here in the woods, Millie thought, so unlike the backroom clubs and underground speakeasies in the city. So crude and isolated, and blacker than the shadows she always handled with ease. *Kind of creepy.*

But experience had taught her that regardless of their outward appearances, these joints often surprised you once you stepped inside, and Millie hoped they'd find the surprise they wanted—hoped their search would end here. The four they'd hit last night weren't much different from this dive, nondescript outposts along miles of forested gravel road. No signs or markings, just vehicles parked outside advertising their purpose, and maybe the hammering of a piano and some off-key bellowing, if you got close enough.

"I don't hear any music, either," she said. "Do you?"

"Not a sound. But five cars and three trucks say something. Rey sure was right when she said this was the only joint for miles."

Millie tried not to think about how many more they'd have to visit, how long it would take to find Rey's trucker snitch. They had to be prompt about setting up Diamond for their "New York" hijacking, to aim him at those mobsters and complete the alignment of a head-on collision. Thanks to the Dazzle sabotage, New York already had Diamond in its sights, and was on course and picking up speed just as planned. According to current rumor, New York blew up Diamond's main garage the other night, and everyone knew Manhattan wouldn't stop there. A hijacking by New York would coax Diamond into battle with a vengeance.

Millie sighed as the clock for Mac's plan ticked in her head. "We need to find this rat soon."

"Yeah, I know. I'd like to get back home one of these days—before it snows."

"Says he who works the Boston docks in February. We've got a job to do first."

"Well, I bet you miss the city." He sent her a goofy grin. "Don't tell me Rey and her stick life are rubbing off on you."

"Well, it's not the Ritz, but I try to think of it as an adventure. After all, who needs a real bathroom or water from a faucet or a stove that doesn't smoke?" She had to smile. "But I really like Rey. She's all right, you know? She's more easygoing than I expected at first. It doesn't seem as though she's bothered by us taking over her place or the changes we made."

"*We*? You mean changes *you* made. Like the yellow curtains you *found* in the closet. She looked pretty shocked when she saw them." Millie shrugged. The curtains weren't anything major, but they kept the forest blackness from seeping into the cabin—and the color was nice, too. Al drummed his fingers on the steering wheel. "It was hard to tell how she felt about you moving the kitchen table way out into the room either, or you changing up the parlor again. You know she fell over the crate by the fireplace last night. Didn't see it in the dark and said a few colorful words." He shook his head. "I suppose she's just keeping her mouth shut about everything, considering we're up here for her."

Millie figured as much. Yes, she'd cringed at that crash in the parlor, and was relieved when the follow-up commentary didn't include her name. The parlor had needed rearranging for their meeting, and she felt certain Rey understood. Secretly, however, she hoped Rey wasn't compiling a list of gripes against her. The sooner they set Diamond in motion, the sooner those forces would let up on Rey and life would return to normal. She wondered how much Rey looked forward to that.

"We have to get lucky at this in a hurry." She adjusted her hat and straightened the front of her dress.

Al glanced at her preparations. "Don't let those bazoombas fall out, Mil. Thought they were gonna at that last joint. I ain't in the mood to take on the whole place."

She looked down at her bosom. "Maybe this *is* too much."

"Oh, it's plenty, all right. Up here, they only see your…your style…in the moving pictures or those Hollywood magazines, so we're bound to catch something with a trap that tempting."

"You just keep your eyes and ears open. I'll take care of my girls." She patted his arm as she opened the car door. "Let's go. We're wasting time."

Inside, laughter and the smell of whiskey and old wood cut through the heavy cloud of cigarette and cigar smoke. The plywood bar and eight shabby tables, half occupied by equally shabby characters, didn't promise success, and Millie sensed another defeat before even ordering a drink. They weren't likely to discover a loose-lipped big spender in this place, and since it was already one o'clock, she resigned herself to trolling Rey's list again tomorrow night.

The wispy bartender with defeated gray hair seemed to have never seen customers like them, because he took their order and just stood, gawking. Millie spoke before Al could reach across the bar and grab him by the throat.

"Al, honey. Got a ciggy? I'm out."

"Huh? Yeah, sure, *Goldie*." He shook out a Chesterfield and lit it for her. "Bartender. Got any smokes back there? Any Luckies for the lady?"

"I might have." He set two brown bottles in front of them and nodded toward the far end of the bar. "Gotta see what I got." He strolled away.

Al slid off the stool. "Be right back. I'm gonna help him."

Millie watched his small, boxy frame lumber away, a cockiness in his bow-legged gait that dared anyone to cross him. The two young women arriving at the bar from across the room watched him, too, eyed him up and down as they waited, and Millie couldn't help but recall those days, barely twenty years old, out with dates. Fun times, mostly.

She noted their amateur makeup and modest attire, the home-spun stitchery, the strapped flats with hardly a scuff, and remembered developing a knack for fashion and making her own clothes when she was years younger than they. A little nostalgic chuckle escaped as she brought her beer to her lips.

One girl turned to her, red hair flashing off her shoulder. "You see something funny?"

"Yeah," the other added, "you thinking we look funny cause we ain't all titties and finery?"

Millie turned a shoulder to them.

The redhead hummed thoughtfully. "Maybe she thinks our guys aren't as good as hers. Or…maybe she's tired of that runt she waltzed in with."

Millie responded with a severe look. "Watch your mouth. I'm minding my own business and you should, too."

"Well, maybe your kind of *business* ain't welcome here, Miss Fancy Dress."

The friend leaned across her to make a point. "Maybe your daddy should take you and that dress someplace the men will fill it with greenbacks. You're not putting it to use here, y'better know that."

Al strolled back to his stool, an eyebrow raised at Millie as he put a pack of Luckies on the bar. "So." He pointed to her cleavage. "The girls aren't striking it rich tonight?" Millie bit back a smirk. He looked at the young women with feigned curiosity. "You saying nobody's got any dough here?"

"Hey," the redhead snapped, "our guys are top dogs at Gramarcy's Smokehouse, been there since they turned fourteen, so they're in the dough, all right, but you ain't getting any of it."

Her friend elbowed her sharply. "These two flimflammers don't know how good we got it." She glared at Millie and tipped her head, side to side. "Why don't you just sashay on out of here, go back where you came from."

"Whoa, ladies," Al said and raised a hand. "Stop, now. That's not being very neighborly."

Millie shook her head. "And I don't particularly like their tone. Not neighborly at all."

"Look," Al tried again. "We're not bothering anyone. We're just here for—"

"Ha!" The redhead pointed in Millie's face. "We can guess what this tramp's here for."

Millie looked down at her outfit. "Tramp, you say?" She grinned at Al over her shoulder. "Should I slap her now?" She heard him chuckle just as an open palm smacked her cheek and nearly sent her off the stool. The sting lingering, Millie ground her teeth in self-restraint.

Across the room, the women's dates laughed and the redhead seemed emboldened by the audience. She straightened, planted a hand on her hip, and stepped closer.

"How's *that*? You think *I'd* take a slap from—"

Millie slapped her with such force, the redhead stumbled back a step. "Took one, didn't you?" Millie said with a smirk.

The redhead seethed. "Why, you... If you think I'm going to let a floozy like you—"

"Honey, you best shut up, if you don't want to end up on your ass."

"Big talk from the flashy little tart. Those big knockers your weapons? Or do you use them for income?"

"You're pushing it, girl." Millie exhaled hard. "Jesus Christ. Look, either you're picking a fight or putting on a show, so either way, smarten up."

"Did you just call me stupid? Y-you hussy!"

She swung with emphasis, but Millie's patience expired first. She smashed the redhead squarely in the mouth, even slid off her own stool doing it. Hurt like hell, hitting teeth, but she'd heard enough. The bitch deserved a solid smack in the kisser. It snapped her head back, staggering her, and before the friend could shove a chair beneath her, the redhead hit the floor. Everyone in the bar whooped at the excitement.

Millie sipped her beer and looked down at her, did her best not to laugh at the teary eyes or the bleeding lip. "Fix your lipstick, little girl."

Al tugged her back and put her purse in her hands. "We're done here. That's enough for one night."

"Ellie couldn't come because she's in the golf eliminations." Mac tightened her grip around Katie on her lap and pushed off on Rey's tree swing. "Mama's really good at golf, isn't she, my Katie?" She grinned at Rey and Jersey on the porch. "Ellie's addicted—and it's the Sagamore's fault. Apparently, the hotel's in some regional tournament and she wants to play." Katie's delighted squeal rang through the woods.

Jersey chuckled from behind her newspaper. "Neither of them will want to go home, you know." She glanced at Rey. "Next thing you know, she'll have us clearing land on her farm for a golf course."

Rey laughed. "Better put in a tree swing while you're at it."

She leaned on the porch railing, watching Katie hug Mac's neck and giggle with each back-and-forth motion. Their love, their bond was unmistakable. A measure of success, she thought, the love of a child. And how stark the contrast between loving parent and shrewd gang boss. But that was what moments like this were for, to let one's heart relax, and she was grateful for this pause in what had been so many mission-oriented days.

The midday sun brightened everyone's mood on this day when idle time actually meant opportunity lost. Millie and Al would try again tonight, and everyone needed them to score. Until then, the master plan sat on hold, and the small army Mac had summoned could only kill time. With associates scattered to the lake and the village, some as far as Saratoga to satiate their city longings, the atmosphere at the cabin was subdued and ponderous. Mac and Katie's arrival had been unexpected but uplifting.

"A tree swing," Mac yelled over Katie's laughter. "That's a definite." She dragged her feet to slow the swing. "And get this.

Ellie checked this afternoon's weather forecast and signed up for a tennis lesson."

"Sports of the rich and famous," Rey said.

Jersey lowered her paper. "Seriously? Golf is bad enough." Katie waddled toward her and Jersey dropped the paper and met her halfway across the yard. She scooped her up and motioned Mac off the swing. "Our turn. Right, my Katie Rose? Let's swing some more!"

"Jezzie!" She patted Jersey's cheeks with both palms.

"Those two," Mac said, grinning. She opened a Coca-Cola from the case she'd brought. "And Ellie says Katie turns *me* into a big kid."

"They think the world of each other. That's obvious."

"Jersey's been a part of our lives almost from the beginning, so, yeah. I was thrilled when Ellie wanted her to be Katie's godmother, y'know, should anything ever happen to me."

"I'd say that's a smart choice, too. Jersey has a steady way about her. And they sure have fun together."

"Katie's been asking for her, so I thought we'd stop by. We've been everywhere, playing tourist, and she's wearing me out. I don't know who's going to be more upset when this vacation ends, Katie or Ellie, but the time's coming and I dread it." She paused and her wistful smile faded. Rey could feel her focus shift. "So, still no rat."

"No, but God knows, Millie's trying. She's got Al crisscrossing the countryside. Tonight will be their fourth time out—and the last places I can think of that might work."

Mac nodded thoughtfully at her bottle. Probably worrying about their timetable, Rey figured, wanting to complete their hijacking so Mac could get her family back to the sanctuary of the farm.

"I heard she saw a little action."

"Yeah," Rey said on a laugh, "and she's got a slice on her knuckle to prove it. Maybe I shouldn't be surprised."

"Nope."

"She's quite a lady. I've never met anyone like her. She doesn't take smart mouth from a soul."

"Never has."

"She's some kind of bearcat, that's for sure." Rey vividly remembered the other afternoon when Millie slammed through the front door, steaming about the outhouse—and the squirrel who'd followed her inside. She hadn't appreciated Rey's laughter, and those fiery eyes had made Rey's heart race like it hadn't in years. Good thing she hadn't complimented Millie about them, as she'd wanted to at that moment. That wouldn't have gone well. "She's a wild one when she's riled up. I hope she doesn't run into any trouble tonight."

Mac stared out at Katie and Jersey. "They have to find this guy."

Mac's economical comments didn't leave Rey hanging any more. She'd grown used to them, but heard deep concern in this last one. Or maybe she was just overreacting, actually hearing her own concerns, but whether it was the set of Mac's jaw, her stoic posture, or her factual tone, something implied Mac had more on her mind than catching a snitch, and Rey didn't know how to ask, or if she should.

Jersey brought Katie onto the porch and they all went inside, where Katie immediately renewed her interest in the wooden blocks she'd left on the parlor rug.

"Ellie knows you brought Katie here, right?" Jersey sank into a chair, her eyes following Mac to the sofa.

"Of course. She's very supportive of all this, but I won't take advantage of that. It's not fair or smart. We'll be heading home soon."

Katie dumped an armful of blocks into Rey's hands. "Wey, bwox."

Rey caught most of them as Katie went back for more. "Getting the family home sounds wise, Mac. You probably shouldn't stick around."

Her arms around five more blocks, Katie struggled to climb onto Rey's lap. "Wey, up," she said.

Rey picked her up in the bend of one arm. Katie giggled, and the welcome on her angelic face made Rey smile. She couldn't remember the last time she'd held a child, or when her own size hadn't intimidated one into scurrying away. Not only was Katie as cute as her mother was beautiful, she somehow had acquired both parents' irresistible charm. Rey helped her stack the blocks on their combined laps.

Mac set her forearms on her thighs. "I want them away from here, far away before any action starts. Trouble is, Ellie loves the Sagamore, so this mess needs to be eliminated. I've been thinking I might surprise her at Christmas, book a New Year's getaway. I know she'd love to come back up for a few days, once things calm down, and kick off the new year. We'd all enjoy playing in the snow."

Rey liked the idea, too. Having friends return to her area certainly would brighten the holidays. "The hotels and resorts offer a grand fireworks show on New Year's Eve. They'd love it." Rey always looked forward to it, even though it was her busiest time of year, with the biggest deliveries of the finest product. But if she could be free of hijackings by then, she'd *really* be in a celebratory mood.

CHAPTER ELEVEN

A l called for a third round of drinks, and Millie twirled a finger through his disheveled hair in appreciation, then swiveled away on her stool. Sitting primly with legs crossed and advertising, she surveyed the gritty, well-liquored drinkers through the smoky haze and let them assess her merchandise.

A wiry black man began banging a tune on the upright in the corner, and just as she hoped, the swarthy big spender she'd been watching for over an hour finally stood and swaggered across the room toward her.

He tossed his head toward the piano. "Time we danced, doll." He took her hand and urged her off the stool. "Unless you'd rather do something else."

Millie shrugged. "I'm not much for all that hot stepping. Too much jiggling, if you know what I mean."

He smiled broadly, eyes roaming her chest. "Too bad. I'd enjoy that show."

Millie sipped her drink and eyed him sideways. She hooked a finger inside a button of his shirt. "How about we sit someplace quiet?"

"Fine with me," he said and bent to her ear. "Smart choice." He cupped her ass as he guided her to a vacant table and signaled the bartender for fresh drinks.

Millie approved of the location, still in Al's direct line of sight. "So, what's your name, honey?"

"Rudy's all you need, doll." He drew out a chair for her. "You sure don't need that lug back there." He pulled his chair closer as she made a show of crossing her legs and revealing her knee. He covered it with his palm. "And what do they call you, besides 'oh my'?"

"My name's Goldie. On my way to fun and friends in Montreal. We's tired of frumpy old Boston. Need some new blood, y'know?"

The bartender delivered their drinks, and Rudy gripped his arm, leaned back in his chair, and announced, "Next round's on me, everybody!"

Millie displayed plenty of delight at his gesture and ran a fingertip along his hand on his bottle. Scraped knuckles stood out even in the poor light, and she figured fighting also accounted for the missing incisor in his smile. He squeezed her knee and inched his fingers higher. *Thank God for years of experience, keeping that .25 on my other leg.*

She spoke before sipping. "I take it you like the dress?"

"What red-blooded man wouldn't? Someone like you shows up? Hell, my luck has changed for the better."

"Oh, please." Millie raised an eyebrow as she swirled her cocktail. "Be serious. With your looks? I doubt you ever have bad luck." She traced the seam of his pants up toward his hip and fanned her fingers over his thigh. "You've obviously got the means to show a girl a real good time."

Rudy leaned heavily into her shoulder. "My dry spell ended the minute I laid eyes on you, good-lookin'." He toyed with her dangling earring, and his eyes drifted with his fingers, along her neck, down to the exposed swells of her breasts. "Snugglin' down in there would make us both feel fine." He dipped a finger into her cleavage and Millie drew his hand away.

"Now, now. We hardly know each other, Mr. Rudy."

"Then let's get to it. Listen, I got plenty of dough for a hot time in Montreal. What do you say?"

"Oooh. Now *that's* tempting." She rubbed between his legs and labored to maintain a playful look. *Cripes, why is this the only trick that works?* "You've got the green, do you? I bet you're a boss man or somethin', aren't you?"

Rudy bit his lip when Millie rubbed a little harder.

"Not a boss. The right people appreciate my smarts, that's all. But I'm big enough to keep you smiling." He pushed her hand against his cock. "Like that, do you? You'll be appreciative, too. I promise. Just like I'll appreciate some of this." He shoved his hand up her thigh.

Millie couldn't back away far enough. "Whoa, fella." She stifled a grimace and found herself comparing the feel to a woman's gentle touch.

"You'll like it. Trust me," he breathed into her ear. "You could take it all night, couldn't you?"

The last thing Millie wanted from smarmy Rudy was this kind of contact. And for a moment, she yearned for the tender strokes of lovers past, the women who'd cared to reach for the soul she held in reserve. How willing, desperate she had been to create *something* with Jackson. How certain she thought she'd been of her needs, of his. Their year-long struggle ended with the admission that their parallel lives weren't destined to intersect at the heart. This life has so many ups and downs, she thought, and sometimes required you pay a difficult price.

The first two stops of the evening had led to this dusty joint, and although she was surprised to find serious spending in such a small dive, she was relieved to get lucky, finally. As skilled as she was at these ruses, this one had dragged on long enough. Intuition told her this was the bastard Rey suspected, the rat trucker with the big mouth. Anyone throwing money around at this hour had to have a special connection, but now she needed to take things a step further. Thankfully, she had plenty of practice holding her liquor, *the good stuff's much harder than this swill,* and could outdrink most men, because this was one of those occasions when it counted. The booze and her flirtation had turned Rudy into a horny hunk of muscle.

"Hey!" Millie grabbed his forearm and tried to push him away as his hand crept higher. "What's your hurry?"

"Come on, doll. What do you say?"

She seized his wrist with both hands, but he had his full weight into it now, his fingers greedily reaching toward the fabric at her crotch. Repulsed, she squeezed her eyes shut as his words gushed against her cheek. "Just a little feel to start, Goldie. We can finish in my Chevy out back, then head for the border."

"Hey, you hick piece of shit!" Al's voice surprised Rudy, and Millie managed to push the hand out from beneath her dress.

He turned to Al's angry mug. "Get lost."

"Show my girl some respect. Keep those fuckin' dog paws off her."

"What did you say?" He lunged to his feet, towering over Al, and grabbed his beer bottle by the neck.

Millie stepped between them. "Stop it. Knock it off, both of you. Al, honey, me and Rudy, we're just talking, okay?" She patted his cheek. "Don't you get all fired up now, baby."

"I saw what he was doing." Al glowered up at Rudy. "Big dumb—"

Rudy lurched forward, sandwiching Millie between them. "You fuckin' shrimp, I'll—"

"No, you won't!" Millie declared and pushed each man away from her. "Rudy, you sit. And, Al, honey, you just go on and finish your beer. Everything's fine here. I promise. Just talking."

Al growled. "If you say so, Goldie." He pointed at Rudy. "Still keeping my eye on you." He sulked back to his barstool as Rudy laughed.

Millie pulled Rudy down onto the chair as she sat. "Don't pay Al no mind. And no more getting fresh like that. What happened to our nice quiet chat?"

He shook his head. "You're a tease, you are, doll. A guy like me doesn't mess around, you know? I see the good stuff and I go after it."

Millie raised her cocktail and smiled coyly. "That how you get so free with your cash?" She looked him up and down, pointedly. "A strong man with money going after what he wants... I like strong men."

"Oh, that's me, baby. I do real well. People know what I'm worth." He chuckled. "You could say I'm a good listener and it's appreciated."

"So you're like an inside guy, getting the goods on what's happening."

"Eh. I make it my business to know." He leaned closer. "Got an ear to the liquor trade around here. That's where the money is." Millie made sure he saw her surprise. "Yup," he said, sitting back and hoisting his bottle. "Some people are just plain stupid with stuff, and that's good for me."

"You're pretty slick, nosing in on things. And you're *so* right about people. Me and Al wound up drinking with a woman last night not far from here, some little joint by the lake where she runs booze. She yapped our ears off, so I get what you mean about folks not knowing when to shut up."

"A woman on Lake George, you say. Big and dumb?"

Millie shrugged. "Some lake. I don't know. But she was a big one, for sure, tall as you. Damn. Never seen a woman that tall, and… and *big*, y'know?"

"She say anything intelligent?"

"Oh, cripes. She whined the whole time, talked a blue streak about business trouble. Desperate sounding, going out in the dead of night tomorrow, all shook up that some hotshot like Jack Diamond will come after *her*." She chortled. "Pretty loose talk, if you ask me."

"She dropped Jack's name?"

Millie laughed. "Yeah, imagine? Probably thinks she's special, going to get her name in the paper with the famous Legs Diamond."

"Dumb enough to mouth off." Rudy's toned softened. "Sounds like someone I know."

"Well, lucky you."

"She say anything about trouble on Bloody Pond Road?"

"Eh, she might've. I ain't sure. I tried to ignore all her slurred yapping." Millie fished through her beaded clutch purse, searching for her compact, and left Rudy waiting for more. He ran a heavy hand across his jaw and she let him stew as she touched up her lipstick in the tiny mirror.

"Goldie," he said, sighing. "So what did she say?"

"Oh, I don't really remember." She puckered into the mirror. "She just mumbled something about a bloody spot on the road, but she was so drunk, who knows what she meant."

"There are stretches that are deserted for miles. There's this curve that's real...unlucky."

"Then you won't catch me driving it." She put her lipstick and compact away, then raised her glass. "And, hey, I'm a real good driver, too, but up here in your damn creepy woods? No thanks."

"You said tomorrow night, huh?"

"As if I care." Millie shrugged. "So, is there *really* a bad rain storm coming?"

"What?" He shook his head as if to clear his thoughts. "A storm? First I've heard of it."

"Well...how far is it to Montreal? I ain't keen on getting stuck on some shitty mud road in this wilderness." Over the rim of her glass, she watched his attention return from somewhere other than their table.

"It's a few hours north."

"The roads get muddy up there?"

"Yeah, but fuck that. Let's run up there now. What do you say, doll? Just you and me."

Millie frowned into her drink. "Sounds like fun, but... Y'see, Al, he... Well, he don't like it when I take off. We's kinda *attached*, if you know what I mean, so—"

"Fuck that, Goldie. I'll just *de*tach him and we can be on our way."

Millie bit back a grin at the thought of Al pummeling Rudy with twenty years of dock brawling and the brass knuckles he kept in his pocket. Chances were, his .38 wouldn't even have to make an appearance.

She tripped a finger under Rudy's chin. "I don't want nobody getting hurt, handsome, so how's about I stop by here on our way back, say, a week from tonight? Could be a good time, y'know. Can I count on you being here?"

"A week?" He pouted as he took her hand. "I'm not a real patient guy."

"What if I promised it would be worth your wait, *boss man?*"
Tickling his palm brought out his broad, sloppy smile.

"I'll be here."

"You better be." With a wink, she left him at the table.

❖

His expensive architect's pencil pinged off the workhouse
wall and settled on the floor amid dozens of rejected calculations, a
mocking collection of paper balls. Lowry propped both elbows on
the table and dropped his head into his hands. No matter which way
he figured it, the money he'd been allocated wouldn't stretch far
enough. And that was costing him time, which clanged in his brain
like a fire alarm bell.

Replenishing construction materials, forcing workers into
extended shifts, and bringing in more equipment, all required more
money and time than the schedule allowed, and he'd been a fool to
promise Bocci so much progress so quickly. He'd put off updating
the big goon yesterday, avoided him today, and practically vomited
at the prospect of facing him anytime soon.

Lowry sat back and wriggled his sore ass on the brittle wooden
chair. His back ached from hunching all day, his eyes stung from the
lousy kerosene light, and he'd been too leery of the little wood stove
to start a fire, so he twitched against the September chill.

"Look at you," he said to no one in the tiny structure, "Mr.
Leave-It-To-Me. They're going to drop the hammer on you."

He took his coat and hat off the back of the door, blew out the
lamp, and stepped out into the blackness of the Dazzle site. "Damn
woods." If only there was money to light it and provide for a night
shift. *Wait till they hear this mess needs more money.* "Jesus Christ.
They can't get blood from a stone."

He carefully drove off the site and sped up at the idea of the
restorative accommodations he'd rented in Saratoga, waiting for
him with electricity, upholstered chairs, and a deep bathtub. He
hadn't the stomach for food at the moment, but the half-empty bottle
of Jameson on the bedside table would take the edge off.

He *had* to face Bocci soon, and he knew the big buffoon would explode about their lagging progress. After all, Bocci answered to Luciano, of all people, so the heat on him to produce *had* to be brutal. And Lowry didn't doubt for a second, that Bocci would pass that heat down the line to him, unless Lowry satisfied him with something—anything. So, tonight, he looked forward to a hot soak and good whiskey to calm his mind and hopefully stimulate a revelation about their nightmare.

Lowry flicked on the light and opened the closet door, then jumped at the noise behind him. Stone-faced and still wearing hats and coats, two men rose from their chairs. Lowry had no idea how they'd gained entrance or how long ago, but they definitely brought the outside chill into the room.

Hands in his coat pockets, the taller one nodded at the closet. "Go ahead and hang up your stuff, Lowry." Like his friend, he remained as deadpanned as his voice, the jagged scar along his jaw hardly moved when he spoke. Lowry fought back a shiver and hurriedly obeyed. "Very good. Now come, have a seat."

Lowry made his way to the parlor and sat. He was thankful when Scarface sat on the sofa, but wished the other guy would stop prowling behind his chair. Having him at his back, out of sight, made it hard to breathe.

"Our boss doesn't like being ignored," Scarface said.

"If you're referring to Frank B—"

The short man spoke into Lowry's ear from behind. "Nice you remember his name."

"I-I'm certainly not ignoring him."

Scarface leaned forward. "Three days without a chat isn't good for business."

"Disrespectful, I'd say," said the short man, at Lowry's ear again.

"You can imagine how a gentleman of Mr. Bocci's caliber hates to be disrespected," Scarface said. "We're here to guarantee you'll pay your respects tomorrow morning at the Adelphi. Ten o'clock, sharp."

"Ten?" Lowry frantically ran tomorrow's schedule through his mind and remembered the critical meeting he'd arranged with site foremen. These thugs weren't likely to care, but he had to let them know. "Look, honestly, I don't want to be difficult, truly, but tomorrow I'm expected—"

The short man clamped a heavy hand onto Lowry's shoulder, tilted him in his chair. "I'm hearing disrespect."

"Do whatever you gotta do, Lowry, but your place is at the Adelphi at ten o'clock."

"Yeah, and the boss wants to start his day on a good note." The short man tightened his grip and shook him. "You'll make his day, won't you?"

"Of course I want to. I-I've been working nonstop, but...but he might not—"

Lowry hit the floor face-first. The pain in his cheek and nose forced his eyes closed. Then the crushing weight on the back of his neck shortened his breathing. A shoe, he guessed.

"We checked out the place today, Lowry, and all you got to show are outside walls and a fucking roof. You think that's going to make the boss happy?"

Lowry felt the weight on his throat increase.

"You got lots of ground to make up," the short one said. "Plus we hear you're spending a ton of dough. Is that right? Huh?" He lifted his foot slightly and Lowry tried to answer, but the shoe came down even harder. "We don't give a shit what you got to say. We ain't who matters. But you know who does, don't you?" He pressed harder and Lowry twisted beneath him, struggling for air. "Yeah, you know."

"Y'see, Lowry," Scarface added, "we're unhappy when our boss is unhappy." To catch a breath, Lowry tried pushing up off the floor with both hands. Scarface stepped on one hand and stomped his other foot onto Lowry's back. "We like being happy, don't we, Packer?"

"We sure do."

"Yes, we sure do. So, I'm sure you'll have good news for him tomorrow morning, won't you?"

The men stepped back. Lowry heaved air back into his system, and coughed violently. The pain in his face, neck, and hand were the least of his problems.

Now, the men yanked him up and dropped him into the chair. Lowry swallowed a mouthful of blood, and the wetness he felt on his upper lip said his nose was bleeding. He hoped the throbbing in his left hand didn't mean they'd broken bones.

"So how's it gonna go tomorrow?" Scarface stood waiting, hands back in his pockets.

"I-I'll give him the b-best report I can."

Scarface bent closer, and his stare shrank Lowry into his seat. "He said he's tired of waiting for results, Lowry, so you better have some. If not, somebody else will, and you know what happens to you?" Nearly shaking, Lowry tried not to picture it. "Come on, Mr. Architect. Take a guess."

CHAPTER TWELVE

Rey fumed as she dug beneath piles of belongings in the parlor, searching for her first aid kit. "I know it's here somewhere, dammit."

Cut on the arm while roughhousing with others at the lake, an associate stood bleeding on Rey's kitchen floor and turned the slow, easygoing morning into a circus. The last thing Rey wanted today was more commotion, and now she couldn't hear herself think, let alone find what she needed.

Jersey scolded the two women responsible for the injury, while a collection of associates tried to explain, talked over her, and blamed each other like stubborn children. Meanwhile, Rey's call for help searching through *their* things fell on deaf ears.

"Son of a bitch!" Rey slammed a trunk lid. "Where the hell are my—"

"Jesus Christ!" Millie flung open the screen door. "I just take a moment to pee, and all hell breaks loose. The wind's carrying this noise all the way to friggin' Canada." She stood at the table, hands on her hips, glaring at the associate's wound. "What happened to you?" She whirled around when Rey stomped out of the utility room, headed back to the parlor.

"Goddammit!"

"And what's *your* problem?"

Rey tossed a hand in futility. "As if anybody cares to lend a hand here."

"Doing what? Why are you throwing stuff everywhere?"

"Because I can't find what I want!" She shoved jackets and boots to the floor and hauled a crate of rifles aside.

"Go easy with those!" Millie commanded. "What the hell are you looking for?"

"I have a medical kit, bandages *somewhere!*"

"It's under the sink."

Rey stopped short and stared at her. "What?"

Millie held up the box. "This?"

"What the hell's it doing over there?"

"I needed the tiny scissors this morning. I put the box under the sink, because that's where you'd most likely need—"

"I have it with me on the boat," Rey said, taking it from her. "That's why I—"

"Well, if anyone else needed it, they'd never know to look—"

"No one else is ever here to need it!"

"Well, lots of people are now!"

Jersey grabbed the box from Rey. "Give it to me!" Eyes afire, she looked from one to the other, and Rey felt like a child. "Jesus," Jersey sighed, "a thundering bear and a whining tornado. Enough, already." She brought the associate to the sink, pumped water into the basin, and set the box beside it. "Clean and bandage yourself up. Don't let it be a problem."

"Sorry, Jers," the associate murmured.

Jersey turned to address everyone. "And no more stupid shit!"

Picking up the mess she'd made, Rey thought the young woman sounded as apologetic as Rey felt. And Millie meant well, but shouldn't have moved stuff without saying something.

Sufficiently bandaged, the associate handed her the medical box and Rey had to step around Millie to put it back under the sink.

"I suppose it can go down here," she said.

Arms folded beneath her breasts, Millie eyed her sideways. "Well, since you're going out tonight on the boat, I suppose you *do* need it with the rest of that stuff. I'm sorry."

Jackson snickered as he went by with a bottle of beer. "Kissy kissy."

In a flash, Millie had one of her pumps in hand and threw it across the room. "Asshole!" Everyone laughed when it bounced off his back.

Jersey picked it up and shook it at her. "I would've left the kids home if I thought they'd misbehave." She followed Jackson onto the porch.

Rey surveyed her kitchen, knowing Millie saw her note all the changes. Canisters, bread box, dish towels, and God knew what else had been moved. Rey just sighed. If she hoped to feed this army in a few hours, she needed to learn her way around.

She leaned on the sink and let the glinting lake restore her sense of calm. Thickening clouds soon would steal the sparkle from the water, would drop the temperature into the feel of late autumn, and she'd definitely need a heavy jacket for the run up and down the lake tonight.

Millie set a hip against the counter. "Penny for your thoughts." She took in the woodsy serenity, too, and Rey supposed it was a rarity for a city girl—if Millie appreciated it at all. But softness had returned to her voice, so Rey risked believing they were of like mind, at least for now.

"Just thinking how beautiful it is, how easily it changes. So comfortable right now and tonight will be chilly. One minute it can sweep your heart away. The next, you can be lost."

"Ah. A touch of poetry from the thundering bear."

Tempted to search for understanding in Millie's eyes, Rey forced herself to remain still. She didn't want to turn and see it missing. She'd rather keep seeing their potential for friendship, maybe even companionship, one that didn't require explanations. She feared her knees would start shaking the way they had that first night, when she'd relinquished her bed and Millie kissed her cheek.

Rey cleared her throat. "Well, every so often, it's good to remind yourself what it's all about, living like this."

Peripherally, she saw Millie still watching, saw her nod, those wind-tossed curls so near to Rey's shoulder.

"It is beautiful. You're very lucky," Millie said. "It's a shame there won't be time to enjoy more of it. I was at the shore earlier and the lake's just enormous, so much bigger than I thought."

"You're always welcome to come back, you know, once all this is behind us." *Don't be a fool. This place isn't set up for a lady.* "It'll be colder, though, and there'll probably be a lot of snow, so—"

"Don't count me out so fast. I'm from Boston, remember, not Florida. The cold white stuff doesn't hold me down."

Hard to imagine anything holding you down.

"I'll keep that in mind."

"You do that, Big Bear. You do that." She set a heavy box of provisions on the table with a thump. "Meanwhile, since it's going to be a long chilly night, we probably should get started on supper. And you're playing sailor in the wee hours, so let's tackle that stew you suggested earlier. You said you have meat?"

Rey grinned at her nonstop style. She hadn't expected Millie to share in the cooking, or even consider Rey's upcoming cold night mission. The pleasant surprises buoyed her spirit.

"Meat. You bet." As Millie pulled a sack of potatoes from the box, Rey produced a large bundle wrapped in white butcher's paper. "Venison."

"Venison? Is that…deer meat?"

Rey began cutting bite-sized chunks. "It is. And you'll love it."

"I've never had it."

"First time for everything, City Girl."

"I thought you said you had beef."

"Why would I say that when I have venison?"

"For Christ's sake." Millie waved the potato peeler at her. "So there's no beef?"

"Nope. And I make the finest venison stew this side of the Adirondacks."

"That so? Well, if we had beef, *as I clearly recall you saying yesterday,* you'd be enjoying the best beef stew of your life tonight."

Rey smirked. "You don't say?"

"I *do* say. I'll have you know that *beef* stew is my specialty. Been making it since I was a little girl. Now, granted, I was self-taught because Mom wasn't around all that much, but I always ended up feeding half the neighborhood. It was the pride of Charlestown, my beef stew."

"I believe you, but we're in Gull Bay right now, not Charlestown, so we're having *venison* stew. Now, you cut those vegetables and let this expert work."

Millie didn't seem too thrilled about the idea, but she attacked those potatoes like a champ. Rey tried to picture her so much younger and alone in a city apartment kitchen, a petite overachiever with an oversized knife and an oversized pot. She pondered such a life with a mother who, apparently, left Millie to her own devices. She guessed the father was out of the picture, and evidently, there were no siblings. No wonder she took to Mac's gang like a family she never had. Jersey had said they were united by background, had tough times in common, but whatever Millie had encountered along the way sure helped create one remarkable woman.

Now riddled with a million questions, Rey stifled the unsettling urge to reach out, make a connection that conveyed her respect for all Millie had endured. A pat on the back just wouldn't do, and Rey conceded she'd best forego touching. But, boy, if she didn't admire her for her success, her fierce independence. Millie had spunk, and no doubt would stand solid against a stiff wind. Valuable traits, and so unlike anyone Rey had ever met.

Millie even survived her first encounter with venison, braving initial mouthfuls of stew until she confessed to liking it. Rey smiled as gallons of it disappeared, and she took charge of cleanup, until only she and her three most important guests remained at the table. Everyone else napped in preparation for the night ahead, but Jackson set out four shot glasses and grinned devilishly at Rey when she cracked open a new bottle of CC.

Once again, they reviewed the plan to retrieve Rey's load by hijacking it back from Legs Diamond. Their attention to detail struck her, the even-keeled approach so steady and professional. Her cause *was* in good hands, that grew more evident by the minute, and she felt another bit of trepidation in her bones ease away.

"Good plan," Jackson said and raised his drink to her. The darkness in his eyes still mesmerized, but somehow relayed confidence, and she appreciated his attempt to allay her worries. She really wanted to believe that he just *looked* evil.

"I say it's a winner," Millie said. Legs crossed and an arm draped over the back of the chair, she exhaled a thin stream of cigarette smoke and winked at Rey. "Much cuter without that hangdog look on your face. This'll go like clockwork. You'll see."

Rey shrugged, a bit embarrassed that her jitters were showing. "It's hard to imagine this is finally going to happen. I've never been on this side of a hijacking before."

Jackson chuckled and clapped Rey's shoulder. "Well, we have."

"After I pull in just north of the village," Rey said, "the truckers will load up and head south around one thirty. Lately, loads don't last an hour on the road before they're jumped, which means Diamond's boys should come rolling up to you before three o'clock."

"We'll be set up by two," Jersey said. "Plenty of woods for cover, so things should go off without a hitch." Millie and Jackson nodded at Rey. "Once the trucks round that curve," Jersey added, "we'll be done in twenty minutes."

Millie sighed heavily. "I still think it's stupid, how New York goons hog-tie people. Takes too much time. We're not rodeo cowboys, for God's sake."

"That's their style, Mil."

Millie tossed a hand at Jersey. "Yeah, well, they shoot anything that moves, too, and we avoid that."

❖

Anxious as usual about driving their old International truck, Millie sat alone in the dark and flexed her left hand around the steering wheel. She polished the shift knob with her other palm, restlessly, and squinted through the windshield.

"Ain't this just swell," she muttered. "Now it's raining." She settled deeper into the bulky canvas jacket she hated. Thank God she wore her favorite wool skirt, but from knees to pumps, she was on her own. She scooted forward on the seat, reassured herself that she could reach the pedals, and went back to grousing about the weather while she and everyone else waited.

She knew they were out there, the people she cared about who put their lives on the line for her—and vice versa—when needed. They were out there in the forest along the road, where everything was just as pitch-black as it was in the truck, and she'd do her part to make sure they all walked away without a scratch, made it back to Rey's cramped little hole in the woods when this was over.

How different this heist was, compared to the many they'd pulled in the past. There'd be no celebrating back at Mac's Victorian when this was over, no twirling with handsome men or glittering women in speakeasies. This job offered far less fun but at least as much adventure. Answering Mac's call actually meant a lot, even if it did dump them in the middle of the damn wilderness with a woman who hadn't a clue about the high life she was missing. Millie wondered what the high life entailed around here…catching some big slimy fish? A meatloaf dinner at one of those tiny joints in the village? A rare trip to one of the grand hotels?

She chortled at the image of Rey, looming so large over the pot-bellied stove and stirring the stew, the wooden spoon a mere twig in those big paws. "She's Little Miss Homemaker, all right." The venison hadn't been so bad after all, but damn, if the bear hadn't gloated about it.

Without a doubt, Rey was a force to be reckoned with, and Millie smiled in the dark, pleased to have caught little snippets of her softer side. Rey spent half their mealtime at the sink, washing her handful of silverware for the next group to use, and ended up the last person to eat. She couldn't wait to feed everyone, even burned her hand rushing cornbread to the table. Rey's probably spent too much time in the woods, she mused, and struggled to picture her at the swanky old Cotton Club in Roxbury. Somehow, Rey in a spiffy suit and shiny shoes didn't jibe, although she could cut a mean rug.

No, Rey belonged in this wilderness. She was part of it, rough and ready for whatever came at her. Millie supposed, in that regard, maybe they were more alike than she'd originally thought. She had to admit Rey made quite a formidable sparring partner, and even though they were a challenge, their exchanges added spark to the endless hours at the cabin.

A shrill whistle broke the silence, and silhouettes of trees coalesced in the blackness ahead. Mellow light cut through the woods as the convoy approached, about to round the bend in front of her, and Millie drew the sawed-off shotgun closer to her side.

A freshly felled pine tree barred the road, separated Millie from the oncoming trucks, and she waited for the moment those headlamps landed on it. Finally, the jostling light filtered through the downed boughs and glazed Millie's windshield. The trucks braked, and Millie countered with her own headlamps.

Associates raced from the woods, many with guns drawn, and surrounded the convoy's three vehicles. Others with clubs pulled drivers and partners from the cabs and out into the steady rain. Truck tarps were ripped aside and two men in the back of each vehicle were ordered out.

Millie kept a keen eye on the process. No trucker would slip away on her watch, although several tried punching their way free.

She pushed her shotgun aside, started the truck, and ground a few gears before finding reverse, but eventually she backed up and towed the downed pine from across the road. Within seconds, their vehicles were alongside the convoy and transfer of the load was underway.

Millie hopped out, careful not to slip in her pumps, and quickly distributed lengths of rope to associates. The truckers added catcalls and wolf whistles to their defiant cursing.

"Hey, honey," a trucker yelled. "What's a babe like you doing with these clowns?" He straightened his portly frame as an associate pushed him deeper into the woods. "Come over here and do us a favor, huh?"

"Yeah," another shouted, "you ain't from here. You from the city, sugar?"

A trucker on the ground, his hands being quickly bound, turned his face up from the turf. "Can't be the city. Those boys use women for other things, not this stuff." The associate clubbed him on the head.

"Naw," said another trucker, who whistled as he was shoved to his knees. "That's big city sassy and sexy, right, doll?"

Jersey spoke softly at Millie's shoulder. "You're making the perfect impression."

"You know," one trucker grunted from the ground, "a piece of New York City ass sounds *real* tasty about now."

Jackson stalked closer, Tommy gun in both hands. "Shut your mouth."

"Hey, little sweetie. You wanna play in the woods with me?" another sniped. He wrestled free of the associate tying his ankles, rolled upright, and took brazen steps forward. "Come here, baby, and see what I got for you. Just loosen this rope."

Millie hurried to him and snatched a club from an associate along the way. "Oooh, you're really something, aren't you?" She cracked his kneecaps with one blow. "You guys just shut the hell up."

One trucker yanked his hands free and darted after her. She calmly sidestepped his lunge and swung the club into his stomach, sending him tumbling onto the road. But when Jersey approached, he scrambled to his feet and ran.

"Don't do it!" Jersey raised the B.A.R. off her arm and fired into the ground ahead of him. Gravel exploded up into his face, and he stumbled blindly until associates caught him.

Finally secured in place with a pair of associates standing guard, the truckers raged, hog-tied and afraid to move for fear of strangling themselves. The road, meanwhile, buzzed with activity.

At the third truck, Millie joined Jersey on the transfer chain, passing crates to a succession of eager arms.

"Almost done," she said. "We're making really good time."

"I'll take it, especially in the rain." With associates covering the loads, Jersey scanned the scene and the very vocal truckers trussed up in the woods. "They'll be out there all night, and it's getting colder by the minute."

"Serves them right." Millie poked a few mussed curls back into place and scowled. "God. You're not going soft on us, are you?" Jersey looked at it from every point of view, but Millie knew they never second-guessed a plan, especially one this well executed. Hell, they had a slew of witnesses, all bound up in perfect Mafia style. "The whole point of this thing is to look like a New York heist. Now, would they give a shit about these guys?"

Jersey swiped angrily at the rain on her cheeks. "Yeah, yeah."

"Hey, eventually somebody's going to notice these guys are late and come looking."

"Yeah," Jackson added over Millie's shoulder. "They'll be pretty frosty and miserable by the time someone finds them but they'll survive." He chuckled under his breath. "As long as they don't get too restless and choke themselves."

Jersey stared off down the road, and Millie could practically hear the thoughts processing. Inside that hard-boiled ruffian exterior, Jersey had Mac's courage, loyalty, and energy, although the latter was often less tempered, and sometimes their big hearts did get in the way.

"Manhattan 'families' don't give a damn about collateral damage." Millie shrugged deeper into her jacket. The warmth of Rey's wood-warmed cabin seemed like heaven right now—and miles away—and she hoped Jersey wanted to be there as badly as she did. Thankfully, Jersey nodded, and water trickled off her fedora. "It's raining pretty good, Jers, and it'll take a while now to get back. *Plus*, I'm out here with no hat."

CHAPTER THIRTEEN

The unexpected glimpse of summer had Rey almost giddy for this boat ride to the village. She knew these gay times with friends would end soon, what with Mac's vacation winding down, but she forced that out of her mind. Over the past few days, life had turned balmy and lighthearted, and thanks to escalating gang warfare, pressure on her loads had lifted. How relieved she'd been, making those two deliveries of her own earlier in the week, back in her familiar routine. Trouble wasn't gone for good, but she suspected it wouldn't be as burdensome in the future, and at least for a while, she could look forward to banking some cash, satisfying her own customers. Only time would tell if Mac's theory proved accurate and a few more hijackings were needed to make a long-lasting statement. For now, however, Rey only cared about taking Ellie, Katie, Millie, and two other female associates to the train depot for their last shopping excursion in Saratoga.

"Sure you won't come with us?" Ellie asked and swung Katie's hand as Rey walked them to the station.

"Yeah." Millie elbowed Rey. "We're hitting every dress shop in town. You'll love it."

"No, thank you."

"Oh, come on. You never know what might suit your fancy."

"Right." Rey had to admit she'd miss this little spitfire once Mac's army moved out.

Regardless of whether she was teasing, flirting or being a wiseass, Millie always managed to come on strong and feminine, a confounding, albeit remarkable combination that shook up Rey's life like a snow globe. Here with Ellie, Millie's presence begged comparison, and Rey enjoyed the mental exercise, appreciated her good fortune to be escorting such proud, vibrant women. Next to Ellie's graceful poise and elegant features, Millie stood tall in her own way, and packed all sorts of attitude and pretty muscle into her little dress. Two smart, powerful blondes of a different color.

"Go," she said. "Have fun. Buy *yourself* something fancy—and don't turn too many heads."

"Gotta give the sightseers something to look at, you know."

Rey thought Millie did that without even trying. Actually, Millie teamed with Ellie meant sightseers would be busy. "Good-bye, ladies." She urged them on. "I'll meet you back here around five." Katie waved with both hands. "Have fun, little cutie."

"Thanks, Rey!" Ellie led the procession into the station. "I think Rey might even miss us when we're gone," she said to the others.

One of the associates laughed. "She turned out to be a teddy bear after all, not the brute I first thought she was."

The other associate tapped Millie's shoulder. "Thank God she gave you her bed, huh? You wouldn't have liked sleeping in the loft all this time."

Millie nodded, a rush of guilt sweeping through her. "I hope that cushy chair has been as comfortable as she claimed."

"Well, I haven't heard her complain. She's tough."

But not so tough on the inside.

Once in Saratoga, the group toured a dress shop and a sportswear store on Broadway, where Ellie found a new golf outfit she *had* to have for her tournament, and practically rushed into the first diner they saw for lunch. Thick milkshakes and greasy hamburgers—and part of a toasted cheese sandwich for Katie—satisfied their urges for "common food," a welcomed variation from the Sagamore's lavish menu and the cabin's camp-style concoctions.

As usual, Katie had Bing on the table, prancing it dangerously from their booth bench up to their plates, and Ellie gently guided it onto Katie's lap.

"Hossie eat, Mama." Katie pressed its stuffed muzzle onto her sandwich.

"No, honey." Ellie wiped Bing's nose with a napkin. "That's your lunch. Katie's sandwich."

"Bing sammish!" Katie insisted and stabbed the sandwich with Bing's muzzle.

"Katie Rose Harrison," Ellie said evenly, shaking her head. "Sandwwwwi*ch*. Not for horses." She turned her grin away from Katie. "She usually can't eat this fast enough. Mac got her started on them."

"Mackie sammish!" Katie held it up. "Mama, Mackie sammish."

"And she's not here, honey. Mac's meeting Rey at the hotel." She offered her a bite. "*You* eat your sandwich." Everyone watched, amused, as Katie studied the triangular piece and then dropped Bing to take it with both hands. After appraising her tiny bite in the middle, Katie went back for a bigger one. "That's Mama's best girl, Katie." Ellie kissed the top of her head. "Is that yummy?"

Now, Katie wouldn't take her eyes off her sandwich. "Yummy."

"Mac will be thrilled," Millie said. "She'd probably get a bigger kick out of watching Katie feed herself their favorite sandwich, than talking business with Rey." She stirred her malted milkshake with her straw. "I think we're coming back, probably in early November. Will you three come, too?"

Ellie frowned, and Millie sensed she'd broached a touchy subject. If Ellie opposed continued involvement, Millie couldn't blame her. So far, they'd kept Mac and family removed from any action, and Ellie had every right to insist things stay that way.

"We won't be back for that," Ellie said. "As much as I adore the Sagamore and hate to leave, coming back won't be necessary. Besides, the Sagamore's so expensive. We've spent a ton on this long getaway, and, with the holidays coming…"

Even though money had to be the least of her concerns, Ellie appeared eager to shift their focus toward it, but Millie couldn't quash a concern about what lay ahead for Rey. Mac and Ellie shared that concern, and most likely had hashed out every aspect of their participation in this scheme, but she sensed Ellie was ready to put all of this behind them.

Everyone knew it wouldn't be long before heat on Rey started building back up, and by November, the goons probably would be all over her again—and needing to be redirected back at each other. In yesterday morning's lengthy discussion at the cabin, Rey, forever the sailor, called it a "course correction" when Jersey suggested that two jobs in two weeks could do the trick, but no one really could be sure how long it would take or if it would work. And Millie wasn't particularly over the moon about another cabin stay, although she enjoyed Rey's sweet humility and respected her honest living.

"Well, at least the casino rebuild isn't going anywhere fast," an associate said, and Millie watched for Ellie's reaction to pursuing the issue. That Hollywood-perfect face revealed little more than a flinch in her creamy complexion. "We snuck a peek at it yesterday, and it's been real slow bouncing back." The associate gestured at Ellie with her last bite of hamburger. "Mac sure is a smart cookie."

"And who's to say it won't run into more trouble and miss the racing season?" the other associate added. "A crying shame, I tell you." She grinned as she scooped the remnants of her milkshake with a spoon. "You know, before I ever let a clown like Diamond drive me crazy, cost me all that cash, I'd play it smart and just dump the whole thing."

Ellie sighed. "God, what a mess they've made up here. Rey's so happy right now. It's good to see her relaxed and smiling again, if only that would last."

"Mil, you had Rey smiling last night." The associate turned to Ellie and smiled broadly. "She tell you about the dancing? How we rolled up the rug and went at it?"

"Dancing?" Ellie raised an eyebrow at Millie. "Do tell."

Ellie definitely prefers changing the subject.

"I turned on her radio and a few of us just started. I refused to let her walk past us, acting like she wasn't noticing, so I grabbed her arm and got her going."

"I see."

An associate added, "I know you wouldn't think it to look at her, but Rey's a terrific dancer, really. Practically put us to shame."

"I beg your pardon," Millie said. "I kept right up with her, thank you very much. And what do you mean, 'you wouldn't think it to look at her'?"

"She's so...so tall—"

"What's tall got to do with it?"

"I think," the other associated tried, "well, what she means is, Rey's...big, y'know? Big boned, big shoulders—"

"Since when don't we like big shoulders?"

"I...well, yeah, I guess—"

"Did you see her tripping over me? Did I fumble around the floor with her?" The two associates withdrew to their milkshakes, and Millie shook her head at Ellie. "We didn't have *any* trouble together. Actually, we danced for quite a while. Everyone had fun, for a change, a lot of laughs, too. What are you grinning about?"

"You, the speakeasy girl, whooped it up in a dusty old cabin in the woods? I'm trying to picture that."

"Oh, you should have seen them," an associate said. "She and Rey took over the floor. Our little Millie and the big dyke in her old flannel shir—"

"So what?" Millie said. "I love to dance and Rey's great at it. No big deal."

"Just not your style."

"Style's got nothing to do with it. Dancing's dancing, and it was good to unwind after all we've been through."

The other associate leaned forward, grinning. "Can't tell me you didn't feel a little swallowed up."

"Stop it. I did not," Millie said, feeling her irritation mount. She hadn't felt small or "swallowed up" in the least as Rey moved her to the music. In fact, their contact had been well timed, almost instinctual, their movement together surprisingly smooth and practiced. Rey had made her feel secure, even special.

"Rey looked a little over the moon, I thought," one associate said to the other. "Didn't she?"

"Most definitely. If that radio show hadn't gone off the air, I think she would've danced with Millie all night."

Millie turned to Ellie. "So what? If you'd been there, she would have dragged you up, too, so stop smirking."

Ellie laughed as she wiped Katie's face and hands with a napkin. "Why do I think she'd prefer to dance with you?"

"Thanks. You're a big help." Millie tossed her napkin onto her empty plate. "You're all impossible." Everyone put a few dollars on the table and Millie lifted Katie from Ellie's lap. "Come on, Miss Katie. Let's you and me go dress shopping." Holding Katie's free hand, she led the way out. "You all go look at lamps, see if we care. We'll catch you on the corner later."

❖

Lowry inspected the polished desk and expensive office trappings and checked his watch again, impatient for the salesman to return with carpet swatches. Almost five minutes now, and as critical as placing this order was, he had to be back at Dazzle to sign off on the mahogany for the grand staircase. He shifted on the thick cushion, straightened his legs with effort, but the pain in his knees didn't subside. Bocci's boy had made sure the message lingered.

Nothing pleased that big man this morning. Not hearing about the roof completion or progress on the interior walls or optimism about striking water on their third attempt at a well. Jesus, the man suggested they use dynamite to speed up that process. Lowry had dared to think his effort stood for *something*, but he'd been wrong. At this moment, he praised the elevator in the Adelphi for sparing him the agony of stairs. That smash to his kneecaps had dropped him to the floor, bawling like a child, and it had taken every ounce of strength to be upright and presentable when the doors opened in the lobby. Walking was torture, and how he'd made it to this store on Broadway was a mystery.

He leaned back and exhaled hard, feeling trapped in the swivel chair, knowing his best efforts would never measure up. Thoughts of the next meeting with Bocci made him nauseous, or maybe that was just his throbbing knees. His eyes squeezed shut, he pushed past the pain and steadied his mind, praying for something to satisfy this monster. *He's really not the one who counts.* The murderous reality of Luciano pressed on his chest, as tangibly as that goon Parker had crushed his throat, and Lowry knew he needed one hell of a prize or achievement to impress him.

The harder he concentrated, the tougher it was to breathe. He stared up at punched tin tiles, meticulously designed and artistically hung, a ceiling he'd always imagined in the home of his dreams on Beacon Hill. With no solution or achievement or prize to save his skin, visions of becoming North Woods's miracle man faded to black and stole away a luxurious future of custom suits, velvet upholstery, and domestic service.

The last image straightened him in the chair.

That homo maid, Elizabeth McLaughlin.

Hijack Mack.

Lowry broke out in a sweat. He stood and slowly began to pace, despite the ache in his knees. They didn't matter right now. Had he stumbled across a solution? An achievement that would mean more to the Mob than the stupid Dazzle deadline? A prize that delivered retribution, revenge, and the last laugh?

Elizabeth McLaughlin, you sick pervert. You've been so clever these past years, haven't you? With whose money? Where'd you get it? There are people who'd appreciate finding out.

"I'd bet a million bucks."

And the beautiful Eleanor Harrison... You corrupted her, too, didn't you? Hijack Mack, you twisted bitch. Eleanor did some serious damage, testifying, and I know people who'd just love to meet her.

He hobbled back to his chair, having thought himself into exhaustion. A plan. He needed a plan. Handing those two over to

Bocci would brighten Luciano's days, let him show off Mob "reach" and authority. Bocci would win points, too. And all that would save Lowry's neck. So he had to devise a plan, and he found himself struggling again. If the damn Feds never caught Hijack Mac, how could he?

But the Feds never knew what "he" looked like and never made the Eleanor connection.

"One will draw the other like a magnet."

The office door swung open and the salesman hurried in with a load of carpet square binders. "So sorry for the delay, Mr. Lowry." He thumped them on the desk. "These top two I had to find out back. Someone misplaced them." He flipped open the first binder and began describing fabric and color options.

But Lowry's attention hadn't left the open doorway. Out in the showroom, Eleanor Harrison and two other nondescript women lingered at an expensive floor lamp. Lowry almost shivered at the coincidence.

"Oh, yes, we love this area," he overheard her tell the saleswoman. "We're at the Sagamore but we're heading home soon. Could you have this one ready for our train ride home Saturday?" They walked out of view and earshot, but Lowry now knew he had five days to do *something*.

Lowry realized the salesman awaited his response.

"Oh, ah… What was that again?" He looked down at the burgundy swatch in the man's hand. "Eh, yes, the color is right for the grand entry, the staircase, and the entire second floor." The salesman scribbled notes as Lowry rattled off requests. "The gold will work in the gaming rooms, and I want that combination pattern in the guest rooms."

"Yes, sir."

"I gave you the floor plans, didn't I? All the measurements?" He wiped his damp forehead with a handkerchief and wished he was better at handling two distinct thoughts at once.

He glanced out to the showroom in time to see Eleanor and the two women leave. If only he could conjure a plan. Right now.

"Mr. Lowry, sir?" The salesman held out an order form and a pen.

Lowry forced his concentration back to business, grabbed the pen, and signed. "Did you say six weeks?"

"Months, sir. Six months. We don't keep your quantity of this high-end stock in house, so I'll be special ordering it for you, and with the winter coming, things could get dela—"

"*Six* months?" He struggled to recall the construction timetable, and looked back to the showroom again. *She's disappearing as you sit here.* "Do it in five." The salesman nodded.

Hat and briefcase in hand, Lowry reached the sidewalk in time to see the three women disappear into a taxi on the far corner. He cursed his ineptitude and the loss of his opportunity to do *something*, and sagged against the lamp post.

CHAPTER FOURTEEN

Mac squeezed Ellie's hand onto her thigh and watched the interaction between Rey and Millie halfway down the table at the Lake Harvest Inn. Rey couldn't take her eyes off Millie in the form-fitting satin dress she'd found in Saratoga, and stuttered each time she spoke. And, for her part, Millie actually appeared humbled by Rey's attention, a reaction Mac hadn't seen in her in years.

Ellie squeezed Mac's hand in return. She enjoyed seeing them get along as much as Mac did. Going home tomorrow wouldn't be easy.

"Well, I couldn't help myself," Millie said, obviously still excited about their shopping adventure. "I *had* to get everyone back to the boutique before it closed. I was tickled to buy Katie that dress. She loves it, doesn't she?"

"Oh God, yes. Red's her new favorite color, although I don't know if all that lace will go over big."

"Or stay white for long," Mac added.

Ellie leaned against her shoulder. "We're putting it away for Christmas."

Rey asked Millie, "So you bought Katie's dress at the Parisienne, too? I-I mean, that's where you bought your dress, right?" She leaned back and whistled under her breath. "Wow. It sure is…well, it's beautiful."

"Why, thank you, Rey." Millie lowered her eyes modestly and reached for her drink.

As she lit a Lucky, Mac caught Jackson's eye roll and wondered what he thought of Millie's demure response to Rey's compliment. Mac didn't think it was an act, but Jackson probably did. They'd rarely seen Millie genuinely reduced to sweet, shy responses, but to Mac, this one seemed legit. Ellie's tap on her thigh said she agreed.

Jersey flashed her a look as she drank, a slight, amused curl on her lips.

"Well, I think *my* new outfit brought me luck yesterday," Ellie said, winking at Mac as she deliberately moved the conversation elsewhere. "We finished second in the tournament."

"How you can get excited about hitting a tiny ball into a hole is beyond me," Jackson said. "More fun trying to shoot it with a gun."

"And too much walking," Jersey said.

"You don't know what you're missing. We had a great time."

"Ellie finished as the high scorer," Mac said, and Ellie elbowed her.

"Baby, shh. I told you, a *high* score isn't good." She shrugged at the others. "I didn't have my best day—but I'd whoop your butt, Miss McLaughlin."

"The Sagamore sure thinks of everything," Rey said. "They should, for what they charge."

"Oh, but the Sagamore does things right," Ellie went on. "Their nursery is worth every penny, it's so well run. The staff is excellent and they always write down where we're going, how long we'll be, the phone number. And that night nurse is the perfect grandmother type. She's crazy about her job."

"And Katie," Mac added.

"Well, I wouldn't object to spending more time at the Sagamore," Millie said.

"You'd own the dance floor, Millie."

"Oh, I doubt that, Rey. Some of those high rollers—"

"You'd dance them right out of their fancy shoes. I'd pay to see that." Rey lifted her glass. "The hottest little number the Sagamore has ever seen."

"Rey." Millie covered Rey's hand on the table. "Look who's talking. Maybe someday we'll show 'em."

Mac hoped Millie saw the bigger picture, knew what was brewing here. And something definitely was—at least on Rey's part. An attractive, spirited woman like Millie *had* to make Rey's heart race, and Mac wished she'd been privy to their interactions at the cabin all this time, wished she had a more accurate assessment of the friendship between them.

If she used tonight as a gauge, she'd have to credit Rey's courtesy and Millie's patience for seeing them through this period—when neither of them had ever been known for having much of either. They'd spent more than half the evening on the dance floor, beaming at each other, and their skill, despite the height difference, drew considerable attention. Throughout dinner, Rey attended to Millie's every need, while Millie responded with plenty of hushed comments and private smiles.

Actually, Mac worried about the growing attachment and feared Rey might be set adrift once they all departed. From where she sat, Mac easily could see Rey relishing Millie's confidentiality, basking in their union on the dance floor, feeling honored and special.

However, unlike Rey, Millie didn't wear her heart on her sleeve, a lifetime of struggles and loss wouldn't allow it. Despite her sincerity, Millie never had much luck with close relationships. The only lasting attachment in her life had been to their gang, aside from that misguided fling with Jackson. At times, her guarded nature served her well; she could play the role of heartbreaker to perfection when necessary.

But Mac wouldn't tolerate any role-playing in this instance. Rey was an honest, trusting soul and a good friend, and Mac hoped Millie saw her as such. She figured she'd learn a lot more about this "friendship," now that they'd be leaving, and especially if a return to the Adirondacks became necessary.

❖

Rey rushed in out of the rain, and tried not to wake her houseguests. She stopped short at the sight of Millie bustling about the kitchen.

"You're up early."

"Coffee's on," Millie said without looking up. "I'm just fixing stuff."

"Fixing?"

"Putting things back," Millie said. "These were over here." She began moving canisters back to where they'd been before the crew arrived. "And this," she hefted the wooden bread box to its original spot beside the sink, "was here."

"Millie, stop. You don't have to do all that."

"I want to. I tore your kitchen apart, remember." She emptied a cabinet next to the stove and filled it with glasses and coffee cups. "There. Your mugs are back where you had them."

Finally, she paused and looked up. Absent her trademark makeup, and dressed in a simple skirt, blouse, and slippers, hair curling wildly in assorted directions, Millie's look of raw innocence left Rey speechless.

"I wanted to get this done before it got crazy this morning." Millie's exuberance eased as she studied Rey's surprise. "I-I didn't think you'd mind."

"Oh—I don't," Rey said quickly, pulling her thoughts from Millie's wholesome image. "I mean, thank you. But you didn't have to. I've kind of grown used to having things your way—ah, that is, the way you had them." She took two mugs from the cabinet and poured coffee for each of them. "You've been going like a wild woman, so sit."

"Thanks, but..." Millie sipped the coffee, set it down, and turned back to the sink. "Not through yet."

"Millie. Sit. Have coffee with me."

"The natives are getting restless. Soon, it'll be insane with everybody up and in my way, so—" She stopped moving when Rey placed a palm on her back. "We're hitting the road early, Rey."

"All the more reason to take a moment now." She handed Millie her coffee.

"You're bigger than me, so I guess you win."

"I am and I do." Winning a concession from Millie was as unique as seeing her "dressed down." Rey knew she'd remember this particular morning long after everyone left. Millie's grin over the rim of her mug struck Rey as the finest start to a day she'd had in ages, left a lump in her throat like a perfect sunrise over the lake always did. She turned to the window, searching for the right words.

"You've been the best hostess, Rey, and we appreciate you taking us in, letting the likes of us run roughshod through your home." Rey looked back at her as she spoke. "We're grateful—I'm grateful. Hell, I know I'm…well, I guess, overbearing, sometimes."

Rey grinned. "Bossy? Domineering?"

"You think?"

"When needed, yeah, but considerate at the same time. And organized and helpful. And I'm the one who's grateful. All of this was because of the mess I'm in."

"*Were* in. And, hopefully, *won't* be in for quite a while."

"Thanks to all of you."

"You may *never* be in another mess. Who knows? But if you need us again, you just have to sing out." She playfully punched Rey's arm. "Then guess what? We'll come and turn your life upside down again. Something to look forward too, huh?"

Rey nodded and meant it. "It won't be the same around here, once you leave."

"Understatement of the year," Millie said. "God knows, we can liven up a place without even trying."

"Like controlled chaos, sometimes, you're right. But I did enjoy the crew. I'm sorry the cabin didn't offer much privacy or… or comforts like you're used to."

"Rey. You have nothing to apologize for. You gave up your bed for me, for crissakes." Millie eyed her sideways. The smirk on those full, delicate lips had Rey eagerly anticipating whatever clever quip followed. "Admit it, Big Bear. Yours truly handled rustic pretty damn well, although, you've *got* to do better than that outhouse. *That* was asking a lot."

Rey conceded that the little shed with its wooden seat must have tested Millie in all sorts of ways—but she prevailed without complaint. Most of the time. Tough as nails. The woman was just as capable as she was adorable. "I think you're amazing." *I said that out loud.* "Y-you've got guts and smarts, and I like how everyone respects you, from the new ones right up to Mac. The way you carry yourself..." *Stop rambling.*

"Well, gee. Thanks, but I haven't even put myself together yet this morn—"

"Millie. That doesn't matter in the least. God knows you're a heart-stopper, all decked out, but...but you don't need..." She sighed at herself. "Well, I think the real you is special."

"You're such a sweetie at heart." She leaned closer. "But can we keep 'the real me' just between us? I have an image to uphold, you know."

"It's a deal." Rey shuffled awkwardly. "You know, I-I like the real Millie Anderson. A lot, spitfire image and all."

Millie set her mug on the edge of the sink and placed both palms on Rey's chest. "Well, guess what? I like *Camille Reynaud* a real lot, too." She rose on her toes and pressed a light kiss to Rey's lips. "I'm going to miss you."

Rey blindly abandoned her coffee and set both hands on the curves of Millie's waist, her heart racing at the feel of such softness in her palms, beneath her fingers. She squeezed gently and took care to avoid any sign of impropriety.

"I'll miss you, too, and I won't hold it against you, wanting to get back to modern conveniences and that swinging city scene."

"Oh, the clubs and speaks? They're really all just...just surface fun, Rey. Hell, the next day, what've you got? A hangover and no cigarettes."

Rey laughed. "I suppose you're right, but you're just as likely to end up with a hangover and no cigarettes up here, too."

"Good point." She crinkled her nose. "There really isn't a lot to do here, y'know. I mean, I might enjoy a little hunting—but fishing? Yuck. Definitely not." A smile reappeared and Rey fought the urge to slip her arms all the way around her. "But you've got a little piece of heaven up here, Rey. The air smells so good, the lake's so peaceful, there's no city hustle 'n bustle, and there's this feel of accomplishment, like pride, in fending for yourself. And it's nice to feel that pretty much all the time. If I hadn't spent this time here, I'd never have known."

Rey tentatively flexed her fingers into Millie's waist. "Maybe you'll come back?"

Millie tapped Rey's chest and grinned. "Eh...there's that outhouse..."

"I'll do something about it."

"Sure you will."

"No, honest. For you, I will." Rey dipped her head and drew Millie closer, thrilled to feel her yield, to know this wasn't unwelcome.

Millie's teasing grin relaxed into a soft smile and she lowered her eyes to Rey's lips. "Well, in that case..."

Rey pressed a tentative kiss to Millie's mouth, and shimmering heat rippled across her shoulders and down her spine. When Millie laced her arms around her neck and kissed her in return, the surge of long-forgotten sensations nearly brought Rey to tears. Gathering all of Millie's plush form against her seemed like the most natural act on earth. Somehow, she managed not to lift her completely off the floor.

Rey cautiously deepened the kiss, then withdrew slightly. "Jesus, Millie. If I'd known what your kiss would do to me, I would've tried the minute we met."

Millie inched away and purred as she cupped Rey's cheek. "Works both ways, darlin'. If *I'd* known, you wouldn't have had to."

"Ahem." Jersey stood several feet away, disheveled and sleepy-eyed. "Glad that's settled. Sorry, but I'm getting everyone up. We're out in an hour."

CHAPTER FIFTEEN

Following instructions in Rey's most recent letter, Mac collected two cartons' worth of groceries in her little hometown market while waiting for the agreed-upon time to place her telephone call. *Will there really come a day when we have one in our home?* Escaping the raw, mid-October air further justified spending time in the popular store, even if it was overheated by the coal stove and jammed to the ceiling with merchandise she couldn't reach without that cursed gripping stick.

At three twenty, she added a box of Rice Krispies and a can of Marshmallow Fluff to her pile of goods on the counter, and hustled to the rear of the store. She stepped up to the telephone on the wall and requested the operator connect her to the number Rey had provided.

"So you heard," Rey grumbled from a café in the Village of Lake George. "Pretty popular topic of conversation hereabouts. All the joints are crying because he upped his prices, yet the locals are all torn up about this. Such a lucky guy, huh?"

Mac preferred not to talk business specifics on the telephone. The news had splashed all over the papers, and she'd heard it on the radio, but the eavesdropping operator would be intrigued by others' opinions of the most recent hit on Legs Diamond back in Manhattan.

"Radio this morning reported he's touch-and-go at the hospital," Mac said into the mouthpiece.

"If you ask me, the bastard's too fucking miserable to die."

"Not apt to slow down his business, I guess."

"Course not. His guys will be back at it soon. No way they'll let New York have free rein just because he's laid up."

Mac frowned at the phone. Their success back in September hadn't stuck, just as they'd feared, and Rey's letters had conveyed increasing hardship. Failure to deliver had cost her five customers so far, and she believed New York goons had stabbed two of her best sailors behind a bar in Glens Falls last week. Four days ago, she caught one of Diamond's boys trying to start a fire on the *Jean Luc II*'s deck and had to fight him off. Both groups grew bolder, more impatient by the day.

Having Legs in a Manhattan hospital would cut Rey's troubles in half but only temporarily. She'd get by if only the big boys were helping themselves to the occasional load, but Diamond's outfit was bound to return in force. And when that happened, a "course correction" to turn them against each other would have to be significant. Permanent, if possible.

"And get this," Rey continued. "Already gossip mongers are bitching about losing out on his easy spending and big tips. You believe that? Cripes."

Mac shook her head. People were fascinated by this thug who magically survived hits from his competition. Publicity and posing for the press had made him a damn folk hero, and throwing money around in these tough times had earned him the appreciation of decent people. Only folks behind the scenes knew Jack Diamond for the thieving, ruthless murderer he really was. The New York Mob knew, too. *Takes one to know one, sometimes.*

"He might not make it this time," Mac said and wondered if Rey's business could survive if it only had to satisfy New York.

"Yeah, but he might. And his boys will pick up the pace until they know, one way or the other."

"True. Well, drop me a note when you think we should get together."

"Might be soon."

"See how it goes, the next couple weeks."

"I expect a rough ride, but thank you."

"Be careful. Keep your guard up."

"Always. Now, go home. And bundle up, feels like snow tonight. Say hi to the girls for me."

"Will do. Take care out there."

Mac hung up, gathered her barn coat around her, and loaded the car with her shopping order. Wet, brisk wind stung her cheeks and nearly claimed her fedora when she turned up Main Street so she gripped the wide brim as she walked, her head tipped down into the gusts. The Hot Stove Diner was only four doors down and she was glad to step in, out of the cold once more.

From behind the counter, Sarah yelled her usual greeting. "Afternoon, Miss Liz."

"Hi, Sarah. How're you doing today?"

Sarah had pet names for all the townspeople. Towel draped over her shoulder and coffee pot in hand, she rounded the counter holding a clean cup and saucer, and addressed Mac as she strode across the checkered linoleum floor. "Coffee, hon?"

"Oh, definitely. Thanks." Mac tossed her hat on the bench at a window booth and shrugged out of her coat as she slid in. She rubbed the chill from her fingers and took paper, pencil, and an envelope out of her inside coat pocket. She had to put Jersey on notice, and this written method proved best. Using the telephone in the market wasn't wise anyway, not immediately after *that* conversation.

"Here y'go. Fresh pot, too." Blocking Mac's view of half the diner, big-boned Sarah poured coffee into the cup before even setting it down. Mac appreciated the round jolly face and flushed cheeks, the cloud of white waves and crooked red bow atop Sarah's head. "Before I forget," Sarah bubbled on, "I have a message for your Eleanor. I swear, folks think this is the post office, always leaving notes for each other."

Mac grinned at her dramatic flair and held up the envelope. "This isn't where I mail a letter?"

"Smart aleck." She set a hand on her broad hip. "So, listen. Make sure Eleanor stops by the town hall to see Abigail. I think she's looking for help again with the census coming up."

Mac nodded as she swallowed a mouthful of coffee. The rich brew wasn't the only thing that warmed her inside. One of the few locals who'd accepted "the city girls" when they moved to town, Sarah sang their praises to neighbors all the time, so much so, that Ellie believed the woman envied their lifestyle. Mac grinned into her cup, remembering when, as "those two women," they'd been the talk of the tiny town. And of course, there was Katie, whose charms had won her legions of admirers within a week. Overall, their humble little town suited them perfectly, and Mac wouldn't trade family life here for the world.

"Thanks, Sarah. I'll tell Ellie. She'll probably stop by tomorrow, if this weather holds up."

Sarah took a moment to stare out the window. "Eh, just a few inches tonight. Now. Can I interest you in our last slice of pumpkin pie?"

"No, thanks, but if you have any of those secret cider doughnuts you make, I'd love to take some home."

"You betcha. Brought some from home this morning. I'll sneak you my last three. Anything for my Little Katie Sweet-thing." With a breezy swirl, Sarah was off.

Mac chuckled as she checked the weather outside again. A dusting now whirled in the twilight, and she knew Sarah probably would start issuing cautions soon, and eventually kick her out for her own good. She gulped down a mouthful of coffee and dashed off the note to Jersey.

It appeared likely that Rey would be drowning in lost loads by the middle of November, and another trip to the cabin would have to resolve this once and for all. Mac counted on Diamond's outfit returning to action and fitting perfectly into the scenario they created.

How does mid November fit into your schedule? Yes, there'll be snow. Chances are, plenty of it. Lots of tough sledding ahead for our pal, so come prepared. Sorry, but can't say if Thanksgiving will be an issue. Stop by on your way so we can catch up.

She scribbled their coded signal, an indecipherable name, on the envelope's upper left corner, printed the address of Jersey's favorite dive in Worcester, and took a stamp and three dollars from her billfold. The money she left for Sarah, the letter went into the mailbox on the post outside.

All the way home, fat, fluffy snowflakes blew in every direction as the wind blustered about winter's potential. Sheltered from the brunt of it on her front porch, Mac paused and inhaled the sweet scent of wood smoke from their stove. It was a welcoming home she'd never take for granted. She stomped snow off her shoes and hurried inside to find Katie amidst a scattering of hefty split logs on the floor.

"Mackie!"

"Hi, my sweet Katie girl. Did Mama make this mess?" She removed her fedora and kissed Katie's head. "Or did her little helper move the pile?"

Her arms loaded with more firewood, Ellie and a blast of cold air entered from the kitchen. "What are you teaching her in the barn, Miss McLaughlin? How to build muscles?" She started unloading by the stove and Mac dashed to help. "Every log I place, Mac, I swear, I find on the rug when I get back. She's going to be as strong as you are."

"As pretty *and* as strong as her mama, I hope." Mac kissed the chilled, rosy cheek, and maneuvered the rest of Ellie's load from her arms. "You ought to see her chuck rocks."

Ellie growled and returned Katie's logs to the stack, much to Katie's dismay. Her cherubic face contorted, Katie staggered to her feet and took aim at the woodpile, but Mac scooped her up.

"Let's go see the snow!" She snatched Katie's coat from the closet as they went to the door.

"So!" Katie yelled, pointing at the window.

"Get that coat on her, Mac. And she needs her hat!"

Mac yelled back from the porch that they'd only be a minute. In less than that, she kicked open the door, set a box of groceries on the floor, and ran back out. Seconds later, she returned with another, but again was gone in a flash.

But only five minutes passed before the pair returned, snow in their hair and Katie's face as bright pink as her clapping hands. Mac settled in the rocker by the stove with Katie in her lap and wrapped a comforter around them both. Katie poked her hands out and slapped them together, her round eyes gleaming at Ellie.

"So cowd, Mama."

Ellie kissed the little hands and rubbed them between her own. "Very good, honey. Yes, snnnnnow *is* colllld." She raised an eyebrow at Mac. She swiped at the snowflakes on both their heads. "Tell me again which one of you is the child."

"Did you see the Fluff I bought?"

Ellie chuckled. "Yes, I did. And I found the Rice Krispies. I gather you're expecting treats?"

"Kispies!" Katie shouted, bouncing on Mac's lap.

"Yes." Mac grinned. "We are."

Ellie brushed her nose back and forth against Katie's. "Then we'll make treats."

Mac smiled devilishly. "I want grown-up treats."

"You be a good girl." Ellie gripped Mac's chin. "And I'll think about treating you."

"Thank you, Mama."

"Tak you, Mama," Katie repeated.

Ellie kissed Katie's cheek. "You're welcome, my precious."

Mac crooned into Ellie's ear. "I love you, gorgeous Mama."

Ellie combed her fingers through Mac's wet hair and brought her lips near. "I love you, Mac." Their kiss was warm and nourishing, lasting until Katie worked herself onto her knees and fell against Mac's chest. Her pinked nose flattened against Mac's, Katie pressed her hand to Mac's cheek.

"Wuv you, Mackie," she said and managed to kiss Mac's lower lip.

Rey stoked up the stove, eager to read the mail she'd picked up in the village earlier and do nothing for the rest of the evening *for a change*. Her old cushy chair let out the same weary sigh she did when she sat. Mentally checking her to-do list, she smiled at having all that work behind her, especially her top priority: sprucing up the outhouse. The surprise would bowl Millie right over, and just anticipating the delight on that radiant face, the spark in those fetching eyes eased some of Rey's exhaustion. Along with the crew, Millie would arrive next week, and that added incentive had driven Rey to attack her chores with purpose.

Gone was the torn window shade in the bedroom, replaced with a new one and topped with pretty blue and white curtains, and she'd washed the yellow ones in the kitchen, so they were brighter, too. After some elbow grease and a few squirts of oil, the hand pump at the sink no longer required a muscle man to use, and she'd hauled out the parlor rug and worked it over good, so it no longer was a mat for wood chips, forest debris, and dirt. The outhouse was her main achievement, though, now that she'd chinked between the wallboards and hung blankets to seal out drafts. She'd constructed a little overhang at the door, replaced the mossy log steps, and even laid a walkway of stones she hauled from the lake.

Today, loading, transporting, and unloading a season's worth of firewood for a customer in the village felt effortless, compared to all that domestic work—until she drained her energy tank and ran aground at sunset.

Millie's letter stood out in the pile of mail, the precise, flowery script revealing more about the lady she was, and Rey could feel that tender hand on her cheek. She'd revisited their kiss many times, even though Millie probably hadn't spared it a second thought. Rey tried *not* to put much stock in their exchange, tried instead to see Millie destroying her kitchen and upending her routine. She tried seeing her as the gal-about-town, bopping with multiple partners in speakeasies, smooching in dimly lit corners. Regardless, the thrill of their kiss wouldn't fade.

So waiting until now to open this letter hadn't been easy. She'd avoided being swept away in the post office again, like she'd been a month ago when Millie first wrote. Her hands had shaken when she opened that letter. Standing in the post office doorway, her heart racing, Rey had read the cordial greeting, the well-wishes, and what seemed like an *implication* that Millie missed her—*"maybe I will get up there again"*—all while customers bumped and teased her about being in their way.

But now Millie *was* coming back. They *all* were coming back, Jersey said in a note weeks ago, and Rey so looked forward to Millie's smile, and maybe another kiss—along with the clutter, organized chaos, overcrowding, and sleeping in this lumpy old chair again. She grinned at the thought of Millie in her bed, of lingering traces of expensive French perfume on the pillowcase.

Knowing she'd already prepped accommodations for everyone, Rey took satisfaction in accomplishing her part of the plan. She'd done all she dared to insure both New York and Diamond craved her product at the right time. She'd manipulated quantities and delivery dates, pushed and delayed recent loads, so hijackings would occur in the right places on the calendar. Neither group had been particularly pleased by her stalling or the shorted amounts, and she'd braved some angry repercussions, not the least of which was an altercation with Diamond's "messenger" last week. Once she knocked his .38 away, it became an even fist fight, and although she'd left him barely conscious behind the depot, she still worried about pushback.

Rey turned her head from side to side and worked out the kinks of rising tension in her neck. Things will go well, she told herself, and those two outfits soon will go somewhere and fight it out. She gave thanks to Mac for her endless generosity, sending help again. At least if the cabin had to be upended, it would be by the good guys. And Millie.

Rey opened the envelope and withdrew just a small, single sheet of stationery. She'd hoped for more pages, to lose herself in all Millie had to say, but it was pink, at least, and that made her smile.

My dear Rey,

How are things in the Great White North? Looks like I'm about to see for myself. Ready or not, here we come! We haven't had much snow in Boston yet, but I bet you have, right? By the way, I'm making beef stew for everyone, so please scrounge up some REAL meat. Ha ha. And get your dancing shoes ready. Looking forward to seeing you, Big Bear.

—Millie."

Rey took a deep breath and exhaled slowly. Damn, that woman kicked up her heart rate every time. No, Millie hadn't said she missed her, or anything mushy like that, but she didn't have to write at all, and she *was* looking forward to coming. Considering Millie loved the city life, that was something.

Beef stew, Rey mused with a grin, and surveyed the kitchen and then the parlor. *Tomorrow, I'll move everything back to the way she likes it.*

CHAPTER SIXTEEN

As she watched her trot up the porch steps, Millie thought Jersey suited the place perfectly in her bulky scarlet sweater, work pants, and that cocky fedora. Likewise, standing with hands on her hips, outside with no jacket, Rey seemed larger than life and just as ready to tackle it. She hugged Jersey off her feet, sent her into the cabin, and met Millie on the second step with both hands extended.

Millie slipped her hands into Rey's big mitts and offered a sideways grin. "Squeeze me like that, Big Bear, and I might break."

"I'll be gentle," Rey said, drawing her closer. "It's good to see you."

Millie stepped into her embrace, instantly enveloped by the large frame with a warmth she felt through the full length of her coat. *No question, Rey invented bear hugs.* She returned the squeeze and leaned back in Rey's arms. "You, too. And we made it in one piece again. But, boy, it's a hell of a ride up here."

"Might have made it in daylight," Jackson said, stopping on the steps and pointing at the cabin, "but *someone* had to finish building a log house on Mac's parlor rug."

"Hey! Not my fault!" Jersey yelled from inside. "We had to finish and then Katie wouldn't eat without me."

Jackson shook his head. "At least we made it."

"I'm glad. And the others?"

"The trucks are about ten minutes behind us." He hefted a duffle bag onto his shoulder and headed for the door. "Believe me, you'll know it when they get here."

Rey looked to the road they'd just traveled and scanned the surrounding tree line. Outwardly, she seemed unfazed by the information, as if all this had become routine, but Millie doubted Rey felt as calm as she appeared.

"Everything okay, Rey?"

"Huh? Oh, yeah. Sure. I'll grab your bag in the car." She squeezed Millie's hands and hurried down the steps. "Go on inside. It's cold out."

Millie surveyed the blackness around them as she stepped onto the porch. There was nothing to see, nothing that *could* be seen, beyond the mellow lamp light at the door, but Rey's hesitation made her stop and look harder.

"Bet the city never gets this dark, huh?" Rey said, joining her, suitcase in hand.

She opened the screen door just as a loud bang sounded from the road. The door snapped out of Rey's grip and a chunk of the wood frame flew past her face.

"Gun!" Millie yelled as a second shot ricocheted off the porch rail. They both grabbed for the door.

A burst of shots shredded wood up the steps, and Millie screamed when fire blazed across her shoulder. The impact slammed her into Rey and sent them tumbling to the floor.

"Millie!" Rey threw an arm around her, pawed the door open, and crawled inside. "Millie's hit!"

"Back here!" Jersey helped Rey situate Millie upright behind the sofa.

"My shoulder," Millie said, eyes crunched shut. "Fuck, it hurts."

"Take care of her, Rey. And stay low." Jersey pulled her .45 from beneath her sweater. "Could be more than one out there."

"Maybe," Jackson said, standing beside the parlor window with gun in hand. "Can't tell yet. Who'd you piss off, Rey?"

"I suppose you could take your pick," Rey said and peeled off Millie's coat. Blood had soaked through her blouse at the left shoulder. She ripped the silky fabric open at the bullet hole. "Shit, Millie."

"Does it look really bad?" Millie asked through a wince.

"Well, th-there's a lot of blood. Hang on." Rey scrambled across the floor to the bedroom. Another burst of bullets traced across the porch and shattered Jackson's window.

Millie heard him swear. "You guys okay?"

"We're good," Jersey said from the kitchen window. "That round took out the porch light, so now we're even."

"Hey, Rey," Jackson said. "You got a back door?"

"Sure, I just don't use it. Here, in the bedroom."

Jersey appeared in a crouch at the end of the sofa. "Until we can get to the car, Mil, use what's above the fireplace." She dashed off.

"Oh, swell." Millie stifled a squeal of pain as she sat up straighter. "Hey, you two shouldn't—Don't go out there. You don't know how many there are." But she knew they'd already left. Neither of them would stand for one of their own being shot. And it was almost impossible to stop *those* two.

Rey scrabbled back across the floor, her arms full of material.

"Rey," she said heavily. "Grab your rifles off the wall."

"What?" Rey tore a bedsheet to shreds.

"The .22 and the shotgun. Get them. And ammo."

"First, I need to see…" Rey wiped away some of the blood at Millie's shoulder. "Looks like it just grazed you."

"Rey. We can't be unarmed in here."

"You're sliced open pretty good, but that's it." They both ducked as successive rounds pinged off the pots above the stove. One slammed into the loft ladder and made it bounce. "Jesus." Rey pressed a wad of bedsheet to Millie's wound. "Hold this tight against it."

Millie did as she was told and watched Rey slink over to the fireplace. It had to be hard for a woman her size to minimize her profile. *Poor Rey, now she's really in the shit, and here I am with hole in my shoulder. How helpful.*

"Are they loaded?" she asked when Rey returned with the rifles.

"They're always loaded."

Millie grinned. "Gimme the .22. I can't use the shotgun with one arm."

Rey checked the safety before handing it to her. "I have to wrap that shoulder, Millie."

"Hell with that," she said and gathered her blouse over the wad of material. "It'll keep for now. We've got to get to the windows. Help me up."

"You're not going anywhere. You're too woozy."

"Oh, for Christ's sake, Rey." She rolled onto her knees and fell against the sofa.

"See? God damn stubborn woman. Sit here at the end and keep most of you behind it." Bullets sprayed across the kitchen window, sending wood chips off the tabletop. Rey's cushy chair rocked with the impact of another shot. Millie groaned when Rey pulled her farther back behind the sofa. "Shit. Never mind. Stay back."

Shooting outside intensified. The long, clattering bursts from what had to be a Thompson were overlaid with louder, single bangs.

"Fuck," Millie said. "They're going at it, now. Those are .45s firing back." Again, she struggled to her knees. "We can't just sit here, Rey."

Clutching the rifle to her side with her limp arm, she inched around the sofa, Rey on all fours beside her, and they swiped aside shards of glass to reach the windows. She took a breath against the pain in her shoulder and ignored the wetness trickling down her chest. The wound demanded attention but wouldn't matter at all if they didn't put a stop to this craziness. Whoever was out there had serious damage in mind, and Jersey and Jackson were up against God only knew how many.

Silence fell upon the area, and Rey spoke quietly as she peered out the kitchen window. "You've done this before?"

Millie took her time answering. "You could say." She'd gone through plenty of barroom brawls, knife fights, hijacking shoot-outs, even shot and killed a Boston Irish mobster back in twenty-eight, but never taken a bullet herself. Tonight, like all the others, she'd been lucky, and not for the first time, she wondered how long that luck would last.

She readjusted the blood-soaked fabric up onto her shoulder and assessed her situation as they watched and waited. Yes, she felt a bit lightheaded, but she still had faith her right arm could do what had to be done. Shivering in the cold wouldn't help. Getting off an accurate rifle shot would be hard enough using only one hand; she didn't need the shakes, too. With the windows broken, the wood stove was no match for the raw wind blowing in off the lake.

She glanced down at herself and shook her head. The skirt she wore permitted too much of a draft, and now the long-time favorite was spotted with blood. And she'd just bought this peach blouse two days ago, to arrive in something new and "ladylike." Hell, this afternoon, Ellie had hinted that Rey would swoon over it, and Millie knew she'd blushed a little. She smirked at the ways her taste in clothes sometimes conspired against her. *Too bad my long, warm, cozy coat is behind the sofa.*

Leaning heavily against the window frame, Millie peeked out. The wilderness looked just as tranquil as when they arrived, a fathomless dark that went on forever, a hushed, pine-scented quiet she remembered enjoying on her first visit. But tonight, it carried a haunting, eerie silence that rattled her nerves. And it had been unsettling when they'd stood on the steps before all this started.

"You felt this coming, didn't you?" she said softly, and Rey mumbled something she couldn't decipher. "This is some stupid shit, Rey, because putting you out of commission really would screw things up for New York *and* Legs. Who'd come after you like this, so hell-bent?"

"Don't really know, except maybe that guy I had a little go-round with a few days back. One of Legs's guys. I…well, I won, so maybe he's looking to get even."

"Sounds like something one of those brainless idiots would do."

"Yup. Whoever's in charge for Legs right now won't be too happy that this clown went rogue."

Millie looked to Rey. She waited until her gaze drew Rey's direct attention. "You *do* realize that this clown's never going to see *anyone* again."

Rey stared back, her eyes dark, unreadable. "I know." She looked out at the woods again and flexed her fingers around the shotgun.

Millie focused on the tree line as questions ran through her head. She hoped Rey never regretted living such an independent life in such a beautiful place, because, even though it was out in the middle of freaking nowhere, this spot really was pretty special, and Rey was meant to be here. Who wouldn't love it.

Rey cleared her throat. "The way I see it, whatever happens in these woods tonight happens. Can't say I'll shed a tear. I've been attacked in my own home, for God's sake, and I'm damn sure not going to shrug it off. But I do hope no one else has found his way up here."

"Me, too." Millie rested the barrel of the .22 on the windowsill, her eyes now adjusted to the darkness beyond the porch. "So, you put a beating on this guy, huh?"

"Yeah. He said Legs didn't like waiting a few more days. I told him I was doing all I could, but..."

"Legs is still hospitalized in the big city, right?"

"He is, but he gets word out. Things slowed for a while, but his boys are used to good money so they hardly missed a beat. Anyway, this goon and I ended up on the ground, and I might have broken his jaw." She shrugged. "I was bigger than him."

"Good for you," Millie said, picturing Rey pounding the schmuck into the dirt. "Problem is, those guys don't take losing very well."

"Tell me about it." Rey shifted on her knees and raised the shotgun. "Hey. Motion in the trees, left of the road."

Millie squinted into the blackness just as the Thompson erupted. Fire from its muzzle exposed its location, and the woods lit up in an ear-splitting barrage of submachine guns, shotguns, and pistols. The roar lasted only a few seconds and the lone Tommy went dark.

Rey stood up on her knees. "Holy shit!"

Millie chuckled as she slid down the wall and sat. "About time they showed up."

❖

"No. No, that can't happen. What do you mean, 'it collapsed'?" His coat buttoned to his chin and collar up around his numb ears, Lowry wiped the outbreak of perspiration off his forehead with a gloved hand. He shoved the role of plans higher into his armpit and cautiously stepped closer to the edge of the well. "I-I don't see it," he said, looking as far down as he dared, which wasn't far.

"You can't. Not from there, anyway," the foreman said. "It's too deep, unless you lay out over the edge, but I'm telling you we're going to need another week. Maybe a few weeks, if this one gives us anymore trouble."

"How the hell did you let this happen?" Lowry felt beads of sweat slide down the back of his neck. They'd been making such good progress lately, so maybe he should have known it couldn't continue. But this, getting water to the site, was big, and should have been wrapped up months ago.

"Shit, Lowry. You think we're just playing around out here?" The foreman threw up his hands. "We've gone through dry spots, tapped shallow veins, broke equipment digging around granite, and waited out replacement parts. We all thought that third one looked good, and it ran dry in a day. This is our fourth one, and we—"

"I know! *This* one was supposed to be 'it,' done, settled, and pumping in two days. Now you want—"

"Hey! It's not about what *I* want. It's *your* damn plan, so decide what you want us to do and let me know." He reset his cap on his head. "Look." He pointed at Lowry's chest. "I'm getting paid for all this, regardless."

He stormed off and Lowry stared back at the hole, pictured himself at the bottom of it, begging for mercy—again. *No, there'll be no more of that.* No part of this project had been easy, but no one was on his back right now, either, and that's how it had to stay. But no quick fix loomed for this well issue, and he began to worry anew.

He shuddered at the thought of returning to those agonizing weeks when Dazzle struggled and he paid the price. Damn, if that sabotage hadn't started a run of horrific luck.

He was in need of another break, and just when the "big people" finally had begun to smile about Dazzle. He kicked the dirt in frustration. Lately, building plans moved from one page to the next with hardly a frown from Bocci. After hearing the progress report last weekend, Bocci even had been amicable at dinner.

Only days from reaching its pre-sabotage stage, the project soon would forge ahead, faster than ever, provided the weather cooperated. He'd given Bocci detailed notes about the exterior finishing, set to start after Thanksgiving, and the interior work about to begin, and told him how furniture, appliances, fixtures, accessories, all were scheduled for delivery by spring. In a bold but fleeting moment of confidence, he'd even intimated that Dazzle could open as early as mid-May.

Sitting in his coat and hat in the workhouse, he stared at the well plans as if waiting for them to speak. Instead, Bocci entered with a flourish and startled him, sending his pulse rate through the roof.

"Jesus Christ, Lowry," he said, shutting the door. "It's as cold as a witch's tit in here." He pulled off a glove and put his palm to the little wood stove. "S'matter with you? Fire this baby up."

Lowry hadn't attempted to start the stove, even though he'd have to some day or freeze to death, but he didn't know the first thing about them. He stood and looked about for matches.

"I...ah...well, I-I don't need—"

"Fuck that. Of course you do. *I* do." Bocci took crumpled papers from the trash basket and stuffed them into the firebox, then placed small sticks from the wood bin on top and some larger ones on top of them. "You open this thing here," he said, turning the damper on the stove pipe, "let the air draw smoke up, and then you light it." He flicked his Ronson to life, ignited the paper, and shut the door. "See? Too complicated for you, hotshot?" Lowry shook his head. Bocci shoved his shoulder and Lowry landed in his chair. "Have a seat. Tell me we're not throwing more money down that fucking well."

Lowry couldn't believe word about the problem had reached Bocci already. He didn't have a solution, not yet anyway, and certainly not a free one. He gestured to the plans. "I'm thinking we could try shoring it up. Cement's already part of the plan, so maybe—"

"Maybe? You're not sure?" He paced the four steps to the far wall and appeared to study the umbrella Lowry had hanging from a stud.

"This all just happened, Frank, and—"

"I know when it happened," he said, turning back, "and I know it don't look good. I know what goes on here, Lowry."

"Yes, I'm sure you do."

"Good. And don't forget it. You know I don't like it when things go wrong."

"I-I know. Neither do I, and I'm doing my best. Things have been going really well lately, you have to admit."

Bocci slammed a fist to the tabletop. "I don't have to admit anything, you little shit!"

Lowry fell back in his chair. "N-no, of course. I just meant Dazzle's doing well."

"As it should. One more hitch in the schedule will cost you— big time. How many second chances have we given you so far, huh? Too many!" He stalked away but came right back. "You know who gets second chances, Lowry? *No one.* We're done with delays."

Lowry pressed his sweaty palms against his thighs, trying not to shake. Another beating probably *would* finish him, and up here in this wilderness, there'd be no one to help him. No one would ever find his body. Perspiration trickled down his cheek, his nerves generating heat while the rest of him shivered. "I-I'll take care of this. It won't set us back."

"You've made promises before. They aren't worth shit. Look at us." He spread his long arms out to encompass the workhouse, and Lowry could picture Bocci hauling the walls down onto him. "We're here, Lowry, in the damn cold, dealing with 'fixes' for problems we shouldn't have. You're not stupid enough to make me another worthless promise, or are you?"

"No. I always do my be—"

"You know damn well that problems make me very unhappy, yet, for some reason, you keep coming up with them. Why is that, Lowry? Haven't you learned by now?" He straightened. "How many times have my associates visited you so far, huh? Three?"

Lowry simply nodded. Each surprise visit, each beating, had been worse than the one before, the last one leaving him unconscious, concussed in his apartment for days.

"Three," Bocci said on a disgusted breath. "Three makes you one lucky son of a bitch and me look like a fool. So fuck that, no more. Now you listen to me good, Lowry, because I promise you, if we need to play that game again at this stage, they'll be the last people you'll ever see."

Lowry dropped his gaze to his shoes. All along, he'd feared it would come to this, but hearing the threat out loud left him dizzy, speechless.

"Pick your God damn head up, you dweeb. You got any guts at all? Christ." Bocci took a cigar from inside his coat and puffed it to life. "So tell me, how are you going to fix things so that *I* don't have a problem?"

Lowry sat up straighter and subtly took as deep a breath as he could. "Ah, well, like I said, we could try—"

"No. No. No. 'Try'? There you go again. See, that's not how this is supposed to work. You're the one who has to *know*."

"But I've only just started looking into it, Frank." Lowry swallowed hard and tried desperately not to stutter. He slid a finger along the well drawing and was relieved when Bocci looked to see for himself. "The issue is down here. So, right now, I figure, if we clear it out, we can build up containment, pump down cement, and set the piping. Of course, I need to sit with the foreman and our master plumber, befo—"

"When you doing that?"

"Well, I...tomorrow morning, first thing."

Bocci nodded and dangled both his gloves over the stove. Lowry hoped warming them signaled an end to this brutal meeting.

"Okay. Tomorrow, first thing," Bocci said, more of an order than a confirmation. "I got business in the morning up to Lake George, so you can buy me lunch at the Sagamore and fill me in then." He put his gloves on and the cigar bobbed between his thick lips as he spoke. "And, shit, Lowry. You're going to be here a while tonight, so put some wood on that damn fire." He opened the door and wintry air rushed in. "Don't be a wuss and freeze your ass off." He grinned as he shut the door behind him.

Lowry closed his eyes as he leaned back in his chair and took some serious breaths. His heart pounding in his ears, he fumbled for his handkerchief and wiped his face and neck. *Focus.* He had calculations to do, for cubic yards of earth to be removed and cement to be poured, for laborers and hours needed, for depth and pressure requirements, and gallons per minute. And that was just for a well that already should be operational.

His stomach grumbled, and he realized he hadn't eaten since breakfast. But he had little appetite these days, plus a long night of work beckoned. Tomorrow, maybe he'd remember to bring something to eat... Tomorrow, after he met with Bocci and told him *something.*

He eyed the stove like a conniving accomplice, Bocci's watchdog, a reminder of his temperament. Conceding he'd have to "feed" it to continue working, he reluctantly picked a quarter-log from the woodbin and turned the firebox handle. Heat seared his fingers and he jumped back, howling and shaking his hand. "Son of a bitch!" He flung the log at the stove and searched for something to ease the burn. Finally, he remembered the jug of drinking water in his car and raced outside.

Bastard's going to be the death of me, he thought, standing in the dark beside his Cadillac, dribbling water on his fingers.

CHAPTER SEVENTEEN

Rey led Jersey over the hill behind the outhouse and down onto the half-mile trail that ended at the *Jean Luc II*'s secluded inlet. "I heard her complaining even before she got out of the car. I give her one day before she ditches that sling."

Jersey laughed. "You're probably right. She's calling herself the one-armed bandit now. But what's worse is that the doc stitched her up right on the top of her shoulder, so she can't wear a bra."

"I noticed."

"Can't help but notice *those* babies. She's determined to wear it though, with one strap if possible." Jersey grinned as they stepped over a fallen log. "I told her one strap didn't stand a chance." Rey had to agree. Jersey stopped, put her hands on her hips, and took a breath. "Are we there yet?"

"Over the next rise," Rey said, waving her to follow.

"God. Canada must be over the next rise."

"Some tough guy you are."

"You're lucky it's cold out, because I'm working up a sweat. Not used to daylong marches across mountains."

"Stop bitching," Rey said. "It's only a ten-minute walk."

"Give me a car any day. Like that drive to Vermont early this morning after the doctor's visit. Now *that* was a fun ride, really pretty, and kept Millie gawking almost the entire time. We hardly saw another car, coming or going."

"Glad it was worth the trip across the border."

"Oh, it was. What you overheard in the village was correct. Dazzle *does* have an order pending for marble. A big order, lots of pieces they're putting throughout the place, and the order's due soon." She chuckled. "We have Ellie to thank for the idea. She wondered about it, because those places are so glitzy. So, when you said you'd heard talk, I thought it was worth checking out."

"She's as clever as Mac, isn't she?"

"They're a perfect match." Jersey jabbed Rey's arm. "And it gets better. Talk about luck. Turns out the quarry boss is one of my Vermont buyers. He runs a little dive on the side, and I've been really good to him—it's brought me quite a few more customers—so we get along great." They paused and looked down through a canopy of trees at the *Jean Luc II*, bobbing alongside a small faded skiff, both tied to a weather-beaten dock. "I made him a deal and he's going to do us a great big favor."

Rey looked over at her coy smile. "Would that be anything like the *favor* that caused their well to collapse? Rumor is that as they were leaving, everyone on the job site heard the yelling in the workhouse. That gossip went all over the region."

"Gee, sounds like the job's hitting hard times, doesn't it?" Jersey said, and they started down to the boats. "Glad a certain guy remembered to do the right thing at the right time, and that he remembered the hot cash in his hand. Mac thought to pull those strings back in September."

"And now this quarry guy you met with… What kind of *favor*?"

"Let's just say measurements for most of the pieces might not be accurate."

"God, what next?"

"Oh, there might be a plumbing issue."

"You're kidding."

Jersey squinted ahead as if trying to summon details. "Yeah, think I heard something about substandard plumbing. There are new regulations, you know."

"Sure there are."

"Yeah, and I guess the local inspector's boss is a real stickler." She glanced at Rey as they approached a stubby gray-haired character waiting on the dock. "Collecting on a favor twice removed, you could say." She looked down. "Millie has a connection in the Massachusetts health department. He's the stickler's uncle."

"Holy smokes." She marveled at the reach of Mac's crew. "So...the project is..."

"Going to get really discouraging by the time winter sets in."

Rey shook her head. "You guys are something, you know that?"

Jersey just smiled and clapped a hand onto Rey's shoulder. "Introduce me to your friend."

Rey struggled to sort out the new information, all the scheming behind the scenes that Mac's gang had set into motion. Meanwhile, her lifelong friend and top sailor, Nettie, awaited an introduction as well, and Rey decided to study the scheming ramifications later.

"This ornery little nugget is Nettie, best sailor on the lake, after me, of course. Thirty years as friends, and we haven't drowned each other yet. Nettie, this city girl is Jersey, a very good, trusted friend."

She watched them shake hands and size each other up. Nettie eyed Jersey warily, while Jersey smiled and seemed perfectly at ease. Both understandable reactions, Rey thought, but she knew Nettie would look right past Jersey's congeniality and not hesitate to snap at this sturdy, confident-looking stranger on her turf.

"I get the feeling there's pretty much nothing you two can't handle," Jersey said.

"We do all right." Nettie didn't take her eyes off her. "You don't look like no gangster."

Jersey laughed outright. "Thanks, I think."

"Well, you don't." Nettie waved a hand at Jersey's frame. "Not with the homemade sweater—and I can tell it is—and those army boots. Maybe the hat says it, I dunno, and maybe that sunshiney smile."

"I'm a businesswoman and I'm here on business."

Nettie humphed. "So, you in charge of this 'help' Rey's told me about?"

"I am, and we'll do our best to take these monkeys off your back."

"Was that you, making all that ruckus the other night? Heard it all the way up to my place. Damn commotion sounded like the

Fourth of July. Don't you know sound travels on water?" She tossed Rey a severe look. "They can't just come here and shoot the place up, Rey."

Jersey took off her fedora and ran a hand back through her hair. "You're right. I apologize for the noise. We should've thought about that."

"Got that right." Nettie hitched up her trousers and mumbled as she stepped over the rail and onto the boat. "This ain't the Wild West, like in them novels, y'know, or the big city, either." She leveled her eyes at Jersey. "We take care of our own up here. Don't need outside help." She looked away, adding, "Not usually."

Rey gestured for Jersey to follow her aboard. "Now, Nettie, cool your motor, girl. You know this mess has grown too big for us, what we stand to lose. Hell, not that long ago, you said you were glad someone else was on our side, so stop giving Jersey a hard time."

"That's cause being on the business end of a loaded .30-06 almost made me mess my britches." She glanced at Jersey. "And I ain't too proud to admit it. Or that I don't want no more of it."

"I don't blame you one bit," Jersey said, "which is why we're here."

Rey found the pint of CC she kept for cold nights on the lake and unscrewed the cap. Tonight would be one of those nights, but right now, she wanted to take the chill off the mood around her.

"Here, take a swig." She handed it to Nettie. "I know it's the afternoon, but this is to friendship. That okay with you?"

"Hm." Nettie took the bottle, threw back a quick blast, and extended it to Jersey, but didn't let go when Jersey accepted. Their eyes met again. "I don't know your line of work, Miss Businesswoman, don't even want to know, but it better not get anyone hurt." She released the bottle.

"That's never our intention. Really, it's all about friendship, and the families we choose. Exactly like you two." Jersey raised the bottle in a toast. "Here's to helping each other." She drank a mouthful and winced at the burn. Rey winked as she took the bottle back. She figured Nettie probably appreciated Jersey's jolted reaction to the whiskey, but *had* to like what Jersey said, because she certainly did.

"So." Rey nudged Nettie. "We're all set for tonight?"

"We are. Pick me up about midnight. By now, the word's out that there'll be a delivery. We made sure the goons who hang out at the café overheard the plan for Old South Road, but we're not telling the truckers until we off-load tonight."

Rey nodded at Jersey. "New York will scoop this load as soon as it can, hand over my thirty percent to the lead trucker, and take off in your direction. Old South is a long one, so pick a spot way down the road."

"We'll be ready."

"So, like before?" Nettie asked and looked to Rey for confirmation. "They're going to look like Diamond jacking from the Mob, right?"

"Right. Diamond's gang will go nuts when they find out they missed the opportunity they've been waiting for, and the Mob will go nuts thinking Diamond took what's theirs."

Jersey grinned, obviously pleased that Rey had full grasp of the plan. Rey handed her the bottle.

"You two are going to kill me, drinking in midafternoon." She upended the whiskey, and this time swallowed without a grimace. "Sounds like we're set, so it's time for me to get back." Nettie and Rey each took another drink before Rey stashed the bottle away, and then followed Jersey onto the dock. "Pleasure meeting you, Nettie." Jersey offered a handshake. "Glad to be working with strong women."

Nettie shook her hand and shrugged. "We've been at it for years, so it's nothing new, but this pressure is, and we need to be rid of it. Guess I'm up for whatever it takes."

They said good-bye and trudged up the trail as Nettie went to her skiff.

Rey sighed heavily. "I can't wait for the day I don't have to see that guy Bocci."

"You have to meet with him a lot?"

"Every so often, yeah, like this morning. Jesus, he's a frightening guy. Always has his two bulldogs, always insinuating things that make your skin crawl, playing games with your head.

Even when I guaranteed him there'd be a delivery tonight, he had to be Mr. New York Goon. He said he's waited long enough, and if he can't count on me, he'll put his own people on my route. 'Take me out,' was how he put it."

"For God's sake, why don't they just take Diamond out? *He's* the real problem."

Rey shook her head. "I know, but he keeps throwing our 'agreement' in my face, and saying Legs is a separate issue, that they're taking care of him."

"But they're not."

"Well, they did put the guy on his death bed, but that hasn't stopped his gang from hijacking my loads. So, no, they haven't taken care of their real problem."

"We're going to do something about that and make it last this time."

They reached the rise and started down the other side. Rey stole a moment to imagine daily life, this walk included, free of life-and-death threats. Months of them had taken its toll and she looked forward to sleeping soundly through the night, running shipments down the lake, and bringing in decent money again. Times when no one got shot or beaten, when you didn't walk with an eye and ear to your backside.

"You guys pull this off," she said, "and the bootleggers in the Catskills will come crying for your help. Nobody out there cooks anymore. Legs has taken over all the small operations, I hear."

Jersey rested at the next rise. "There's a big difference in the Catskills, Rey. Here, we can play Legs and New York against each other, use Dazzle to drive the Mob into throwing up its hands. But in the Catskills, it would be just us against Legs, simple, all-out war. No conniving, just killing."

Rey nodded as they walked on. She prayed that when Bocci learned tonight's "guaranteed" load had been lifted, he'd go after Legs. Jersey and the crew *had* to be convincing.

❖

Commotion ahead sent Rey and Jersey running the rest of the way. Only when they reached the outhouse and saw the crew milling around the yard, did they realize Millie and Jackson were shouting at each other in the cabin.

Jersey shook her head. "Damn it. Leave them alone for a second and something blows up."

"Listen to her," Rey said, content to just eavesdrop where they stood. "She's raging." Rey pictured fists flying, or Millie's one available fist, or worse, household objects. "She's not a thrower, is she?"

Jersey chortled. "Not usually, although years ago she clocked me with a two-by-four."

"Really?"

"Took my legs right out. Well…I suppose it was my fault. We'd been working on our old house, and were just joking around, and I dropped a chunk of ice down the front of her blouse. I didn't mean to rip it."

"Show time."

"Oh it was, for sure. You know how she is about clothes, not to mention having *the girls* exposed an' all." She shook her head again, smiling at the memory. "Jesus, was she mad. Hornet in a hurricane."

"Remind me never to tick her off." She pointed at Jackson storming down the steps, headed for the road. "Well, he's ticked off."

"Yup, but, deep down, Jacks is a gentleman and knows to walk away."

They approached the porch with caution, and Rey turned to her. "You going in or should I?"

Jersey frowned. "I'll go."

"She may not go nuts if I go in. Look." She pulled a quarter from her pocket. "I'll flip you for it. Heads, I go."

"You are a glutton for punishment."

Rey slapped the coin onto her forearm and slowly revealed the result. "Wish me luck."

She passed through the crowd of smirks and eye rolls, and stepped into the silent cabin. Nothing seemed out of place, no overturned furniture or broken dishes. Millie sat with her back to the door in a chair by the fireplace, remarkably with her arm still in the sling.

"Knock knock," Rey said. "Is it safe to come in?"

"It's your place."

"It's a lions' den, by the sound of it."

"Sorry."

"Anything I can do…or…or help with?"

Millie gripped the arm of the chair with her free hand and pulled herself to her feet. "No, thank you." She headed for the bedroom. Her mussed curls and smudged makeup said this argument had been a battle, and Rey tried to picture her pulling her hair out, crying as she countered everything Jackson said.

"Wait." Rey stopped her at the door, a hand on her arm. "If you talk, I'll listen."

Millie closed her eyes and moved her head from side to side. "It's all too stupid to talk about. I'm sorry there was a scene—that *I* made a scene."

"Hey, you've been through a lot in the past twenty-four hours, give yourself a break." She risked tugging Millie back to the parlor. "Come on. Sit and let me hear it."

"Rey, no, but thanks. I need to go put myself together." She stopped at the coffee table and looked through the half-open door. "Good thing the windows are boarded up right now. The less everyone sees the better."

Rey straightened and gripped her arm. "Oh, no. Now you *are* going to sit." She pressed her onto the sofa and sat beside her. "Cut the poor-me routine. Where the hell did the feisty, good-looking dame go? You can put yourself together in a minute, and everybody can just stay outside a while longer. Talk."

"You don't want to—"

"If you don't tell me what that was all about, I'll…I'll take back my bed."

Millie looked up at the ceiling and chuckled. "You really know how to get to a lady, don't you?"

"I'm still waiting."

Millie blew out a breath. "If you laugh, I'll hit you."

Rey grinned. "It'll be worth it."

"It's about tonight, and maybe even the job after that."

"What about them?"

"Jackson says I'm out. Because of this fucking thing." She raised her sling too quickly, and was unable to disguise the pain in her eyes.

"I see. You think Jersey or the others want you to risk it? You can't drive a truck, Millie. You know that, right? And you can barely hold a rifle, let alone shoot one."

"You want to see what I can hit with a .38?"

"Easy there, Annie Oakley. Okay, fine. You're a good shot. But if something goes wrong, you could be putting anyone of them at risk, not just yourself." Some of the steam appeared to dissipate in Millie's bearing. She looked out to the porch and front yard again and seemed to be reconsidering. Believing she was making headway, Rey resorted to the point she thought carried the most weight with Millie. "Mac wouldn't want anyone taking unnecessary risks, would she?"

Millie sighed. Her distant look traveled from her lap to Rey's flannel shirt to Rey's face. In that moment, the spitfire became a bruised, disappointed lady, and Rey didn't think twice about caressing the tear-streaked cheek.

"It's my job, Rey."

Rey knew that if she looked into those eyes much longer, she'd succumb. She slid an arm around Millie's back and drew her head to her shoulder. There. No more seeing disappointment. Just the tenderness of the lady in the circle of her arm.

"God, Rey. You're such a soft-hearted soul. Sorry to be such a crybaby."

"Well, you know, you may be right on both counts." Rey gave her a reassuring squeeze. "But like I said, it's been a hell of a visit so far, don't you think? You drive for hours out of Boston, visit Mac for a few more hours, drive more hours on dark dirt roads to get here, and by then you're trance-like, half asleep, and boom! You get frigging shot off your feet, and before you can blink, you're in a gunfight. Personally, I think that's a bit much. When you're overtired and need to recover in so many ways, everything gets magnified. You rest and I bet you'll see things differently."

Millie hissed at the pain when she tried to shrug. "Maybe you're right. I apologize for letting everything get to me, and I need to apologize to everyone—and Jackson. God, the poor guy." She sagged heavily within Rey's arm, weariness winning this battle. "But, you know, this…craziness… It really is normal. It's what I do. It's my life."

Rey sat her up and settled her back against the sofa. "Only if you say so," she said softly. "But don't let it run you, Millie. You can have any life you want."

Millie reached to Rey's face and trailed her fingers through her hair. Rey almost quivered.

"Thank you, Rey. I know you're right. I think these woods have made you a wise woman."

She raised her head off the sofa and pressed her lips to Rey's. So soft, so plush and warm, the kiss practically melted Rey where she sat. Her heart pounded in her throat as Millie withdrew, and she watched the long lashes flutter open. She had no words for the world she saw, the greeting of a blue-sky morning, a soul deep as any sea.

Millie ran a finger across Rey's eyebrow, down to the tip of her nose, and smiled.

"Would you mind if I lie down for a bit?"

At this moment, there isn't one thing you could do that I would mind.

"Of course not." Rey managed to find her feet and help Millie up. "Get some rest," she said at the bedroom door. "I'll explain to the others. Don't worry about them."

"Obviously, I have some apologizing to do, once I get my wits about me." She set her palm on Rey's chest. The touch and its warmth held Rey in place, even when Millie tugged her down by the shirt and kissed her again. "Thank you."

CHAPTER EIGHTEEN

Millie found a jazzy station on Rey's radio and settled onto the sofa with the tattered copy of *Photoplay* magazine she'd brought from home. Hollywood gossip would keep her mind from wandering back to the activity going on without her. Alone in the cabin for three hours now, she understood the meaning of "stir crazy."

At the sound of footsteps on the porch, Millie cocked the .38 that Jackson left her and pointed it at the door.

"Hey, Mil. Just me coming in."

Millie blew out a breath to steady herself as the door opened. She lowered the hammer and set the gun beside her. "Cookie, for God's sake. Sing out *before* you stomp up the steps, okay?"

Cookie leaned her shotgun against the wall. When she removed her cap, her ball of red curls bounced to life and she looked comically contrite. "Sorry, Mil." She unbuttoned her thick jacket as she went to the stove. "My turn to warm up." She rubbed her hands together. "Smells good in here. How fresh is the coffee?" She poured herself a cup without waiting for an answer.

"Fresh enough," Millie said, staring at the door. "Help yourself to the bread." She wished she could see the hijacking preparations underway, somewhere far from where she sat.

"The other guys will be coming in soon, I imagine. It gets cold in these woods when you're just hanging out. It's tough to keep your guard up." Cookie looked around the cabin and sat on the arm of the cushy chair as she drank her coffee. "Cute place, isn't it? Nice having a little music on. Keeping you company, huh?"

Millie tried not to sulk. As much as she appreciated the associates guarding the cabin, she hated being reminded that she wasn't part of the action. To pass the time initially, she'd taken a hot bath in the tub Rey put in the bedroom for her. Pumping, heating, and lugging water had taken over an hour, and bathing had left her relaxed and drowsy, neither of which she wanted to feel on this important night. So, after she failed at sweeping with one arm, she whipped up two loaves of banana bread, put on a pot of coffee, and tidied up the cabin. A homemaker she wasn't, but being productive kept her sane.

Cookie spoke around a mouthful of bread. "Hey, this is real good, Mil. Thanks. How's the shoulder?"

"Grumpy. Just like me."

"You just got a tough break, Mil, especially up here. Bet you can't wait to get home."

"I'd be just as aggravated with myself there."

Cookie put her cup in the sink and buttoned her jacket. "At least you'll have company here when Rey shows up. She's due any time now." As she went to the door, she poked her hair into her cap. "Don't shoot any of us when we pop in, okay?" She chuckled as she left.

Millie looked down at the .38 beside her and grinned at the thought of greeting Rey at gunpoint. But she dropped that thought quickly. Rey wouldn't see the humor in it, not like Millie's friends would, and definitely not after a cold night of dead-serious work on the lake.

She leaned back against the arm of the sofa to read and realized, as she swung her feet up and nestled in, that she still wore Rey's heavy flannel shirt over her blouse. She'd slipped one arm into it and draped the other side over her injured shoulder after she dressed from her bath. Hanging on a hook behind the door, the roomy, red and black checkered shirt offered the coziness of a blanket, and she hadn't hesitated, but with Rey about to arrive, Millie second-guessed herself. Would Rey understand she'd borrowed the shirt for warmth? Or would she interpret Millie wearing it as something more?

She chortled at herself. "You didn't worry what she'd think when you put it on, did you?"

"Hello inside!" Rey's gravelly voice drowned out the radio as well as Millie's thoughts.

"Oh well," she mumbled. "She'll think what she thinks, and that's okay."

"Millie? Is the night owl still awake?" Clomping up the steps was followed by the door opening, and Rey's hat appeared on the end of a shotgun like a truce flag. "Cookie said don't shoot." Rey peeked around the door.

"Get in here," Millie said, sitting up. "Let in any more cold air and I *will* shoot you."

Rey took a giant step across the threshold, shoved the door shut, and tossed her sea bag aside. Maybe it was the boots or the long canvas jacket with its upright collar that sealed out the wind, but somehow Rey seemed taller and broader than ever, practically blocking the entire doorway. A cross between lumberjack and Yankee fisherman, Millie mused, a mixture of rugged readiness that should make women everywhere proud. Rey tugged off her leather gloves and sniffed the air.

"Holy smokes, Millie. It smells awfully good in here. You've been busy."

"Look who's talkin'. Everything's hot, so have some."

Rey stuffed her gloves into her pockets and hung jacket and hat by the door. "Boy, what a great surprise. Thank you." She went to the stove and extended her hands over the heat as she surveyed the bread and coffee pot. "You were bored to death, weren't you?"

"Cripes. You know me too well already."

Rey sent her a quick over-the-shoulder look, a mischievous spark that lit up her weary face, and Millie had to admit, she'd missed Rey's company.

"Here," Rey said, approaching with bread and coffee for two, "you're joining me." She took a bite and sat back with both hands around her cup. "I haven't had banana bread in years. Jesus, this is delicious. Thanks so much."

"I'm glad it came out okay. Baking in a wood stove was a first for me. I hope Al appreciates losing all his bananas. He shouldn't have bought so many in the first place."

"You made good use of them, though. And thank God, because this place was started to reek of them."

Millie laughed. "I don't even know what possessed me to bake because I never do, and with one arm, it took forever."

"But you tackled it for all of us."

Millie sipped her coffee and looked down at herself and was reminded of the shirt she wore. "You give me too much credit. I don't know if I was bored or just frustrated."

"I understand, and I'm sorry it's dull for you up here, being out of action with that bad wing. If you wanted out, I can't imagine anyone would blame you."

Millie agreed. She'd considered going home, but common sense told her it was better to be among these close friends than regular co-workers any day, even if she couldn't do her part. So going home wouldn't help matters. And when she took a *really* hard look at this wilderness adventure, she knew it amounted to a constant challenge—abilities be dammed—and she'd stopped shying away from challenges years ago. She'd learned they held her interest, kept her mind sharp, her blood running hot, and often expanded her world in surprising ways, so staying right here made the most sense.

"You're not to blame for my situation, Rey, but thanks for the thought."

"You know, um…" Rey folded her hands together and cleared her throat. "I mean, just in case you don't know, Saratoga has connecting trains to Boston. I-I could get you to the depot in the village—if you wanted, that is."

The worry lines across Rey's forehead deepened with her obvious concern, and Millie watched the fervent color in her eyes recede to a weaker, softer hazel. So remarkable that such a strong, self-made woman would yield so visibly, undermined by emotion.

Rey didn't really want her to leave any more than Millie wanted to, and she accepted both facts with an unexpected dash of optimism.

"Believe it or not, I like it here," she said, "and I don't want out."

"You're sure?"

"Mind you, it does get boring sometimes, but maybe that just takes getting used to."

"And your frustration will fade right along with that gouge in your shoulder. Before you know it, you'll be back in the swing of things."

"That can't happen soon enough."

"I'm really happy you're here. I couldn't ask for finer company."

"And I enjoy yours, Rey. I'm glad you're back. This place is empty without you." *Yes, I think I missed you.* "So, how did it go tonight?"

"We moved right on schedule. A bit colder than usual, but the lake behaved, smooth as glass, and I imagine Jersey is taking back my load from New York as we speak."

"God, I hope so. Waiting is rough."

"You might be good to go for the next job, Millie. Legs will be screaming for a replacement load by tomorrow night, so that job could come early next week. You've been a real trooper through all this, considering you're wounded and things here aren't as modern or easy as what you're used to."

"Thanks, but honestly, being here hasn't been so bad. You know, in the beginning, I figured I could *put up with* this area, this job, and even you for a week or two, but I was wrong. I'm not *putting up with* anything. Truth be told, I'm enjoying all of it very much."

"That makes me really happy to hear, surprises me, actually, because you're such a city girl, and this place surely doesn't offer what Boston offers. And I'm grateful I haven't run you off, sent you kickin' and screamin' into the woods."

"Aw, just when I thought you knew me well." Millie placed her hand over Rey's. "Listen, those are two different worlds you're talking about. Believe me, completely different, which is perfectly fine. You need to stop underestimating yourself, okay? Happy is the woman who lives as she chooses."

"Oh, I like the way you think." Rey raised her cup. "A woman after my own heart."

Millie touched her cup to Rey's. "Besides, can you *seriously* picture me running, kickin' and screamin' anywhere?" She thoroughly enjoyed the smile that brightened Rey's face.

"You've done a great job with the stove," Rey said. "You'd never know it's thirty-six degrees outside. Were you chilly?"

Millie felt her face heat as Rey inspected the shirt she wore. "I was, right after I took a bath and dressed, and I saw this hanging—I'm sorry. It was presumptuous of me to borrow it."

Rey fingered the collar near Millie's chin. "How could I mind when you look so adorable in it? Please wear it as much as you want."

"Nothing adorable here, Rey. It's definitely you."

"Makes you look cuddly."

"Ha! You didn't just say cuddly. Jesus, that's a new one."

"Well, it's true." Rey finished her coffee and set both their cups on the table. "It's a comfy shirt, right?"

"Well, yeah, very, but—"

"Then let me show you." She drew Millie to her chest and enclosed her with an arm around her waist.

Millie welcomed the snug security, the gentled strength that enveloped her, and the easy, comforting heartbeat beneath her ear. Millie relished the cool cotton of Rey's work shirt against her face, along with its crisp, fresh scents of lake and forest.

"See?" Rey said, her breath warm in Millie's hair. "Cuddly on a cold night is good."

Millie rubbed her cheek against Rey's breastbone. "No argument from me, Big Bear." She managed to raise her left arm in the sling, fanned her fingers over Rey's ribs, and squeezed.

Rey sighed. "I could stay here all night, you know."

"Mm-hm. Me, too, but we'll probably have company soon. Gill and then Louie will be in to warm up."

"Let 'em."

"I'm so comfortable right now, I just might." She closed her eyes, thinking Rey's hand stroking her back could put her to sleep. She figured Rey was bound to nod off as well, no doubt short-changed of quality sleep lately by that damn cushy chair. Millie considered going to bed and giving Rey the sofa, or vice versa. The other option, sharing the bed, forced her eyes open because it appealed in a big way.

Rey spoke into her hair. "Please tell me we're not lying on a handgun right now."

Millie froze. "Oh, shit. Don't move." Cautiously, she wrangled herself into a sitting position and delicately probed between the cushions. She pulled out the black .38 and rolled her eyes as she showed it to Rey. "Jesus Christ. I completely forgot about it."

"I like that you did."

"And what if someone had blown through that door while we… while we were, you know…"

"Guess we would've gone out with a bang."

"Oh, you're a riot." Millie straight-armed Rey back against the sofa. "Bang, my ass."

"Well, if you'd just keep your gun hand free and an eye on the door, we could continue."

Millie grinned as she put the gun on the table. Continuing could be risky in more ways than one.

Rey pulled her back down against her chest and Millie's breath caught in her throat. "Now," Rey said, sounding quite pleased with herself, "would you look at this. I've captured the infamous cuddly one-armed gangster."

Millie smirked at very close range. "Camille Reynaud. I believe you have me at a distinct disadvantage."

"I'll tell you what I believe, Miss Anderson." Rey raised her head enough to bump their noses. "I believe you are a first-class lady, and I don't care if you have one or two or no good shoulders." She trailed her fingers around Millie's ear and into her hair. "In fact, I don't care if you can shoot the wings off a butterfly, or black bottom me clean off the dance floor. You can even date a new man or woman every day of the year. So what. To me, your spirit and your big heart make you very special."

Millie let Rey draw her down into a kiss because she damn well wanted to kiss Rey. Now. Sweet nothings never included her spirit or heart before. For once, her appearance, the fancy clothes, the glamorous makeup, and, thank God, her boobs, didn't matter. Rey put more stock in who she was *inside*, and boy, if that didn't make her head spin. A stream of blazing heat coursed through her body to a critical spot that made her squirm in Rey's arms.

Their lips met softly, tentatively, as if for the first time. She could lose herself in this, and apparently, Rey felt the same, intensifying their kiss, squeezing her closer. Millie desperately wished she had two good hands simply to cradle Rey's face right where she wanted it.

Rey ventured beneath the flannel shirt, stroking slowly over her blouse from shoulders to hips and back again with hands so large that, together, they covered her entire back. They didn't claw their way beneath her clothes, or toss her about, as they well could. No gruff mauling, no frenzied pawing or gobbling kisses. Quite the opposite, and so different from what she'd endured in the past. Millie reveled in Rey's remarkable tenderness, welcomed her own vulnerability for a change. The touch soothed and relaxed her and had her senses clamoring for more. There was a kindness in Rey's hands, a sanctuary in her embrace, and an unexpected reverence in her kisses. Millie found herself eager to convey as much, willing to bare her soul for the first time in years.

Rey kissed beneath her ear and along her neck.

Her eyes closed, Millie trembled beneath Rey's touches and heard the surrender in her own voice. "God, you're so sweet, Rey."

"*You're* the sweet one, Millie. Sweetest I've ever known."

Millie drew back to speak against Rey's lips. "No one's ever made me feel this way." She kissed her lightly.

"What way's that?" Rey kissed her lightly in return.

"I-I can't explain it," Millie said and lowered her mouth to Rey's for more. "Just…special."

"Because you are." She claimed Millie's lips in a long, languorous kiss. "God, you're special. Gets me all choked up that you feel it. And the way you make me feel..."

"So, tell me." Millie inched up on Rey's body and traced the rise of Rey's cheekbone with her nose. "How do I make you feel, hm?" She set a featherlight kiss on her eye.

"Like I'm flying." She sought Millie's lips and kissed her pointedly. "That such a special lady could grant me this. Me, the big dyke bear who lives in the wo—"

Millie kissed her hard. "Mmmm," she murmured, pulling back. "I won't listen to that. I admire you for living this way. Takes guts to do it, and I know guts when I see it. And I just adore the 'big dyke bear,' the broad, strong feel of you." She lingered over Rey's lips. "The way you hold me, touch me... Honey, a lady dreams of that."

Rey slid her hands up Millie's sides and wrapped her tightly, burying her face in the crook of Millie's neck.

"I'm going to miss you."

"You know, right now I'd give anything to be able to put my arms around you." Rey rolled them slightly to one side and Millie pulled her right arm free and slipped her fingers into Rey's hair. "I'm going to miss you, too."

"Would you consider staying for Thanksgiving? It's only a few days away."

She set her nose on Rey's. "Do you go out and hunt your own turkey?" Rey laughed and Millie liked the feel of it beneath her. "So, really, do you?"

"Not usually, no. Why? You want to traipse through the woods with me?"

Millie studied the sparkle in Rey's eyes and smirked. "You think I can't take it?"

Rey shook her head. "Wouldn't doubt you for a second, Miss Anderson." She cupped Millie's head and drew her into a kiss. "Please say you'll stay."

"You make it awfully hard to refuse, Rey." She stroked errant strands of Rey's hair off her forehead with her fingertips. "Ellie invited Jersey, Jacks, and me, and you, hell anyone we wanted, to have Thanksgiving at their place, but we have to consider work back home. These next few weeks are busy for us—for you too, I imagine, with the holidays ahead." She traced the upper ridge of Rey's top lip. "But, at the moment, work's the last thing I want to think about."

She set her lips to Rey's and felt her tremulous foothold on propriety drift away with the air in her lungs, like the last cloud in the sky. Rey's tongue grazed hers and Millie's danced across it as she inched higher on Rey's frame, a palm to Rey's square jaw.

Rey hoisted Millie onto her fully, effortlessly, and Millie straddled Rey's hipbone, her own thigh pressed between Rey's legs. Hunger seared through Millie, from her deepest reaches to her lips, and she kissed Rey with a desperation that surprised even her. Rey moaned, holding Millie's head in place with one hand, while the other roamed her spine, curved onto her ass, gripped it, and squeezed.

She pressed Millie into her, rocked her higher, until they both groaned into their kiss.

Taking a quick, much needed breath, Millie drew back and dropped her forehead onto Rey's. She wanted more, and the profound craving scared her. This yearning ran deep, hard, and sure, a desire stronger than she'd ever experienced, one that wouldn't easily fade.

"Hello in the cabin!"

The announcement and then deliberate stomping doused everything like a bucket of water. Millie lifted her head and brushed her nose across Rey's twice.

"Damn."

"You can say that again."

They sat up as Gill rushed in, a shotgun slung across his back.

"God, it's cold out," he said. "You got coffee?" His eyes widened at the pot on the stove. "Yes!"

"Hang in there a little longer," Millie said, glad he'd made a beeline for the stove. She straightened her blouse quickly. "They should be on their way back by now."

"Good," he said as he poured the hot brew. "We could use the relief. It feels like winter out there. At least those other guys saw some action tonight."

Missing out on tonight's hijacking couldn't have been further from Millie's mind now. She still reeled with the pleasure of Rey's affection, the apprehension of where it could lead. Her body still hummed insistently.

She sat back, crossed her legs, and picked up the magazine to appear occupied, but, damn, if feelings didn't demand attention. Dare she identify things like desire, arousal, contentment? *Simmer down, girl. Really, this was just necking on the sofa, wasn't it?* But somehow, it felt like far more, and she wondered, should there be a next time, if it would call to her like this.

Rey ate the last morsel of her banana bread. Looking just as flustered as Millie felt, she leaned forward where she sat, quite taken by her coffee cup and then the rug. Millie ran the back of her fingers along Rey's side, just to signal she shared the feeling, and admittedly, to enjoy one more bit of contact. She truly hoped Rey didn't regret what they'd done, because she didn't. In fact, practicality aside, she wanted to risk more such moments…before the reality of city life returned.

CHAPTER NINETEEN

Mac lifted Katie off her shoulders and set her into the ankle-deep snow. "Time for you to go inside for a while."

Katie spun around, reaching up for more. "Mackie, up."

"Honey, look," Mac said, crouching to her. "See Mama? She's calling you." Through the onset of tears, Katie eyed Ellie on the porch steps. "We'll play more later, okay?" Mac wiped away a tear with her thumb. "First you have to warm up with Mama." Just as she took the mittened hand, Katie gripped hers and pulled toward the porch. Mac laughed up at Ellie. "We had fun, Mama."

"And you, your pants are soaked so stay by the fire." She lifted Katie into her arms and they waved to Mac. "Love you."

"Love you both." Mac blew them a kiss and Katie sent one back.

Mac returned to Jersey at the fire ring, where extra pots of potatoes and squash cooked and a cauldron of spiced cider simmered on the side. With six guests in for Thanksgiving, the kitchen stove needed help and, thankfully, the cook fire she'd built for previous gatherings had come to the rescue once again.

"So, what's really going on between them?" She ladled cider into mugs for Jersey and herself and waited. Apparently, Jersey needed to think hard.

"A lot's happened in the past few weeks."

"So I gathered, but they haven't said more than two words to each other since you all arrived. Rey's been so quiet, I can't figure her out, and compared to her usual self, Millie's like a wet blanket. Is she upset that Jackson went home with the others?"

"Oh, no. There's nothing like that between them."

"Is it that Rey invited Nettie along? She's a character, isn't she? Tough, a real down-home sort."

"She is. I don't think she knows what to make of us, though, or how to deal with Rey bringing strangers with guns into their world. She's defensive, guarded. But that doesn't faze Millie. No, I think her issue is Rey."

Mac frowned at the fire. "Ellie thinks Rey and Millie may have started a little something up at the cabin. Is that true?"

"Oh yeah." Jersey set her mug down to light a cigarette. "They tried to keep all the smooching and little touches a secret but didn't fool any of us. It was pretty cute. But now, I think she's afraid of getting in too deep, and it looks as though Rey got the message and she's thinking twice, too."

"Who'd have seen that coming? Both of them know a relationship would take a hell of a lot of work." Mac blew across the top of her cider and sipped carefully. "So, how close…like…"

"Have they slept together?" Jersey shrugged. "I don't think so. They haven't had time alone, to tell you the truth. Since the morning of our second job, there's been trouble in paradise."

"Oh, for God's sake." Mac lifted the lid off a pot and poked a potato with a fork. She put the lid back on and did the same to the squash. "Bet Millie went with you on the second job, shoulder or no shoulder."

"She was hell-bent. No way she was staying behind again."

"How'd she do?"

"Solid as ever. Maybe even more fiery than usual."

"That's a relief," Mac said and slipped two cut logs beneath the cooking grate. "Sounds like you would've had a nightmare on your hands if you'd tried to make her step aside. If we need to go back, will she even consider it?"

"Consider what?" They turned to see Zim trotting down the back steps. "Not sending everyone north again."

In typical black topcoat, fedora cocked back on his head, Mac's long-time associate strutted to the fire and helped himself to cider. Glad as she was to have two more of her original cohorts with her for Thanksgiving, Mac knew Zim and Roxie, now his wife, wouldn't welcome loaning the bulk of their crew again. They needed all hands for their Boston operation at this hectic time of year.

"It's possible," Mac said, and Zim muttered a curse toward the fire.

Jersey added, "It would be the icing on the cake, to pick off a New Year's load. They're the biggest, most expensive loads of the year." She watched Zim shake his head and turned to Mac. "By the way, that shooter who got Millie, we dumped him the next night at the first job. Guess he must've caught some rounds from New York goons during the hijacking."

"Must have." Mac lit a Lucky, reassured to hear they'd left no loose ends. "Look, Zim." She exhaled smoke over his head. "I know another job puts you both on the spot and I'm sorry about it, but according to everything Rey and Jersey have said, pulling off something this big will push them all over the edge."

"Jesus, Mac. You're timing sucks. You know what New Year's is like, what the demand is, and we've got the biggest client list we've ever had. We'll be scrambling to deliver. Tell me you don't want eighteen again, right before the holiday."

"A run this important will have an escort, Zim, and *you* know what that means." She gestured to Jersey. "Fill him in on the last two, what you ran up against."

"Well, the first job was a cinch, but they came ready on the second and we took a few nicks. I suppose we did have enough for that, but like Mac says, they'll load up for a New Year's run, and we'll have to be prepared."

Zim loosened his tie as he paced around the fire. The calculating mind that had made him Mac's successor in Boston practically ticked out loud. He'd come so far from the scruffy, petty thief she'd met on the South Boston streets many years ago, and she was proud of him and his success. She didn't relish squeezing him for help.

She hated to burden either of them by lessening their resources for a friend. She never liked taking risks.

Zim stretched his back and sighed. His frosty breath mingled with the wood smoke.

"So you can't get by with, say, ten?"

Jersey shook her head. "My outfit will be hurting, too. I've got miles and miles of godforsaken territory to cover." She tossed her Chesterfield into the fire. "Say fifteen total."

Now Zim shook his head, and Mac feared they'd end up severely shortchanging themselves. She wondered if Rey had any idea what this "favor" could cost and considered calling her outside to join them, but decided to keep the needs of their operation private. The less Rey knew about these details, the better for Rey.

"What do you say to eight from Boston, six from Worcester?" she offered. "Use Rey's trucks. Keep yours for your routes."

"The trucks we can manage," Jersey kicked at the snow, "but I'm not nuts about losing four bodies when we'll need to be at the top of our game." She and Zim squared off, and she lifted both palms haplessly. "Well, hey, wouldn't be the first time we beat the odds, would it?"

Zim hiked a shoulder. "True." He rubbed snow from his left toe against the back of his right pant leg. "So you said Luciano's and Diamond's boys have been picking each other off up there. That's a good sign, isn't it?"

"It is, so I hear," Mac said. "Things have really heated up, apparently. Everything's falling into place."

"New York took out one of Diamond's snitches last week," Jersey reported. "And we heard that right before our second job, a Luciano goon sleeping in his car went bye-bye at a dive outside of Glenns Falls. Legs likes blowing things up."

"God damn. You all better watch your step." Zim looked beyond Mac and his expression softened. "You warm the coldest day, Miss Eleanor."

Ellie blew Zim a kiss as she joined them. "Ever the sweet talker, you are." Mac gathered Ellie's jacket together and buttoned it for her. "Hi, sweetheart." She kissed her softly. "We're coming in. How're things going inside?"

"Well, Millie and Katie gave up on Lincoln Logs and are using *real logs* to build this mountainous thing in the parlor. Roxie kicked me out of the kitchen, and Rey and Nettie went to see your shop masterpiece."

"Masterpiece?" Zim asked.

"If you'd come by once in a blue moon," Jersey injected, "you'd know Mac's turned the little barn into a repair shop/bunk house thing. Most of us are sacking out there tonight."

"You and Roxie get the guestroom," Ellie assured Zim, "being mister and missus."

"Best way to solve that problem," Mac added and squeezed Ellie to her hip. "Are Millie and Rey speaking at all?"

"Not much to each other. There's definitely something going on there, and it doesn't look good." She patted Mac's chest. "Now, look. I have a pretty good idea what you're really cooking out here, Stick McLaughlin, but please just give our potatoes and squash another five minutes?" She tripped a fingertip over Mac's bottom lip, kissed it quickly, and went back inside.

Jersey shook her head as she watched Ellie leave. "She knows everything," she said to Mac. "You *are* the luckiest woman in the world."

Mac stood taller. "You're absolutely right."

"She's glad you're not participating in all this, I'm sure," Zim said.

"Very. This is as involved as I get." She shifted the coals with a long stick. "Too bad, in a way, because she loves that area and the shopping and restaurants in Saratoga. But I'm thinking of surprising her at Christmas with a New Year's getaway at the Sagamore. She and Katie would have a ball." She straightened and looked from Zim to Jersey. "We should all do it."

"French champagne at midnight?" Jersey asked.

"Sure," Mac said with a laugh. "On me."

"Then count me in. It'd be nice to be there just for fun."

❖

Despite Katie's impatient fussing, Millie managed to tie the hat beneath her chin and slide mittens onto her hands. "Okay, Miss Katie, off you go!" Katie wobbled as quickly as she could to Rey, who waited with outstretched hand at the door. Before stepping out, she sent Millie a long, curious look, one Millie didn't want to see.

Breakfast had been only slightly less awkward than yesterday's feast. All the table talk, laughter, and overlapping conversations exhausted her, and keeping a smile on her face for so long left her drained. If she didn't stop kicking herself for growing attached to that woods woman, her ass would complain all the way back to Boston.

"Thanks for getting Katie dressed," Ellie said as Millie returned to the kitchen. "Here, sit. Join me for a moment of peace and quiet. You've got time for another cup." Ellie poured and slid the coffee toward the vacant chair across from her.

"She's too adorable for words," Millie said, "and she loves everybody. She won't like it when we all leave, you know."

"Oh, there's a tantrum on the horizon, for sure. Mac and I are taking her to the diner this afternoon. Seeing everyone there will cheer her up, and it's amazing, what a cider donut can do."

"Thanks for everything you guys did, by the way, hosting Thanksgiving and all. It felt good, us being together. My little Charlestown flat will take some adjustment. I might have to hunt down some cider donuts for myself."

"Last night," Ellie said, "Mac told me about needing one more job up there, a big New Year's job."

"Yeah, we figured. When those animals go on a feeding frenzy, you make the most of it. They're running around, frantic now, doing outrageous things to each other. We think both outfits are stressed to the max, so the timing is right for a big hit."

"Thank God things are working out the way everyone hoped. I gather that casino is playing its part, too?"

"They're still having well problems. A foot of new snow didn't help, and plumbing trouble is going to start." She smirked. "But my favorite part is all that expensive marble. It'll arrive soon, cut to the wrong sizes, *somehow*. Reordering will cost them a fortune, if they can even get any more of that stuff. Cripes, when the New York heavies find out who screwed that up, they'll bury him in the woods."

"Will you go back? You sound excited."

"Oh, I-I doubt it. I *am* glad the plan is working, though. Who doesn't like it when a plan comes together, but it's not a good time for Boston to be shorthanded."

"But wouldn't it be worse to be shorthanded up there, in the middle of a gang war? That Legs Diamond bunch supposedly is so sneaky and vicious—and the whole world knows better than to irritate the New York Mob. Isn't this the moment you've all worked for?"

"Hey, I thought you wanted no part of this stuff."

"Well, I really don't. As a family, there's no way we should, but Mac's doing what she can, and that's as far as she'll take it. I'm just surprised that you, of all people, won't be seeing this through."

Millie eyed her sideways. "Damn. You and Mac make the perfect team." She still could hear Mac making the same points right before breakfast. And, like then, Millie knew her half-hearted response didn't measure up. "I think it's best that I don't go."

Ellie patted the back of Millie's hand. "Does Rey know?"

Millie slipped her hand away as she sat back. The comforting touch brought emotion to the forefront, made concentrating on being practical so much harder. "I haven't mentioned it, no, but I'm sure she understands."

"Uh-huh. Understands you two aren't clicking anymore."

"We get along just fine. Sure, it was nice to get closer during those trips up there, but, really, that's all it was. Couldn't go anywhere, realistically. She knows we live in different worlds."

"Different and distant."

"Exactly."

"Better to play it safe on your home turf, doing what you're good at, than—"

"The writing on the wall is pretty big, El."

"Forgive me, but the writing on your face is, too."

"Look, I lost my head a little, spent too much time escaping, I'll admit, but it's pretty obvious we're cut from different cloth and I should've known better, that's all."

"Simple as that. 'Thanks for the fun, it was nice, I'm outa here'? You're just going to vanish, ignore what happened, force yourself to wake up from the dream?"

"God, Ellie." Millie grabbed the pack of Luckies Mac left on the table and shook out one for herself. "When you put it like that, I sound like such a bitch, like I led her on. The attraction was mutual, you know." She went to the stove for a match.

"I've no doubt it was," Ellie said. "I think it *still* is."

Millie scratched the match off the stovetop and puffed the cigarette to life. "Come on. Rey and me as a couple? *Seriously*, El?" She exhaled toward the ceiling as she sat down.

"So you think it was a mistake, what you two shared up there?"

"Maybe it was." Millie waved away a cloud of smoke. "We didn't go *that* far, if that's what you're thinking, but far enough to know…well…"

"To know you both wanted to, that you both felt that spark."

"But so what? Jesus. It wouldn't work out, that's pretty obvious. I have to face facts, El. I can't take a chance like some schoolgirl. As I said, I just should've—"

"But life's all about taking chances, Mil. You're a smart, attractive thirty-year-old woman with your whole life to live. Make it a life you want. Stop looking at what you two shared as a mistake. Hell, Rey's moping around just like you are. She shares your bleak, *practical* outlook?"

"It's disappointing, okay? I'll admit it. Somehow, we got too attached and I think we both started daydreaming. Actually, I can't imagine what we were thinking because we know better."

"Look, I don't mean to upset you, but we've known each other too long for me to let this go." Ellie folded her hands on the table. "You know, if I hadn't taken a chance years ago, it would've been my biggest mistake ever. Katie would have suffered, too. When Mac reappeared in my life, I turned my back on the handsome character

in the custom suit with gangsters all around her, and I walked out."
She tossed a look at the ceiling, as if thanking God. "Talk about
cut from a different cloth. I was newly widowed and a brand new
mother, and the Stick I'd known was someone named Mac, running
a gang, dodging bullets and the Mob, the Feds. She was a wanted
felon. Cripes, she *still* is."

Millie could guess where this was going, but she didn't mind.
They'd been each other's sounding board for years and Millie
cherished her. So when the raucous sound of everyone arriving at
the back door threatened to interrupt this moment, she found herself
hoping Ellie could complete her spiel in time.

Ellie reached across the table again and squeezed Millie's hand.
"Look, hon. My point is—and I'm preaching, I know, but you're
like a sister, so I'm allowed—please beware of overthinking and
using too much of your smarts. Sometimes a chance comes along
that's worth taking."

CHAPTER TWENTY

Rey left her plate and mug on the table and went searching for her boots. It wasn't the first time she'd forgotten where she put them, these past few weeks. She stood in the middle of the parlor, looked around again, and knew where her old habits had gone.

At least when Millie rearranged her things, they usually could be found. How quickly she'd grown accustomed to Millie's preferences baffled her. Maybe the half-hearted attempt to undo Millie's touches had led to this, this disorganized chaos in the cabin. In her life.

Shame on me, she thought, for ignoring the fine print. No flashy, cosmopolitan spitfire like Millie could seriously be interested in a big, scruffy lug like herself. So what *was* that all about? A quick sample of something wildly different? A change of pace to spice up her life?

Doubting Millie's motives made her question her own, and she cursed her reckless behavior. *I'm as much to blame.* The change of pace, something different, appealed to her, too, but, damn, if Millie hadn't reached deeper than that and touched her heart. Not that she'd had any say in the matter. Dangerous stuff, she thought, letting her heart in on the action.

The lift in her spirits, that bounce in her step, they'd returned to normal even before everyone left for Thanksgiving at Mac's, and she'd returned here to reminders of her lost common sense. No wonder she put some things back where they'd once been, and grown a stack of dirty dishes in the sink and amassed overdue laundry on the bedroom floor.

"Jesus Christ," she muttered, discovering her boots beneath a pile of jackets. "Pull yourself together. This is ridiculous." She cursed at the time as she pulled on her boots, knowing she'd kept Nettie waiting at the boat and that their sail up to her Canadian connection had fallen behind schedule.

A noise on the porch stopped her with only one boot on, but she hobbled to the fireplace and snatched the shotgun off the wall. She pumped a shell into the chamber just as Nettie called out.

"Hey, you better not be nappin'." Nettie waltzed in and gave Rey the once-over. "Shit, woman. Put that thing away."

"Sorry." She hung up the gun. "Just playing it safe. You never know, these days."

"You been hanging around those gunslingers from the city too much. They got you all jumpy."

"Not true. You get your place all shot up and see if it puts you on edge. Better to be safe than sorry."

"Bah." Nettie tossed a hand at her and went to the stove. She lifted the coffee pot and gently shook it. "Good. There's some left. I need a bit before we scoot out. Damn cold."

"And quit putting down those 'gunslingers from the city.' They're our friends, and they're trying to save our hides up here."

"Right." Nettie searched the cupboards for her favorite mug. "I liked it better when you kept these on that side."

"I like them where they are now," Rey said, "and stop messing with my stuff." She stomped her foot into the second boot. "You know those guys are doing an amazing job. You're just too crotchety to admit it."

"I am not. You forget that I can shoot, too? Just wasn't necessary to bring in hired guns."

"They're so much more than hired guns, dammit. And don't start this again. Do you even realize that, if it weren't for them, I'd be dead right now?" She yanked her coat off the hook. Sometimes, Nettie's parochial ways drove her crazy. "You could be a little more thankful."

Nettie narrowed her eyes at Rey as she sipped her coffee. "Well, I ain't thankful they left your sorry ass in the state it's been in lately. Half the time, you're not on the ball. One big sad sack, you are. Look at this place."

"I'll get to it. I've just been busy, that's all."

"Busy broodin' about that woman."

"*That woman*'s name is Millie. Show some respect."

"She's a city player, ain't she?"

"She's a lady. A strong, smart, thoughtful lady who's on our side." Rey poured the last half-cup of coffee for herself and stood beside Nettie as they drank. "I don't want to discuss it any more. We're late enough as it is."

"Thinking about her has cost you."

"Nothing I can't handle."

"She worth the trouble, Rey?"

Rey lowered her mug. "She's worth everyone's attention, but I'm not pining for her. Got it?"

"Right." Nettie put her mug in the sink and headed for the door. "We need to shove off, not waste time dealing with your need for a gal to warm your nights."

"Give it a rest, Nettie."

They hurried by flashlight to the *Jean Luc II*, single file along the snowy trail, with Rey wondering when Nettie would drop the subject.

"How long ago did Alice break it off with you?" Nettie asked without looking back.

"She jumped ship and left us shorthanded, remember? I broke it off with her."

"So, a hell of a long time ago. When you gonna get back in the saddle?"

"You should talk, you grouch."

"At least I know when I got it made, smart aleck. Daughter and son-in-law, grandkids, they make for a nice home."

"Moocher."

"Crybaby."

"I'm not crying about anything."

"Horse shit. You've been sulking around for weeks, since she's been gone. Don't even want to put your place back the way you liked it before she came in. You let her do whatever she wanted."

"I like the way things are. You're being—"

"And you miss sharing your bed."

"We didn't share my bed, God dammit. I let her have it."

"Ain't fooling me. Those big knockers of hers didn't fire you up? You losing your—"

"Watch your mouth, Nettie. You're making me mad."

"She seems the type who's used to getting her way. Let her go or you'll get your heart broke."

"Enough already. Knock it off."

"Rey. She's a looker, all right, cute and sassy, but a woman's got to be more than that to handle you. She's one *tough broad*, if you catch my drift."

Rey followed Nettie aboard, lost in thought. Yes, Millie was a "tough broad." She smiled at the many varied meanings. How Millie would have ignited at that remark, barked right into Nettie's face.

She remembered the cut on Millie's knuckle after that altercation in the dive bar. The way Millie gritted her teeth against the pain, holding the .22 on the windowsill the night she was shot. The very sight of her, so undone, in slippers and free of makeup, that early morning when they revealed how much they cared, when she bravely took Millie in her arms and kissed her. That first time she left.

So different from the last time. They'd only had a minute alone in Mac's parlor, and even that had probably been by accident. Millie had avoided her in the few days leading up to and through Thanksgiving as well as the next morning, probably deciding they'd been foolish to start something they weren't destined to finish.

And once Katie wrapped herself around Rey's leg, refusing to let her leave, the brief opportunity with Millie slipped away. They'd barely managed to mumble well-wishes before heading to separate vehicles, and Rey wondered if they parted equally disappointed.

She remembered strolling around to the backyard with Mac, prior to leaving, and the hushed conversation they shared.

"Your people have risked so much, Mac. I could never thank you enough."

"Hey, you have your own risks, my friend, running up and down this lake with the goods, and making sure deliveries look 'normal.' Just set aside a few cases each time and plan your private drop-offs for the twenty-eighth. We'll do the rest."

"When will your guys arrive? Are they all coming back again?"

"The twenty-eighth will be a busy day. Jersey said most of the same crew will come. And I'm hoping Ellie, Katie, and I will be checking into the Sagamore that day, too, for a New Year's getaway. I'd like you to join us and some of the others to ring in the new year."

"That's very generous. Thank you. Will Millie be coming back, too?"

"Sorry, but I don't know. She's a key player in Boston, and Zim might not be able to spare her."

"I understand. I wouldn't blame her if she didn't want to do another job up in my area."

"She didn't indicate one way or the other before leaving, so I can't say. In fact, she pretty much kept to herself the whole time, seemed a little out of sorts. Would you know anything about that?"

"No, we're good friends, but she didn't share anything with me."

"Good friends. That's not what I heard or saw in my parlor."

"Well, sure, we got pretty chummy for a while, but there's no future in that, Mac. We're too different from each other, so that's all you saw."

"From afar, friendship can look like something entirely different."

"I don't know what Millie's thinking, but I doubt a city girl would understand."

"Thank God Millie's not as stupid as you sound."

"I-I didn't mean it that way. I know she has plenty of smarts. It's just that a city lifestyle's so opposite of mine, hard to adapt one to the other."

*"Jesus. You're slinging the shit now, Rey. It better not be me
you're trying to convince. You two didn't even talk before she left,
did you?"*

"No. There was no good moment for it."

*"Well, that's a damn shame. Listen, if Millie comes back for the
New Year's job, you two better iron this mess out."*

Reggie Lowry entered the offices of Terrazzo and Schultz in
Albany, no longer worrying about the loose fit of his suit. Everything
seemed to be a little off these days, including this peculiar, time-
consuming mission to the capital city. Bocci's messenger had
slipped him the word and accompanying business card as soon as
he'd driven onto the Dazzle site, and he had to speed to make it
down to Albany in time. All the while, he worried about this fancy
architectural firm's role in his project.

Both Terrazzo and Schultz welcomed him with coffee and a
seat at their long conference table, and seemed eager to learn about
Dazzle's progress, shaking Lowry even further when they unrolled
their own copy of the site plans. But when Bocci walked in and
shook the partners' hands, all Lowry's questions vanished.

"Good to have backup for a project as important as ours,"
Bocci said and socked Lowry in the arm. "These gents have been in
the business for thirty years. They've seen it all and know the right
fixes to keep jobs on track. So explain Dazzle's troubles, Lowry. Fill
them in."

Lowry barely managed to keep the quiver from his voice as he
detailed his design, the progress, and the many tribulations that kept
dragging the project behind schedule. His index finger trembled
when he pointed to various areas on the plans, so he reverted to his
pen and tapped the points of interest instead of letting his instrument
shiver in place for everyone to see.

Beleaguered though he was, Lowry couldn't imagine being
replaced, couldn't bring himself to see that scary picture. But
Bocci's oddly congenial manner signaled exactly that. The big goon

refilled their coffee cups, laughed at Terrazzo's jokes, and joined in the conversation without being his normally obtrusive self. Lowry grew distracted by the behavior, knowing Bocci well enough to fear what lay ahead.

Lowry struggled to stay on point throughout the presentation, and with his concentration lagging, he fumbled often as the hour dragged on mercilessly. He noted the glances between the partners and the quick, knowing looks they sent Bocci. As much as he wanted out of this meeting, Lowry dreaded its conclusion.

Schultz treated them to a fine luncheon and promised to have remedies and innovations on paper for their perusal within the week. The timeframe gave Lowry pause, actually had him calculating when Bocci would dismiss him—and how. He ate little, but drank all the wine Terrazzo offered, and later found his legs a bit unsteady as Bocci walked him to his car.

"Those two sure know their stuff, don't they?" Bocci said.

Lowry opened the Cadillac door, grateful to steady himself on the handle. "Yeah, they do." He slid behind the wheel and could feel Bocci studying him. "I heard their firm is one of Albany's best."

"Better be." Bocci stepped into the car's open doorway and slammed a hand onto Lowry's shoulder. "You know this is costing us a fucking fortune, don't you, Lowry?" His heart pounding in his throat, Lowry just looked through the windshield and nodded. He held his breath when Bocci leaned down. "And after that fucking inspector pulled that stunt with the piping, we're *really* unhappy about spending more money."

"I'm still working day and night to stay on top of things, Frank. There just seems to always be another issue slowing us down. I'm on each one of them, though."

"Uh-huh. These guys will get Dazzle moving forward. We ought to see something from them real soon."

"I-I appreciate the help."

"Yeah, I bet you do." He straightened and shut the car door.

Lowry forced himself to drive away routinely. His hands still shook and he took deep breaths to steady himself. Too many horrendous images came to mind, wherein he was "removed" from this project. The Albany firm was no one's backup. The long trip north passed in a haze, shadowed by a thickening winter sky that matched his mood.

If only that damn plumbing inspector hadn't pushed them to the brink. Two weeks had been lost just in scheduling his visit and then waiting for all the paperwork, only to learn all the piping didn't adhere to the latest building code. And a third week passed before the guy agreed to let the matter slide, a third week and a fat envelope under the table.

But this, this hotshot Albany firm had to be the last straw. Lowry couldn't picture Bocci begging Luciano and Lansky for such expensive help. No, retaining Terrazzo and Schultz had to have come from the top down, and Lowry broke out in a sweat, believing his ineptitude had drawn Luciano's rage, those devil eyes afire because of him.

Lowry scrubbed a hand over his face as he drove, glad snow hadn't started. Enough of it banked the roadsides, but at least the way was clear enough for mindless driving. And that's how he found himself: mindless, fraught with fear, and wracked by anxiety, his mind spinning uselessly. Snow, he pondered, don't slow us down again, please. The first shipment of marble would arrive soon and truckers needed good traction on the site.

Lowry pushed the Cadillac up another steep grade, rounded the bend at the top, and pumped his brakes before starting down. However, the pedal offered no resistance beneath his foot, and both went flush to the floorboard.

"No!" He drew his foot back and tried again, repeating what now was a desperate stomp to slow the accelerating car, but the brakes would not engage. "Come on! Jesus Christ!"

He shot downhill, swerving into and out of tight curves, clutching the steering wheel to avoid being tossed aside. He pumped the foot brake again in panic, then remembered the emergency brake. He grabbed the stick and yanked back but cursed his lack of strength. He abandoned the wheel to use both hands.

The tires locked, but momentum sent the heavy car into a slide. The Cadillac skidded and rocketed diagonally across the road, climbed the snowbank, and landed on its side in the wooly boughs of four massive balsam firs.

Covered in snow, branches, and broken glass, Lowry blinked away the blood that trickled from his forehead and flexed his arms and legs. He drew his body from beneath the steering wheel and pulled himself up to the broken passenger window. Before climbing out, he located his briefcase behind the driver's seat and sent it out ahead of him.

Standing in the woods in shin-deep snow, wobbly with shock, he looked back at the automobile he cherished, its glass missing, smoke rising from beneath the crumpled hood, and he counted his blessings. Apparently, he'd had one left, because, in this region, brake failures always ended badly. But this hadn't been a maintenance issue, some growing concern he'd procrastinated fixing. He always kept his cars in top condition, and his brakes had been fine to this point. Somehow, they'd let go.

He high-stepped back to the road and began walking. A classy businessman shouldn't have trouble catching a ride, especially on such a well-traveled road. Until then, he walked accompanied only by the crunch of his dress shoes in the snow, the whirl of cold air through the foothills, and those recurring, ominous thoughts.

God only knew what it would take to outshine the likes of Terrazzo and Schultz, but he needed to come up with something quickly to save his own skin. Maybe a big cost savings somewhere, a miraculous fix, or a way to jump ahead in the work schedule. Some financial gain, because that was all the likes of Luciano cared about. That ego fed off status and success like no creature Lowry had ever known. Defeat, failure weren't in his vocabulary, and should anyone associate them with Luciano, they'd pay the heaviest price.

Lowry struggled to recall any hard times befalling the infamous Mob boss. Not long ago, he'd been badly beaten and left for dead for his role in a big-time killing. And there was the time the Feds took down Boston's ethnic gangs, and Luciano's outfit lost dozens of connected lawmen, politicians, and soldiers, on top of millions in revenue. To this day, he hadn't avenged those losses.

Stopping to catch his breath, Lowry looked back down the hillside but saw no oncoming rescue. His thoughts ranged afar, to that woman, the Feds' witness, Eleanor Harrison. How Luciano would relish that opportunity for revenge, even more so, if "Hijack Mack" came packaged with her. Too bad there wasn't a way to deliver them and become a hero in Luciano's eyes. "Getting rid of that pervert would be such a bonus," he said on a sigh.

He walked on, wishing he could conjure both Eleanor and Elizabeth. Snatching one would do the trick, because the other was bound to follow.

Lowry waved his arm at an approaching car. *If only the break I need would come along like this.*

CHAPTER TWENTY-ONE

A few more feet and we're done," Ellie proclaimed. "Honey, if you eat any more we won't have enough to finish."

Mac shoved the fistful of popcorn into her mouth and wiped her hand on her trousers, hurrying back to her job threading their garland for the Christmas tree. Like Ellie and Millie beside her on the sofa, she diligently worked a sewing needle through alternating cranberries and puffs of popcorn. Katie sat at their feet, supplying each of them one meticulously selected berry at a time from the wooden box on the rug.

"Katie," Ellie said, "shall we make popcorn for Santa?"

The little baby blues widened at the concept. Berry selection ground to a halt.

"Santa's coming soon, Katie," Millie said, "and he'll be hungry."

"But Santa likes cookies," Mac reminded everyone and scooped a handful of berries into her lap.

"Cookies, Mama!"

Ellie sent Mac a look. "Yes, we'll bake Christmas cookies for Santa, *together*."

"Kissmiss cookies!" Katie exclaimed, clapping her hands and sending berries around the room.

"I can't wait for Christmas with a little one in the house," Millie said. "It's been ages since I spent holidays with a family. Thanks for letting me come out ahead of everyone and share it with you guys."

"You're always welcome, sweetie," Ellie said and squeezed her shoulders. "I'm glad you decided to come. Not sure you're really enthused about going up to Rey's, but you're here and I'll take it."

Mac tossed a piece of popcorn past Ellie and hit Millie's hand. "You're family and always will be." She cupped Katie's chin. "We need more berries, cutie. Can you find them on the rug?"

"Well, I thought about it for weeks," Millie said, "whether I wanted to do the ol' pioneer woman thing again or not, whether I wanted to deal with the emotional drama. I'll be honest. I *do* think Rey's a honey, y'know? But, I'm not overlooking that big dividing line between us."

"One you're not willing to cross?" Mac asked, a bit surprised by Millie's reluctance to tackle this challenge.

"We're not exactly cut out for each other, Mac." She shrugged and the cardigan draped over her shoulders slid off, exposing the thin straps of her emerald holiday dress.

"I guess you've got a point," Mac said with a smirk. "After all, you'd have to change your wardrobe, for starters. Trade it in for warmer things. That little number you're wearing just might be wasted up in the boondocks."

"Personally," Ellie said, "I think if a relationship is meant to be, it'll know no bounds."

Mac kissed Ellie's shoulder. "Very prophetic of you, my love."

"Well, it's true. Obviously, there are a lot of miles between Boston and Gull Bay, but…but things can change. You never know."

"But first, you have to be interested in a relationship," Mac added and raised an eyebrow at Millie.

"Right," Millie said. "I'm past that." She tugged her sweater back onto her shoulders.

"You are?" Mac asked.

"Well…I suppose a little fling would be okay."

Ellie stopped threading her garland and stared. "Something tells me Rey wouldn't agree. And I just know you don't see Rey that way."

Katie toddled into Ellie's knees. "Mama, Wey, cookies. Go boat."

"Rey is far away, my precious, but we'll see her soon. I promise. No boat, though." She hugged herself and shivered. "Boat's too cold."

Katie dropped to the rug, pouting. "See Wey."

"You miss Rey, don't you, sweetie?" Millie said, and Katie scrambled up and leaned against her legs.

"Wey, boat," she said, her mouth contorting as she began to cry.

Millie took her face in both hands. "Don't cry, honey. You'll see Rey sometime soon." Millie looked over Katie's head to Ellie and Mac. "Wouldn't this melt the big bear into a puddle?"

Mac chortled. "Yup. Rey's definitely the meltable sort."

"And therefore wouldn't do something as superficial as a fling," Ellie added.

"Okay, I guess not." Millie sighed as Katie rolled cranberries across the rug. "Regardless, I told Zim I wanted to go because it's right to see this through. Third time's a charm, huh?"

"My money says it will be," Mac said, hoping that their time together would lead to better things. She lifted the five-foot-long strand of garland she'd just completed. "How's this?" she asked Katie. "Okie-dokie?"

Katie bounced as she shouted her customary response. "Dokie!"

"We can make our chain now?"

"Twain," Katie interjected and crawled back to the box to deposit a berry. "Choooo-choooo."

Mac grinned at Ellie, knowing Jersey soon would arrive with a little windup train.

"Ch-chain, honey," Ellie said, "around our Christmas tree. To make the tree pretty, like this." She stood with her hands full of garland, and Mac and Millie helped her drape the strands onto the branches.

Dotting the tree with many intricate glass ornaments took them until supper, but afterward, Mac took Katie into her arms for a closer inspection of each one. Most of the decorations she remembered from Ellie's family in her youth, and the memories of those fun-filled holidays returned to her so suddenly, so vividly, she nearly shed a tear. She found Ellie's misty eyes beyond Katie and swallowed hard.

"I'm glad we decided on a big tree this year," she said gently. "Last year's was tiny and we didn't bring out these fine things."

"She'll really remember this tree," Millie said, tickling Katie. "The lamps make all the decorations shine so bright. Such a pretty tree."

"Pitty twee."

"See this one, Katie?" Mac asked, pointing to a glistening porcelain star. "It was Mama's favorite when she was barely older than you. Like a star in the sky. Can you say 'star'?"

Katie nodded vigorously. "Stah."

"And this one," Ellie said as she lifted a fragile wooden figure with her fingertips, "was Mackie's favorite. A drum."

"Dwum, Mama."

Ellie kissed Katie's nose and ran a hand through Mac's hair before moving aside to let Millie reach the tree.

"What's this, Katie?" Millie tapped her finger on a crystal snowflake.

"So!" Katie answered with gusto.

"Very good! Snnnnowflake."

Mac drew a tiny ornament closer for Katie, and they examined the hand-painted glass angel, its hair a tuft of golden silk. Katie carefully touched its starched lace wings.

"See, Katie? She's an angel, just like you." Mac squeezed her tight. "You're our angel. When I was little, your mama was my angel."

Millie dropped her head and turned away. "Oh, great. I have to sit before I cry."

Ellie moved in. "And this simply must be on our family tree at Christmas." From a loop of satin ribbon, she dangled a hefty piece of green glass, roughly ground into the shape of a heart. "Many years ago," she said to Katie, "Mackie gave me her heart." Ellie closed it in her hand.

Mac wrapped her fingers around Ellie's and pressed it to her own chest. She leaned closer, around Katie, and kissed Ellie deeply. "I love you more each day."

Ellie wiped away a tear and looked back at Katie. "Mackie's heart," she told her, still holding the ornament to Mac's breast. Then

Ellie brought their hands to her own chest. "Mama's heart." She placed them against Katie's. "Katie's heart."

❖

Mac thought it a bit flashy, the colorful automobile array at her front porch, but what really mattered was that it had brought the most important people in her life to her home this Christmas day. She turned back from the window and Zim handed her another glass of warm hard cider.

"Tell the truth, Mac. You guys made this?" he asked, sipping his third of the afternoon.

"Good, isn't it?" Mac smiled at Ellie on the sofa. "Rey taught us."

Jersey suddenly crashed to the floor, exaggerating Katie's push, and Katie giggled as she piled her toys on Jersey's stomach.

"Oh, careful there, Katie. This belly is really full."

Katie watched Jersey pat her stomach. She slapped both palms to the same spot and Jersey guffawed. Katie only laughed harder.

"Jezzie, baby!"

Jersey's expression blanked. She popped up on her elbows. "There's no baby in my belly!"

Everyone roared.

"That's not what she means, Jers," Ellie managed around a laugh.

Katie retrieved her new baby doll beneath the tree, took aim at Jersey's prone figure, and hustled back, promptly thumping it onto her stomach.

"Oh, Katie!" Jersey jerked into a sitting position, one arm protecting her gut. "Careful or our yummy turkey dinner will come back up!" She pointed menacingly at her stomach.

Katie held the doll up to Jersey's face. "Jezzie, kiss."

Jersey stretched forward, pecked the doll on the cheek, and set it in Katie's arms. "Baby is sleeping now," she said with a finger to her lips.

Katie checked and the doll's eyes had indeed flipped closed. She looked back up at Jersey then hurried to the sofa and nestled the doll onto Ellie's lap. She mimicked Jersey and tugged on Zim's trouser leg. "Shhh," she said and turned her attention to the train on the rug.

When she pushed the wooden locomotive over Zim's polished loafers, he knelt beside her and drew the box of train cars and tracks closer.

"Here, Katie." He took the locomotive and attached the coal car, spinning its wheels with his finger. Katie nearly tumbled headfirst into the box to grab a coach and sat captivated as Zim clicked it into place.

"Caboose," Jersey said and handed Katie the last piece. "Can you say caboose, Katie?"

"Boose."

"*Ca*-boose," Mac said as she aligned sections of track.

"Ca-boose."

"That's my girl!" She kissed Katie's nose. "Very good!"

Millie shook her head at the adults playing on the rug. "Oh, El. Your car will be full of toys when you go to New York."

"I know. The Sagamore's nursery has everything you could need, but the grown-ups will be heartbroken if we don't take some of these with us." She winked at Mac across the room. "I can't wait to see the Sagamore again. It's always so beautiful, and it must be magical, all decorated for Christmas."

"Well, I wish Zim and I could go," Roxie said, "but there's too much work to be done." She followed Ellie to the kitchen. "We'll have a post-New Year's celebration at the house and you guys can all come and stay a while."

Ellie slid pumpkin pie from the oven and set it next to the apple already cooling on the counter. She joined Roxie in hovering over them, inhaling the delicious aroma. "There's plenty more cider, so drink up. The rum's in the cupboard right there, if you want more."

Roxie refilled her mug, sipped, and shook her head. "God, no. This is perfect." She brought dishes and silverware to the table, then turned with a sigh.

"How are you dealing with this trip, El? A major job, I mean. Are you okay with it?"

Ellie straightened and shrugged, her cheeks flushed from the stove's heat. Conscious of what her hesitation revealed, she saw the compassion rise in Roxie's eyes. "I'm as okay with it as I can be."

Roxie moved closer and rested a palm on her shoulder. "I worry about you worrying. Everything's going to be fine, you know."

"Well, we'll be up there this time, and I know Mac will have things planned to the minute, but even though she won't be involved, the rest of our family will be. Mac and I both worry about that, and probably always will. We worry about you and Zim in Boston, too, even though you're not doing this dangerous stuff anymore."

"I know there's no sense telling you not to worry, because you will anyway, but I wish you wouldn't fret over us. We're fine. And listen, things will go smoothly up there. They've done this before, don't forget. Er...maybe a time or two."

Roxie's lighthearted understatement was well intended, but hardly reassuring. Ellie looked back as she moved to the table. "How do *you* do it, Rox? Don't you want it to end?"

Roxie hurried to her side. "Of course I do and it will. Soon. For us, just one more year and we'll be off to Chicago, because Zim and I want a family just like yours. We want to be done with this, like you guys. You know Mac wouldn't be anywhere near action like this if she didn't feel it was necessary." She draped an arm around Ellie's shoulders. "You think any of us would've stayed this long, grown so loyal, if she wasn't the best?"

"You're very sweet." Ellie handed her a slice of pie. "Believe me, I know she's special, and true to her word. And she always manages to think of everything. I've been reminding myself a lot lately, it seems, but anything can happen, especially up there in that wilderness."

Roxie set a shoulder against Ellie's. "You, Mac, and Katie get settled in Sunday afternoon, relax, play in the snow, eat like royalty, and Jersey and the others will check in after the job's done Tuesday morning. You'll all be primed for the fireworks, come Wednesday night."

CHAPTER TWENTY-TWO

Lowry sat in his rented LaSalle outside the Sagamore Resort Hotel and prayed he wouldn't have a heart attack. The owner of the Vermont quarry had agreed to meet him for lunch, but Lowry now doubted either of them would have an appetite after their talk.

Months ago, the company had been exceedingly pleasant, naturally thrilled to receive Lowry's massive order, and Lowry counted on that easygoing, old Yankee demeanor today, when they would go head-to-head about the disastrous shipment that arrived. All the rare polished marble destined for Dazzle's grand lobby, tabletops, counters, sinks, and various floors had been manufactured too short of the specifications Lowry supplied. He had all the paperwork to prove what he ordered, but the quarry foreman had his as well, and they didn't match.

The time constraints involved with reordering were bound to be crippling, but in his gut, Lowry knew the expense, the setback would be fatal.

Seated at a small rear table, he gave thanks that only a dozen or so parties occupied the large dining room, and that his business wouldn't be overheard easily.

He ordered Scotch and waited, appreciating the pastoral view outside, the snow-covered lawns and vibrant blue of the lake beyond, and envied the tourists and hotel guests for their happy, relaxed time in such a luxurious place. He set his fingers to his glass and watched the tremors disappear when he tightened his grip. He shook often nowadays. Who wouldn't. Any minute, any day could be his last. Hopefully, he'd somehow survive this incredible nightmare with the quarry.

"Mr. Lowry? I'm Dan Creighton. I own Vermont Mar—"

Lowry practically jumped to his feet to shake his hand. "Yes, of course, Mr. Creighton. Reginald Lowry. Thank you for meeting me."

"Call me Dan, please." He laid his coat and fedora on the adjacent chair. "Reginald you said?"

Lowry tried to assess the man's approach, but he'd never been good at it. He *could* tell that Creighton probably had thirty years on him, and the deeply furrowed brow indicated he thought long and hard about things. The quarry had been in Creighton's family for generations, so Lowry believed the man knew the business as keenly as the trade. This mixup certainly wasn't Creighton's first, but it might be the biggest.

"I appreciate you coming all this way, Dan. I hope it wasn't terribly inconvenient."

"Not at all. My wife seized the opportunity to tag along. She's visiting an old school chum in Saratoga, so we've made a day of it." He smiled up at the waiter. "Scotch, please." Creighton unbuttoned his sweater and adjusted his tie. "So. Reginald. My foreman tells me we have a serious dilemma here. He gave me the paperwork on your pieces, and I've examined it all quite closely. It's our largest order of the year, you know."

"Is it? I do know it's substantial, yes."

"Well, first off, I thank you for your patronage. We take great pride in our work, have for many years, and do our best to please every customer. This issue is extremely upsetting, to say the least."

"Unfortunately, Dan, the need is critical now."

Creighton took the folded papers from inside his coat and laid them open on the table. "I'm sorry to hear that," he said, nodding when his drink arrived. "You see, because your specs call for a particularly rare stone, I'm afraid we won't be able to provide a rapid turnaround."

"How long will it take?"

"Possibly by May."

Lowry sat back hard. "May? *Possibly*? No, that's…" He shook his head. "That can't be."

"Pink marble, Reginald. It's Italian. Imported."

His mind spinning again, Lowry rubbed his forehead to clear his thoughts. "Yes, I realize that, but May? We're hoping to open in May. I can't wait that long. I can't have laborers doing such major work at that stage, not surrounded by finished walls and woodwork, carpeting, furnishings…Jesus."

"Have you considered a different stone?" Creighton slid a brochure across the table as he sipped his drink. "We have a vast inventory, as you can see here. If we can eliminate the import delay, we could have you set up in March."

"If I skimp on quality."

"Well, you'd preserve your timetable and save a considerable sum."

"*I'd* save?" The waiter arrived with menus, but Lowry waved him away without looking. "Dan, this was an error on your part. I shouldn't be paying anything for you to correct it."

Creighton's shoulders stiffened as he set down his glass. "It's quite evident that the error was not on our part." He picked up the job forms. "Dimensions are clearly written, I believe by your own hand." Now, the overworked eyes and aging face appeared defiant and stern.

Lowry quickly produced his own copies and indicated the discrepancies. "This is what I provided your sales office. What you have appears to have been altered."

Creighton looked closer but shook his head. "I disagree, sir. There's nothing overwritten here. You can look for yourself." He offered his papers and Lowry frantically searched the notations for changes.

"Well…well, how do you account for the differences? A change on my part would have been ridiculous."

"I can't explain it, but I know what I see, and I *don't* see any alteration on our forms." Creighton took a much larger drink this time.

Lowry slouched in his chair, a wave of defeat rising over him. "Of course you don't. It would cost you a mint."

"I beg your pardon?"

"I said finding an issue with your paperwork would be an admission of fault and obligate you to remedy this mess, *spend a lot of money*. Of course you wouldn't see anything wrong."

"And neither did you."

"Look, I know my paperwork is correct. *I* didn't change anything after I left your office."

"Exactly what are you implying, sir?"

"Not implying anything. I'm telling you outright. I didn't touch up the numbers, so it had to have been your people."

"It's obvious we're just going in circles here, and further discussion is useless, if not completely ludicrous." Creighton stood and finished his Scotch. "We would appreciate it if you took your business elsewhere, Mr. Lowry. Please be advised, there's a sizeable balance due and we expect payment in full." He picked up his hat and draped his coat over his arm. "Our business here is done."

Lowry jerked forward. "Oh no it's not. Far from it. We need to work this out. We have to."

"I don't care for your insinuation, Mr. Lowry, and I don't care to do business with you. As a matter of fact, I don't care for *you*." He turned and strode through the dining room.

"Creighton! Come back!" Lowry shouted, and every head in the room turned his way. He didn't care anymore. He had nothing to lose now. "I'll see you in court!" He lurched upright on wobbly knees and pounded the table. "Do you know what you've cost me?"

Lowry dropped into his chair.

The world felt safer here in this upholstered dining chair with serenity everywhere he looked outside, the smells of exotic cuisine and the comfort of friendly conversation inside. In contrast, home, his rented accommodations in Saratoga, offered nothing like it, and work, that rustic wooden shack with poor light and dangerous heat, certainly offered far less. And neither place provided sanctuary like the Sagamore. No harm would come to him as long as he stayed right here.

"Excuse me, sir. Could I refresh your drink?"

Lowry peered up at the waiter, who clearly wanted his own escape from this loud exasperated patron wilting in the chair. "Y-yes. Do that."

He sat up properly and loosened his tie. He chose to think about the filet mignon he'd order for supper, about finally learning to play poker in the saloon downstairs, and about drinking enough to ask any attractive lady he chose to dance, once the big band started in the ballroom.

He chose not to think about the monumental expense of Dazzle's marble, the costly hell the plumbing inspector created, or that his own replacement had been retained. Or Frank Bocci's temper and the final punishment he would mete out. Convinced that an attempt already had been made on his life, Lowry respected the Mob enough to know that, given a second opportunity, he soon wouldn't have a care in the world.

As he let his new drink burn its way down, Lowry decided to stay in this lap of luxury until his money or his luck ran out. Maybe he'd make it through New Year's.

He snorted at the thought and slugged down another mouthful. The prospect of returning to the job site chilled him, although he'd like to collect the few personal belongings he'd accumulated at the workhouse. He could make a quick stop there and hopefully be gone before Bocci or his henchmen caught up with him. But why bother, unless he wanted to run for his life and start anew someplace the Mob wouldn't find him.

"God, this is impossible," he sighed and lowered his face into his palms. "How did I let this happen?"

He stretched his back and headed for the men's washroom. A good splash of cold water might restore some brainpower, and he took his time hunched over the sink. He found no answers in the mirror, however.

"Look what's become of you, you mousey fool. They played you from the start and you were just too headstrong to see, too full of yourself, and now look where you are. Talking to yourself in a damn men's room, completely frazzled and no balls, just waiting to be erased like the flunkies they erase every day."

He dried his face and hands and used the tiny comb he kept in a back pocket to straighten his hair. "Show some self respect, for God's sake." He wiggled the knot of his tie back into place and nodded at his reflection. "Better late than never."

A cluster of new arrivals chatted gaily at the registration desk as he crossed the lobby, and, eyeing the expensive top coats, fur-collared shawls, and adorable children, he wondered which parts of this holiday season they enjoyed most, and if he'd ever see another one. A little boy ogling the glittering Christmas tree turned excited eyes up at him when he passed.

"Mister, what does this one say?"

Lowry stopped and looked at the shiny ornament in the boy's hand. He bent lower to read the Victorian script. "It says, 'Good will toward men.'"

"I know what that means," the child said, smiling up at him. "It means be nice to everybody."

Lowry somehow managed to return the smile. "Yes, it does."

He took a moment to appreciate the spectacular tree, its dozens of varied ornaments, the draped tinsel, and the garland that wound around its girth. His own childhood trees had been beautiful, but he'd never had one this tall or so meticulously decorated. A wave of nostalgia threatened to close his throat and he swallowed with effort. The Douglas fir dominated the spacious lobby, broadcast the season with its refreshing scent and classic profile. In the background, excited guests organized their belongings with bellhops, and, there, beyond the tips of several branches, Lowry spotted a familiar face.

The new arrival in matching charcoal topcoat and fedora lifted a toddler from her carriage and spoke with an elderly couple nearby. Lowry stared in disbelief, as Elizabeth McLaughlin reappeared in his life. He quickly scanned the group for Eleanor Harrison, and she literally strode right past him from the powder room and kissed the child's cheek.

"My God," he murmured. "Fate twists again."

He sidestepped farther behind the tree but kept them in sight and remained close enough to catch some of their conversation.

"I signed us up for the sleigh ride," Elizabeth said, and the child bounced in her arms.

"Mackie, hossies!"

Ellie removed the little girl's hat and smiled. "And tomorrow we'll go sledding and build lots of snowmen."

The child reached out for her. "Mama, pay so! Go out!"

"Snnnnnnow," Eleanor said.

"So, Mama!"

Elizabeth laughed as she slid their luggage toward the bellhop's cart. "I think Katie's a snow bunny." She leaned closer and rubbed her nose against Katie's. "We'll go out just as soon as we get squared away in our room, okay?"

"Mackie, go out!"

Lowry nodded at the name. *Hijack Mack, isn't it, you sick piece of garbage.*

"Long ride for you folks?" the bellhop asked, turning the cart to leave.

"Just a few hours," Eleanor said with a brilliant smile. "But when you're this excited to come back, it seemed like days. We're thrilled to be here for New Year's." She pressed a shoulder to Elizabeth's. "Best Christmas present ever."

Lowry's stomach roiled at their affection. The hotel staff probably don't know what to make of them, although "Mackie" easily passed for a man. *Twisted bitch. To think she has that lovely Eleanor under her spell. And with an innocent child, no less. So disgusting, so horrendous, what she's doing to the little girl, Katie, misshaping "normal" to her own perverted ways.*

He watched them exit the lobby and returned to his drink and table in the corner, still stunned from seeing them, and overwhelmed by renewed hope. Fate had dropped salvation into his lap and he vowed to make the most of it. Life just might go on, after all. If he could stay alive long enough.

❖

Jersey sighed so heavily she fogged her windshield. She swore under breath as she cleared the glass with a gloved hand. "It's a long way to go in silence, Mil. Might as well get it off your chest."

Millie looked out her passenger window. "Nothing to say, that's all. But thanks for driving, letting me leave my car at Mac's."

"Uh-huh. Does Jackson do all the talking when he drives or do you actually converse with each other?"

"Stop it. You know what's on my mind. Isn't that enough?"

"No. We all put up with the awkwardness between you and Rey last time, and that was plenty. At least then, we were leaving. This time, we starting a job and we've got to be relaxed, good with each other, so get it out now."

"Dammit all. I'm not sure what to say to her, how to act."

"Try saying 'Hello. Good to see you.' You *will* like seeing her again, won't you?"

"Of course. That's not the point."

"Look, Mil. You two are sweet on each other, admit it."

"I have admitted it. Just doesn't matter."

"Well, that's a crock of shit."

"You have such a delicate way with words."

"Well, it is. What do you mean, 'it just doesn't matter.' Sure it does." She resettled the cap on her head and took a long drink of Coca-Cola. "Now, listen."

Millie continued to stare out the window. "Here it comes."

"Just hear me out, okay?" She cleared her throat. "Staying in the cabin's really cozy, and I believe that you, Miss High Fashion, like being there. You like cooking on that clunky stove, the freshness of the outdoors, cruising the lake, and poking around the cute villages. And I think Rey's special. She's not like your friends back home, that's for sure. She doesn't give a damn about appearances or having 'stuff' to show off. She's genuine and actually cares about people." She paused so long Millie finally looked at her. "You know I'm right," Jersey continued. "Know what else I think?"

"Oh, I can hardly wait."

"I think you'd be happy there. With Rey. I doubt you'd miss the Boston scene much at all. Remember, there's always the high life in Saratoga. I'm sure Rey would love to hit that with you once in a while. Hell, you'd have a ball, dancing the pants off people." She took another drink, but Millie passed on the opportunity to sneak in a response. "So, I think you both could be very happy. I don't see why it's impossible."

Millie turned back to the window. She'd told herself all that already, but Jersey meant well, and it was nice that she'd put so much thought into the situation. But give up her little apartment with electricity, running water, and telephone? Say good-bye to her favorite speaks and jazz clubs with their ever-changing characters and flamboyant styles? What about the corner market, the morning paper, the streetlamps…?

"Cripes, Jers. Did you do all that thinking from Rey's point of view, too, or just mine?"

Jersey took forever lighting a cigarette. No, Millie thought, she hadn't looked at it from Rey's side.

"You see?" Millie went on. "Either way, one of us would be a fish out of water, not knowing how to function. We'd be giving up our livelihoods, too, not to mention our sanity."

"But Rey's more invested up there than you are in town, Mil. She's got a home, a boat, a business."

"So *I'm* supposed to give up everything for her?" That would be asking a lot, even though Jersey had a point.

"Well, not necessarily, I guess. You work things out together, start brand new, with a partner at your side for a change. Someone who matters. Hey, I'm no expert, but I think love works that way, sometimes."

Millie pondered that word, the all-consuming power of the emotion. She didn't think it applied in her case because she certainly would know it if she felt it. Or thought she would. She wasn't an expert, either, in fact had never experienced that head-over-heels thing found in songs and poems, the "thing" that made you surrender heart and soul to someone else.

But, to be honest, she'd spent weeks missing Rey, imagining life in her world, and wondering if Rey was doing the same, so did that mean she felt more than simple attraction?

"I'm not sure love is a player here, Jersey."

"Fair enough." Jersey exhaled smoke out her partially opened window and turned onto the long snow-packed dirt road that led to

Rey's cabin. "Maybe things will be clearer after our stay here this time."

"Maybe."

"Find time to talk, please. Otherwise, you two will have it tough, come New Year's Eve. I'm looking forward to whooping it up big. Mac's paying."

Millie laughed. "Where would we be without her."

"Got that right. Now, snap out of this and be your happy self. We'll be there soon, and Rey's probably just as rattled as you, so shake it off."

Millie studied the world of skyscraping evergreens and dense woods as they approached the cabin, and tried to see herself in such a place. Not an impossible sight, but sketchy. Wild times of a totally different kind. No frolicking in the latest fashions or jiving among mobs of frenetic dancers out here. No making the rounds to all the right nightspots, either, or exhausted walks at sunrise up her two flights on aching feet. Just wooded trails and low-hanging branches, darting animals that startled you, and fun you made yourself. *Who knows if I'd even have what it takes? If I wanted to try, that is.*

Jersey parked in her usual spot at Rey's porch and shut off the car.

"Happy self," she said in a commanding tone. "And don't forget to talk."

Millie gave her a quick little salute before they stepped out.

With a typically wide smile, Rey burst through the screen door to greet them.

"Welcome back," she said. "Perfect timing. I just put the coffee on." She trotted down the steps. "Give me a couple of those." She took two of the duffels Jersey pulled from the trunk. "It's good to see you both."

"Same here," Jersey said, slinging a bag onto her back. "I'll take this inside."

Millie touched Rey's arm. "How've you been?"

"I-I've been well. Surviving the winter so far, but it's really just getting started. I, ah, I didn't expect to see you this time."

Millie lowered her head, not especially proud to admit she'd wrestled with the decision. "At first, I wasn't sure, either, Rey. But I realized that it's my place to be here, to finish what we started."

Rey nodded. "I appreciate that, Millie, but…" She exhaled hard. "Well, are you talking about the job or…or us?"

The softness of her usual grumble struck Millie as particularly sweet, and the wary expression begged honesty. Millie smiled up at her. "Both. But, you know, there isn't much of 'us,' Rey."

Rey shrugged one shoulder. "That's true, I suppose. I'm sorry I brought it up, with you guys just getting here. Hell, you haven't even come in yet, and I'm—"

Without thinking, Millie slid her palm over Rey's hand. Such a strong and weathered hand, apparently oblivious to the cold. "I don't want it to be a sore subject."

"Me neither. It's just that, the way we left things here last time—"

"And after Thanksgiving at Mac's."

"Yeah. We should've made time to talk, Millie. I hated that we went our separate ways without clearing the air."

"Me, too. Let's make a point to do that this time."

Rey's stiff posture relaxed noticeably. "I guess that's a good plan." Millie watched her gaze travel the length of her and back up. "God, Millie. I can't help it. Just a look at you stops me in my tracks. It's so good to see you."

"Well, you're looking fine yourself, Big Bear, rough and ready as always."

"Eh. Don't know about that." She tossed her head toward the cabin. "Come on. You must be freezing. Let's get inside."

As she hurried up the steps to open the door for her, Millie realized that Rey's pointed inspection had melted away the cold.

CHAPTER TWENTY-THREE

Try as she might, Rey couldn't hide her grin. Millie in a pair of Jersey's trousers, complete with suspenders, was a sight she never thought she'd see, and wouldn't mind seeing every damn day. Al and Sid hadn't stopped teasing her about the uncharacteristic look since they left the cabin, and now, an hour into loading a truck at Rey's storehouse, Millie seemed to have taken enough.

"What? So, I'm wearing pants," she snapped at Al, then turned to Rey. "And you can wipe off that shit-eating grin. I'm being practical, like you suggested. A girl can't lug these damn things in a dress, can she? No." She grunted as she hoisted a crate of whiskey bottles up to Nettie in the truck.

"I appreciate the help," Rey said, picking up another and watching Millie struggle from her shorter height. "Can't believe you said yes to doing this delivery with us."

"More hands make lighter work," Millie said through clenched teeth and lifted another crate. "No sense just sitting around, twiddling my thumbs, waiting for tomorrow night's job."

Al passed another up to Nettie. "We all got here just in time. The five of us should take care of this in a jiffy."

"Three hotels, Rey?" Sid asked, hopping into the truck to help Nettie.

"Yup. We'll take this east road down and come up along the west shore. The Sagamore's last, so the back half of this load goes to them." She swung another crate up. "It's not too late, so we won't be suspicious."

"I can't believe you skimmed this much off your loads, these past few weeks," Al added as he passed. "Your best customers better appreciate the risk you took."

"Got some freebies from up north," Nettie said. "That was a big help, otherwise a place like the Sagamore would've been furious with us."

"Last one," Millie said and blew out a frosty breath. "Thank God."

"Okay. Let's secure this and hit the road." Rey removed her gloves to begin the tie-down process but found Sid and Al already on the job, and doing it faster and better than she ever did. "Thanks. Sometimes I forget that you've all done this before."

Millie climbed in from the passenger side and slid to the middle. Nettie followed her in as Rey moved behind the wheel. Two raps on the cab wall, from Sid and Al beneath the canvas in back, sent them on their way.

"Mind if we take this truck with our two tomorrow night?" Millie asked.

"No. I'd rather you do. It's the best of my three."

Nettie asked, "So you're one of them who're doing the hijacking tomorrow?" She produced a tobacco pouch from her voluminous coat, and began packing a miniature corncob pipe.

Millie observed closely, much to Rey's amusement.

"I am, of course."

"Hm" was Nettie's response.

"It's not my first, if that's what you're wondering."

"Nope, wasn't wondering that." Sucking on the stem, Nettie concentrated on drawing fire from a match.

"Well, all right, then."

Rey thought the two of them would carry on the staccato conversation all night, if she let them. "She's been with this group a long time, Nettie. She knows what she's doing."

"Hm."

Millie looked at Nettie sideways. "Long time for you, too."

Nettie nodded. "What part of the city you from?"

"Charlestown."

"Oh. You know about guns?"

"I do."

"What kind?"

"Pick one."

"Ever killed anybody?"

"Why?"

"Just curious, little sassy thing like you."

"Well, this little sassy thing doesn't mouth off about her work."

Nettie leaned forward to speak to Rey around Millie. "She's okay."

Rey winked at Millie. "We're glad you approve."

"Just hurry up," Nettie grumbled, and smoke fell out of her mouth. "Want this done and over with, pronto. Lot safer on the damn water."

At nearly eleven o'clock, they drove onto Green Island and the sprawling Sagamore compound. Rey noticed how intrigued Millie appeared, captivated by the dimly lit backside of the majestic hotel.

"Damn, what a huge place," Millie said. "I can't wait for New Year's Eve here."

"The back's almost as impressive as the front," Rey said as they rumbled around to the freight area. The hotel's victuals manager opened the storage doors right on cue, and Rey backed up to unload.

Hand-to-hand, they passed the crates inside, keeping their efforts methodical and quiet. Just five minutes in, a tall lean figure in coat and hat approached from a wing of the hotel, and Rey felt Millie grip her arm.

"One second," Millie said in a hush and waved Al and Sid into the truck for their shotguns. Millie positioned herself to the opposite side of Rey from the stranger, and drew a .38 from her jacket pocket.

Silhouetted in the backlight, the stranger walked closer and exhaled a cloud of smoke.

Rey squinted into the poor light. "Evening. Something we can do for you?"

The stranger laughed. "Who were you expecting? Santa?"

"Jesus, Mac," Millie hissed. "You scared the hell out of us." She stepped forward and hugged her. "What are you doing out here?"

"Just out for a little stroll. Right time, right place, huh?"

"All settled in?" Rey asked. "Ellie and the baby?"

"God, yeah. And if Katie doesn't see you soon, we're going to ship her to your place."

Rey laughed. "She misses big ol' me?"

"Hell, yeah. And your cookies and your damn boat."

"Well, I'm glad." She puffed out her chest. "That makes me an aunt."

"Get in line, Big Bear," Millie said. "So, you all had a good night?"

"We wore ourselves out on the dance floor after dinner, and Ellie decided to get Katie from the nursery and go up to bed. I thought I'd check out my lucky table downstairs, but then I remembered when you'd be hitting this place, so I decided to get some air."

Al jumped down from the truck and waved to Mac before lugging a crate inside. Sid appeared next, but set his crate on the ground. Hurrying to Mac, he grabbed his cap off his head and extended a hand. "Just had to meet you," he said, vigorously shaking Mac's hand. "Name's Sid. I'm kinda new, about a year now, and I-I've heard so much about you. Real happy to meet you. Never thought I would." He finally stepped away and slapped on his cap. "Ah…well, back to work. Happy New Year, *Mac*." Giddy as a kid, he hustled to the truck.

Rey clapped Mac on the back. "Damn movie star, for Christ's sake."

Millie shook her head. "If he asked for your autograph, I would've kicked him in th—" She glanced at Nettie. "Keister. I would've kicked him in the keister."

Nettie chuckled. "So," she asked Mac, "you're the boss, huh? Had an inkling, back at your place on Thanksgiving."

"We're all just old friends, Nettie."

"Uh-huh. Well, you're dressed slick enough. Good for you, having yourself an outfit of your own."

"Well, I'm not actually—"

"It brightens my day, seeing a woman in charge, God dammit."

Rey sighed and planted her hands on her hips. "Oh joy," she said to Millie. "Nettie's day has been brightened. Okay, look. Social hour is over. Sorry, Mac, but we have to square this load away and clear out. So should you."

"Eh." Nettie tossed a hand at Rey as she addressed Mac. "Hope we meet again, Mac. Maybe we'll chat over a few cold ones sometime." She nodded at Mac and climbed into the back of the truck.

"Rey's right, Mac," Millie said. "You get out of here. We'll be done in a flash. Wish us luck tomorrow night, huh? We'll catch you the day after."

Having spent all afternoon and evening trying to plot his own salvation, Lowry never expected the solution to fall into his hands this way. When he finally left the confines of the tiny room he booked at the Sagamore and ventured toward the bar, the keys to his every scheme appeared like a gift from God, some fifty feet away. As he stood shielded by a framework of lush evergreen garland, Elizabeth McLaughlin sauntered down the west wing hallway toward the far exit, and Eleanor Harrison entered the nursery. In the minute it took Lowry to decide who to follow, Eleanor emerged with Katie and rode the elevator up.

Lowry chose Elizabeth and hurried to the fire door. Keeping to the shadows, he followed her to the rear of the hotel and watched her rendezvous with truckers. Bootleggers, he surmised, as crates went from one man to the next and into the building. He wished he could move closer to hear their words but didn't dare risk exposure.

What he *was* willing to risk instead was getting to the lovely Eleanor, who now was alone. With a pretense of simple conversation, he would lure her into a vulnerable position and overpower her until Bocci could arrive. And right now, time was of the essence.

At the front desk, he asked for her room number. He would only need a minute to snare her with his belt, stuff his handkerchief into her mouth, and squirrel her away.

"I'm sorry, sir," the young host said, "but we're not at liberty to give out that information."

Lowry presented his most humbled, pleading look. He patted his suit jacket pocket. "I only need to return her brooch, you see. She left it at our dinner table and she'll be devastated to find it missing come morning."

"Very well, sir. You can leave it with us and we'll guarantee she receives it at eight o'clock sharp."

"Oh I couldn't," Lowry said, straightening with flair. "It's priceless. A family heirloom. No disrespect intended, but I simply couldn't entrust it to a stranger. You *do* understand, I'm sure."

"Certainly, sir. However at this hour," he checked his watch, "it's approaching midnight. But if you'd like, I could ring her room."

"Absolutely not. That would wake her child. Listen, young man," Lowry pressed, and opened his billfold. "I'm sure there's *some* way to make this easy?" He slid a ten-dollar bill across the counter.

The host fidgeted with his bow tie and glanced around at the empty check-in area. The ornate foyer was similarly void of potential witnesses. He searched Lowry's eyes for so long, Lowry thought he'd have to put up more of a fight. And he was in a frantic hurry to get upstairs.

Finally, the young man sighed and flipped several pages of the registration book. "The McLaughlin party is in room two seventeen."

Lowry almost bounced on his toes. He tapped the bill on the counter and walked as casually as possible to the stairs. He wouldn't chance being seen in the elevator.

Lowry pulled his fedora down almost over his eyes. He shook violently as he removed his belt and gathered it in one hand, and then plucked his handkerchief halfway out of his pocket in readiness. He glanced in each direction of the deserted hallway, then knocked gently three times.

"Mac?" The feminine voice sounded groggy with sleep.

Lowry rapped again.

"Mac, honey?" Her soft lilt now closer to the door, Eleanor yawned and then chuckled. "You forgot your key, didn't you?"

Lowry jumped when the door swung open. Forcing himself to act and not think, he stepped across the threshold. Eleanor gasped in shock but didn't move aside.

"Who—"

"Eleanor?"

"S-stop! Who are you?" But she didn't wait for an answer. "Get out of here!" She grabbed the door with both hands and labored to shut it on him.

"Wait! Eleanor, we need to talk!"

She pressed her weight into the door. "Get out!"

Lowry staggered back a step. He slapped a palm against the door to keep it open. "You're going to listen!"

Eleanor's next shove nearly crushed Lowry's fingers in the jamb. But suddenly the pressure abated, and as the door drifted open, he saw her dash to the nightstand, heard her yell.

"Get out! I-I've got a gun!"

Lowry backed away with a long step and ran to the stairs. He heard Eleanor's door slam as he raced down. At the bottom, he paused and gulped air, shoved his belt into his jacket pocket, and straightened his hair with both hands. He entered the side lobby unseen and somehow managed a leisurely walk to his room. Once locked in, he collapsed on the bed, defeated.

Mac removed her fedora as she slid her key into the hotel room lock. She heard the release, but couldn't budge the door. Instinctively, she stepped back and drew her gun.

"Ellie?"

"Mac?"

"What's going on? Open the door, please."

"Is it really… Mac?"

"Of course, Ellie. Come on."

"Well… W-what's your old nickname?"

"Huh?" The query took Mac by surprise, but the tremble in the voice scared her. "Honey, are you all right? Open up."

"Tell me," Ellie insisted.

"What? Er…my nickname? Why?"

"Just tell me!"

"Shit…" Mac's own fear temporarily blanked her mind. "Stick. Now, please open the door!"

At the sound of furniture being moved, Mac swung the door open with a fury and stepped in, gun first.

Ellie gasped at the sight of it then threw herself into Mac's arms and burst into tears.

"Thank God!" She squeezed Mac's neck so hard she nearly cut off her breath.

Mac slipped the .45 into her trouser pocket and took Ellie in a secure hold, rocking her from side to side. "Jesus, honey. What is it? Are you all right? Is Katie okay? What?"

Ellie's sobbing quieted and she spoke muted assurances into Mac's jacket collar.

Mac held her out at arm's length and looked her over carefully. She stroked back Ellie's wild hair and cupped her teary face.

"Jesus, please, Ellie. What happened?" She led Ellie to the bed and leaned into the adjacent room to check on Katie, who sighed in a slightly restless sleep.

Holstering her gun inside her jacket, Mac returned to Ellie and sat beside her, an arm around her shoulders. "Easy now. Take a breath, okay? What happened?" She covered both Ellie's hands with one of hers, but Ellie pulled them away, waving them as she spoke.

"A man… A man came in—"

"In here? With you and Katie in bed?"

"I don't know who he was, Mac. Some guy, pretty much a silhouette. It was so crazy, I-I couldn't recognize him."

"How—what did he say? Did he know you? What did—Jesus, I'm sorry." She pushed out a steadying breath. "Go ahead, please."

"There was a-a knock. I just thought you'd forgotten your key." She buried her face in her hands and Mac pulled her to her chest. "God, Mac, he scared the life out of me."

"Shhh. It'll be okay." Mac reeled with the possibilities. "Then what happened?"

"Well…I called your name. I should never…" Ellie straightened and expelled a breath toward the ceiling. "I opened the door before hearing you answer."

"Did he come in?"

Ellie nodded. "He called me by name. Eleanor. I couldn't recognize him, Mac. I'm sorry."

"Shhh. God, you have nothing to be sorr—"

"He was just a…a suit and fedora. About my height. And I was practically asleep. But I asked who he was and he just said we had to talk, or something." She shook her head at herself and dropped it into her hands. "I tried to shut him out, close the door, but he pushed back."

"Son of a bitch. What else did he say?"

"Nothing. I kept telling him to get out. And finally I gave the door a shove and made a dash for the lamp. Something told me to say I had a gun. I guess that was good, because he ran."

"He just turned and ran?"

"Yes, and I ran back to the door and locked it."

"Shit, El." Mac crushed Ellie to her again.

"Oh, Mac. I shouldn't have stayed." She gripped Mac's shirt in her fist. "And with K-Katie right here…I-I just wasn't thinking. I should have taken Katie and left."

"No. It sounds like you gave him enough reason to stay away, honey, and it's not likely he'll be back. How long ago did this happen?"

"Maybe…fifteen minutes?"

She kissed the back of Ellie's hands. "Trust me. We're all going to be okay, sweetheart." She unstrapped the small pocket gun at her ankle and wrapped it in Ellie's palm. "You know how to shoot this."

"I-I do. And I will, trust me."

"See? Together, we've got this. Now, I'm going down to the front desk. Give me just a few minutes."

"But, Mac—"

"Just a few minutes, El." Mac pressed a gentle hand to her cheek. "When I leave, lock and jam the door again, then go back to bed with this under the pillow." Ellie's tears had slowed, but Mac wiped the wet cheeks with the bedsheet. "Let me do this, okay?"

Ellie could only nod. "Only a few minutes."

Mac lowered her lips to Ellie's and delivered a long, promising kiss. As she left, she tried to send a reassuring smile past the furor rising within her.

She descended the two flights in a blur, scanning the steps and landing for anything the intruder may have dropped or discarded. She burst into the lobby but wasn't surprised to see no other hotel patrons milling about. Even the front desk was deserted.

She stepped around it and into the back room, where the young nightshift host sat reading a novel at his desk. He leaped to his feet, eyes wide as she barreled toward him.

"I'm sorry, sir—er—ma'am, but you can't—"

Mac seized his upper arm. "Come with me." She hurried him out to his station.

"Hey! Let go of me!" He twisted to free himself. "Just what do you think you're—"

"Shut up and listen. You on duty here all night?" She hauled him behind the counter and he yanked his arm loose.

"How dare you manhandle me!" He straightened his tie and vest and looked up defiantly. "I'm having you removed at once."

Mac swung an arm around his neck and bent him backward, almost off his feet. "I'll remove your fucking head from your neck. Now shut up and answer me." She clenched her arm around his throat and, when he began to gag, she thrust him to the floor. "Get the fuck up and don't make me help you." Coughing and rubbing his neck, he stood carefully. "One more time, kid. You on duty here all night?"

"Since ten o'clock."

"Anyone else but you work the desk at night?"

He narrowed his eyes and lifted his chin before speaking. "No, no one. I'm here during the overnight. I'm the night manager. You *have* to tell me what this all about."

Mac turned him to face the registration book and slapped her hand onto it. "Two seventeen," she snarled in his ear, watching his eyes drop to the leather-bound book. "Name's McLaughlin. Sound familiar?" She watched him stare at her hand and curled it into a white-knuckled fist just for effect. "Someone asked for the room number tonight. Do you remember *that*, night manager?"-

"Er... N-no, not that I recall, si—ma'am." Perspiration dotted his upper lip as his face paled.

"Better think harder." Mac shoved his shoulder, resisting the urge to jam her .45 under his mousy chin. "Who'd you give it to?"

"I beg your pardon, but are you insin—That's cause for dismissal! I'd never do such—"

She slammed a hand to his chest and pushed him all the way back into the office and down into his chair. She leaned on both armrests and glowered into his face.

"Now you fucking listen to me good. A stranger came to two seventeen tonight while an innocent woman and child slept. Someone gave him that number, and my money's on you." She stabbed a finger into his chest and he winced. "Now, who and when was it?"

He blanched. "D-did someone get hurt?"

Mac's jaws flexed. "Answer me or I swear I'll take you out where you sit!"

The manager avoided eye contact and stared straight ahead at Mac's torso. Mac knew what he saw, the white silk shirt, form-fitted vest, and because her jacket draped open, the leather holster. His wide eyes began to fill.

"I-I didn't want to. He said he had...some expensive brooch she'd left."

"Uh-huh. How much was your cooperation worth?"

"T-ten dollars."

Mac straightened but didn't move away. She crossed her arms and stared down at him. "What else did he say?"

"I don't... Um, that I couldn't call up because she had a child that was probably slee—"

Mac lunged for his throat and twisted his tie until he gagged. "And you still gave him the fucking number?" She shoved him away and his chair rocked on its rear legs. "You get his name?"

"No. Honest." He swiped at his wet forehead. "He probably arrived during the day shift. I'd never seen him before."

Mac spun away, hands on her hips. "Fucking idiot." She hadn't been this worried, this furious, or this helpless in a long, long time. She smoothed a hand down the back of her head, trying to think.

"What time was it?"

"Ah…almost midnight, I think. Yes, eleven fifty. I remember looking."

Mac paced back to stand between him and his desk and crossed her arms again. "Describe him. In detail."

"Ah, well…God, I-I can't rem—"

Mac lowered her face to within inches of his. "You damn well better remember."

"Er…well… A-a-a thin—a thin face. B-boney. And maybe my height and build. I'm five seven, one twenty-eight. Regular hair—I mean, brown."

"Combed how?"

"Um…from right to… No. From left to right."

"Over his forehead?"

He shook his head. "Real short, business like. Like a banker."

"A banker?"

"Yeah. And g-gray suit."

"Vest? Buttons on the jacket? Like mine? Shoes?"

"Jeez…um… No vest. A single-button jacket. Yours has two. I-I didn't notice his shoes."

"Eyes?"

"Damn. I don't think I… Well, they weren't dark. Maybe gray or…or hazel."

Mac nodded pensively as she wandered away again. "That's good." She handed him his half-empty Coca-Cola bottle. "Here, take a drink. Anything else you remember?"

The young man sighed after gulping almost all that remained. "Nothing. Before I knew it, he had his billfold open—" He flashed hopeful eyes up at Mac. "I saw a business card with trees on it, only… Well, they weren't trees. They were dollar signs, all lined up like a forest on a mountain."

"You didn't see any of the printing?"

"Uh-uh. Things moved too fast. Besides, I was impressed by the wad he was carrying."

Mac couldn't figure it out, some professional type with cash to spend but not enough to go all-out. Someone with high ambitions. Too much cash to be a G-man. Too inept to be a mobster.

"All right, now. Pay attention." She clamped a hand onto his shoulder and he straightened in the chair. "You're going to find me a vacant room. Right now. Get up." She pulled him to his feet. "Let's go." She shoved him back to the front desk. "You got a bellman handy? Someone I could wake up if I bang on your shiny brass bell here?"

He looked from his reservations register to the bell to Mac.

"Well, I-I could call back there, sure. The overnight quarters are behind the kitchen."

"Good. So, find a room. The party in two seventeen is moving to…where?"

"Er…I'm afraid, we…I'm sorry." He looked to Mac with hesitation. "We don't have anything tonight on the second floor. I'm sorry. It's one of our busiest weeks. It's entirely out of my control. It's New Year's, you—"

Mac raised a palm. "First floor, then."

"Ah…" He slid a finger down his list. "I do have a double bed with private bath in the west—"

"Done. Get your bellman up to two seventeen in half an hour and move everything into that room. We're here till Friday, so I want the first suite on the second floor that becomes available." She grabbed his chin and yanked his head around to face her. "Don't fuck this up."

"B-but how will I explain—" His eyes widened again. "You won't speak to the general manager about this, will you?"

"Trust me. That's the least of your worries right now."

CHAPTER TWENTY-FOUR

A fifty-dollar bill to the overnight auto attendant netted Mac no information or clues, but did allow her to borrow his Pontiac Big Six early the next morning. As Ellie and Katie finished breakfast in the main dining room, Mac raced to Rey's cabin.

Tearing up the forest road, she tried to picture the man and his motive, who had sent him and why. She couldn't imagine that anyone had learned of her past or Ellie's, but all her rationalizations kept returning to that premise...unless the guy just was some whacko after a beautiful woman.

A quarter-mile from the cabin, two heavily cloaked figures stepped from each side of the road and leveled shotguns at the Pontiac. She slid to a halt.

"What's your business?" one shouted.

"That you, Gill? It's me, Mac."

"Yeah, right. Get out."

Mac opened the door and raised both hands as she emerged. "Yeah, it's me. It's early, I know, and I'm in a damn hurry."

"Jeez, Mac." Gill and the other man relaxed. "Haven't seen you in ages. You came up like a house afire." He waved her on. "Go, go."

Mac sped on, the powerful motor announcing her arrival.

Rey stepped onto the porch, and Jersey, Jackson, and then Millie appeared behind her, all carrying guns. Two more faces appeared in each window, rifles ready.

Mac hurried up the steps and didn't give anyone time to speak. "Back inside. Something's come up."

"What is it?" Jersey said as they gathered in the parlor.

"I need a few of you at the Sagamore. Now. Until you guys have to go out tonight. Some clown tried to nab Ellie last night, forced his way into our room." She looked at Millie and Rey. "While I was with you. I don't know why or who he was."

"Jesus," Jersey said. "Are Ellie and Katie okay?"

Mac nodded. "Somehow, Ellie managed to shove the door on him and pretended she was going for a gun. Thank God the son of a bitch took off."

Millie set a hand on Mac's shoulder. "She must have been scared to death."

"A total mess. She didn't recognize him, didn't get much of a description, but I got some information out of the night manager."

Jackson nodded in approval. "I bet you did."

Jersey pulled a heavy sweater over her rumpled shirt. "So you're thinking this guy's still there?"

"He could be, yeah. The auto attendant said no cars came or went after midnight."

"Fuck," Jackson said and grabbed his coat off the wall hook. "Let's go."

"I'll take a bunch of us in a truck," Millie said. "We'll park in the back of the place."

Rey went to the door with Mac. "I can take my woody. It's behind the cabin."

"Good," Jackson said from the crates in the corner. "I'll take Jersey's Studebaker." He stuffed a box of bullets into his coat pocket and tossed another to Jersey.

"And, Mac, I'll ride with you," Jersey said. "You can fill me in." She turned back to the others. "We should put on the most decent things we brought. Can't be traipsing around the la-la crowd looking like thugs."

"Excuse me?" Millie said with a smirk. "*I'm* in a dress."

Rey hustled away to the bedroom. "I'll throw on my good shirt."

"I appreciate this," Mac said. "We need to play this as cool as we can." She watched Millie direct four associates in old work pants and battered wool jackets into the truck. "Might be difficult."

"Don't you worry about them." Jersey urged Mac through the door. "Step on it, and start talking."

Mac relayed every detail she had to Jersey as the Pontiac led the others back to the Sagamore. It wasn't much comfort to hear Jersey echo her own concerns about who and why someone wanted to get his hands on Ellie.

"But, Christ, Mac. No one specific comes to mind. I mean, there's no way anyone would know what Ellie did in the past, or you, for that matter. Not up here, anyway. Maybe he's just some local yokel, a boozehound after some—"

Mac shook her head. "He called her by name. *Plus*, he knew to ask for *my* last name at the desk. Whoever he is, he knows something." She pounded the steering wheel. "Shit, I hated leaving them unprotected at the hotel like this."

"Hey, they were with a ton of people having breakfast and then going with a big group for sleigh rides, right?" Mac nodded. "They'll be fine, but I'm glad you came and got us. Damn shame Rey has no telephone."

Catching up with Ellie and Katie in a crowd of guests at the horse barn brought Mac overwhelming relief. So did having eight armed associates prowling the compound. She'd handed out enough cash to a few so they could linger in the bars and dining and gaming rooms, and made it worth the auto attendant's time to keep tabs on which cars left.

Nevertheless, not knowing the bigger picture ate at her nerves, and she struggled to keep Ellie from worrying. This wasn't how a fun holiday escape was supposed to go, and Mac was determined to eliminate this hitch in their plans. Ellie and Katie deserved to enjoy themselves, and Ellie certainly didn't need a resurgence of their past and the anxiety that came with it. Mac's promise to keep her family removed from "the life" weighed heavily.

She just hoped the crew spotted him soon, because she wouldn't have its help after this evening. All these associates had to return to the cabin by nine o'clock and prepare for tonight's most critical hijacking.

But by the time they regrouped in the downstairs pub for supper, Mac's hopes had dimmed. She saw the disappointment in the faces at their table, and held out hope that the other four associates still milling around the complex would get lucky.

Katie, the brightest light among them, delighted in sharing Rey's soup, and her clapping after each spoonful seemed to entertain everyone in the place. Mac slid an arm around Ellie and squeezed.

"Highly unlikely there'll be any more trouble, sweetheart," she said, knowing Ellie couldn't trust the sentiment any more than she could. "Let's just focus on having another fun day tomorrow. Katie's had a great day today. She'll sleep like a rock again."

Ellie sat back into Mac's arm and sighed. "It *was* a relief, getting that nightmare off my mind today. I just wish we knew it was over."

"Odds are he's long gone," Millie said, her shoulder against Ellie's.

"That's right," Jersey said. "He had to be some wimp, not some heavy, because you scared him off just by saying the right thing."

Mac squeezed Ellie again and moved her wine goblet closer. "Enjoy this. Let it help ease your mind."

Jackson leaned low over the table. "Hey, Mac. Dapper old gent sitting at the bar is trying to get your attention."

Mac turned and Gordon Merriweather beckoned with a grand wave.

"I'll be back in a minute," she told the others. "Merriweather. He's an investor in Dazzle." She wiped her mouth with her napkin and stood. "*My pal.*"

Merriweather appeared mesmerized by the jazz band setting up across the room, but revolved in his chair to greet her.

"Good to see you again, Miss McLaughlin. I thought that was you over there."

"Mr. Merriweather. Good seeing you as well. Yes, the gang's all here, gearing up for the big night. May I buy you a drink, sir?"

"I don't mind if you do. That's quite kind of you. Won't you have a seat?"

"I'm afraid I can't stay long, but wanted to say hello." She waved to the bartender and ordered their drinks. "I'm surprised to see you here. I didn't expect to run into you until we met at Dazzle next summer." An unmistakable flash of suffering crossed his eyes.

"Nothing but trouble, that place is. I swear." He exhaled cigar smoke toward the ceiling.

"Not *more* difficulties, I hope?"

He shook his head. "June isn't looking too promising any more. So many issues. Your observation about it being a difficult project was on the money, young woman, and I fear my associates are reaching the end of their rope, shall we say."

"The North Woods Consortium?" He nodded as he puffed away. "You don't mean they're reconsidering the project."

"It's been one thing after another, each issue more troublesome—and expensive than the one before it. Not sure if it's wise to hold out hope, you see," Merriweather went on. "That bastard Jack Moran, the gangster, his bunch has been raising hell in the area, on top of all this."

"Isn't that Legs Diamond, the one you see in the papers all the time?"

"The same. He's finally due out of the hospital any day now, but his crew has been keeping him afloat at our expense. Many fine businesses rely on my partners' efforts, and it all trickles down to Dazzle, you know, how reliable our *resources* will be." He tapped the bar with emphasis. "The back-and-forth has been brutal, and now my associates are trying to decide whether to put a stop to Diamond's operation once and for all, or to ditch the whole idea."

"No! Oh, but cheer up, Merriweather. After all your group has invested, I can't imagine it would throw in the towel." She leaned closer. "If your partners got rid of Diamond somehow, wouldn't that solve everything?"

He pointed to her and then himself with his cigar. "You and I might think so, but to them it's all about the money they've been putting out, not to mention Diamond's track record. Who knows when they'll be rid of him."

"Good point. I've heard the jokes about him, that he gets all shot up but won't die."

"True. So true. We're spending double on resources because of him when that money should be going into Dazzle. And the way project expenses have been going lately, my associates are leaning toward an architect change as our last hope." He shook his head. "So unfortunate, too. Ours is a good man, but he's run into some terrible, extremely costly luck on this job."

"Sounds like big decisions, big changes are ahead."

Merriweather snickered and sent her a sideways look. "Like an iceberg ahead of the *Titanic*, if you ask me. Makes you lose sleep at night. I feel bad for our architect, in particular, because I believe his time is up."

"I can tell that you think highly of him."

"I do. I think Lowry's given his best, but my associates have lost patience with him. They're moving toward an older, more established firm. It's a last-gasp move."

"Lowry."

"Reginald J. Lowry III," Merriweather said with a forlorn smile. "Young man has old-school polish. He's from Cambridge, Massachusetts, you know."

Mac felt the blood drain from her face as a vengeful ghost emerged from her past. She found it difficult to speak past her racing thoughts. *Say something.*

"Lots of smart people come out of Cambridge." *How astute. Obviously, I'm not one of them.*

It took all Mac's self-control to raise her glass and swallow the whiskey. Lowry in the vicinity put a whole new slant on things. She felt her pulse quicken and her mind begin to whirl. This conversation had to end and she had to have another, much bigger one with friends she'd left across the room.

She steadied her hands and willed her breathing to level off.

"So, you think he'll be fired. That's tough, with the project so far along."

"Fired, yes, I suppose. Maybe the consortium will see a way to give him other, smaller projects, because he's very dedicated. Do you know, he even took a little place in Saratoga to stay on top of things daily? I would've invited him here tonight but couldn't reach him. Maybe his telephone hasn't been connected yet. You know how slow those things are."

"That I do," she answered, not hearing anything except that Lowry was in the wind—and local. She sighed openly and stood with her drink. "I'm terribly sorry for your difficult situation. I'll root for your good luck, Merriweather. But, in the meantime, I'm afraid I should get back to my table. I've left that crazy bunch unsupervised for too long." She offered her hand. "But I do wish you well, sir. Hopefully, you'll see clear to have a happy New Year."

Merriweather reached to an inside pocket and smiled as he handed her his business card. The North Woods Consortium insignia was embossed in dark green ink across the left side. A forested mountain of dollar-sign trees.

Merriweather took her hand. "Thank you for the drink—and for listening to the liquored ramblings of an old fool, once again."

"Not at all."

"Please look me up next summer if you're in the area. It's been a pleasure."

Mac managed a warm smile and strolled back through the assorted tables to her own.

CHAPTER TWENTY-FIVE

Timing of all this stinks to high heaven, Mac." Millie gathered her coat around her as they all walked to the Sagamore's parking area. Leaving now to prepare for the hijacking had her oddly unsettled, and she didn't like it.

Intuition told her Mac would ensure Ellie's and Katie's safety, so that left the heist as the probable cause of her unrest. And that didn't make sense. She'd participated in countless hijackings over the years, played every role. Did knowing they'd enrage the New York Mob rattle her? Was it the location, in these consuming, unforgiving forests, or was it this job's potential for killing or being killed? Maybe that was it, the severity of this particular heist that made it so unlike others in the past. Mac's gang had never been known as killers, even though a scattering of lives had been taken over the years, but tonight, by spoiling the plans of the mighty New York Mob, anything could happen, and she hoped for more strength, resolve, and pure luck than ever before. "Much rather we all be together during this."

"Sorry it's working out this way," Rey added. "Helluva night for this, and I feel bad about all of it."

"It's not your fault, Rey," Ellie said and nudged her arm. "We'll get through this." She smiled at Katie half dozing on Mac's shoulder. "I do believe we're quite safe here. *You're* the ones who need to be careful tonight."

"You really think it was Lowry?" Jackson asked Mac.

"I do now. It's been ages since I've seen him, but that description fits, and the business card."

"Just hard to imagine a wimp like Lowry would have the guts to pull what he did," Jackson added. "How would he even know Ellie? The only way is if he recognized you, saw her with you."

Millie sank onto one hip. "Yeah, but after all these years, he'd never recognize Mac. Dressing the way she dresses now?" Inwardly, she cursed their luck on this night. As if stepping on the Mob's toes wasn't serious enough, they now had a crazy man on the loose, too.

"What gets me," Jersey said, "is why bother. That stunt seems like overkill for your average bluenose with hateful thoughts. Too hard core for him, way out of his league—unless he knows about you two." She held Mac's even stare. "Unless he knows you're of *value* to his bosses."

"For a sap like that to take that much of a chance," Rey said, "he'd have to be pretty damn desperate."

Millie watched Mac's shoulders broaden as she took a deep breath. Mac appeared to temper whatever emotion had been about to emerge, and when she glanced at Rey, Millie intercepted the heavy message in her dark eyes. This deadly, irrational threat to her, her family, to all of them, actually, afforded a rare peek at the soul of the woman Millie had loved and respected for many years. And now that soul was plagued by worry and rage.

Mac lit a cigarette and exhaled a harsh stream of smoke. "Desperation's a powerful motivator."

"Obviously, the guy's not bright," Jersey said on a sigh. "Look, now we know Dazzle's in major trouble, and Lowry's on the brink. And you can bet North Woods Consortium won't use a friggin' pink slip to get rid of him. He's probably been taking the heat for a while and has to know it's not going to end well for him. Maybe he's desperate enough, stupid enough to try getting on their good side."

"You mean, after all this time," Rey said, "he thinks he'll get revenge at Mac—*and* save his own butt in the process? Maybe he has half a brain after all, killing two birds with one stone." She rolled her eyes at herself. "Sorry. That didn't sound good."

They arrived at the cars and Jersey folded her arms as she rested against her Studebaker's front fender. "Holding a grudge all this time and wanting revenge is one thing. It's something else completely, if he's trying to give Ellie or Mac or both to the Mob."

"No kidding," Millie said, looking up at Rey to explain, "because that means he knows what they're worth to them." She turned to Mac. "But how could he have learned that? You haven't seen him since you left the estate, and we didn't start up till well after that."

Jackson leaned toward Mac. "When's the last time you saw Olivia? She's the only other person who knows, the only connection."

"Wasn't it last June?" Mac asked Ellie. "When she came to the farm for Katie's birthday party?"

Ellie took a sleeping Katie into her arms. "It was. We don't see Liv that often, but she never sees Reggie. She can't stand that S.O.B., so she'd never speak to him, let alone bring up Mac's name."

Jackson rocked back on his heels. "He needs to be taken out."

Leave it to Jackson, Millie thought, dark and direct as always. Rey looked a little stunned by Jackson's cavalier approach to justice. Rey's innocence in all this was telling, and Millie appreciated Jersey's refusal to include Rey in tonight's hijacking. She'd rather Rey stay home. It was more than a matter of being recognized by any of the goons; it kept her safe and honest, free of blame for whatever might happen. That's exactly who Rey was and should always be. Jersey tossed a hand in futility. "Well, it sure looks like Lowry knows *something*."

"It looks that way," Rey said, "but what if he's just after revenge for the divorce and doesn't know anything about your hijackings or Ellie's testimony? Maybe he's clueless about all that."

"Unfortunately, there's a lot we don't know," Mac said and drew Ellie and Katie closer. "We have no idea if he's told them about us. If he tried, did his 'hot news' get their attention? Or what if he was following orders to prove it to them by delivering one or both of us? And now that he's screwed it up, will they come looking?"

"Jesus," Rey said, exhaling hard.

Jersey linked an arm with Ellie and leveled her eyes at Mac. "Don't be without your piece. I know neither of you want that, but until we fix this mess, you pack that .45, full-time."

"We know you often don't anymore," Millie said, "but think about it." She placed her hand on Katie's back. "That bastard opens his mouth about the *pretty witness who talked*, or reminds them of all those connections, the millions they lost because of some pain in the balls named Hijack Mack… Shit. One word to Luciano…" She held up a finger. "Just one."

Jackson coughed into his fist and looked around before speaking. "Like I said. We do this job tonight, then come back and take out this piece of shit."

Mac sent him a cautionary look and tossed her cigarette aside.

Millie glanced at Rey again, wondering how all of this was sitting with her, if Rey expected to hear Mac literally order an execution. Millie knew, as they all did, that Lowry would be taken care of as promptly and delicately as possible, but that Mac would never request such an act. Feeling a need to reassure Rey, Millie ran a fingertip across the back of her hand.

Mac leaned against Rey's wagon. "I have to say, this really is one damn turn of events." She sighed as she adjusted her fedora and grinned distantly. "But you know, over all the years, *through it all*, I've never doubted that each of us will do what needs to be done when the time is right. Trust has served us well and nothing's changed." She stood and slid an arm around Ellie's waist. "Ellie's right, what she said earlier. We'll get through this. We'll manage, and we appreciate everyone's effort here today. Make sure you tell the guys that when you get back."

Jersey gestured to her car. "I'm leaving the Studebaker here, Mac. You shouldn't be without wheels. The three of us will ride back with Rey."

"A lot warmer that way," Millie said and bumped her shoulder to Rey's bicep.

They turned to Rey's woody, but Millie saw Jersey take Mac's arm, and sensed what Jersey would say. An echo of her own sentiment made the whispers easy to understand.

"Bright and early tomorrow morning," Jersey told Mac. "We'll be back and take care of this once and for all. Stay sharp."

Jersey and Jackson gathered around Millie as she put a flashlight to her Bulova and confirmed that the convoy was now a full hour late. They were all frozen to the bone, waiting in the snowy woods, and seriously contemplating abandoning the heist. It was a decision Millie knew Jersey fought hard to avoid.

"Everyone's up, walking off the cold," Jackson said needlessly. "We can't hold out like this much longer."

"We have no choice and you know it."

Millie wanted to say she could hardly feel her feet anymore, but figured she wasn't the only one. "We won't be much good for anything, if they don't—"

"Lights!" an associate called from the darkness farther down the road.

"Thank God," Jackson said on a hard breath.

"I agree completely." Jersey turned to the group milling about. "Okay, everyone. Let's do it."

Associates scrambled, retrieving rifles and darting off the road, back into the cover of the woods.

"Wait on Millie's whistle!" Jersey yelled as she high-stepped in the shin-deep snow.

The rickety Model T they'd borrowed from Nettie lay on its side, angled across the road, and Sid threw himself into a prone position beside it, after dousing the snow pack with blood-like tomato juice. If it didn't stop outright, the convoy would have to inch past against the snow bank, either way enabling associates to overtake the occupants. Stationed a significant distance away, Millie knelt behind a large oak and sited the lead vehicle off her rifle, following along until the headlamps lit the area.

The impressive Chrysler led three trucks, and wasn't unexpected, considering the value of the cargo, but the car bringing up the rear *did* surprise her. She hissed the word "five" back, along the line of associates, and counted on their staging and the long monotonous drive to take the convoy off guard.

The Chrysler lumbered around the curve and slowed almost to a stop when its lights fell upon the upended car and the "injured" driver in the road. With the convoy abreast of her associates, Millie put two fingers to her lips and sent a shrill whistle into the night.

Like ants in a feeding frenzy, associates poured out of the woods onto the illuminated road, rifles poised, a multitude of voices yelling commands. But drivers and partners opened fire from both cars and all three trucks, the noise deafening, muzzles flashing, and three associates fell in the snow. Others dove for cover.

The gunfire was relentless, as truckers shot wildly, often blindly into the trees. From the dark, associates responded with more success and picked off truckers who dared lean into the light.

Millie focused on the rear car, took aim at the passenger with his rifle out the window and fired a shot that slammed him back in his seat. He tipped sideways and then slid down and out of sight. Maneuvering for a shot at the driver, she spotted Jersey far ahead, racing for cover behind their overturned car. She'd seen Sid scurry behind it when the shooting began and hoped Jersey found him unharmed. Suddenly, Jersey rose into clear view and unloaded four rounds from the B.A.R. through the Chrysler's windshield. When the blast echoes subsided, Jersey yelled over the din.

"Hold your fire! Hold your fire!"

Shots from the woods ceased but sporadic fire continued from the truckers.

"Come on out! Hands up and no one gets shot!" she shouted. "You're outnumbered. Step out!"

The scene fell silent as both sides waited. Millie tried to remember how many associates she'd seen go down. Despite their varied duties, they'd always been a close-knit group, and not knowing who'd been shot gnawed at her insides. Back when she'd been attracted by Mac's invitation to join, the appeal of "family" had been her deciding factor. To lose any would be heartbreaking. She'd shoot, kill if she had to, to defend any one of them, but sometimes, living on the edge like this asked a lot.

She itched to know their status and wondered if they still had a numbers advantage over the convoy. Hopefully, they were better shots than the truckers and hadn't lost it.

"Don't be stupid!" Jackson yelled, and Millie located him behind a large pine, midway along the road. In a blur, he slapped a replacement drum of bullets onto his Thompson. "Enough blood already. Step out now!"

Directly across from his position, a trucker with his own Thompson leaped out. Jackson edged just beyond the tree and both Thompsons fired. And each man hit his target.

Millie watched the trucker spin wildly and drop, and then saw Jackson crumble onto his face in the snow. Her heart rammed into her throat, silencing her scream.

"Everybody out!" Jersey shouted. "Now, God dammit!"

Gradually, legs and raised arms emerged from the vehicles, and associates cautiously left their secure positions to round up the remaining five men who could stand. Two more with leg wounds were dragged to the others, and as associates set about tying them, Millie scrambled onto the road and raced along the convoy to Jackson.

"Jacks!" She dropped to her knees and gripped his shoulders. "Jackson! Hang in there, Jacks!" She rolled him onto his back. A trail of bullet wounds ran from his midsection to his forehead. "Oh, no, Jacks! God, no!" She cupped his face, his cheeks still warm, and she sobbed.

Jersey fell to her knees at her side and Millie let herself be drawn into her arms. "Son of a bitch," Jersey mumbled.

"Four hits, Jers," Millie cried, refusing to let go of Jackson's arm. "Four."

"So fast, I doubt he felt much. Jesus, I hope not." She lowered her head, rubbed her eyes on her sleeve, and squeezed Millie closer. "He told me once, that this was how he wanted to go, in a blaze of glory." She stroked Millie's back. "He always did read too many novels."

Millie slumped onto her heels and grazed a finger along Jackson's goatee. "I loved this little beard," she said, her voice breaking. "I loved him, too."

"W-we all loved him, but what you guys had, past and present, was special, I know."

Millie shook her head as she cried. "Fuck, Jers. It's like a piece of me has been cut off."

"Yeah, it hurts like hell." Jersey removed a glove and closed his eyelids. "He'll always be with us, you know, the tiger in him, those haunting eyes, the way he stood up for us. He's in here," she said, gesturing to her heart.

From somewhere on the road, Millie heard Al calling out that the load transfer had been completed, and realized they'd been kneeling at Jackson's side for some time. She never heard the crew move the trucks into position or perform the heavy lifting. And she didn't care. Right now, she didn't care if she ever heard such sounds again.

Al, Sid, Louie and several others ran to them, gathered around and removed their hats.

"God damn," Al said. "I can't believe it."

Jersey hugged Millie to her again. "We have to move him, Mil. It's time to finish this and go." Millie nodded against her chest.

They wrapped Jackson's body in blankets and laid him in the truck with three wounded associates. Millie ignored Jersey's suggestion to stay with him, and in turn, ordered two associates to sit alongside the body. She wanted—*needed*—to face the men who caused this.

"Then come with me," Jersey said, the B.A.R. still tucked into the crook of her arm. "We'll leave Mr. Diamond's calling card."

Now carrying Jackson's machine gun, Millie looked around at the dark splotches in the snow as she followed Jersey to the men who were bound and chained to the trees, and decided not to travel this road again any time soon.

Jersey approached the most vocal of the truckers. "You got a really big mouth. Wanna put it to some use?" She pressed the barrel of the imposing rifle onto his boot until he winced.

All the truckers shouted back.

"Every one of you shut the fuck up. Now you, big mouth. Who sent you here ready for war?" The trucker simply stared down at his foot, not daring to move. "I asked you a God damn question!"

A trucker shouted from behind him. "Ain't saying nothing to no dyke!"

"Yeah," another snarled, "you fuckin' took out four of our guys!"

"I'll fuckin' take *you* out!" Millie screamed back and pointed the Thompson at his chest.

The trucker's mouth snapped shut, but then his cohorts started shouting.

Jersey twisted the B.A.R. barrel harder onto the trucker's foot.

"Take a good look, you son of a bitch, because unless you start talking right now, this pretty little foot's gonna be gone in one twitch of my finger." He met her eyes, his face pale. Jersey's jaw flinched. "I'll count to three and then you're crippled for life. Got it?" Tongue-tied, the trucker's mouth gaped. "Have it your way, then, and you have no friggin' idea how much this will please me. Ready? One…" He swallowed hard. "Two." His chest heaved as he sucked air. "Thr—"

"Don't!" he cried. "It-it's not…I mean…" Jersey tucked the B.A.R. under her arm and waited as he stammered. "We just g-got an env-envelope. Our pay. We don't know any names."

"Think hard. WHO?" Jersey blared into his face and he jumped.

"A-a big guy. Big. Italian. Met him a f-few times. Fancy, eh, ugly clothes. Had an accent, even."

Jersey's expression slackened. "He's a pretty greedy guy, this Italian friend of yours."

"He'll come after you for this," another trucker said, and his eyes flitted from Jersey to Millie and her Thompson.

"You think he's big enough to do it?" Millie asked and stepped closer. Punishing all of them wouldn't bring Jackson back, but definitely would relieve some of her rage.

A trucker snickered at her. "Oh, he'd have a good time with you, doll."

"So, you're a tough guy, huh?" Millie slammed the Tommy into his throat with both hands, and he fell back against his friends, choking. "How about I use this thing the right way and shoot your balls off?"

Jersey told them, "Make sure you tell your big Italian friend that this load wasn't his to take." She turned to Millie. "Anything else he should tell his friend?"

"Yeah. Happy fucking New Year, love, Jack."

CHAPTER TWENTY-SIX

Rey heard the truck before she saw it and waited until she recognized it pulling into her front yard before going out onto the porch. They were several hours late, but the crushing worry lifted from her chest when the driver's door opened and Millie slid off the seat to the ground. Jersey emerged from the other side, both of them looking worn and bedraggled, but unharmed. *Thank God.*

"Boy, you guys are a sight for sore eyes." She held the screen door open for them.

"It's been a rough night," Jersey said, stopping in the doorway. She removed her hat, and her anguish gripped Rey where she stood. "Jackson's gone."

Rey recoiled. She felt her heart leap, her breath catch, and she looked to Millie. *Is that blood on your coat?* Her ghostly pallor brought the reality of death within reach.

"Oh, my God."

Jersey exhaled hard and went inside. Millie's vacant stare made Rey hesitant to move at first, but she gently pulled her into her arms.

"I'm so, so sorry, Mil. God, I'm so sorry." Arms at her sides, her head heavy on Rey's chest, Millie felt lifeless against her, and Rey wasn't surprised by the absence of tears. The spent form said they'd already been shed. "Come inside." She urged her through the door.

Millie dragged off her hat as she went to the sofa, and dropped her coat on the floor before sitting down. She leaned forward and held her head with both hands. "Wish I could just wake up from this nightmare," she mumbled, and finally looked up at Rey. "I *am* glad to be back. Thankful."

The simple statement struck deep, and though Rey knew it was irrational to think otherwise, she still wished Millie meant it in more ways than one. This loss would leave a mark on all of them. Indestructible, they weren't, and losing someone as close as Jackson drove that point home. Mac's gang must have had its share of losses over the years, but Rey figured none compared to this.

No amount of makeup could cover the agony on Millie's face, and Rey had never felt more helpless. Nothing she could say or do would assuage the loss of such a dear friend, and Jackson and Millie certainly had been close. She knew little about their past relationship, except that they'd been young and helped each other grow, to realize that friendship mattered above all else. Jackson might have been a bit of mystery, but Rey knew she'd miss his spirit and strength, even his sinister style.

Al entered with a case of whiskey and set it down on the rug. His expression hard and resolved, he adjusted his cap before leaving. "Tullamore single-malt," he said before going back out. "Kept it for us. Jacks would've wanted some."

Jersey nodded at him and he left. She pried open the crate and pulled out a bottle. Rey hurried for glasses.

"The others will be coming in soon," Jersey said. "They're unloading the trucks in your storehouse, Rey. We visited your doctor friend on the way back, had him patch up our hits. Three minor ones." She handed drinks to Millie and Rey. "The doc has Jackson. We'll have to go back in the morning to arrange things."

"We need to tell Mac," Millie said in a droning voice.

Jersey shook her head at their plight. "As if she doesn't have a nightmare on her hands already. She's expecting all of us to show up and catch a nutcase. When she hears this, she'll…I don't know." She lifted her glass. "This is for you, Jacks. Our brother gone too soon. We love you. Rest in peace, my friend."

They saluted Jackson and Jersey refilled their glasses as Millie wiped her eyes with the sleeve of her blouse. Rey couldn't imagine the hurt coursing through her, and wished a way existed to help Millie ease the pain. Maybe they'd talk it out. Soon, Rey hoped.

Jersey started sorting bottles of the prized Irish whiskey. "We'll finish our bottle," she said, "and can each have our own, and the gang can polish off the rest. These four go to Mac to take home. We can toast Jacks every time we get together at her place."

"I like that," Millie said.

During the next hour, they emptied their bottle, mixed with stunted conversation, and Jersey stood tentatively. "I'm going up to the loft. The crew will be here any minute and I'm in no mood to rehash everything." She paused at the ladder and looked back at Millie. "If you want, I'll gather Jacks's things up here."

"I…" Millie swayed where she sat. "Go ahead. I don't think I could take seeing them."

Jersey continued her climb and Rey moved to sit beside Millie.

They'd drunk far too much of the good stuff to be talking, but Rey couldn't help herself. She ached to assure Millie that she wouldn't feel this lost forever, but didn't know where to start or if she was correct. Rey had felt lost, too, while she waited—and waited—for them to return from this damn job, and tried to remain occupied, to keep from noticing how cavernous, empty, the cabin seemed without Millie.

And those suspenseful hours had led her, inescapably, to the resolution that Millie would return to the city life she preferred, that they were bound to part ways once the job was completed. Millie's "glad to be back" didn't refer to her attraction to Rey's rustic life, of that Rey was certain. And now, Millie surely longed to be home, away from the reminders of this tragedy, and never return.

As subtly as she could, she took a steadying breath. "Are you injured anywhere?"

Millie sat back and puffed an errant strand of hair off her forehead. "No, and none of us should have been. We knew New York would load that convoy with protection. We shouldn't have been caught off guard."

"At least it's over now."

"Yeah. It's been a few years since we found ourselves in a mess like that." She wiped her eyes. "There was so much gunfire. Those guys were wild, blasting at everything. Thank God we were able to take care of things, once we recovered from the surprise."

Millie's business approach reminded Rey of Jackson's. But then, they *all* had a touch of Jackson's attitude, a survival skill, of sorts. Millie's just came packaged with gumption and a smile. She wasn't smiling now, however.

"Oh, Rey." She closed her eyes and dropped her head. "He'd had a tough life since he was a little boy, and only let a few of us past that hard shell. You felt special, grateful, being one of those, being let in. You give back without a second thought."

"I caught some of that, although I wish I'd had the chance to know him better."

"You never think about this happening to you or someone you care about. How are we supposed to cope with it, when it does?"

Rey laid an arm across Millie's back. "I don't know, but we do, somehow. And Jackson would want that."

"Yeah." Millie's mouth formed a painful little smile. "Yeah, he'd want us to knock it off and get to work." She looked up at Rey, besieged and sad. "Helluva business, isn't it? When it comes down to kill or be killed, what does that say?"

"That caring about someone else over yourself comes first. My guess is all of you have stories similar to Jackson's. You all give back so unselfishly. No matter the cost."

"Tonight, that cost grew pretty steep, Rey."

"I-I was worried."

Millie rested a palm on Rey's chest and the gesture nearly stole away her thought. They flustered her, Millie's touches, made her heart skip and conversation difficult. "It's a...a pretty helpless feeling, sitting around here just waiting and wondering, not able to do anything," she covered Millie's hand with her own, "not knowing if you'd been hurt."

"The job didn't turn out a one hundred percent success, but we did come out on top, and it's over. It's sweet of you to worry, but I'm sorry you did."

"Oh, don't be sorry, Mil. I worried becau—" Rey stopped at the sound of many voices about to disrupt their moment. "I guess they'll be coming in now. It *is* after four o'clock."

"I need to collect myself and get to bed. We're all going to need strength tomorrow." Millie struggled to her feet and rocked back on her heels. Rey quickly rose and steadied her. "Thanks. Past my bedtime. Past my limit, is more like it."

"This way," Rey said and led her by the hand to the bedroom. "I dug out the winter comforter, so you should be plenty warm. Try to get some sleep."

Millie answered around a yawn. "You, too."

"I will. I'm just going to stoke the stove and—"

"I should help you."

"No," Rey insisted and took Millie's hands in hers. "Thank you, but you're not too steady on your feet. Besides, the last time you did that, you burned your fingers."

"No, no. Not fair to you. I know how." Side-stepping around Rey, Millie stumbled. "Damn. Lemme show you."

Rey slid an arm around her waist and drew her in. How easy it would be to hold her like this all night. And on *this* night, Millie might welcome the closeness. On the other hand, in her current state, she might not.

"Thank you, Mil, but no. Don't worry about the damn stove. You've had a long night and need to get to bed."

Millie peered up at her, obviously trying to focus. "I hate it when you're more stubborn than me."

"I'm sure you do," Rey said. "I'm the stubborn ol' bear, remember." Rey felt her weaken and wrapped a second arm around her.

Millie's cheek dropped to Rey's chest. "You are a stubborn ol' bear," she mumbled, "stubborn ol' honey bear, and I like you a lot. Thanks for holding me up."

"I like you a lot, too." Rey bent at the knees, counting on them to survive the quiver Millie just delivered, and lifted Millie into her arms. "You need bed."

Millie raised her head sleepily. "You're carrying me?"

"Just your imagination."

"Uh-uh."

"Sure it is."

"I don't feel my feet on the floor."

"Doubt you'd feel them if they were." Rey laid her on the bed and set a pillow beneath her head.

"Maybe I'm tired."

"Maybe." Rey shook out the comforter over her. "Stop talking and go to sleep."

"You sleep, too." Practically asleep already, Millie reached out and snared Rey's hand.

Looking down at her in the dim light spilling from the parlor, Rey fought the overwhelming desire to kiss her. This is no fairy tale, she thought, especially after a night like this. And there was no happily-ever-after ending on the horizon, not when there were two vastly different horizons. This was too real and just as dangerous as what happened on that road. *If only our stars had crossed differently.*

Millie's eyes were closed, the remnants of her makeup just a faint reminder of how valiantly, how typically she'd tackled tonight's mission. Rey lightly swept more curls from her forehead and dared herself to stroke the satin of her face.

"You'll be my princess who got away, won't you, Miss Anderson?" she whispered. She lingered a moment longer, enchanted by the easy set of her mouth, the plush texture of her lips.

"Rey," Millie murmured as she drifted off.

Rey bent lower and kissed her lips as lightly as she dared and reeled to feel Millie respond.

Millie's hand slackened in her grip, and Rey slipped it beneath the comforter.

❖

"One of the most emotional days I've ever experienced," Ellie said, and conversation paused as the Sagamore waiter delivered fresh drinks and cleared their table of empty ones. "One minute, you're escorting us everywhere like royalty, and the next I'm crying

my eyes out in the powder room. Repeating that all day takes a toll."
She patted Millie's hand. "Thank you for stealing Katie away during
my breakdowns."

"Thank you for understanding when I had mine," Millie said,
"but keeping up appearances was a bitch. We kept filtering through
the crowd, searching, and kept our teary faces from being seen too
long in one place."

"I almost slugged a groundskeeper." Rey tossed a thumb
toward the wall of windows. "I thought he was going to throw a fit
when Mac rolled up a snowman and exposed the grass."

Mac sent her a thumbs-up. "Nice restraint, Rey. Katie was in
her glory."

Mac smiled her first easy smile of the day. Instead of jumping
into the family snow sculpture contest after breakfast, Mac first
endured a torrent of tears at the death of her long-time friend.
Together with Jersey and Millie, she arranged transport for Jackson's
body back to Boston, and for all of them to attend funeral services
on Friday. Zim broke down when Mac reached him by telephone.

Rejoining her family and participating in the snow games with
an uplifting attitude had been unbearably hard. She'd held out hope
all day that *some* good news would boost her mood, but flooding the
Sagamore compound with associates did not raise a trace of Lowry.
She swung her thoughts to their family time and did her best to
remain strong, hoping that the worst now was past.

"Katie wore herself out," she said. "I think she was sound
asleep before I even left the nursery."

"Isn't bread and butter her favorite?" Rey asked. "She didn't
finish that."

"In my opinion, the animal competition was rigged," Millie
said bitterly, her anger with the world still simmering. "Your snow
cow deserved the blue ribbon, not the dog those bratty kids made."

"They were bratty, weren't they?" Jersey said, frowning as
she rejoined them. Mac noted her discreet nod and knew she had
dismissed the last quartet of associates still prowling the compound.
At nine thirty, she agreed they'd put in a long day, particularly after
last night's trauma.

"I thought they were too," Ellie said. "Thank God Katie's not like them."

"All I know is that the slush cones helped me get through the day," Rey confessed.

Millie poked her side. "The grown-ups' slush cones were spiked, weren't they?"

"Bourbon. I had four of them."

Ellie exclaimed, "Four? How'd you function all day?"

Mac tipped toward her. "Remember, they were on the job since breakfast, honey."

Jersey swirled the ice cubes in her glass. "Too bad it didn't get us anywhere."

"Well, I'm pretty convinced Lowry left," Ellie stated. "I mean, as you've all said, he was scared away by the *idea* of a gun, so I agree. He's not brave enough to try again."

"Absolutely," Rey said. "The brave ones are here, at this table."

"Excuse me, ladies and gentlemen." A waiter appeared at Mac's shoulder and handed her a small sheet of Sagamore stationery. "A note for you." Mac tipped him a dollar and unfolded the paper. *Urgent. See me immediately. Vincent Davison, Night Manager.*

Mac looked at everyone quickly and gripped Ellie's hand. "I'll be right back, okay, sweetie?" Wordlessly, she implored her, waited for her reluctant nod. She kissed her and stood up. "Jers." Jersey rose alongside her and they hustled out of the lively dining salon.

Waiting for her in the middle of the lobby, Davison looked almost as frantic as he had the night before. "Miss McLaughlin." She saw his hand quiver as he pointed. "I just saw him again. The man I told you about. He went down the east corridor."

"Where'd he come from?" Jersey asked sharply as they hurried in that direction.

"Er…" Davison turned in a circle as if lost in his own hotel. "The nursery."

Mac and Jersey nearly fell over each other, coming to a sudden halt.

"Jesus!"

Mac raced down the opposite hall, Jersey right behind her, and they roared into the plush, silent room, where nearly a dozen youngsters slept in cribs. Knowing exactly where she'd checked on Katie less than a half hour earlier, Mac ran to the crib and felt all the air rush from her lungs. Katie was gone. Mac gripped the rail with both hands so hard, it cracked against the strain.

"NO!"

"Fuck no!" Jersey gasped.

"NO! NO! Oh, God, no!" Mac buckled, and Jersey threw an arm around her waist.

"Excuse me, you two!" The nursery matron hurried to where they stood, hissing and waving a scolding finger at Mac. "You be silent! Don't you know—"

Mac seized her by the shoulders. "Where's Katie?" she screamed. "You're responsible!" The woman shrieked when Mac shook her violently. "Where is she, God dammit?"

Jersey pried Mac's hands off the frail shoulders, and the matron staggered at the release. She looked into the empty crib and her hands flew to her face.

Jersey grabbed Mac's arm and pulled her into a sprint. "Come on! Run! Maybe we can catch the sonovabitch!"

They bolted across the lobby and down the east corridor.

"Do we check these rooms?" Mac yelled as they ran past doors she could barely see.

"Just maintenance shit!" Jersey shouted back. She blew through the fire door and stopped dead in the snow, Mac a half-second behind. Their expelled breaths fogged the air. "He wasted no time." Car and truck tracks went in all directions, but there were no vehicles in sight.

"FUCK!" Mac screamed into the night, and collapsed to her knees. "God help her, Jers." She sobbed into her hands. "Not this, our little girl!" She looked up, struggled to see Jersey through her tears. "She's so little, she'll be s-so scared." Mac dropped so low, her head hit the snow. "Fuck, Jers. It's…I did this to her."

Jersey wrapped her arms around Mac's quaking shoulders and drew her up. "No, Mac. You're wrong." Mac couldn't breathe. Her heart pounded so hard she expected it to explode. "Hey, we'll find her. Katie will be all right." She held Mac out at arm's length and gave her a shake. "Come on, boss. Where's your fucking fight, huh?"

Mac forced in a ragged icy breath. Her hands trembled, as did her voice. "Jesus, I have to—how am I going to tell Ellie?"

"You just will." Jersey pulled her toward the door. "Don't break down on me now, Mac." She leaned in close enough to kiss her. "I'm going to open this door, so pull yourself together. For Katie and Ellie." Trying to wring out her eyes, Mac squeezed them shut for a moment and took another breath. She needed a level head and sharp mind, now more than at any time in her life. Jersey raised an eyebrow. "Ready?"

"Shit, no, but go."

CHAPTER TWENTY-SEVEN

Lowry sat in the near darkness of the Dazzle workhouse, sweating from the wood stove he'd managed to start. He took another swig from the CC bottle on his work table and continued listening for just the right sound in the desolate woodsy construction site outside. Almost an hour passed before it came, the distinctive rumble of a large expensive automobile. He hoped Bocci had come alone, as he'd cryptically instructed on the phone.

Lowry opened the door two inches and peered into the dimness. Bocci left the luxurious confines of his Packard, and picked his way across the uneven, snow-covered terrain in his three-hundred-dollar Italian wingtips. "So nice to see you again, Lowry," he growled. "Been looking for you. This better be good."

"Keep your voice down. And yes, it's good."

Bocci's formidable presence filled the small shack. He grinned like a fiend before hanging up his coat and dropping into one of the two available chairs.

"So. Long time no see." He nodded at the whiskey bottle. "Start pourin'. I left the finest piece of ass I've had in ages just to drive way the fuck out here, so let's hear why you're so fired up you can't talk straight. And what's with the dim light? Turn that up." He squinted at the kerosene lamp and took the glass from Lowry. "So, where you been lately, huh? You wouldn't be hiding out, would you?"

"Shh. Lower your voice," Lowry hissed. "Forget the lamp. And I've been...busy."

"Busy. Well, you ain't started talkin' yet, and I ain't happy enough yet to sit here in your mood light, so what the fuck?"

Lowry jutted his chin toward the pile of blankets on the workbench against the far wall.

Bocci glanced over his shoulder. "Yeah? Blankets. So what? Y'wanna get cozy or somethin'? Didn't take you for a swisher, Lowry, and you *know* I ain't no perv."

"No, Frank, God dammit. Over here. Look." With Bocci looming behind him, Lowry approached the pile, delicately moved a corner of the blanket aside, and revealed a child's blond curls and the side of her face. She slept on undeterred.

Bocci straightened like he'd been shot. His face aghast, he backed away until his legs hit his chair, and then sat, hard.

Lowry reveled in the reaction. "She cried for a while and called for her mama, but fell back to sleep on the ride here." He could feel Bocci's stare on his skin as he reclaimed his seat.

"Ho-ly shit!" Bocci gushed as gently as he could. "What the fuck is that? I mean, what the fuck you doing with some kid?"

"Better question: How does Meyer Lansky show his gratitude?"

"Huh?"

Lowry poured more into their glasses and sat back. "With this kid, you can get your hands on the local gang boss who's behind the product losses."

"What? This is Legs's kid?"

"Who?" The name caught Lowry off guard. "Oh, you're thinking Legs Diamond? Oh no, no. Hardly."

"So you mean it's been somebody else hitting us all along? You gotta be shitt—"

Lowry held up a hand. "Wait, there's more. Just so happens, it's the same one who cost Luciano and his pals millions a few years ago in Boston, when the Feds raided all the locals."

The distant look on Bocci's face said he was laboring to recall the event, but finally, he bobbed his head, his eyes wide.

"Yeah, I do remember now. Yeah. Helluva show, families fightin' because each was jacking from the other. Lots of big money connections went down in that." He moved to the edge of his seat.

"So, you sayin' they were all set up? And you know who was behind it? *You* know?"

Lowry wasn't positive that "Hijack Mack" was actually Elizabeth McLaughlin, but this was a gamble for his life. Plus, the prospect of finally eliminating the sick bitch, combined with Bocci's astonished respect made the risk all the more worth taking.

Lowry sipped his whiskey, feeling emboldened like never before. "And that same person is up here now, behind all our product losses. Doing it all over again."

"You know this guy?" Bocci tossed a thumb toward the workbench. "And this is his kid?"

Lowry simply nodded, ridiculously pleased by the amazement on Bocci's face.

Bocci glanced at the workbench again, and then back at Lowry. He shook his head and smiled. "Well, fuck me."

"There's quite a story behind it all, so settle back. We've got plenty of time." Lowry relaxed and crossed his legs. "The child's untraceable, so don't worry. I'm counting on you to find a suitable place where we can wait for our fish to take the bait."

Bocci chuckled and shook his head again.

"Didn't think a little shit like you had it in you, Lowry. I may have to rethink my plans for you." He took two cigars from his jacket pocket and handed him one. "Cause for a little celebration here. I want this guy alive to give to Lansky. Gotta say, it'd be nice to go up a notch with him. It takes a lot though, so you better produce, cause, holy shit, man, you got one helluva situation here."

"Find us a map." Mac squeezed night manager Davison's shoulder as he sat surrounded at his desk. "If you thought our little 'encounter' last night was rough, just wait."

"But I *have* to call the police." He blindly pulled a road map from his center drawer. "A child has been kidnapped. I'll lose my job if I don't notif—"

"Give me that." Jersey grabbed the road map from him, and he tried pleading his case to her.

"Seriously, I *have* to call."

"Shut up." Jersey cleared his desk with one sweep of her arm and flung open the map.

"There are only a couple roads out of this area," Rey said, running her finger along the blue lines.

"Well, we have two vehicles," Millie observed.

"Doubt he'd go north," Jersey said at Mac's shoulder.

"Ah, excuse me?" Davison interrupted, looking from one face to the other.

Millie grumbled. "He's too much of a pansy to venture into scary mountains alone."

"Not too much of a pansy to kidnap a little girl," Jersey countered.

Mac tightened her arm around Ellie, who stood trembling with a handkerchief at her nose. "Merriweather did say the sonovabitch took a place in the area, but…"

"He could be anywhere, even Saratoga," Rey muttered.

"That'd be his style," Mac said.

"Unfortunately," Millie said, "the only place *we* know to look would be…" She pressed a finger to the name on the map, "Luzerne."

"Er… Look, I'm sorry to interrupt," Davison tried again, "but I'm required to call the police."

Jersey's head snapped up. "Shut up, dammit."

Frantic, Davison reached down for the telephone. "But you don't understand." He pulled it toward him along the floor. "I have to do this." He set the phone on his lap and put the receiver to his ear.

Jersey's Colt .45 suddenly appeared in his face. "You don't listen well, do you?" She used the gun's long barrel to swing the receiver aside.

Millie grabbed the phone, ripped it from the wall, and tossed it into the corner with a loud, ringing crash. Davison fell back in his seat.

"Well, okay. Luzerne, then," Rey said, frowning at the map. "We have to start somewhere."

Mac tossed her head toward the lobby, and everyone backed away from the desk and filed out. Mac hovered in the doorway while Jersey dealt with Davison.

"This is a private matter, Vincent," she told him evenly, deliberately posing with her Colt in her folded arms. "You have a talk with that nursemaid and get your damn stories straight. Understand what I'm telling you?"

Davison sat forward cautiously. "I-I believe I do, but I could get fired. They could fire us both, if—"

"Could've lost a whole lot more than your damn job last night, but you didn't, did you?"

She leaned on his desk with the Colt. Davison's eyes kept bouncing to it. The gun's menacing size left a distinct impression beyond the dent she'd pressed into the wood.

"Listen carefully, Vincent. Okay?" She waited for his nod. "Good. See, you're off the hook here, because the family flat-out refuses to involve the police. And that means your hands may be tied, but they're clean. Got it?" He nodded again, and she tapped his shoulder with the Colt barrel. "Very good. And don't you worry. We're coming back, and we'll be sure to speak to the right people. You and that nurse just keep in mind that nobody, not this family, not you and her, and definitely not this posh resort, *nobody* wants this kind of publicity. Do they?"

Davison just stared up at her, hands gripping the armrests for all he was worth.

"*Do they*?" Jersey closed in and he recoiled. She pressed her cheek to his, facing the Colt she held up for his inspection. "A gun this size can be very persuasive, don't you think?"

"Y-yes."

"So, I'm going to ask you one more time, and I think you'll answer because you're a bright guy. You're a night manager, after all." She slammed the Colt flat to his chest and Davison gasped. "No one wants to hear anything about this, do they Night Manager Davison?"

Shivering now, Davison shook his head. "N-no."

"Excellent." She straightened, holstered the Colt, and socked him in the arm. "See you soon, Vinny."

❖

The seldom-traveled lumber road Rey chose to Luzerne took them on a winding course through dense forest, and Millie braced herself with a palm against the passenger door.

"This woody of yours sure can fly. You know this road, huh?"

"Sh. I'm concentrating." Rey wrangled the wagon through the deep snow, sliding around curves, her leather gloves squeaking on the wheel. She sped up on a straightaway and eyed Jersey's headlamps in the rearview mirror.

She saw Millie look back and check for herself. Cutting through the cloud of flying snow, the Studebaker ran less than two lengths behind, and the big lights made her blink. She sat back and stared into the onrushing darkness. "Sure as shit hope he has Katie at this place."

Rey felt her studying her profile and wondered if Millie saw the fear pumping through her veins. Her nerves jangled so hard, she surprised herself by asking, "There's going be a killing tonight, isn't there?"

"Oh, you got that right. Won't be much left of that bastard when Mac's done."

Rey skidded sideways around a turn and struggled to keep the woody on the road. *Best to just think about driving.*

She pointed ahead. "A ways up, there's an access lane cut through the woods, going into the site from the back." She pumped her brakes to signal Jersey, slowed to a stop, pocketed a flashlight from her glove box, and shut off her headlamps. Jersey followed suit, got out and hurried to her trunk. Rey and Millie joined her, and thankfully, Mac arrived with her own light.

Rey watched with fascination as Jersey unwrapped a burlap bundle of guns and handed a Thompson to Mac, a shotgun to

Millie, and loaded her B.A.R. Rey didn't expect Jersey to hand her a box of shotgun shells. *How'd she know about the gun I hide in the woody?*

Mac grabbed an extra .38. "I know Ellie isn't happy with me right now, but... She'll be able to protect herself, that's for sure." She glanced up at Rey and then Millie as she loaded the gun. "We argued about it, driving here," she explained, "and El's furious about staying in the car, but I don't care. She shouldn't even be here. For God's sake, I promised her we'd never face this craziness again, and look at this mess. So, I'm damn sure not leaving her defenseless."

"Mac," Millie said and took hold of her arm. "I'll stay with Ellie. We'd all feel better about it, right? I would and so would you. Can the three of you manage?"

"We will."

Rey stared at Millie, thinking she was the bravest woman she'd ever met. "I can't imagine you're—"

"You just go and be safe," Millie said, prodding Rey's chest. "You guys just go and take care of this. And...and fucking hurry."

Jersey closed the trunk with a soft click. "Listen. Just a thought about all this firepower. Until we know where Katie is... Let's be careful."

Now in near complete blackness, the vehicles crept along the lane, curled around the last bend, and shut down to roll the last few yards in silence. Dazzle's sprawling silhouette rose through a significant buffer of woods.

"Just what we need right now," Millie muttered to Ellie, "a dark and spooky shell of a building. At least it's not old enough to be haunted."

Mac turned around and knelt on her seat. "Keep that blanket over you both and stay warm."

Millie patted the shotgun beneath it that spanned their laps. "We're all right."

"Pretty damn ticked off," Ellie answered heavily, "but fine."

Mac reached over the seat and drew her closer. She kissed her tenderly, mutual tears wet each other's cheeks.

"Oh, Mac. Are these tears? I've been crying for all three of us, baby. Don't you lose it, too." She wiped away Mac's tears with her fingertips.

"Don't worry," Mac said and managed a wry smile. "He won't hurt her, honey. He's just using her to get something else."

"Yes. Me." Ellie fought back a sob.

"Or me. But he's damn sure going to get something else, and Katie'll be back with us in no time. Just sit tight and keep your eyes open, okay?"

"I love you, Mac."

"And I love you, Ellie. More than the air I breathe." She kissed her again, praying she soon would have the loves of her life safe at her side.

CHAPTER TWENTY-EIGHT

They hustled through the woods to the packed terrain closer to the construction scene and silently assessed the tiny workhouse and the Packard and LaSalle parked on the drive.

Mac pretended to blow smoke from a cigarette upward and pointed at the little building. Jersey stared harder at it until she nodded at the wood smoke rising from the chimney. She drew a flat circle in the air and they separated to surround the building, maneuvering behind trees, machinery, and supply stockpiles for cover. Mac raced across open ground to the side of the workhouse, while Rey settled behind a steam shovel, and Jersey dashed around the Packard.

Mac liked their odds as well as the lines of sight all three of them had to the workhouse and, if needed, Dazzle. Evidence of heat in the little building made it Mac's sole objective, but now she worried about a Thompson barrage penetrating the simple construction. Jersey's B.A.R. would reduce the shack to kindling. Whoever had Katie in there knew it, too, and obviously was smarter than Lowry. She ran to Jersey's position to air her concern.

"We can't fire on the shack, I agree," Jersey said in a hush. "But we could wait him out. I know it's not my most brilliant idea, but he'll have to move her before workers start showing up in the morning."

"Let him have Katie that long? No. Not brilliant."

"Door's open." A shotgun muzzle protruded from a slim opening in the workhouse door, and a blast clanged off the steam shovel. Smoke hung in the opening, backlit by faint, amber lamplight.

"You in the shack!" Jersey shouted. "Stop the stupid shit. Bring the girl out and no one gets hurt!"

Beside her, Mac snorted. "Fuck that. Soon as I get the shot I want—"

"Took you fellows long enough to get here," a booming baritone answered. The shotgun reappeared and fired in their direction. "Think I ain't serious?"

"That's no wimpy voice," Jersey mumbled, glaring at the doorway. "Wonder who he is."

"You guys looking for a sweet little thing, maybe?" The man's deep laugh echoed through the pines. "We're going to have us a chat. The sooner you see I'm serious, the better."

"Definitely an Italian accent," Jersey said. "New York truckers last night, they have an Italian mob boss up here."

Mac responded without looking away from the door. "Half the gangsters in the damn world have Italian bosses."

"Hey, Reggie Lowry!" Jersey called. "We know you're in there! Bring us the girl, Lowry! Bring her outside and step away."

The Italian laughed again. "How about you come and check the merchandise?"

Mac shouted from her crouch. "She better be all right or you're fuckin' dead!"

Jersey gave her arm a squeeze and shook her head. "He's fucking dead anyway. Don't be taking his bait."

The Italian yelled, "Ready to talk trade?"

Now Rey yelled from across the clearing. "Stop stalling, bring out the girl and step aside!"

Jersey hissed at Mac. "There it is. A trade."

Mac couldn't think about that at the moment. The picture of Katie, terrified and lost, wouldn't leave her mind.

"Time you faced some music, Bocci," Rey added.

"Who the fuck are you?" he yelled back, and Katie's soft cries drifted from the workhouse.

Mac tensed. Despite the cold, her hands had begun to sweat on the Thompson. "I'll kill these guys if it's my last act on Earth."

Jersey squeezed her arm again. "Sounds like Rey's recognized this goon. You just stay steady. You'll get your chance. I promise."

Mac took a deep breath. At least she knew Katie was alive.

"Bring the girl out!" Rey shouted.

Bocci shot at the steam shovel again. "*I'm* in charge here! You out there, McLaughlin? Ready to give some maid service, Hijack Mack? Come out with your skirt up, you homo perv!" Laughing, he swung the door open.

"I can take him right now," Mac growled.

Lowry moved into view, holding a crying Katie wrapped in a blanket. He stepped in front of Bocci.

Mac lunged to her feet, but Jersey yanked her back down behind the car. "Don't be an idiot!"

"Hey!" Bocci began, and pointed at Katie with the shotgun. "This what you're looking for? Well, this is what's going to happen. Too claustrophobic in this cardboard box, so we're going to take a little walk over to my hotel, okay? Us three. And *Daddy* is going to join us for a get-together. You catch all that?"

Every nerve in Mac's body knotted. Lowry had finally figured it all out. Who she was, who Ellie was, their connection, and their past. And he'd talked to the Mob. Life, family, home, none of it would ever be the same.

"What the fuck?" Jersey said. "He's calling you Daddy. The sonovabitch expects you to—"

Katie's crying penetrated Mac's racing thoughts, swirled around her heart, and squeezed. Katie would come out of this unscathed. Whatever it took.

"I'll do it. I'll go." She offered her Thompson to Jersey.

"The hell you will." Jersey waved the gun away.

"No. Here." Mac thrust the rifle toward her again. "If it'll get Katie away—"

"And you'll what? Go have tea with Lucky at the Waldorf? Take them down with your bare hands?" She shoved the Thompson back. "This is going to end our way. Knock this shit off."

Shielding himself behind Lowry and Katie, Bocci ushered them outside and onto the Dazzle veranda. He opened one of the three massive center doors, and backed them into the casino and out of sight.

In the black void of the grand lobby, Bocci hurried to a window and mumbled instructions to Lowry without taking his eyes off the open area out front.

"You took that flashlight from the shack, right? Take her downstairs and hide her in the alcohol vault. And seal the fucking door. I'm not listening to her shit any more tonight."

"We're just going to get McLaughlin and go. We don't need—"

Bocci whirled on him. "Do what I said!" He turned back, shivering as he squinted into the night.

Carrying Katie to the basement, Lowry remembered the painstaking effort, the detail he incorporated into the secret chamber. Thanks to Prohibition, every such establishment had one. The vault door was several inches thick of solid beech and disguised as a wall next to the laundry. The ideal hiding place. *Jesus, no one would have reason to open it until spring.*

Above him, he heard Bocci yell from the front window again. "Come on in, *Daddy*, and step on it. I'm fed up with the kid's bawlin'!"

Lowry heard him fire and wondered if he hit anyone. Katie cried incessantly in his arms, and thrashed inside the blanket. She had a case of the hiccups, too, and that aggravated Lowry even more, reminded him of how utterly helpless he was in this situation.

Another blast sounded, and then two more. By now, Bocci *had* to have eliminated a few friends of that sick bitch. "Vindication," he said to bolster his nerve.

He set Katie on the wood floor of the vault and backed out. She was screaming as he turned the flashlight away and swung the heavy door shut. Silence returned to the basement and brought calm to his senses. He rushed back up the stairs, listening to Bocci spout off again at the window.

"We're waiting, *Daddy*! You know, the kid's been okay until now. Too bad her mommy isn't here. Oh, wait. Are you a mommy, too, or just her daddy? Bet you can't even tell anymore, can you?" He took a breath and yelled even louder. "You fucking hearing me? We're getting impatient just like the little brat! So you get the fuck over here before I lose my fuckin' temper!"

Having run to the rear of the building, Mac still could hear his threats, and she wondered if they carried as far as Ellie and Millie in the car. But the shouting helped, because as Bocci roared, Mac hammered a rock onto a pry bar Jersey held until she broke open the freight door lock.

After pausing to listen and let their eyes adjust to the dark of the cellar, she and Jersey climbed the stairs, silent and grateful for the lack of creaks in the fresh pine. The building was still little more than a maze of broad, lengthy hallways and hollow rooms that amplified every breath, including those grumblings in the front lobby.

From what resembled the future kitchen, they made their way through a cavernous space, a formal dining salon, no doubt, and edged toward its opening at the grand foyer. They managed to discern Bocci pacing at the windows like a caged animal, head swiveling in constant surveillance, his attention never leaving the clearing out front. Behind him, seated on the impressive central staircase, Lowry sat wringing his hands.

Mac flexed her fingers around the Thompson, reacting to the sight of him, calling on every last ounce of self-control to keep from splattering his brain on the steps. But not before she found Katie. Jersey elbowed her and mimicked rocking an infant, then tapped her ear. There was no sound of Katie now and they peered out into the lobby, searching as best they could.

Bocci took a long swig of CC, set the bottle on the windowsill, and reached into his coat. "Lowry, take my .38. You ever shoot a gun?" Lowry stared at it, turned it over in his hands, and Bocci snickered. "Didn't think so. Well, you better when the time comes, God dammit. I ain't going down on this scheme of yours."

"You were quite enthusiastic a while ago."

"Well, this is for the birds. Who knows how many guns they got out there. They've been smart about what they show."

"Maybe we should've stayed in the workhouse. It was warmer."

"And where would we have stashed the kid, huh? Genius architect. I should've dumped you long ago. In fact, I got a mind to take her *and you* for a ride right now…if only I's sure about what's out there."

Considering Lowry's profession, Mac now feared finding Katie here could take hours. He designed the place, knew every potential hiding spot.

Bocci opened the window again and yelled. "I'm done waiting, *Daddy*! It's time we gave the kid a real reason to cry!" His voice dropped to a muffled growl. "Pay attention, Lowry. That's gonna get the perv to come to us. Go make sure the cellar is clear for us to get out. And leave the kid down there. We'll come back for her later."

Lowry gingerly tucked the .38 into his coat pocket and left by way of the grand salon. Mac and Jersey watched him go, heard him shuffle through the dark and descend the stairs.

Mac pressed her mouth to Jersey's ear.

"A minute head start and he's all yours. I'm going after Katie." She watched Jersey go to one knee and aim the B.A.R. at Bocci's back. No longer worried about his fate, Mac headed for the staircase and made her way down in a crouch.

❖

Wishing she had Mac's slim physique, Rey pressed herself as flat to the wall as she could and edged inward from her corner of the veranda. Bocci's shotgun protruded from the window like a ship's cannon, now only several feet away. She counted on her agility and strength to get to it the second he began another tirade. *But then what? If he pulls out a handgun…* Eyes locked on the motionless gun barrel, she focused her energy on repaying all the damn misery he caused.

"So!" Bocci yelled at a bone-rattling volume, so close that Rey almost fell from her pose. She took a breath and geared her muscles to pounce. "You want me to punish the kid, you sick perv? Time you paid the price to the big boss. Hijack Mack's all done!"

"*You're* done." It was Jersey's voice from inside, and as Bocci spun to her, Rey lunged and yanked away his shotgun—just as Jersey unloaded.

The impact blew Bocci backward through the window and into Rey, knocking both her own shotgun and Bocci's from her hands and sending her tumbling off the veranda. Scrambling to her feet, she watched him writhe amidst shards of glass, gasping for air and pawing at the grotesque hole in his stomach.

Jersey appeared at the shattered window and finished him on the spot. She looked out at Rey, her trademark devil-may-care expression exchanged for one of steadfast, resolute calm. The split-second turn of events left Rey stunned. She'd never witnessed a scene like this, never been a part of a gang takedown, yet here she was, standing with blood splattered on her coat and pants, and murder at her feet. And still, Jersey loomed tall in her eyes.

"Jesus, Rey. That was close. I didn't know you were right here. I almost hit you."

"Yeah," Rey said, trying to blot that image from her mind. "I-I'm glad you didn't."

"Katie's in the basement somewhere, and Mac's followed Lowry down. I'm going after her. You take the back."

Rey gathered her wits as she ran around the building, no easy feat on a snow-covered construction site with one puny flashlight. She didn't expect to see Mac bolt out of the freight door, and they barely avoided a collision.

Just as winded as Rey, Mac pointed toward the woods and grabbed Rey's arm. "Get that fucker for me." She spun back inside.

Rey took off for the tree line, unable to remember the last time she'd run this much. But thoughts of her truck-horse breathing quickly changed when she realized she didn't like *this* setup at all. The forest blackness ahead was where they had come onto the site, and their cars—and Millie and Ellie—weren't that far away.

Halfway through the forest buffer, she switched off the flashlight and stopped to listen. She muffled her heavy breaths long enough to strain—in vain—to hear movement. Fumbling on, barely able to avoid trees and maintain her own silence, Rey focused on the lightening in the woods ahead, the truck lane where they'd parked. Voices carried to her as she neared the edge of the trees, and she stopped before venturing into the open. Two figures stood beside the Studebaker, one holding a gun to the other's back.

"Ellie," Rey murmured. "God damn." And no sign of Millie.

Rey hefted her shotgun and clicked off the safety.

"Now you hold your friggin' horses! You just wait one God dammed, fucking minute!"

Hearing that attitude in that Boston accent, Rey grinned in the dark.

Millie's diminutive form burst out of the car, a jumble of blanket in her arms. "Look, fella, you can't just appear out of nowhere and *take* somebody! Who the fuck you think you are?"

"Shut up, lady!" Lowry said and inched Ellie backward. "She's coming with me. This isn't about you."

Stalking forward, undaunted, Millie waved her arm in outrage. "Of *course* it is, you sick bastard!"

Lowry drew Ellie back another step. "Listen, bitch, whoever you are, get back in the car! I-I've got a gun here!"

"Oh big deal. A wimpy ass with a wimpy-ass gun! Bet your dick ain't half as big! Now you listen to *me*, you sonovabitch!" She shook her fist as she advanced. "She's a friend of mi—"

"You better shut the hell up and back off!"

"If you think for one minute, I'm gonna let you sneak up here, whip her out of this car with your wimpy-ass gun, and just waltz her off into the night, you've got a fuckin' screw loose!" She wrestled with the blanket against her coat as she raged at him. "Too damn cold out and I'm in no mood to be playing games."

She flung the blanket over his gun, heaved the bundle up into his face, and kicked him where it counted. As he howled from his knees, she pressed the .38 to his forehead and cocked it.

"Gotcha, you miserable dumb fuck," she said, bending over him. "Honey, your troubles have just begun."

CHAPTER TWENTY-NINE

With the Thompson slung around to her back, and Jersey scanning with the flashlight, Mac ripped Dazzle's basement apart. They called out for Katie constantly over their noise, and yanked open boxes, chests, even crates probably not big enough. She searched the laundry, its many cabinets and closets, and inside the five huge tubs designated for washing machines.

Where the hell is she?

She went to the other side of the floor and began another systematic search, bumbling along in the poor light and upending everything in her path. Reaching the far corner and doubling back, she swiped cobwebs from her ear, tried in vain to settle her nerves, and had to stop and breathe. This time, the tiny voice reached her. Unless it was her aching will playing a trick. She dropped back against the wall to collect herself and heard it again. Behind her.

"Katie!" Mac turned and smashed her fists to the wall. "Jersey! She's here!"

Jersey rushed to her side. "Where?"

"I know I heard her. I know I did."

They surveyed the wall from ceiling to floor, and Jersey reset her cap in frustration.

"But I don't see…"

"It's a wall *and a door*! It's a damn stash room!" Mac exclaimed. She'd seen her share of them, designed to protect alcohol supplies, and usually they were airtight. Fleetingly, she considered the air supply as a frightened Katie floundered in the pitch-black. She slapped her hands all over the wood repeatedly, pressing every inch for a hidden release. "Katie! Mackie's coming!"

The meager voice from inside could barely be heard. "Katie kwying."

"Oh Jesus." Mac's voice broke. "D-don't cry Katie! It's gonna be okay!" She clawed at the wall. "Don't cry, honey! I love you! O-okie dokie?"

There was a long pause and Mac and Jersey held their breath, but Katie finally responded with a weary, "Dokie."

Jersey retrieved the pry bar by the cellar door, and hauled Mac aside by the shoulder. "Lemme at it." She jammed the snipped end of the bar between the planks and began pushing, but succeeded only in chipping chunks off the surface. "Fuck." She threw the bar into the laundry room.

Mac pressed her face and now bloodied hands to the wall. "Find me an axe. I'll chop this God damn thing—"

"Mac!" Ellie pushed the Thompson aside to hug her from behind, and Mac turned blindly into her embrace.

"Oh, God, baby! I-I can't get—Katie's in the stash room, El. We have to find the way in!"

Ellie looked past Mac to the solid wall streaked with blood from Mac's palms. Her eyes filled. "She's in there? But y-you know she's…?"

Mac nodded vigorously. "I can hear her, but, I…" She took a deep breath. "I can't fucking get this door open." She pounded it with both fists.

Ellie yelled through the door. "Katie? Mama's here, sweetie!"

At the sound of her mother's voice, Katie cried louder. "Mama! Dark!" Her sporadic sobs grew into long terrified wails.

Winding up to take another swing at the wall, Mac spotted Millie, and when she stepped aside, Mac saw Lowry, hands bound behind him, standing in front of Rey's gun. Rey shoved him forward and he fell over a crate onto the dirt floor.

"Look who we brought," Millie said. "Bet the wimpy architect knows how to get in."

Everyone jumped back as Mac swooped down on him. She seized his collar in both fists and slammed him against the wall. He blinked several times.

Inches from his face, Mac snarled. "Long time no see, Lowry. Open this fucking thing right now or I'll kill you."

Lowry glared back, and Mac could see the hatred. She hoped he could see hers, because it flamed through her every pore, and she wasn't sure she could control it. And when Lowry spit in her face, she didn't.

She dropped her hands to wipe her face and Lowry settled into a defiant stance. Mac spread her arms, pushed the others away, and pulled her Thompson around from her back. Lowry's eyes grew wide and, before he could speak or even flinch, she sprayed his feet at point-blank range.

Lowry screamed as he fell into a fetal position.

Mac shoved the gun behind her and hauled him upright, jamming him onto his feet. He screamed louder, and began sliding down the wall. She pinned him in place with an arm across his throat, and leaned on it.

"You'll tell me how to open this door, won't you?" She threw her weight against his Adam's apple and his face darkened. "Just a little nod will do." But Lowry turned his face away and tried to gasp for air.

Mac let go and he dropped onto his side, heaving and moaning. She swung the Thompson up into both hands again and put three quick rounds into his left shoulder. The impact bounced him onto his back as he screeched. His arm limp in its shattered socket, he squirmed in the mud of the blood-soaked floor.

Mac stood over him, the Thompson still smoking, and watched his eyes threatened to roll back into unconsciousness. She pulled his head up by the hair, waved the barrel beneath his nose, and let smoke trail into his flaring nostrils until he coughed. She rammed the muzzle against them and twisted.

"You listen to that little girl in there. Oh, don't think you're going to pass out." She yanked his lolling head upright. "You're going to stay conscious till I get an answer. I only want one in particular: how this door opens. I'm waiting." She thrust his head to the floor. After a second, she pushed the Thompson behind her again. "I'm done waiting."

Mac jerked him off the floor and hurled him against the wall, left shoulder first. He screamed long and hard, and fell into a heap. "Not what I want to hear, Lowry! Speak!" Mac rammed her shoe into his crotch, and grabbed the Thompson again. As he folded in half, she hammered his jaw with the gunstock and sent him rolling onto his other side.

Mac straightened. "Y'know, I *will* get our little girl out of your God damn vault, and when I do… You think you're suffering now?"

Coiled in agony, Lowry coughed deeply and blood poured from his mouth.

Mac kicked his chest and flattened him onto his back. She drew her .45 and stabbed it into his manhood.

"Time's up, you piece of shit." He squirmed beneath her and Mac snorted. "Wait till you see what's left of your stuff."

"N-no." Lowry tried to say more but gagged. He huffed hard breaths and his eyelids closed to slits.

"Ceil-ceiling," he uttered, and everyone looked up.

Rey, with the longest reach, poked and pulled at one cross member after another until one shifted in her hand. She yanked it back and a barely audible click set a section of the wall ajar. Mac shoved her fingers into the narrow space and pulled the door open. Flashlights lit the small room.

Katie sat in the middle of the floor blinking in the light.

Ellie practically fainted. "Katie Rose!"

"Mama!" The little face crinkled into a rainstorm of full-fledged tears.

Ellie erupted into a deluge as she scooped Katie off the floor and out of the vault, and buried herself and Katie in Mac's arms.

"About God damn time," Jersey said. She looked down at Lowry and kicked him in the head.

❖

Mac ordered the Packard and LaSalle nuzzled right up against Dazzle's veranda. Next, she tried to persuade Ellie and Katie to return to the Sagamore with Millie, but lost that argument.

She took Millie aside by the cellar door. "Position our cars to go out the main drive. We're not leaving on that sled run we came in on. And please convince Ellie that waiting with Katie and you in the Studebaker is the smart thing to do."

"I'll remind her that it has a decent heater." She glanced over Mac's shoulder, watched Rey adjust a blanket around Katie and Ellie. "What's your plan?" she whispered. "Gonna get a little toasty around here, isn't it?" She waved off that thought. "No. Never mind. Too many options." She led Ellie and Katie out, and Mac stepped around Lowry's writhing form to speak to Jersey.

"The goon upstairs?"

She shook her head. "Frank Bocci, Rey says. A New York regional captain, the one who's been squeezing her. He's had a *very* bad evening." She pulled Bocci's billfold from inside her jacket. "About two grand in cash. Should make for a humdinger of a New Year's Eve."

"I like tying up loose ends."

"Got more souvenirs for you, Mac," Rey said and handed her Lowry's billfold and .38.

Mac drew a North Woods business card from the billfold. "Jesus. Meyer Lansky."

Rey's face went blank. "*The* Meyer Lansky? God damn."

"With his telephone number." Mac exhaled hard. "I need to tell Ellie."

"Not right now, you don't," Jersey said. She held Mac's gaze for an extra second and Mac knew they both were considering how much Lowry might have revealed and to whom.

"You think he or Bocci talked about you to Lansky?" Rey asked.

They all looked down at Lowry who was barely conscious.

"No time to dwell on that," Mac mumbled.

Jersey nudged her back. "Come with me. Something I want you to see."

As they hurried out, Rey found herself virtually alone in a very dark place. But she had the flashlight, and that said everything. Early conversations with Mac sprang to mind in detail, and just how they'd led her here, to this, confounded her. But that proverbial light at the end of her tunnel shone unimpeded now, and business would return to normal. That should help her overcome the nagging ache in her heart. This was Millie's world, after all, and Rey knew the sooner she accepted that, the better.

Rey peered down at Lowry, who whimpered in a fetal position, his lifeless left arm still tied to his right at his back. A deep purple ring marked his throat, and blood pooled on the floor beneath his head, both feet, and where it soaked through his coat around his shoulder.

"Can't imagine a piece of garbage like you ever thought this would work, Lowry. What were you thinking? For someone smart enough to build something like this, you're one stupid bastard." She sighed. "I bet Dazzle would've been your shining moment, huh? You even had Meyer Lansky, one of the biggest hotshots in the world on your side. Jesus. Did you and Bocci win points with him for finding Hijack Mack? Huh?" She nudged his chest with the flashlight and he groaned and turned his head farther aside. "Well, didja? This sure must've been worth a lot to you two."

Lowry coughed and the motion led to more howling.

Mac returned with a wooden crate, and Jersey a reel of cord.

"What'd you find?" Rey asked, shining the flashlight on the crate of TNT. "Mother of Jesus. They must've had this to speed up the digging around here."

Mac eyed the volatile contents and nodded. She couldn't have asked for a more decisive finish to this whole mess. "I'll put a few down here and you guys spread the rest upstairs. Run the fuse out, off the veranda."

Jersey snorted. "It'll wipe this place clean off the map."

"That's for sure," Rey said heavily. "This area will rock for miles."

Mac took Rey's flashlight and turned it on Lowry. "There'll be nothing left." She looked back at Jersey and Rey. "I want to close the book on trouble. This should do that for all of us...for Ellie and Katie, for me, for you, too, Rey. Odds are, New York will send an entire regiment after Diamond for doing this, and with any luck at all, say to hell with doing business up here."

Rey stared back at her. Mac could see that the impact of the words and what they were about to do, what it would mean in the long run, swamped her mind. Finally, Rey looked down into the box and took a deep, nasal breath. "I hear you, Mac."

Keeping four sticks of dynamite for herself, Mac gestured to the crate with her chin. "Take it up." Jersey hefted the box, and Mac waved them away with the flashlight.

She made her way to the far end of the cellar and laid two sticks on a bundle of copper piping, then returned and set the other two on the floor near Lowry. He turned his head as far as he could to see, and coughed, trying to muster his voice.

"You... You'll n-never...get a-away...with this. Wretched d-devil woman. That's...what you are."

Mac knelt on one knee beside him and spoke quietly.

"Sunny days on horseback, Reggie. Tea in china cups on those lazy summer afternoons in the orchard. The beautiful Olivia in your bed. That's what you need to bring to your pathetic, sick mind right now."

She shined the light just off his face for him to discern hers. His red wet eyes hardened and revealed the rage that still burned. His lips trembled when he grimaced.

"I'll...I'll s-see you in hell."

Mac smiled. "Don't think about being a failure, Reggie. Think about what you had. Remember being king of your domain, being waited on hand and foot by that maid you hated so, how you had her at your beck and call, how she helplessly catered to your every whim. Well, she's here now, Reggie, and she's not helpless any more. She's going to serve you one last time, serve you up to whatever god you choose. And you *do* need to choose, because your time has come."

She stood and took a last look around, at the blood on the walls, the opened vault that yawned in the dark. She would dream about it all for a while, but the dream wouldn't be a nightmare. She closed the cellar door to the outside and, from the bottom of the stairs, she shined the light on Lowry one last time. He craned his neck to watch her, his face contorted by agony, sheer terror, and his last shred of hate. He yelled weakly and gagged at the pain it caused.

Mac shook her head. "I'd say it was a pleasure, Reggie, but it wasn't."

She met Jersey and Rey in the lobby and exhaled hard. "We ready?"

Jersey led them out, over the ignition cord that meandered from the lobby, snaked around Bocci's body on the veranda, and ended at the stairs. They stepped respectfully over all of it. "It's for the best," she said. "We all agree."

Rey set her beefy hand on Mac's shoulder. "Gotta say, Hijack Mack, this has been one helluva ride. We need some serious drinkin', so," she glanced down at all the ignition cord, "so best get on with it." She gave Mac a pat on the cheek and went down the steps to her car.

Joining Mac on the second step, Jersey lit a Chesterfield and slapped her Ronson lighter into Mac's palm. "Use mine and let's get the hell out of here."

Mac hung an arm around her shoulders. "Tell me it's all over."

"A *grand* finale, boss. Happy New Year to us." She hugged Mac to her hip and slipped away to the Studebaker.

Mac stared into Dazzle's dark interior, and a vision of Lowry flashed through her mind. Followed by one of Bocci, and then one of Ellie and herself holding Katie.

She turned back to the cars and found Ellie watching through the rear windshield. *I love you. And thank God you love me.* They shared a nod, and Ellie returned her attention to Katie in her lap.

Mac crouched and touched Ronson fire to the end of the ignition cord.

CHAPTER THIRTY

Less than twenty-four hours later, the Sagamore buzzed with the celebratory anticipation of New Year's Eve. The younger set had given way to adults-only festivities, and well-liquored, uninhibited dancers filled the ballroom, dining salons, bars—and sun rooms, hallways, the lobby and everywhere floor space permitted. Waiters flitted among the partygoers, offering an endless supply of appetizers and cocktails as if Prohibition were prohibited.

Dressed in black silk shirt and trousers beneath white dinner jacket and bow tie, Mac stopped as she entered the ballroom, and actually thought hard about celebrating. The calendar called for it, and without doubt, they deserved it. But this New Year's Eve, as new came and old went, they would reach deeper into their hearts. For family, for its loss *and* its gain.

She took a breath to steady a swell of emotion, and waded into the throng to her table. She placed a long, earnest kiss on Ellie's cheek before sitting.

"Sorry to take so long. I went back to our room and checked on Katie. She's in dreamland with Bing and that teddy bear Rey gave her today." She squeezed Ellie's hand as she added, "No one's getting past those two guys Rey assigned from her crew. They're sharp." She leaned toward Jersey. "Solid additions to your group, by the way, if Rey would let them go. You two might want to talk."

"I feel so much better, knowing they're there," Ellie said, "even if we don't need them anymore. Katie's happy and safe."

"And will stay that way," Mac stated. "So, then I ran down to the pub to find Rey and tell her the good news." She reached for her drink and grinned at their expectant faces. "Dazzle's dead. New York's dumped the project and gone after Diamond. Rey's home free."

Jersey raised her glass and Ellie sat back in surprise.

"We saw you talking to Merriweather and that other man at the bar earlier. That's what they told you?"

"Actually, his associate, Meyer Lansky, told me."

Jersey almost dropped her drink. "*That's* who the other guy was? Guess a really big boom shakes out some really big rats, huh?"

"I almost lost it when Merriweather introduced me." Mac lit a cigarette and exhaled with relief. "Best acting job I've ever done, thank God, and couldn't have heard the news from a better source."

Ellie rubbed Mac's thigh under the table. "And it couldn't have come at a better time, either, New Year's Eve. What a way to start the new year. I'm so proud of you." She pulled Mac closer and kissed her. "And Rey must be overjoyed."

"Oh, she was happy, all right, but I don't think the news really registered. She and Millie were getting awfully cozy at their table for two. Don't be surprised if they're not up here with us at midnight."

Ellie inched to the edge of her seat. "They'll be celebrating by themselves? Maybe celebrating something other than New Year's, I hope?"

"Are they getting serious down there?" Jersey asked. "Like, they're finally talking about 'them' and stuff?"

"Oh, I hope they are," Ellie said. "They've beat around the bush long enough. It's time they admitted they want to be together…somehow." She practically wiggled in her seat and caught Mac smiling at her excitement. "You're not fooling me, Stick McLaughlin. You're hoping for it, too."

"Well, if they aren't, at least they can celebrate the clock striking twelve," Jersey said. "I mean…if nothing else. But it would be nice if they joined us. Hell, I want to see them burn up this dance floor. They *are* good together."

Mac pointed at her. "Then *you* go and drag them up here."

"Uh-uh." Jersey shook her head. "Interrupt Millie? Ha. Not me. *You* do it."

Mac leaned back in her chair. "Nobody has to do it. Here they come." She watched Millie lead Rey toward them, holding her hand as they wove around the tables, waiters, and clusters of laughing partygoers. "And they look happy."

Ellie tilted toward Mac. "Is she glowing or am I drunk already?"

Mac laughed as she signaled the waiter. "You're not drunk, sweetheart, and yes, I think she's glowing."

"I think they both look like they swallowed canaries," Jersey said. "Boston just might have lost the life of the party, and if she leaves, the city will never be the same." She lowered her voice. "But do you think Millie would really do it?"

"I think we're about to find out," Mac said.

Ellie pouted at her empty glass. "I'm definitely going to need a few more of these."

The waiter delivered three bottles of champagne as Millie and Rey joined them at the table.

"Well, now," Mac said with a smile. "You made it with just minutes to spare. Big night like this and you guys called it close."

"We had a big night already," Rey said, "but we're glad to be here with you, too."

Millie patted Ellie's hand. "Took a lot of hard thinking, but we got past a few tears and ended up reaching a decision we both can live with." She flashed a coy smile around the table as she linked an arm through Rey's. "This wilderness adventure of ours has been eye-opening. Maybe losing Jackson and almost losing Katie pushed me over the edge, I'm not sure, but I've had enough wild times and scary moments, cried too many tears. I'm done. Rey's coming back to Boston with me for Jackson's funeral, and then she's going to help me pack. I'm moving out here, where I actually can have love in my life. With Rey."

"Woo-hoo!" Jersey exclaimed, and everyone cheered. Neither Millie's makeup nor Rey's ruddy complexion hid their blushes. "Took you guys long enough to decide, for crissakes."

Ellie ran to hug them. "I'm so happy for the both of you. I know it took a lot of soul searching. There's so much to consider, and I'm sure there's still a lot to work out, but…well, just looking at your faces says it all."

"She had to stay," Rey said. "Hard times are gone, but I can't get by without this one-woman army, this incredible lady by my side." She clutched Millie's arm tighter. "I wouldn't want to."

Millie kissed her lightly. "They say the right one will come along if you're patient, and, boy, have I been patient." They laughed in agreement. "Who would've thought a big ol' bear would be the right one for little ol' me? I certainly didn't, not at first, anyway, but I've seen what I've been missing, how sweet life can be—*if* I'm willing to take that step." She winked at Ellie. "And I am."

Rey tugged her out of her chair, onto her lap, and kissed her roundly.

"Hey!" Jersey shouted, and jumped to her feet. "It's almost time! Let's pop a bottle. Hurry!"

Mac stood and launched a cork into the crowd, filled glasses for Ellie and herself, and passed the bottle. Her face hurt from smiling, and she felt her heart reach out to Jackson. She'd envisioned this scene when the idea had come to her originally, ushering in a fresh new year surrounded by everyone who counted. She found solace in knowing his spirit would forever linger with each one of them.

She hoisted her glass. "Everybody? To Jacks. Rest in peace, my friend." They raised their drinks and echoed her words.

Mac turned and lifted Ellie's chin.

"I was tempted to wake Katie, but figured all this would be too much for her, considering what she's been through. This really isn't the place for a little girl, and she needs her rest, I know, but I miss her right now."

"My love." Ellie cupped Mac's cheek. "I miss her, too, but you're right. Don't forget, she really enjoyed the children's celebration earlier, the little fireworks show, all the balloons, and way too much cake and ice cream." She set a light kiss on Mac's lips. "She had an absolute ball today. She's safe and very happy, honey. That's what matters."

Millie whirled from Rey's lap and slapped her hands onto Rey's shoulders. "Up y'go, my Big Bear!"

They gathered together as the countdown approached single digits, and Jersey nudged Mac.

"A New Year's toast, boss."

Mac held out her drink again and all glasses met within their circle. "To friends and the family we choose, to those of us here and those who smile upon us: May the coming year and all that follow be filled with the happiness and love we share right now."

Hundreds of revelers chorused "Happy New Year!" and confetti filled the air as the band struck up "Auld Lang Syne" right on cue.

As Jersey popped open another bottle, Rey swung Millie off her feet and spun in a circle, both of them lost in their kiss.

Mac and Ellie slipped into each other's arms automatically.

"Happy New Year, my Stick McLaughlin. I love you with all my heart. Always have and always will."

"And you are my one and only, my forever love, Eleanor Harrison. Happy New Year, sweetheart."

THE END

About the Author

A recent telecommunications retiree, CF Frizzell ("Friz") is the recipient of the Golden Crown Literary Society's 2015 Debut Author Award for her novel, *Stick McLaughlin: The Prohibition Years*. Friz discovered her passion for writing in high school and went on to establish an award-winning twenty-two-year career in community newspapers that culminated in the role of founder/publisher.

She credits powerhouse authors Lee Lynch and Radclyffe, and the generous family that is Bold Strokes Books, for inspiration. A lifelong Massachusetts resident, Friz is into history, New England pro sports, and singing and acoustic guitar—and living on Cape Cod with her wife, Kathy, and their chocolate Lab, Chessa.

Books Available from Bold Strokes Books

Captive by Donna K. Ford. To escape a human trafficking ring, Greyson Cooper and Olivia Danner become players in a game of deceit and violence. Will their love stand a chance? (978-1-63555-215-7)

Crossing the Line by CF Frizzell. The Mob discovers a nemesis within its ranks, and in the ultimate retaliation, draws Stick McLaughlin from anonymity by threatening everything she holds dear. (978-1-63555-161-7)

Love's Verdict by Carsen Taite. Attorneys Landon Holt and Carly Pachett want the exact same thing: the only open partnership spot at their prestigious criminal defense firm. But will they compromise their careers for love? (978-1-63555-042-9)

Precipice of Doubt by Mardi Alexander & Laurie Eichler. Can Cole Jameson resist her attraction to her boss, veterinarian Jodi Bowman, or will she risk a workplace romance and her heart? (978-1-63555-128-0)

Savage Horizons by CJ Birch. Captain Jordan Kellow's feelings for Lt. Ali Ash have her past and future colliding, setting in motion a series of events that strands her crew in an unknown galaxy thousands of light years from home. (978-1-63555-250-8)

Secrets of the Last Castle by A. Rose Mathieu. When Elizabeth Campbell represents a young man accused of murdering an elderly woman, her investigation leads to an abandoned plantation that reveals many dark Southern secrets. (978-1-63555-240-9)

Take Your Time by VK Powell. A neurotic parrot brings police officer Grace Booker and temporary veterinarian Dr. Dani Wingate together in the tiny town of Pine Cone, but their unexpected attraction keeps the sparks flying. (978-1-63555-130-3)

The Last Seduction by Ronica Black. When you allow true love to elude you once and you desperately regret it, are you brave enough to grab it when it comes around again? (978-1-63555-211-9)

The Shape of You by Georgia Beers. Rebecca McCall doesn't play it safe, but when sexy Spencer Thompson joins her workout class, their non-stop sparing forces her to face her ultimate challenge—a chance at love. (978-1-63555-217-1)

Exposed by MJ Williamz. The closet is no place to live if you want to find true love. (978-1-62639-989-1)

Force of Fire: Toujours a Vous by Ali Vali. Immortals Kendal and Piper welcome their new child and celebrate the defeat of an old enemy, but another ancient evil is about to awaken deep in the jungles of Costa Rica. (978-1-63555-047-4)

Holding Their Place by Kelly A. Wacker. Together Dr. Helen Connery and ambulance driver Julia March discover that goodness, love, and passion can be found in the most unlikely and even dangerous places during WWI. (978-1-63555-338-3)

Landing Zone by Erin Dutton. Can a career veteran finally discover a love stronger than even her pride? (978-1-63555-199-0)

Love at Last Call by M. Ullrich. Is balancing business, friendship, and love more than any willing woman can handle? (978-1-63555-197-6)

Pleasure Cruise by Yolanda Wallace. Spencer Collins and Amy Donovan have few things in common, but a Caribbean cruise offers both women an unexpected chance to face one of their greatest fears: falling in love. (978-1-63555-219-5)

Running Off Radar by MB Austin. Maji's plans to win Rose back are interrupted when work intrudes and duty calls her to help a SEAL team stop a Russian mobster from harvesting gold from the bottom of Sitka Sound. (978-1-63555-152-5)

Shadow of the Phoenix by Rebecca Harwell. In the final battle for the fate of Storm's Quarry, even Nadya's and Shay's powers may not be enough. (978-1-63555-181-5)

Take a Chance by D. Jackson Leigh. There's hardly a woman within fifty miles of Pine Cone that veterinarian Trip Beaumont can't charm, except for the irritating new cop, Jamie Grant, who keeps leaving parking tickets on her truck. (978-1-63555-118-1)

The Outcasts by Alexa Black. Spacebus driver Sue Jones is running from her past. When she crash-lands on a faraway world, the Outcast Kara might be her chance for redemption. (978-1-63555-242-3)

Alias by Cari Hunter. A car crash leaves a woman with no memory and no identity. Together with Detective Bronwen Pryce, she fights to uncover a truth that might just kill them both. (978-1-63555-221-8)

Death in Time by Robyn Nyx. Working in the past is hell on your future. (978-1-63555-053-5)

Hers to Protect by Nicole Disney. High school sweethearts Kaia and Adrienne will have to see past their differences and survive the vengeance of a brutal gang if they want to be together. (978-1-63555-229-4)

Of Echoes Born by 'Nathan Burgoine. A collection of queer fantasy short stories set in Canada from Lambda Literary Award finalist 'Nathan Burgoine. (978-1-63555-096-2)

Perfect Little Worlds by Clifford Mae Henderson. Lucy can't hold the secret any longer. Twenty-six years ago, her sister did the unthinkable. (978-1-63555-164-8)

Room Service by Fiona Riley. Interior designer Olivia likes stability, but when work brings footloose Savannah into her world and into a new city every month, Olivia must decide if what makes her comfortable is what makes her happy. (978-1-63555-120-4)

Sparks Like Ours by Melissa Brayden. Professional surfers Gia Malone and Elle Britton can't deny their chemistry on and off the beach. But only one can win… (978-1-63555-016-0)

Take My Hand by Missouri Vaun. River Hemsworth arrives in Georgia intent on escaping quickly, but when she crashes her Mercedes into the Clip 'n Curl, sexy Clay Cahill ends up rescuing more than her car. (978-1-63555-104-4)

The Last Time I Saw Her by Kathleen Knowles. Lane Hudson only has twelve days to win back Alison's heart. That is if she can gather the courage to try. (978-1-63555-067-2)

Wayworn Lovers by Gun Brooke. Will agoraphobic composer Giselle Bonnaire and Tierney Edwards, a wandering soul who can't remain in one place for long, trust in the passionate love destiny hands them? (978-1-62639-995-2)

Breakthrough by Kris Bryant. Falling for a sexy ranger is one thing, but is the possibility of love worth giving up the career Kennedy Wells has always dreamed of? (978-1-63555-179-2)

Certain Requirements by Elinor Zimmerman. Phoenix has always kept her love of kinky submission strictly behind the bedroom door and inside the bounds of romantic relationships, until she meets Kris Andersen. (978-1-63555-195-2)

Dark Euphoria by Ronica Black. When a high-profile case drops in Detective Maria Diaz's lap, she forges ahead only to discover this case, and her main suspect, aren't like any other. (978-1-63555-141-9)

Fore Play by Julie Cannon. Executive Leigh Marshall falls hard for Peyton Broader, her golf pro...and an ex-con. Will she risk sabotaging her career for love? (978-1-63555-102-0)

Love Came Calling by CA Popovich. Can a romantic looking for a long-term, committed relationship and a jaded cynic too busy for love conquer life's struggles and find their way to what matters most? (978-1-63555-205-8)

Outside the Law by Carsen Taite. Former sweethearts Tanner Cohen and Sydney Braswell must work together on a federal task force to see justice served, but will they choose to embrace their second chance at love? (978-1-63555-039-9)

The Princess Deception by Nell Stark. When journalist Missy Duke realizes Prince Sebastian is really his twin sister Viola in disguise, she plays along, but when sparks flare between them, will the double deception doom their fairy-tale romance? (978-1-62639-979-2)

The Smell of Rain by Cameron MacElvee. Reyha Arslan, a wise and elegant woman with a tragic past, shows Chrys that there's still beauty to embrace and reason to hope despite the world's cruelty. (978-1-63555-166-2)

The Talebearer by Sheri Lewis Wohl. Liz's visions show her the faces of the lost and the killers who took their lives. As one by one, the murdered are found, a stranger works to stop Liz before the serial killer is brought to justice. (978-1-635550-126-6)

White Wings Weeping by Lesley Davis. The world is full of discord and hatred, but how much of it is just human nature when an evil with sinister intent is invading people's hearts? (978-1-63555-191-4)

A Call Away by KC Richardson. Can a businesswoman from a big city find the answers she's looking for, and possibly love, on a small-town farm? (978-1-63555-025-2)

Berlin Hungers by Justine Saracen. Can the love between an RAF woman and the wife of a Luftwaffe pilot, former enemies, survive in besieged Berlin during the aftermath of World War II? (978-1-63555-116-7)

Blend by Georgia Beers. Lindsay and Piper are like night and day. Working together won't be easy, but not falling in love might prove the hardest job of all. (978-1-63555-189-1)

Hunger for You by Jenny Frame. Principe of an ancient vampire clan Byron Debrek must save her one true love from falling into the hands of her enemies and into the middle of a vampire war. (978-1-63555-168-6)

Mercy by Michelle Larkin. FBI Special Agent Mercy Parker and psychic ex-profiler Piper Vasey learn to love again as they race to stop a man with supernatural gifts who's bent on annihilating humankind. (978-1-63555-202-7)

Pride and Porters by Charlotte Greene. Will pride and prejudice prevent these modern-day lovers from living happily ever after? (978-1-63555-158-7)

Rocks and Stars by Sam Ledel. Kyle's struggle to own who she is and what she really wants may end up landing her on the bench and without the woman of her dreams. (978-1-63555-156-3)

The Boss of Her: Office Romance Novellas by Julie Cannon, Aurora Rey, and M. Ullrich. Going to work never felt so good. Three office romance novellas from talented writers Julie Cannon, Aurora Rey, and M. Ullrich. (978-1-63555-145-7)

The Deep End by Ellie Hart. When family ties become entangled in murder and deception, it's time to find a way out... (978-1-63555-288-1)